MW00936401

Uncontrollable Urge

ISBN: 1482068133
ISBN 13: 9781482068139

Library of Congress Control Number: 2012919150
CreateSpace Independent Publishing Platform
North Charleston, South Carolina

To my loving parents, Horace and Theola;
my adorable son, Cody Austin;
and my sisters; Yohanna, Tonya,
Sheryl and Chequeta who never wavered
in their love and support.

May your light continue to inspire others to
achieve the unimaginable.

LGT

CHAPTER 1

The day was anything but typical for Tracy Hudson. Weeks of preparation had to be orchestrated like a well-run machine. Months of planning and years of waiting had almost led her to the breaking point. After her second failed marriage, it was time to throw in the towel. She went about her business as if nothing out of the ordinary was going to happen. But leaving the city and her husband behind was exactly what she was determined to do. She wouldn't give him the satisfaction of walking out on her and ending their ten-year marriage. Not this time. She had been burned too many times in the past by ex-lovers and the married guys she kept on the side.

"Good morning, Ms. Tracy," her housekeeper said as she scurried about, getting breakfast on the table.

Tracy was shocked to see her. Rhonda had been with her for the past seven years. Tracy always admired her loyalty and discreetness, so she was sorry that she couldn't even share her plans with Rhonda. She didn't want to deal with the sad good-byes and having to explain why she had decided to leave town. Some things were better left unsaid.

"Rhonda, this is your day off. Why are you here?" Tracy asked, trying to keep the fear out of her voice.

"Don't mind me, Ms. Tracy, I haven't any big plans for the day."

Rhonda had been faithful through the years, a quality she admired since her husband, Stephen, couldn't keep his zipper up. She could no longer tolerate the silence between them, which had consumed all she had to give. She didn't blame her husband or herself. In life some things were just not meant to be. Tracy had to get her thoughts together since the moving van would be there within the hour.

"Oh, Rhonda, I forgot to tell you that we are remodeling and will have new furniture arriving at the end of the week. I have donated some of our used furniture that we have no use for to a homeless shelter for young unwed mothers. The van will be picking those pieces up this morning."

The look on Rhonda's face said more than words. Rhonda knew not to press her boss for any more information.

"Well, it's a good thing I decided to come this morning. You'll need some help rearranging things."

Tracy had to think quickly. She needed to get Rhonda out of the house and fast. Stephen was representing a client in New York for the next several weeks and wouldn't be returning until the trial was over. Stephen would enter a very quiet and somewhat empty house upon his return. She was only going to take a few items with her … her mother's piano, the sofa in the entertainment room, a bedroom set and a couple of pictures. Stephen could have the rest. It meant nothing to her now, and scaling down to a two-bedroom town home or condo didn't lend itself to a whole lot of furniture. She also wanted to decorate her new place in a more contemporary, upscale fashion.

"Rhonda, I want you to spend the day at CoCo's Day Spa. You deserve to be pampered. Go there now and tell them to put everything on my account."

And without another word, she ushered Rhonda out the door and on her way. That was a close call. She called her husband on his cell to make sure he hadn't changed his business schedule. Stephen answered on the second ring.

"Hi, sweetie, how are things in New York?" The crude words and coldness in Stephen's voice said it all.

"Did you call me out of a meeting to check how things are going?" And with that she heard a click on the other end.

She was tempted to redial his number, but she thought better of the idea. Why waste her time and words on a relationship that was doomed from the start? The thoughtful man she married was now as cold as ice and never showed his emotional side. Since this would be her last day in their home, she was suddenly overcome with emotion.

Tears filled her eyes as she thought about her decision to leave. It wasn't the decision but the way she decided to exit. What if Stephen followed her and made a scene? What would her new employer think of her? Tracy wiped her eyes. It was too late now to turn back the hands of time.

Tracy was a very attractive woman. In stocking feet she stood five feet eight. She had emerald-green eyes that seemed to follow you around the room like Mona Lisa. Her shoulder-length, golden-brown hair was thick and shiny like that of a new fur coat. She wore a size four dress and had a figure that any modeling agency would be proud to have on the runway. In high school and college, Tracy was always the most popular girl on campus and had guys wrapped around her little finger. Not only were her looks to die for, but she was also equally as smart.

She grew up in California as an only child, completely adored by her parents. Her father had a very successful law practice in San Francisco, and her mother was a plastic surgeon. Her parents met while on a ski trip in Denver. They immediately connected. Tracy's mother found her future husband quite fascinating. Her mother was intrigued by his brilliance, sense of humor, and love for life.

Her father always said life was not a dress rehearsal but one's final performance. Her father relished every waking moment. He slept only four hours a night and worked diligently each day to allow time to enjoy the weekend. He got up early on Saturday mornings, went to the office to clear off his desk, and left by noon to play golf and tennis with his friends, and to enjoy the theater when shows appealed to him. To let her father tell the story, it took him almost two years before her mother agreed to move to California from New York.

It was a hard decision for her mother, leaving friends and family and going west in search of eternal happiness. Her mother had agreed to move on one condition; they would marry within the first year of their engagement.

Tracy grew up with lots of love and devoted attention. She attended the best private schools that money could buy and had her own full-time nanny. As a family they always tried to eat dinner together at home three to four nights a week. On Friday evenings Tracy still remembered her parents keeping their "date night." She couldn't comprehend nor understand the significance of "date night" then, but once she became a spouse, she finally understood why her father was adamant about having private time with her mother.

After graduating from high school, Tracy was determined not to leave California. She had applied to schools back East and had gotten accepted at a number of the Ivy League schools, but decided she would call the University of Southern California home for the next four years. She majored in economics with a minor in Spanish.

Not sure of what she would do with the degree and all of her knowledge, Tracy decided to enter USC Gould School of Law. Her father was so proud that she was following in his footsteps. Her father had suggested that she do her internship at his firm before her final year of undergraduate school to make sure that law was what she wanted. Her father remembered a number of his classmates majoring in law who realized too late that they neither had an interest in law nor a desire to practice it.

School was easy for Tracy. She got As with little effort. Her roommates always hated how easy everything appeared to be for her. While they spent hours and hours at the library, Tracy spent her time enjoying campus life. She was never short on brains or dates.

She graduated with honors and in the top 10 percent of her class. During her senior year at USC, she met Matthew Warwick, whom she married in an elaborate ceremony the following summer. Just hours before she was scheduled to walk down the aisle and become Mrs. Warwick, Tracy got cold feet. Somewhere deep down in her gut that inner voice told her Matthew wasn't the man for her. Instead of following her heart, she listened to her best friend who convinced her that, in time, love would come. Love never came for Tracy, and after just one year of marriage, she called it quits. She never looked back or had one moment of regret.

Matthew wanted to start a family right away and wanted Tracy to sit at home and play Susie homemaker. Thirty days into the marriage, she knew she had indeed made the biggest mistake of her life. She felt nothing for Matthew and wondered what had possessed her to marry him. Since they had not purchased a home together, it was easy dividing up their personal things and the few items they had accumulated during their brief marriage. Thinking back on all of it, she wondered if anyone was truly happy after the "I dos." There was no time to dwell on that now.

Tracy called CoCo's and spoke with the manager who reassured her that Rhonda would receive the very best care. She started to tell the manager about her plans for leaving the city, but she thought it wouldn't be wise to take the chance since she hadn't told her housekeeper. Before her mind could drift back to the past again, the doorbell rang. It was the movers, slightly ahead of their scheduled time.

She pointed out the furniture to be loaded on the truck, and showed them the boxes in the garage and the closet in the master bedroom that needed to be packed and loaded. She had already sent about ten boxes to her temporary apartment in the city.

"Ms. Hudson, is there anything else we need to pack?"

Startled at first by the voice, she discerned that the driver was asking for permission to lock the truck and move on to his next assignment.

"I think that's all for now. Thanks for a quick and professional job. I'd like to give you this," Tracy said, as she handed the driver three hundred dollars. "Please divide it among your men. They've done an exceptional job taking care of my valuables."

With that the driver shook her hand and thanked her for the money. "We appreciate this tip. You're so kind. It's rare for my men and me to be rewarded for what we're getting paid to do."

She took one last walk through her home. She started to get cold feet. Why was she running away and not facing the music? Wouldn't it have been better to sit down with Stephen and explain why she had made the decision to take a job on the East Coast? What would Stephen think, and how would he feel returning home to an empty house and a wife who had left without saying good-bye?

Stephen was twenty years her senior. He was a partner with Pearson, Broderick, Mason and Scott, a very prestigious law firm specializing in corporate law. They had met shortly after Tracy landed her first real job as a human resources director with a family dining company headquartered in Los Angeles. Stephen never understood or accepted her decision to not practice law. Tracy tried to explain that she was dealing with legal issues everyday, protecting the rights of the company and its employees. He would hear nothing of it. To him, she should have chosen a job that would allow her to practice and use her craft.

She and Stephen dated for two years before saying their marriage vows in a simple ceremony at the courthouse. Only family members and a few close friends attended the reception at the prestigious Olson Country Club. He had wooed Tracy the moment their eyes met.

Stephen was six feet four with piercing, deep blue eyes and dark brown hair that always looked like it had been recently cut. He was an immaculate dresser. He only wore Armani suits, always conservative in color, with a faint hint of cologne. Stephen was well shaven with no facial hair. His nails were always buffed, and he constantly got pedicures to keep his feet soft and well groomed. He wore a Rolex watch underneath the cuff of his shirts, and dress shoes with a military shine. His speech was impeccable, and he sounded more English than American. His family had spent a considerable amount of time in England when his father was in the Navy.

He was a man of few words, but when Stephen spoke, all eyes focused on him. Her mother had tried to warn her of eventual problems because of the huge difference in their ages, but she was determined to marry Stephen and at the time thought age didn't matter. Tracy went so far as to tell her mother that age was only a number. She now realized how wrong she was and how right her mother had been.

At almost sixty years of age, Stephen was no longer fun or interesting. During her prime, instead of enjoying life's moments, she had become homebound, always waiting for a trial to end or for him to return from a business trip. While Tracy was climbing the corporate ladder, Stephen had already built a successful law practice and was dedicated to his work.

The passion and excitement in their relationship had long since died. He was a workaholic with a type "A" personality; demanding, self-centered, unaware of her personal needs, and always wanting immediate gratification. His job was his life. Early in the relationship, Tracy felt like a trophy wife. During later years she felt abandoned and alone.

She was glad they never had kids. There was never time, and she definitely didn't want to become a stay-at-home mom while Stephen's career soared. She had carved out a nice niche for herself in corporate America. She was now working with her third food company at the executive level. With base salary, bonuses, long-term incentives, and executive perks, she easily made a million dollars annually. She was sought after by all the major companies on the East Coast.

As a successful human resources executive, she knew how to engage employees in order to bring more dollars to the bottom line. Companies needed her expertise since employees were the glue that held it all together. She handled million-dollar budgets and was responsible for thousands of employees under her domain. Tracy had an impressive portfolio and was considered an expert in leadership development, executive compensation, organizational effectiveness, and employee engagement.

Tracy was both confident and skilled at what she did. She wasn't afraid of top management or the board of directors. She worked because she loved it. She had her own money. Her parents had died in a terrible automobile accident on Christmas Eve two years ago. Sometimes at night when she shut her eyes, she could still hear the screeching of tires and see lights flashing everywhere.

Why her life had been spared was a mystery. She and her parents had been out shopping for last-minute Christmas gifts on a clear day in December. There wasn't a cloud in the sky. The temperature was in the mid-seventies, and they were singing Christmas carols as her father drove the car. Tracy sat in the backseat discussing, between songs, what they would have for breakfast on Christmas morning. Her mother was an excellent cook. Tracy gave the impression she wanted to become a great cook one day, but deep down inside, she could care less about preparing a meal and getting it on the table.

Out of nowhere, an 18-wheeler swerved to miss a dog and lost control, plowing into the front of their SUV. Her parents were killed instantly. She remained in a coma for three weeks, suffering only a broken arm. When she finally woke up and received the news of her parents' death, she cried uncontrollably. What was even more heartbreaking was the fact that their funeral had already happened, and she'd missed it all.

Tracy felt all alone in the world. She had no siblings and few friends. Her parents had left everything to her, which totaled approximately twenty-five million dollars. She was not planning on seeking alimony from Stephen. All she wanted was a simple divorce for irreconcilable differences. As a major partner in his law firm, Stephen was worth double that amount.

She wished her mother was still alive; she missed her so much. Tracy could hear her mother's voice pleading with her to take her time in marrying Stephen. Her mother liked Stephen a lot but felt he was too close to her father's age. She felt Tracy hadn't completely gotten over her first marriage. She thought Stephen would only slow Tracy down and would never be there for her with his current lifestyle and very demanding job.

The car she had reserved came to pick her up at 4:00 p.m. Tracy told the driver to give her five minutes. Almost on autopilot, she went to Stephen's office, turned on the Tiffany lamp, and opened the top drawer, where she read for the thousandth time, the program and arrangements for her funeral. How surprised Stephen must have been when the doctors informed him, his wife was going to live. Had Stephen planned on moving one of his mistresses into their home? Holding back tears, she closed the desk drawer for the final time, trying to ease the pain that stabbed at her heart.

She left her keys on the table next to the door with a note that simply read, "Our life together was great while it lasted. I'll call you soon," Trace. As tears rolled down her face, she closed the front door, waved to her next-door neighbor, and gave her bags to the driver. Life as she knew it was over.

CHAPTER 2

Once at the airport, Tracy called her dear friend and colleague Don Johnson with Brock Consultants. Don had worked with her on a number of reengineering efforts and outplacement assignments at her last company. Don had gotten out of the corporate world years ago. He was now a principal at Brock offering consulting and outplacement services to employees who were fired or let go. Brock Consultants always encouraged companies to offer outplacement services and severance packages to those employees who were being severed during a reengineering effort. Tracy would constantly remind management that the employees whose services were no longer needed were still potential customers for the company. In reality it kept sane employees from going postal.

Don answered on the second ring. "Well, I've done it. I left Stephen, and I'm headed to Florida to my new job."

Don was a very patient man with great wisdom. He had tried to encourage Tracy to tell Stephen face-to-face of her desire to leave him. Don felt the passive approach would only anger her husband. The last thing Tracy needed was for Stephen to make trouble at her new company. Don wasn't a fan of taking the coward's way out. In his years of counseling and working with people who had faced difficult situations, he knew all too well that there was a fine line between sanity and insanity. Life was just too short to play with someone's livelihood and life.

"How are you feeling about your decision?" he asked.

"To tell you the truth, I feel rotten. I know it was the wrong thing to do, but I just needed out. I'm tired of having to explain myself. After all, it isn't like we were great lovers. Since the death of my parents and my recovery from the coma, we've hardly spoken to each other. I think my mother was right. Age is more than a number."

She could sense from the words Don had chosen that he felt her pain. He just didn't know how to bring her comfort.

"Hudson, what's done is done. You need to take care of you. Tomorrow isn't promised for any of us. Do you think you should perhaps call Stephen and let him know that you've decided to leave? After all, what do you have to lose? His plane ride back to Los Angeles will give him an opportunity to clear his head."

She knew Don was right. Walking into a deserted house with some of the furniture gone would drive Stephen's blood pressure up. She wouldn't want to be placed in that position. Even if the marriage was over, they still needed to be civilized. She needed her divorce and didn't need any complications. She ended the call and decided Don had made a valid point. She had a two-hour layover in Atlanta and decided to call Stephen from the airport. If he got aggressive or hostile, she would hang up the phone.

The flight to Atlanta was uneventful. As the plane taxied into the Atlanta terminal, Tracy felt her stomach doing somersaults. She probably shouldn't have had those two cocktails on the plane. All she needed now was food to calm her nerves. She suddenly felt faint. Why had the captain turned off the air? She felt like screaming at those slow passengers in front of her. My god, why don't people just check all that gear and pick it up in baggage claim? How much time could they be saving, dragging that stuff through the airport?

Once she had deplaned, she grabbed a chicken salad and a banana. She wolfed down the salad and threw the banana away. Her stomach wasn't in the mood for fruit. She looked cautiously and anxiously around the terminal for some private space. It seemed that every seat and every inch of space was taken.

Even in Delta's private lounge, there was no privacy. She didn't want to air out her dirty laundry in front of total strangers. What if Stephen went off and threatened her? What would she say? She didn't need him interfering in her life. She dialed Stephen's number, and there was no answer. Well, Don, she thought to herself, at least I tried. She decided to wait for the fireworks. Maybe she'd get lucky, and he would just have his attorney draw up the papers for her to sign. Once the house was sold, they would split the profits, which would be a hefty amount.

She decided she would call Rhonda once she had settled into her apartment and explain why she left so abruptly. For now all she wanted to do was focus on her new life away from her problems.

Tracy arrived at Miami International Airport just a couple of minutes shy of midnight. She picked up her luggage at baggage claim and her rental car and drove directly to the corporate apartment. Her plan was to stay in the corporate apartment until she could secure permanent housing.

All of the amenities were waiting for her. The company had thought of everything. There was a wonderful basket full of chocolates, fruit, cheese, and wine. A large duffle bag held many of the company's promotional products, along with copies of recent company newsletters. This would be excellent bathroom reading, she thought.

There was also a note from the CEO that said, "Glad you chose us. This is the start of an exciting and rewarding career. See you on Monday." It was signed "Judy."

As she entered the first bedroom, she recognized the boxes she had packed and sent ahead of time. They were neatly stacked in the corner of the room. As she ventured into the master bedroom and bath, she noticed a large plush robe next to satin slippers. She eased out of her stilettos and slipped them on. Not only were her feet sore, but she was also exhausted from the long trip East. She undressed, took a long, hot shower, and went to the kitchen to see if there were any edibles.

To her amazement, the kitchen was well stocked. There was milk, juice, and wine in the refrigerator, along with a meat platter of ham, turkey, roast beef, and an assortment of crackers.

The cabinets were stocked with cans of soup, peanut butter, quick packaged meals, and cereal. There were plenty of pots and pans as well as silverware and china. The living room was quaint and adorable with a comfortable leather pullout sofa, flat screen TV, chaise lounge, accent chair, end tables, and an antique French desk with a four-drawer file cabinet. There was a huge picture on the wall of the Miami skyline.

On the desk was a corporate cell phone with instructions. A note was attached informing her that IT would set her up on a company computer on Monday.

It looked like the company had thought of everything. Tracy had two days and the weekend before she would start her new job. She was scheduled to spend time with the realtor on Thursday, Friday, and during most of the weekend. She didn't know if she would rent or purchase a town home or condo. She already missed the West Coast and looked at this opportunity as temporary. She ate a bowl of cereal, checked her e-mails, set the alarm clock for 9:00 a.m., and called it a night.

Tracy fell into a deep sleep and didn't awake until she heard soft background music in the distance. She got up, turned off the alarm clock, and decided to sleep until noon. After all, it was 6:00 a.m. on the West Coast. She felt entitled and knew her body needed more rest.

She didn't wake again until one. Realizing that the realtor would be in the lobby of the complex at two o'clock, she showered, blow-dried her hair, ate a piece of fruit, and drank a cup of black coffee.

There was an immediate connection with Linda Scott, her realtor. Linda was casually dressed in a navy Moschino pantsuit with Gucci flats, and she carried a D&G shoulder bag. Tracy could see that Linda was at the top of her game, selling real estate in a very depressed market. Linda looked to be in her early forties. She wore her hair in a sleek ponytail with soft ringlets framing her face. She had natural beauty and barely wore any makeup. On her wrist was a Louis Vuitton timepiece, and a gold wedding band circled the ring finger of her left hand.

"Hi, you must be Tracy," Linda said, as she introduced herself. "I thought we could spend about an hour over lunch, so you can familiarize me with what your current plans are and the type of housing arrangement you're looking for. There's so much to choose from and a host of decisions to make. I can show you property on the ocean, property in gated communities, condos … you name it, and we'll find it."

She could tell that this lady wasted no time whatsoever. She was focused, direct, and a go-getter.

"What type of food do you like?" Linda asked.

"Any place with fresh seafood and great salads," Tracy responded.

"I know just the place."

For lunch they dined at Fifi's Seafood Restaurant near South Beach. Linda took time to show her ocean-view condos, apartments, and town homes. After seeing property on South Beach, Tracy had pretty much made up her mind to live either there or on Miami Beach. However, she wanted to remain open to properties further north and south of the corporate office. That way she wouldn't be too close to the corporate office building on Brickell Avenue and could enjoy the city and her privacy. She wasn't one to start friendships with coworkers. Having her own space was a way to protect and guard her privacy.

She arrived back at the corporate apartment around eight in the evening. Tracy was too tired to see another property. They agreed to have dinner on Friday at Joe's Stone Crab in Miami Beach.

"You'll enjoy the service and great food. People travel from around the world to dine at Joe's. They're only open during select months and refuse to take reservations. You're seated on a first-come, first served basis. Everything is fresh, and their desserts are to die for," Linda said.

"Oh, Linda, that sounds like fun. I've read articles about the restaurant, but I've never dined there."

They agreed to meet on Friday for dinner at five and to spend most of Saturday looking at additional properties on South Beach, as well as in Boca, Key Biscayne, Kendall, and West Palm Beach. Living in LA Tracy was very accustomed to spending hours on the freeway, trying to get from point A to point B. She wasn't sure she wanted to sacrifice that much time to the roads. She planned to spend a quiet Sunday reading The New York Times, organizing her clothes, and preparing for her first day in the office.

As expected, Linda picked her up on time for dinner. They arrived early at Joe's, and to their surprise the wait was short. Tracy dined on lobster, while Linda said she just couldn't pass up the stone crabs. For dessert they each had a slice of key lime pie.

"This pie is heavenly and rich. I'll need to spend an extra hour at the gym," Tracy commented, although she had no intention of starting an exercise program right away. She felt getting in and out of the car to look at all of the various properties should count for something.

Tracy rolled into bed around 11:30 that night but couldn't get to sleep. She wondered why Stephen hadn't called. That seemed odd. She was praying that the trial hadn't ended early. She checked her e-mails. There was an e-mail from Stephen. All it said was that the trial had been delayed so don't expect him home anytime soon. It wasn't even signed with see you soon, miss you, or thinking about you. There was no sign of affection or concern. He'd chosen to send an e-mail as opposed to calling. After ten years of marriage, there was nothing left but an empty shell.

Tracy turned off the bedroom lamp and stared at the ceiling, thinking about her two failed marriages and whether she should have taken the job on the East Coast. About the only thing LA and Miami had in common were palm trees and great tropical weather. She only hoped, she could survive the lifestyle of her new place. She was here now, so she tried to get those negative thoughts out of her head. Where had the time gone?

When she woke up on Saturday morning, she quickly dressed and met Linda in the lobby of the apartment complex. It was late October in Miami, and the weather was warm with an occasional cool breeze. They saw several more properties before she fell in love with a two-bedroom condo right on South Beach. The terms of the arrangement by the owner were ideal. The owner wanted a tenant who would lease the place for a year with the option to buy. Tracy felt great when she returned to the apartment. She was having the realtor draw up the papers and was happy not to be tied to a house. If she decided to vacate the city, there wouldn't be a property-owner noose around her neck.

CHAPTER 3

The phone rang early Sunday morning. Tracy leaped to her feet with her heart racing. For a moment she thought something terrible had happened to her parents. Then she remembered that both her parents were dead. If anything had happened, it would be her husband Stephen, who discovered much too soon, that she, had left him. She dropped the receiver as she attempted to answer.

"Hello ... hold on please ... Hi, this is Tracy," she finally said.

"OK, sleepyhead, get up and get dressed. I'll be there within the hour. If I can't sleep in on Sunday morning, neither can you."

It was her friend, Leslie Klein. She and Leslie had worked for a family dining company in California when Tracy was fresh out of graduate school. At that time, Leslie, who was seven years older than Tracy, was the assistant general counsel. Leslie was now the general counsel at Sunset Pub and Grill, her new company. Leslie was so excited when she got the news from the CEO that Tracy had accepted the job. The executive leadership team at Sunset Pub and Grill were all women, with the exception of the senior vice president for real estate and franchising. The company was fairly young, housed in an industry of older, more established, casual dining enterprises.

"You've got to be kidding me," Tracy said, as she glanced at the clock and saw it was 7 o'clock in the morning. "Who in their right mind would phone someone on Sunday morning at this ungodly hour unless it were an emergency?"

"You just get yourself dressed and be out front in an hour, my friend," Leslie said, and with that she heard a click on the other end. Leslie had disconnected and was probably at Starbucks getting her favorite drink.

Sunset Pub and Grill was started by two brothers, Marc and Erik Beckham. The cofounders graduated from the University of Miami and, after trying to fit into the corporate box, decided to become entrepreneurs. They had tried several business ventures before realizing that Miami and other cities needed a sports bar where all ages could enjoy themselves while they watched sports, games, and fights on the big screen.

The company had opened its first restaurant on Miami Beach some thirty years ago. The concept was simple; provide a place where individuals and groups could meet in a relaxed atmosphere and enjoy great food at a reasonable price with a wonderful selection of both domestic and international beers and wines.

Sales were now three billion dollars for the company, which owned about 1,000 restaurants in thirty-two states. Twenty-five percent of the restaurants were company owned, and 75 percent were franchised under a licensed agreement. The company had gone public ten years earlier, and their stock traded on the New York stock exchange. Sunset employed approximately twenty thousand employees. Most of the employees were hourly, who were paid minimum wage.

At first, Tracy was hesitant to take the job because of the lack of diversity in the upper echelon and the fact that the company was female-dominated at the top. Her new boss, Judy Page, had worked for the company twenty-one years. Judy was initially hired by Marc Beckham to handle the books. The company had only about one hundred restaurants at the time and was struggling to keep afloat. They were selling franchises to keep the company going.

After about six months, Judy was handed the CEO job on a silver platter. Judy didn't have to interview for the job. Marc said, "It's yours if you want it." After her promotion, Judy brought her friend Sheila Newbury on board to replace her as chief financial officer. Judy and Sheila had been roommates at Florida State University. They had remained friends and, in a lot of ways, complemented one another. Even now in her late forties, Judy was a striking woman, standing six feet one. Her complexion was fair and free of wrinkles. Judy kept her blonde hair cut just above her shoulders. Her eyes were the color of the ocean on a clear day, and her teeth were pearly white and even. Judy had worn braces in junior high school, and they had served her well in later years.

Tracy was taken aback by her beauty when they first met. Although Judy was quite smart and stunning, Tracy felt Judy was somewhat cold and distant. Judy said all the right words, but her body language didn't convey warmth, kindness, and concern for others. Tracy was shocked when Judy shared with her during the interview that she and Sheila, the company's chief financial officer, had been roommates in college, had shared boyfriends, had worked together for only two companies, and had traded maternity clothes. Tracy thought that was an odd thing to say to a perfect stranger.

Upon meeting Sheila Newbury, it was clear who had the brains of the outfit and why their relationship had survived. Sheila was of average height with auburn hair cut in a short bob. Sheila looked to be about fifty pounds overweight. She wore no makeup and although she and Tracy had only talked twice, her clothes looked to be less expensive than those worn by the other executives in the company.

Sheila was definitely a plain Jane. A hint of makeup would have greatly enhanced her appearance. She wore no jewelry on her arms or hands with the exception of a small, gold wedding band. It was clear that she was the wallflower of the two. Because Sheila appeared so plain, Tracy was stunned to see that she wore two earrings on each ear; diamond studs in the first hole and small gold hoop earrings in the second. Sheila stayed back and ran the company as Judy traveled the country serving on boards, accepting speaking engagements, attending seminars and joining professional organizations.

Both Judy and Sheila lacked in-depth corporate experience. They had learned on the job, and unlike most of the world's executives who had the pleasure of working for many different companies under leaders who used various management styles, Judy and Sheila only had each other and what they were able to glean from magazine articles, books, seminars, and membership in professional organizations. Several times during the interview, Judy commented that she was looking forward to the corporate experience Tracy would bring.

Leslie was on time as she blew her horn for Tracy to join her. The two drove to Coral Gables to have breakfast.

"What have you been up to, Tracy? I practically had to kill your new assistant to get your address and phone number. Sharon felt whatever I had to say to you could definitely wait until Monday."

It was like old times with Leslie. She was direct and frank. Nothing escaped her. Leslie spoke up and made her feelings known. Leslie was bright and highly intelligent. She graduated in the top 5 percent of her class at Harvard. Her staff loved her. She put the needs of others ahead of her own. Leslie got the best from her handpicked team of attorneys because she was inclusive, approachable, and showed empathy and compassion.

Leslie was five feet seven, with a shapely figure, blonde hair and turquoise eyes that seemed to change to various shades of blue and green when she became angry, which was seldom. Leslie was naturally beautiful and spent little time fussing with makeup or over herself. Others enjoyed her company immensely. Leslie knew how to get results and constantly encouraged her team to strive for excellence by exceeding expectations and business objectives.

"Tell me, Leslie, what have I gotten myself into? I've the funny feeling that I'm not stepping into utopia," Tracy said, as she looked straight at Leslie over breakfast. "I've the distinct impression that there's more to this puzzle."

Leslie knew what her friend was asking, even though she thought it was best not to be totally honest with her at the moment. She had been on a couple of interviews and was considering leaving the company. She felt that Judy and Sheila were too close as friends, and it had ruined their objectivity. All decisions had to be agreed to and accepted by both Judy and Sheila. The two talked about a collaborative environment and decisions being made by the executive committee, when in essence they were the final decision-makers.

"Where's this place called utopia? Tell me so I can sign up. I don't think you'll ever find it in corporate America."

Tracy knew Leslie was right. Utopia didn't exist. The name of the game was to survive, enjoy the perks, and keep your resume current.

"I'm leaving Stephen. It's just not working out."

She brought Leslie up to speed, telling her about the death of her parents and slipping into a coma; and finding arrangements for her funeral. She thought Stephen had already buried her long before she came out of the coma.

"I guess I have to take some responsibility for what has happened. When my parents died, I should have sought therapy. I lost my way. I was so hurt that I blamed anyone in my path. Stephen sought affection from his mistress. He claimed she was just a one-night stand. I couldn't accept what he was saying. His unfaithfulness was too much for the marriage. I shouldn't totally blame him," Tracy said.

Leslie couldn't believe her ears and held up her hand, signaling her to stop. "How dare you take responsibility for Stephen's actions? Did you forget you spent weeks in a coma? Stephen wasn't there for you. When a spouse is suffering as you were, you don't turn your back and find love in the arms of another woman. Give me a break."

She had missed her old friend and their honest, frank conversations. Leslie didn't pull any punches. She called a spade a spade and kept going. She didn't cloud the issue, looking for the silver lining. Sometimes she wondered if Leslie saw shades of gray. They finished breakfast, drove around the city, and stopped at Target so Tracy could buy a few household items she needed. Leslie encouraged her to sleep well so she could hit the ground running on Monday.

As Tracy opened the passenger door and got out of the car, Leslie yelled out to her, "We've some self-centered, self-promoting divas on the executive team. Trust no one. Be safe, my friend. Now go and enjoy what's left of your Sunday."

Here we go again, Tracy thought. I come all the way out here only to find cutthroat individuals who aren't about creating an engaging environment for the employees, but only seeking personal gratification for themselves. Why do companies interview candidates? All it is, is a dance of survival. I see nothing has changed.

"Well, bring it on Sunset Pub and Grill. May the best man or should I say, may the best woman win," she said out loud as if others could hear her.

At about nine in the evening, Tracy decided to phone Rhonda and explain that she and Stephen had decided to separate. There was no need to give her all of the details. She saw no need to tell Rhonda that not only had she left Stephen, but she had also departed the state.

They spoke for about forty minutes. Rhonda wasn't surprised. She had noticed many signs that indicated the marriage had ended some time ago. Rhonda would now be working for Stephen and would probably only need to be at their home two days a week instead of three, or whatever arrangement he decided. She told Rhonda she would continue to transfer the money into her account twice a month. Rhonda wished her well and assured Tracy that she wouldn't say anything to others about their separation.

Tracy tossed and turned the entire night. She was up several times, going back and forth to the bathroom. When the alarm clock went off at 5:30 a.m., she was physically exhausted. Where had the time gone? She knew she needed to make a good impression on her first day by being in the office ahead of time. She dragged herself to the kitchen, made a cup of coffee, and carried it back to the bedroom. She showered, did her hair and makeup, and by 6:45 a.m. she was headed to the office.

There was very little traffic at that hour, so her commute was less than twenty minutes. The building and parking lot were deserted. After parking her car, she had the security guard, who had received clearance the previous Friday from Judy's administrative assistant, unlock the outer door of the corporate office.

The office was empty and quiet. As she moved about the floor, there wasn't a soul to be found. Tracy located the office with her name on the outside of the door, turned on the lights, and proceeded to get organized when a shadow came over her. She looked up, somewhat alarmed.

"Hi, Tracy, welcome aboard. I'm Sam Mason. I run the IT department. I didn't expect to see you here at this hour."

"Hello, Sam, it's good to meet you. I thought I'd come in early to get things organized. I understand there is a staff meeting starting at eight o'clock."

She and Sam spoke briefly about the company; the companies she had worked for, and when she could expect to have her computer. Sam was very articulate. He had interned at the company during his last year in graduate school at the University of Miami. Sam joined the company the summer after he graduated as a manager in the IT department. Over the past eight years, he had worked his way up the corporate ladder and now headed up IT.

He looked to be in his early forties. He was slightly under six feet, had a muscular build, and salt-and-pepper hair, definitely a sign of premature aging. Tracy liked him the moment they met. Sam was very friendly, knew his craft, and had a nonthreatening personality and style.

"Tracy, I'll get out of your hair. I can see you have things to do. If you need anything, just come up one flight, and let me know. I can direct you to the best restaurants, doctors you should stay away from, and where to take your clothes to be cleaned." And with that he was gone.

As she unpacked a couple of personal items, the office started coming alive with the voices of people sharing how they spent their weekend. After placing a couple of pictures on the credenza, she removed her Bose radio music system from her shoulder bag.

Tracy loved music. It was so soothing to hear classical music as she went about her work. It served as soft background music, which seemed to put the employees and her visitors at ease. She chose instrumentals and preferred piano concerti by composers such as Chopin, Beethoven, Schumann, and Bach. She had the complete classical library with more than fifteen hours of high definition sound. Her taste in artists spanned the globe. She loved country, blues, reggae, jazz, rock and roll, alternative, and classical music. Somehow, she never acquired a taste for hip hop.

She placed her Tiffany Francesca table lamp on the small table next to a beige sofa. In the center of her coffee table she placed a couple of motivational books and a glass paperweight. She was now in business.

She had learned a valuable lesson when she started her career. She saw firsthand how cold and callous corporate America was. Bottom-line results and keeping shareholders happy were all that mattered. She only brought things to the office that she could carry out in her shoulder bag. If at anytime during her career she was asked to leave, all she would need was ten minutes to pack up her things and exit the facility.

At 7:45 a.m. Leslie Klein was standing in her doorway, signaling her to wrap things up so they could head to the boardroom.

"Well, my friend, did you sleep well?" Leslie asked, as she pulled the door closed.

She wondered why Leslie felt the need to close the door. It was apparent that employees were moving about the office, even though no one in human resources had officially come in to introduce himself or herself. Her style would have been to gradually get to know her staff by moving around the office and personally saying hello. Starting her first day with an executive staff meeting was awkward.

"Has something happened since yesterday that I need to know about?" Tracy asked, as she waited for Leslie to speak.

"Just some protocol to be aware of. Judy schedules these 8 o'clock meetings, but she generally arrives fifteen to twenty minutes late, giving some half-assed reason for her lateness. Judy is the head honcho so, if I were her, I'd start at eight-thirty or nine o'clock. Those are more decent times; especially given these meetings always follow a weekend. The only saving grace is we only have to stomach them twice a month."

The more Tracy listened to Leslie talk about the rules of engagement, the more she wondered what had she gotten herself into.

"OK, let's have it. What cardinal rule shouldn't I break?" As she said the words, her stomach started to turn. Leslie looked at her with concerned eyes.

"It's not that bad. Just don't take the middle seat on the right side of the conference table. Judy always sits there. Sheila usually sits on the other side, as they play cat and mouse with humans. I think Judy sits in the center to give the impression that it's a democratic form of politics here. Don't believe it for a minute." With that Leslie opened the office door, grabbed her things, and motioned for Tracy to follow.

As expected, Judy arrived at eight-thirty with an excuse about work on the expressway and traffic being backed up for hours. Tracy watched as Judy took the middle seat. The meeting started with introductions and each executive giving a brief update of key initiatives, any new hires who joined the company, and a quick budget review.

Tracy felt all eyes were on her as they tried to pierce through the exterior. What they didn't know was that she was quite astute at the political games in corporate America. She had played them well. It was laughable when Judy said during her interview that politics didn't exist at Sunset Pub and Grill. Only a fool would think or believe that politics didn't exist in all walks of life. There was no escaping office politics.

The leadership team broke for lunch at noon. Food had been ordered by Judy's administrative assistant and there was enough to feed a small army. There were only seven members on the executive team. She couldn't imagine who would eat all the leftovers. Perhaps they gave the food to a homeless shelter. It would be a sin to just throw it away. She wouldn't dare ask such a trivial question. She would just observe and make a mental note to ask Leslie later.

Once the lunch break was officially announced, the executive team scattered like ants, making a mad dash for the door. No one seemed to take the food, which was even more puzzling. She took her lead from Leslie who also headed for the door. Leslie explained that most of the team rushed back to their office to read e-mails, return phone calls, and handle unpredictable situations. The staff slowly wandered in as the clock was approaching one. Each person grabbed a plate, loaded it with samples of each entrée, and reached for a canned drink or bottled water.

Judy spoke first. "We're indeed very fortunate to have Tracy on our team. Tracy comes to us with loads of corporate experience. I think she'll be good for all of us here. I'm sure by now, Tracy, you've read our biographies and realize that we all have limited corporate exposure and experience, except perhaps for Lauren Hanks."

She had read their biographies and had even questioned previous colleagues about them. Lauren had worked for Mrs. Fields Cookie Company, Best Buy, and Disney. Lauren was hard-core and ruthless. She had focused her career on human resources and had somehow convinced Judy that she could handle operations. She was responsible for about 90 percent of the employees, who were mostly hourly. Lauren ran a tight ship and her staff had little respect for her. All of her direct reports had worked their way up through the ranks. They were crushed and heartbroken when Judy announced that Lauren was being promoted to chief operating officer. What a joke. The only time Lauren had spent in operations was when she worked at Disney with responsibility for field human resources.

Lauren kept her deficiencies well hidden from Judy. To talk the lingo, she spent about 90 percent of her time in the field learning the job and keeping the real superstars on her team out of sight of the CEO. Whenever Judy would visit the field, Lauren rehearsed every stop and visit with her team. She left no stone unturned and would often cut her staff off as they attempted to explain things and to make a name for themselves.

Lauren was about five feet seven, with bleached blonde hair and hazel eyes. She had a serious acne problem that had scarred her face during her teenage years. She was constantly putting on makeup throughout the day, touching up the pimples. Although Lauren made a very good salary, she didn't invest a lot of money in her clothes. She was known in the industry for sleeping with her bosses to get ahead. Now that she was reporting to a woman, she used other unethical tactics. Tracy was sure Leslie had some tidbits to share regarding her.

During her interview with Lauren, she was so nice, that it appeared insincere. Her candor was too much to handle. Lauren had shared many personal things that you would only tell a close friend, not a person you had met the hour before. Tracy had worked with that personality type before at one of the casual dining companies in California. These were women who would claw their way to the top, destroying anyone who got in their path. They were ruthless, heartless people who would sacrifice a loved one to move ahead. They played on your emotions and, at that critical moment, would stab you in the back and watch you bleed.

Elizabeth Carmichael, Judy's assistant, knocked on the door and quietly entered. Elizabeth asked if anyone wanted seconds before taking the food away. She said the natives were waiting to enjoy what was left. Tracy thought it was a nice gesture to order enough food so the employees could partake of it as well.

"Our next item of business is to discuss upcoming promotions for the quarter," Judy said. The executives around the table pulled out their lists and started to share their recommended nominees.

Tracy chimed in, "What set of criteria are we using to nominate our candidates?" You could have heard a pin drop. Sheila was the first to speak.

"We don't use a set of criteria; we come prepared with our list of who should get promoted, and we discuss each person put forth."

Tracy spoke up. "Aren't you afraid that you may be promoting people for selfish reasons in some cases? By that I mean people we want to keep in our own departments or at the company but who, may not have the skill set to be successful at the next level."

Tracy knew before anyone spoke that she hadn't chosen her words carefully. The emotional word "selfish" sent bullets flying through the room. She watched the looks and expressions on the faces of the executives. The last thing they needed was having a neophyte change the rules of the game.

"Let me give you some food for thought," Tracy said, watching Judy's expression the entire time. "As we promote employees, I would think that they should at least be above-average performers. We need to make sure that on our performance appraisal rating scale; they're rated by their supervisor as having excellent or outstanding performance in meeting team and individual objectives. I know we don't have a succession planning system in place now, but these candidates should be able to manage a staff and a budget, have good leadership skills, be rated high on core competencies, and have been mentored by an executive. These would just be the basics. We could build the criteria as a team."

Sheila spoke up immediately. "Well, I'm OK with those as the benchmark we use to get these folks promoted. Let's see, I'm recommending Emily Morrison as director. Using Tracy's criteria, I rated Emily as exceptional last year on her performance appraisal, and I think she could one day replace me. Emily hasn't managed a large budget, but she has that skill set. I don't think any of us have mentored these people formally, but informally we have."

Tracy was getting a massive headache. These people were clueless. She could see that it had already been decided who would get promoted. She watched as Judy and Sheila ran the show. They gave their approval sparingly. Each executive put forth the names of one or two of their top people only for Judy and Sheila to find reasons why the person shouldn't be promoted. Only two executives got the nod to move ahead with their candidates. So as not to discourage the team, Judy asked that the subject be revisited at their next meeting.

"So that this process has a set of criteria that makes sense for the company, I'll meet with each of you prior to our next staff meeting to work on the promotional criteria we should use. Then we can discuss where we are and what needs to change," Tracy said, as she watched the faces of the group.

Interestingly, it didn't seem to bother the team that most of them had lost their bid for their candidate to go to the next level. It was as if they knew that the CEO and CFO would decide. She saw firsthand the amount of work to be done to get the team to act as executives.

"One final note about our promotional criteria is to be sure that our employees understand the criteria and what he or she will need to do in the future to be considered."

She watched Judy's face, which had turned several shades of red. Judy stumbled on her words.

"I'm not sure we want to do that since it will give our employees the wrong impression. Getting promoted is a decision we make. They don't have a say in this matter."

Tracy could see that Judy was uncomfortable and was probably wondering why she had hired her. Tracy was a mover and shaker. It was apparent that Tracy too had opinions and was not shy about voicing them. Sunset needed help and even if she decided to have a short tenure, there was no way she wouldn't attempt to get the company into the twenty-first century.

Tracy was able to calm the team and reassure them that together they would create the criteria. She told them that the best way to keep senior leaders was to keep them involved and informed. Talented senior leaders were in demand and could jump ship at any time.

Her head was now pounding. She was praying she wouldn't get a migraine headache on her first day on the job. She didn't need to spend the evening in bed, curled up with a pillow. She had work to do. There were so many systems lacking in human resources. She was also anxious to meet her team. When she went down to her office during the lunch break, the staff had all gone to lunch except for her assistant. She apologized for not introducing herself earlier. The staff meeting had definitely been scheduled at an inopportune time.

Tracy made a note in her Day Timer to, at some point, talk with the executive team about not having senior leaders start on the day of a scheduled staff meeting. It made it too awkward not meeting their team members on the first day. Anytime a new executive joined the company, the team was anxious to meet him or her. This allowed the team to form their own opinions. The anticipation of waiting to meet one's manager was a lot to handle in an industry plagued with downsizing efforts.

Following the five-minute afternoon break, Judy asked the team not to share the information she was about to divulge with their senior leaders and vice presidents. Tracy was curious to see what was so sensitive that only the executives would be privileged to the data.

"It's difficult for me to say that after thirty years of positive sales and a constant stream of revenue, we're going to have to lay off about 10 percent of our employees. If we don't reduce our overhead, we'll fall short by about twenty million dollars, which will not sit well with our shareholders and the board. I see no other course of action," Judy said.

What had she gotten herself into? Tracy didn't want to believe she was brought in to be the hatchet man. Employees would lose trust in a heartbeat. This was her first day on the job. She hadn't had an opportunity to get to know the employees and gain their trust. She had no credibility with the Sunset team. She was new and hadn't established herself. Why had Judy failed to mention that important detail during the interview process? Maybe she wouldn't have come. She didn't need the money. She enjoyed working and being part of a team. She was at a point in her life where she wanted to work for a company that was just as passionate about their employees as they were about the business.

This would be a major setback for the company. Whenever the media interviewed an executive from the company, usually Judy, the question would always be asked; how much longer can you survive without reducing your overhead? The finance side of Judy would always play that well-orchestrated speech of managing overhead better than their competitors, mainly due to her strong financial background and that of the CFO.

Tracy couldn't hold back any longer. "Judy, what's the timing of this layoff, and are we sure the only way we can save the twenty million dollars is through the elimination of positions? Are there any other options?"

Tracy sat there watching as the expression changed on Judy's face. You would have thought she was hit by a ton of bricks. Judy was careful with her choice of words.

"Tracy, I wish I had a better answer for you. This type of thing is always difficult. I think the sooner we get this over with, the better. Then we can return to normalcy. I thought either this Friday or next Monday."

Tracy was losing her cool. Why would anyone in their right mind schedule a layoff for four to five working days from the time it was announced, especially given the fact there hadn't been a human resources head to coordinate the effort.

"Judy, it generally takes a decent amount of time to plan and orchestrate a layoff of this magnitude. Is the senior leadership aware of the pending separation of some employees from the company?" Tracy asked.

As she watched the faces of the other executives, who seemed unmoved by the pending layoff, Leslie shot her a look that said now you understand why this place needs your leadership.

For the next three hours, Tracy took control of the meeting. One skill a number of companies had admired in her background was that of a reengineering guru. She was a master at coordinating rightsizing events. Each and every time she had to lay off employees, it brought tears to her eyes and left her stomach in knots.

At her last company, she had to let five hundred people go. No one was exempt. Executives along with directors and managers got caught up in the process. In the past, Tracy had always convinced the companies that employed her, to be humane in their treatment of employees during the separation process, so as not to cause major disruption and chaos in the business. Companies were helpless in the face of fate. Somehow she got the distinct impression that these people either didn't get it or just didn't care about the underlings.

Tracy was stunned by the marketing head's comment that employees were a necessary evil. Nora Lane was as insensitive as they come. She was centered only on her career. Life was all about Nora and what she could get out of the deals she negotiated. She wondered if Nora would appreciate someone labeling her as a necessary evil. If only the tables were turned, and Nora was on the receiving end. In the corporate world, it was just a matter of time. Life atop the corporate apex wasn't about how brilliant one was; it was simply about the chemistry between the executive, the CEO, and the board of directors. An individual with average skills could be successful if he or she was astute at playing the political game and staying ahead of the competition.

CHAPTER 4

The staff meeting was still going on as the hands on the clock approached six. Tracy wasn't sure that any of them had a true sense of the hours that would need to be invested to pull the separation off with no legal ramifications.

"Judy," she asked, straight out, "is the board of directors aware of the timing of the layoff? The reason I ask is that we want to minimize our exposure and not have the media catch board members off guard." One thing about Judy was her honesty, no matter how naive she sounded.

"They know we have to cut jobs, but I haven't discussed the timing with them because frankly, I was waiting for you to get on board to spearhead this effort."

Tracy explained to the team that she would need a minimum of three weeks to coordinate the layoff. Judy was a little reluctant to give her the time. However, she convinced Judy that with the additional time, which was still by most standards unrealistic, she could reduce their legal exposure and keep their corporate image in the community untarnished.

The next fight she had on her hands was obtaining severance packages for those who would be affected. Since the company hadn't laid off anyone in their thirty year history, and most reductions were due to attrition, Sunset didn't have a severance policy. It was foreign to both Judy and Sheila to give employees money to leave. The other executives got it and tried to convince them it was protocol. It was the accepted standard in the industry to provide severance dollars to help employees transition into a new company or another field.

Tracy went on to explain that typically administrative support staff received four to six weeks of severance, managers received three months, directors four to six months, and executives from six months to a year.

Sheila chimed in, "Why in the world would we pay employees who are losing their jobs that amount of money?"

Tracy was hoping to get some support from the team, but they all remained silent. She was beginning to understand how the team operated. They probably feared Judy and Sheila and didn't want to jeopardize their relationship or put their job on the line. It was every man for himself. Tracy had taken a personal oath when she entered the human resources field to protect the company and its executives, employees, shareholders, and customers. She was a leader for all of the people, not just those favored by Judy and the executive team.

"Sheila, some of the severance dollars can be written off, which minimizes the cost to the company. The employees we separate from the company will need some money to tide them over until they get hired by another company, and above all we need to keep them as customers."

Tracy could tell by the look on Sheila's face that she wasn't buying it. Tracy mentioned the high unemployment rate in

Florida and the nation and, according to The Wall Street Journal, how long it would take for a person at the manager or director level to find employment. Sheila still sounded and looked unconvinced.

The next fight would be getting them outplacement services, which seemed foreign and out of the question when Tracy broached the subject. That definitely opened up a can of worms. Both Sheila and Judy had become millionaires on the backs of the hourly employees working in the restaurants. When the company brought Judy and Sheila on board, there were a number of struggling years. When their base salaries couldn't be increased to keep up with the industry, they were given tons of company stock, which was now trading at sixty-four dollars a share; a nice nest egg, no doubt.

To end the challenge of the unknown for the executive team, Tracy suggested that they meet the next morning at nine to go over a preliminary schedule for the upcoming event, which she named "code red." She knew it was useless to continue to throw ideas on the table that seemed beyond their grasp. She was sure some of the executives understood and had decided not to participate in the discussion.

Her heart always went out to the underdog. Even though the layoff wouldn't affect hourly employees and restaurant managers, she couldn't help but wonder why companies treated hourly employees like second-class citizens. Companies would rather lose millions and millions of dollars to turnover than invest in their hourly employees by making health care insurance affordable. Society kept these poor souls in their place. Some of them worked two jobs to get a forty-hour work week.

As the executives were gathering their things, Tracy told them that for the next three weeks, they should plan on team meetings each day for about an hour to go through the details, so critical decisions could be made. To make it easier on the group, she suggested they alter their time each day. Those who wouldn't be able to make it could be brought up to speed by an assigned designee, one of their colleagues.

Tracy also informed them that aside from their daily group meetings, she would also be meeting with them individually. That brought moans and groans and sounds of disenchantment. She was sure they were moans of despair. Tracy walked out of the meeting with her friend Leslie, who was rushing to keep dinner plans.

When she got back to her department, it was deserted. Everyone had gone for the day. She made a mental note to circle the floor early Tuesday morning to introduce herself to the team. She gathered a few things, stuffed them in her briefcase, and clicked off the lights. On her way to her car, she ran into Lauren who assured her that they were all glad she had arrived.

"Give it some time, Tracy. We'll all adjust to you and the priorities necessary to keep the bottom line strong," Lauren said, as she turned to go back into the office building. Tracy threw up a hand, gesturing her a good evening.

She wasn't looking forward to the long night ahead. Thank goodness she had several prototypes to get the job done. Tracy was sure the executive team would freak out when she communicated to them that senior leaders of the organization would need to be brought in to the fold by Wednesday. That would give them plenty to think about.

What she wouldn't give to be a fly on the wall when Judy and Sheila got together. She was sure they were sizing her up and wondering what they had missed in her interview. Why hadn't they seen the charismatic, self-assured qualities of this direct, very assertive woman? Tracy could only imagine them saying how they wished they'd had the hindsight and foresight to do the layoff before her arrival. Yes, the roller-coaster ride for the next three weeks would be anything but pleasant.

Tracy wasn't sure of restaurants near her apartment, so she stopped off at the corner Starbucks; a cold sandwich and a cappuccino would have to do. It had been a long day, and her patience was wearing thin. She spotted a guy leaving and rushed to secure his table. As she did, a handsome man placed his cross-body bag on the table.

"Sorry about that. I'm sure you didn't see me, but I've been waiting for this table for about five minutes," he said.

She looked up, completely taken aback, and decided she'd take her order to go.

"That's quite all right. It's been a busy day at the office, and I'm not sure I'm totally with it. By all means take the table."

With that she removed her stuff and headed for the counter as he extended his hand.

"By the way, I'm Eric Sears. I'd be happy to share this table with you." Tracy shook his hand and took him up on his offer.

"That's so kind of you. Do you mind watching my things while I place an order?"

There was one person in front of her. As Tracy waited she started to reflect on her day. What was she thinking, leaving California and moving to Florida? She was alone and had deserted what few friends she had there. What she wouldn't give at this moment to be back there … anywhere but here.

When they called her name, she collected what would be her dinner and returned to the table. She hadn't paid much attention before to the man who was now watching her very closely. She noticed his scrubs, no doubt a doctor.

Eric was totally gorgeous. He looked to be in his late thirties or early forties. His smile drew you in and his eyes seemed to focus beneath the surface. He was friendly and easy to talk to.

Eric had solid black hair with just a hint of gray above each ear, ocean-blue eyes, dimples in each cheek and a deep bronze tan. His muscles popped out under the sleeves of his top. Eric smelled of cologne. She checked his fingers ... no wedding ring, she thought. She was sure that a specimen this gorgeous was either married, gay, or bisexual. After all, this was Miami.

Eric stood up and tucked her chair under her; a gesture women seldom saw in this day and age.

"Thanks, Eric, for sharing your space with me. I hope I'm not imposing," Tracy said, praying the whole time that he wouldn't mind. There was something about Eric that was mesmerizing. What a handsome man.

"I don't think you told me your name," he said, closely watching her the entire time.

"I'm Tracy Hudson. It's so nice to meet you. Is this one of your favorite spots to hang out?" Eric shook his head while taking a bite of his cake.

For the next thirty minutes, Eric and Tracy shared background information. She told Eric all about her new job and moving from Los Angeles to Miami. Eric grew up in Connecticut where he had gone to medical school. He relocated to Miami nine years ago after completing his residency at Yale New Haven Hospital. He was a plastic surgeon and had a private practice in Miami Beach. She could tell that Eric loved what he did. He looked at plastic surgery as a form of art—creating a person in his or her best image. Eric saw beauty in every woman and man; it was that simple.

Maybe to get to know him better she would take his card and use him for her next injection of Botox and fillers. She was against getting a facelift even though she didn't currently need one. The aftermath of facelifts wasn't pleasant. She had seen so many disfigured women in California trying to prolong the fountain of youth only to prematurely age themselves. Their faces looked distorted. Once a facelift went bad, there was no correcting the mistake. It was now approaching eight, and no matter how enjoyable the conversation was, Tracy knew there was much work to be done.

"My new friend, I'm going to have to leave you," Tracy said.

"Is it time for beddy-bye or do you have that special person waiting for you back at the ranch?" he asked.

"Neither," she responded. "I've a ton of work I need to do before I call it a night."

He could see that her demeanor had shifted from being jovial to serious, so they exchanged business cards and said good night.

As Eric sat there, he wanted to know more about Tracy Hudson. Thank goodness for the Internet. Life no longer had to be a mystery. Whatever you wanted to know could be found there. He had second thoughts about stepping into her past. It wasn't as if he was a free agent. He did have a somewhat steady girlfriend who was practically living with him when she was in town, although she had her own place.

Eric knew it was just a matter of time before he broke off the relationship with Priscilla. Priscilla was pressing him for a greater commitment, and Eric wasn't at that stage in life. Playing the field was more exciting than devoting and giving himself to one woman. Eric continued to check his messages and a short time later he headed home.

Forty minutes later she was at her computer in her apartment, drafting the schedule of events. She was sipping a glass of wine and enjoying the quietness of her surroundings. She jumped when the phone rang. As Tracy picked up her cell, she heard her friend's voice.

"How was your first day? I see you are still alive and well," Don Johnson said, as she made a horrible grunting sound. Don's timing was always on cue. She had planned to call him tomorrow morning about working with the team and her in orchestrating the layoff.

"Yes, I'm alive but barely surviving. I think there should be a law against working with people who are still in the dark ages, screwing helpless employees," she said, taking another sip of chardonnay and thankful that her apartment had been well stocked.

She brought Don up to speed, telling him about the personalities at the company and the challenges ahead. She knew with his help she would be able to pull off the layoff and not have any hiccups in the process. She enjoyed working with Don. He had a charming wit about him. He was so smooth that you never saw the sales pitch coming. Don had also worked with her in the past and had pulled off some difficult separations in a relatively short period of time. Tracy knew that she could have met the Monday deadline, but it would have left too many disgruntled employees, not to mention serious damage to the company's image in the industry.

They spoke for another ten minutes. She promised to call him Tuesday morning following her nine o'clock meeting with the executives. When she hung up the phone, she felt so much better.

Now she had the insurmountable task of convincing Judy and Sheila that not only did they need to provide severance packages and outplacement services, but also needed to rent space in a separate facility or use Brock's regional office so the laid-off employees would have a place to go to in order to find new employment. It was hard enough to lose one's job, but not having professional counselors and consultants to work with was even more devastating. Waking up the morning after being fired and not knowing what to do next could cause even a well-adjusted person to slip into depression.

Tracy worked until two a.m. She was totally exhausted from her lack of sleep the previous night and thinking about all of the upcoming challenges at Sunset. Her head hit the pillow at around two-thirty. When she awoke and dragged herself out of bed at six, she felt a little refreshed.

She was in the office at five minutes to eight, walking around and introducing herself to the human resources team. At ten minutes to nine she headed to the boardroom. She was the first to arrive. The room was dark with the shades drawn. She opened up the shades and set up her PowerPoint presentation. She located the easel at the back of the room and searched frantically for Magic Markers. Not locating any, she called her assistant, and within minutes Sharon was standing in the doorway with boxes of markers. She could tell that Sharon was both efficient and had a sense of urgency about her.

Sharon was Hispanic with long curly brown hair. She was in her early twenties and had worked at Sunset for six years. She was five two with slight freckles underneath her eyes and on the bridge of her nose. She had married young and had a small child whom her mother kept while she worked.

The executives started coming in around five minutes after nine. With the exception of Sheila, all executives were in their seats by ten minutes passed nine. Judy suggested they start, given the schedule and priorities of the day.

Tracy reviewed the schedule with the executives, highlighting the fact that they needed to meet with senior management tomorrow to make them aware of the layoff. She suggested that anyone who was traveling could be conferenced in. She told the team that the layoff would take place the Wednesday, prior to Thanksgiving week.

Judy wanted the layoff to happen the Friday before, but after Judy listened to the rationale, she thought better of the recommendation. Tracy explained that they had to think about the survivors, those employees who would not be affected. It would also be a very sad and difficult time for them, seeing their friends and peers leave without jobs as they remained gainfully employed.

The executives were surprised when Tracy said she would have a nurse on board and security would be notified to keep separated employees from returning to the building. She explained that they would encourage employees to pack their personal items up on the day of the event, or return later that evening or on another day to pack their things under the watchful eye of a human resources representative. If employees preferred, the company would designate a person to pack up their things and have them delivered by courier. She stressed that the employees must leave with dignity and that security guards not under any circumstances would escort them out like criminals.

The discussion went south when she approached the subject of severance packages and outplacement services. Judy was the first to speak.

"Won't we be establishing a precedent, giving away packages to people who are talented and sure to find work somewhere else?"

She took a deep breath. Judy was sounding like a leader who ruled with an iron fist in the 1970's and felt employees could "do it my way or the highway." What had she gotten herself into? The conversation went on for the next thirty minutes. She'd finally had enough and put a compromise on the table.

"At this point I recommend that we offer four weeks of severance to administrative support individuals, two months to managers, and four months to directors. If any officer is affected, let's offer six months," Tracy said.

To win at the game of verbal diarrhea, Tracy proposed a stipulation to the plan. "If any employee gets a job before his or her severance runs out, we'll discontinue paying so there will be no double-dipping."

She knew that was a language they understood. In their minds employees would never use up all the money, so they would never have to pay out full severance packages. Tracy wanted them to keep thinking that was the case. In today's market, it would be rare for employees to get employment within the allotted amount of time. In a more sophisticated organization, she would have asked for a safety net to accommodate hardship cases where severance packages ran out before employees secured employment.

She asked to meet with Judy following the meeting and asked that Sheila join them. Might as well kill two birds with one stone, she thought. Why prolong the agony? She wasn't willing to give up on offering outplacement services. Tracy had a speech prepared and had highlighted key points that she knew finance people would understand. She was prepared to use scare tactics with them. The last thing Sunset needed were employees going postal. She explained that there was a fine line between sanity and insanity.

"Sometimes when employees become distraught, their behavior can escalate to violence. We don't need any crazed employees hanging around, strategizing on how to get even," Tracy said.

After explaining how outplacement services could humanize the process for the terminated employees and ease the pain for those who remained employed, both Sheila and Judy hesitantly agreed. Things were moving according to her plan.

As she was leaving, she turned back and said, "I'll explain to the team tomorrow afternoon that the supervisors of separated employees will meet with them on the day of the event and tell them face-to-face. In the room with the supervisor and the employee will be a human resources representative. An outplacement counselor from Brock Consultants will be housed in a different office which will allow individuals to openly discuss their concerns and vent their emotions. You'll see that having a human resources representative in the room will lessen the stress on the supervisor. Everything will be scripted. I'll be available for anyone who needs me."

She pulled the door shut and left Sheila and Judy to ponder everything she had said.

When Tracy returned to her office, she motioned for Sharon to come in. She told Sharon that for the next month they would be joined at the hip. She reiterated the confidentiality agreement Sharon had signed when she joined the company and the high need for candor, and confidentiality. Sharon was instructed to schedule afternoon meetings with three of the executives, an afternoon meeting on Wednesday with the total team, and to alternate between morning and early afternoon meetings with the executive team. She also asked for the personnel folders on each of her team members and for Sharon to schedule individual meetings with each of her direct reports. After receiving her marching orders, Sharon left.

Tracy phoned Judy's office. When Judy picked up the receiver, she could hear Sheila in the background. "Judy," Tracy said, "I forgot to ask if each team member is supposed to reduce his or her team by 10 percent, or if there are sacred areas that shouldn't be touched or should be reduced by a lower percentage. I'll be up after lunch so I can get the details."

Judy agreed on a time, and she hung up. This was no time to be modest and walk softly. Sunset had created the monster, and it was now up to Tracy to reengineer the company. This would also be excellent training in case they had to trim the staff in the future. There was still so much to do and so many things that could blow up in the process. The executives would soon realize that they were all in it together. She wasn't going to be viewed as the hatchet man, and she wasn't going to allow the layoff to become a human resources directive.

Tracy met with Judy after lunch and shared the particulars. Judy was a taskmaster, and in a lot of ways, Tracy felt sorry for her. She knew loneliness at the top from experience. As she was climbing the corporate ladder, it was easy to be part of the group and talk about "those people" who made the decisions. Now she was one of "those people."

Life did seem a lot simpler when she didn't have the total responsibility for the lives of others. At the time, even though Tracy was not yet a member of that secret society at the top that was making all of the decisions, she always had a knack for connecting with people, whether they were board members, executives, or custodial staff members.

She didn't pull any punches. She was fair and consistent in how she handled people and situations. She was true to her word. Playing corporate gamesmanship only led to disaster. Her reputation was too valuable to her. Tracy always made it clear to employees that she would remain confidential and keep what they were saying in the confines of the office, provided what they were sharing wasn't in violation of the law or company policies and procedures. She would counsel people who found themselves in difficult situations and would give them the opportunity to disclose the information first.

As Judy was talking about where the cuts needed to be made, Tracy felt in her gut that the executive team hadn't been privileged to that conversation.

"Judy, are your direct reports in receipt of this information?" she asked.

Judy told her that she would send each an e-mail within the hour, so there would be no reason to have another meeting that day. She tried to convince Judy to meet with the group as a team and perhaps take a more democratic approach to getting at the same results. She cautioned Judy that her decision could backfire and make her team feel as if she didn't value their input. Judy didn't agree with her, but Tracy didn't give up easily.

"Judy, I realize this is your decision, but I think there could be some backlash if the team thinks their feedback isn't important. I think you may want to rethink your decision," Tracy said. She continued to expound on the reasons why the team should be involved but to no avail.

She left Judy's office feeling somewhat defeated and feeling sorry for her team members. Wait until they understood where the cuts would be made. It was obvious whose Judy's pets were. There was no rhyme or reason to her choices other than personal bias. There was little objectivity to her decisions. Tracy had fought a good fight and negotiated her percentage for the human resources department. Others on the team weren't so lucky.

There would be no cuts in Sheila's department. To let Judy tell the story, finance was understaffed. Tracy made a mental note to check that out. Operations, marketing, and legal would all have to trim their departments by 5 to 8 percent. The bulk of the cuts would have to come from the real estate and franchising departments. Tracy was hoping that Judy could get ahead of her by notifying the team of the amount of money each would contribute to the pot.

She looked at her watch. Where had the time gone? She quickly sent Don an email so he could free his schedule in order for his team to help with the layoff. She now would be about ten minutes late for her meeting with Lauren Hanks, the company's chief operating officer. Lauren had a soft demeanor about her that gave the impression she was in your corner; however, Tracy could feel the claws beneath the exterior. There was still something not right with her. Lauren motioned Tracy to come in the moment she saw her face.

"Come in, Tracy. Have a seat. I just need to give these to my assistant."

Tracy looked around Lauren's office, which looked junky on its face. There must have been about fifty pictures in a collage on the wall and a dozen family pictures in frames on Lauren's credenza. There was an oversized lamp on her desk, and the floor was littered with company mugs, tee shirts, and pictures from years past. Her conference table was covered with magazines and books, and in every corner of the floor were piles and piles of paper. The bookshelf had many out-dated business books. All in all the office décor was tasteless.

"To what do I owe this pleasure?" Lauren asked, as she took a seat opposite Tracy. Tracy watched as Lauren appeared to be trying to read the notes she had in her hands.

"I apologize for being late. My meeting with Judy took a little longer than I'd planned. We have our work cut out for us. We're about two weeks out from the time when everything will need to be done, except for last-minute changes," Tracy said.

"I wasn't aware that the time was so short. I thought we had three weeks total. Maybe I misunderstood, or perhaps my memory is failing me," Lauren said.

Tracy told Lauren she hadn't misunderstood. The last week would be needed for last-minute changes. It was clear from her meeting with Judy that the cuts weren't about organizational effectiveness. Judy merely wanted to meet the shortfall. As long as Sheila's department remained untouched, Judy probably cared little about the feelings of the others.

"Are we all supposed to cut our teams by 10 percent?" Lauren asked, as she looked on with curious eyes.

Tracy knew it was too soon for Judy to have sent the email explaining how the cuts were decided and each team member's share. Tracy watched as Lauren double-checked to make sure the office door was securely closed.

"Let me give you a bit of advice, Tracy. I know you're new here, but I want to prevent you from falling into a land mine as you navigate your way through this maze. I had your position about eighteen months ago. I was the chosen one until my colleagues decided to gang up on me. They wanted to get me fired. Just be careful of those you let into your inner circle."

Tracy couldn't believe what she was hearing. What happened to all of the bullshit she got during the interview process? She heard nothing but what a great collaborative team they were, how everyone worked for the good of the company, and how caring each one was. She recalled Judy stating that each one had the other's back. Well, that wasn't proving to be true. The question was; why would Lauren open up to her so soon? It wasn't as though they had developed a relationship.

Lauren was a dangerous person, one not to be trusted. Tracy knew how to play the game. Keep Lauren talking and make her feel more and more comfortable with her new peer was Tracy's objective.

"Why were your colleagues trying to get rid of you? Had anything happened among you guys?" Tracy asked.

She knew there were always two sides to every story. Why would her colleagues be out to get her, was the question that remained unanswered? Lauren shared how flighty Nora Lane, the marketing guru, was. Lauren described Nora as fickle and a lightweight, and shared that the only reason Nora was successful was due to her relationship with a particular board member. Nora also knew how to wow board members, which apparently bothered Lauren.

Nora wasn't viewed as a marketing guru in the industry. She had been with the company for eleven years. Nora was of average height with long strawberry-blonde hair and light brown eyes. She had gone through two divorces. Nora's second husband was a field marketing director at Sunset when they married. There was a big stink about the head of marketing marrying one of her own. Judy and Sheila stopped the dialogue by making it clear to company employees that Nora was there to stay and that she was a contributing member of the executive team.

Nora's affair was kept from board members. Judy found a job for Nora's new husband in the human resources department, but the marriage went belly-up about a year later when her spouse was caught sleeping with one of the general managers. There they were at the company's annual conference, shacking up like teenagers. The general manager was demoted, and her spouse resigned shortly thereafter. Thank goodness Tracy hadn't been there at the time to deal with company dating. Nora should have been fired for violating company policy.

Had Tracy stepped into Peyton Place? Did these people do whatever they wanted to no matter who it hurt, and weren't there any repercussions? Didn't they know the law? What if Nora's spouse had challenged the company's decision, claiming that Nora made unwelcome advances toward him?

Dating was allowed in the work environment as long as human resources intervened and made sure that each contributing party was aware of the company's position, what happened if either party decided they wanted out, and that there couldn't be a direct reporting relationship.

There was something known as a love contract that each person involved in the relationship needed to sign. That guaranteed employment to both if suddenly the relationship went south. The document was legal and would stand up in court. She remembered in California when an executive had decided to date one of his department managers. Tracy had tried to discourage the relationship, but since they were both consenting adults, she had legal draw up the contract. She asked the executive and manager to decide who would be leaving the department. The decision had to be mutual. The woman could not be forced out because she was in a lower-paying position.

In the end the consenting executive and manager had agreed that the manager would move to another department, managed by one of the other company executives. Like so many office relationships, the arrangement didn't last. The wandering eyes of the executive soon chose his next victim.

She and Lauren worked for the next hour on the upcoming layoff. Lauren felt a little more at ease after Tracy told her she would only have to cut her team by 5 to 8 percent. Lauren continued to press her for how much each of her colleagues would need to contribute, but Tracy told Lauren she didn't have that information. Tracy assured her that Judy would be sending each one an email by the end of day. Tracy didn't feel it was her place to share what her colleagues would have to reduce their staffs by; that was Judy's job. Deep down in her gut, Tracy knew Judy wouldn't send an email. Judy was leaving that job to her.

As Tracy was leaving Lauren's office, she couldn't help but notice a small picture on her desk. In the picture were Judy, Sheila, Nora, and Lauren with some unrecognizable guy—or at least she hadn't met him. They were all holding fishing poles with odd caps on their heads.

"That looks like fun. What were you guys doing?" she asked Lauren.

Lauren explained that each year a small team gets flown on one of the board member's planes to Alaska to fish. The board member pays the expenses, and the trip is generally over a weekend. Lauren explained that not all executive members were privileged to an invitation. It took Lauren about two years to be asked; actually Lauren was only "invited" after she questioned Judy and made somewhat of a scene after discovering that Nora attended each year.

Tracy now had a better understanding of how things got done. She was careful not to criticize anyone or to rationalize anything that Lauren shared. What a zoo, Tracy thought. The company needed so much help. The executives were all jockeying for a position and to remain in Judy's good graces. The executives had lost all sense of judgment. To them it was about power and influence. The friction between Nora and Lauren was obvious. Judy and the others just sat back and let them duke it out, figuratively speaking.

Maybe she had wanted to get away from Stephen so badly that she had jumped at the first offer. Utopia was definitely not here at Sunset Pub and Grill.

One of Tracy's biggest mistakes and regrets prior to joining the company was not meeting with the board members. To her surprise human resources had never been involved with the compensation committee. She found that unusual for a company its size. Judy assured her that she would have a critical role working with the compensation committee.

The executives and the board all felt that Sunset was very unique in comparison to other companies in America. The board members had never worked for any major companies, with the exception of the newest board member, John Bailey. Each member was a millionaire who either came from money, made millions after starting his own company or earned millions while working for small boutique firms.

Tracy was beginning to realize that it was like the fox guarding the hen house. She would have the pleasure of meeting the chairman of the board today at four; she could hardly wait.

In the meantime she wanted to check in with Leslie to see what light she could shed on Lauren and Nora. She didn't need anyone sugarcoating anything. These were two devils in the forest, Tracy was sure. She needed to understand Nora's and Lauren's motives and rationale for going up against each other. There had to be more to their disagreements. The two were already at the top of their careers. She surmised that Nora was envious of the salary and perks Lauren received.

The chief operating officer position was a bigger role and as a result carried more weight than marketing. They were at odds with each other. Nora had the most tenure with the company, other than Judy and Sheila. In a lot of ways, Judy felt compassion for Nora and mothered her like she was her daughter. Nora had been quite successful with all of the company's marketing and advertising campaigns and had made a decent name for herself in the local community. Nora had Judy wrapped around her little finger. It was just a matter of time before the cat fight between Nora and Lauren went live.

CHAPTER 5

Tracy returned to her office and made a few calls. She had to make sure Don could fly in tomorrow to meet with Judy, Sheila, and her before meeting with the team. Don had already made arrangements to fly out that evening and would be joining her in the morning. Since his flight was arriving after midnight, they made plans to have dinner the following evening.

Tracy met briefly with Sharon concerning the day's activities and tomorrow's schedule, and instructed her to call Don's assistant with hotel information and directions to the corporate office. Tracy apologized to Sharon for not having much time to spend with her but reassured Sharon that things would calm down after thirty or so days.

She knew it was no way to win friends and influence people, but she had no other recourse at the moment. Thank goodness she had arrived at Sunset when she did. If nothing else, at least the employees, whose services were being terminated, would leave with dignity and some money. Too many things could go wrong if you put people on the street with no funds.

She called Leslie's office only to find that she was meeting with outside counsel concerning a pending lawsuit. Her assistant, Lynn, said Leslie would be free around five. Tracy got on Leslie's schedule for five-thirty in case her meeting with the chairman of the board went a little long. She had about twenty minutes before meeting with the board chairman, Zahn Durk.

She asked Sharon to pull together some information on the chairman as she surfed the Internet to get facts as to how Zahn had become a multi millionaire. Zahn had made his money in real estate. He grew up poor and had gotten a late start in school. After graduating from high school, he attended the University of Boston for two years. Finding it difficult to adjust to college life, Zahn dropped out and started buying real estate with an investor he had met while on a skiing trip. Zahn was quite convincing and had made the investor, who took a chance on him, a hefty amount of money. He was now in his late sixties and enjoyed life traveling around the world. He had homes in France, Dubai, Italy, San Francisco, and West Palm Beach. He spent most of his time in Paris or traveling on his yacht.

She was taken aback when she met Zahn. He was short and soft-spoken. There were no signs of gray in his hair, and he was immaculate in his dress. Just looking at him, you could tell that his suits were tailor-made. The letters "z.a.d." were embroidered on the cuffs of his shirt. His silk tie had diagonal stripes in shades of red, blue, and yellow. He wore no jewelry. His face had few wrinkles, and his broad smile pleasantly took you in. Zahn's eyes were the color of the sky after a hard rain as a rainbow was forcing its way in. He didn't look to be a day over fifty.

Zahn stood as Tracy entered the room, acknowledging her presence. He shook Judy's hand as she entered the conference room and embraced Sheila with open arms. After the introductions, they got down to business.

Judy took a backseat, allowing Tracy to highlight the upcoming layoff. If she had known that Judy wasn't going to take an active part, she would have come better prepared for the meeting. Tracy still sounded like a pro, explaining all that needed to be done before that critical Wednesday. Zahn was polite and gracious. When he didn't understand something, he didn't fly off the handle or into a tirade; he asked questions and processed the information.

The conversation shifted to Tracy's involvement with the compensation committee. Judy chimed in, almost apologetically. It was obvious that the discussion had never taken place; you could tell by his reaction. Another slip-up. Maybe Judy wanted to see what type of reaction she got from Zahn, so if it were negative, she wouldn't have to take ownership. She had let the cat out of the bag. Might as well go for the bull's-eye, Tracy thought.

The meeting didn't last long. Tracy convinced Zahn of the importance of her being a part of the compensation committee. She wouldn't be a voting member but would be there to help guide the discussion, to explain executive compensation and what had to happen within the parameters of the law, and to be responsible for all supporting documents. She was surprised that the board relied on the company for all its information. She explained to Zahn why it was necessary for the compensation committee to hire its own consultant. It was as if she was in a time bomb. Was the company just a sleeping giant, not paying any attention to its judiciary duty and responsibility?

Judy made it clear that both she and Sheila would still be at each and every meeting of the compensation committee. Tracy was beginning to piece the puzzle together. Sheila and Judy were everywhere. They were not going to relinquish any power or authority anytime soon. These were two non-trusting individuals. What Leslie had shared was true to form. For Judy and Sheila, Sunset Pub and Grill was their baby. They still ran it like a small enterprise. There was no letting go.

She also saw another side of Judy. In the presence of the chairman of the board, Judy was mild and meek. Judy waited for Zahn to speak before she offered any comments. Judy's participation in the meeting was laid back and unassuming. As the CEO, Judy should have taken the lead regarding the upcoming reengineering effort. Instead, she just sat there, offering very little.

Judy's colleague and close friend, Sheila, wasn't a whole lot different. Sheila took her cue from Judy and allowed Tracy to run the meeting. Maybe that was how both Judy and Sheila had survived all of those years, by letting the men on the board run the show in their presence.

The other disappointing feature of both the executive committee and the board of directors was the fact that all the members were white. The board lacked diversity in its make-up. The only diverse employees she had seen in the corporate office were in low-level positions.

Once she returned to her office, she would have her corporate director for compensation and benefits run a diversity report. That was the next project she had to tackle. It was so odd to Tracy that being in a city like Miami, the company was not more diverse at the top, given the heavy Hispanic population.

With the exposure in the media these days, with its lily-white leadership team, she wondered why diversity hadn't been mentioned as an initiative or a concern when she interviewed. Technically, it probably would have been better if her job had gone to a minority.

Tracy said good-bye to Zahn and reiterated that she was indeed looking forward to working with him and the other board members. They shook hands, and she quickly left in order not to engage in another conversation with Judy. She wanted to see Leslie before she left for the day. Upon exiting the conference room, Tracy explained that she had a five o'clock meeting with Leslie.

On her way to the meeting, Tracy wondered if she could make the impact in the company she needed to make. There were a lot of skeletons in the closet. The company didn't appear to want to invest the time and energy it would take to go from a mediocre company to a great company. They were very comfortable being in second place. She was now questioning her judgment coming to a place so archaic. Nevertheless she would see that some changes took place before she left, which was quickly becoming a reality.

The meeting in Leslie's office was breaking up as Tracy approached her door. Leslie's visitors were collecting their belongings and wishing her a pleasant evening. When all was clear, she entered Leslie's office, collapsing on the sofa in the far corner.

Leslie's office was exquisite. Leslie had always loved antiques and had a flair for taking odds and ends and making them look fantastic. Leslie's rosewood desk was heavily carved. Her mahogany 1800 Victorian conference table was surrounded by four banker's chairs. There were two art nouveau side chairs opposite the sofa, and to the left of her desk was an oakwood bookcase with glass doors. To make her office look more inviting, Leslie had added throw pillows and an Oriental rug on top of white carpet. At the end of her desk were fresh flowers and a silver tray that held bottled water.

"My goodness, Leslie," Tracy said. "I pity the person who will have to relocate you out of this office. I've never seen so much furniture, and might I add, you once again have demonstrated impeccable taste."

Leslie just laughed, telling her how she had confiscated the furniture from the warehouse. The furniture had belonged to one of the cofounders.

"I think people in Miami prefer comfortable, easy living furniture. Antique furniture does not suit their taste. It's too heavy for them. I grew up with antiques, so I fell in love with this furniture the moment I saw it."

Leslie's office definitely did stand out. Most of the corporate offices had Herman Miller modern furniture. Although the furniture was very much overpriced, it was practical and user friendly. It also took into account ergonomics in its workplace design, so employees were more efficient.

Tracy got up and closed the door since you couldn't be sure who lingered outside, especially since she was the new sheriff in town. Once Tracy made herself comfortable in one of the conference chairs, she was ready to get the facts from Leslie.

"Give it to me straight, my friend. What's going on in this place? I spent over an hour with Ms. Motor-mouth Lauren who spilled her guts, which I found quite strange. Then I had the pleasure of meeting Zahn Durk where both Judy and Sheila were non-assertive and timid. The two of them chose their words carefully, and oddly enough waited to be given permission to speak. What have I gotten myself into? I don't recall any of this being shared with me during my interview."

Leslie just looked at her for a moment. It hadn't taken Tracy an enormous amount of time to figure out most of the executives. She was reading them right. They were all self-centered, grabbing whatever they could as they dragged the other one down. If the team spent as much time running their departments as they did playing politics, maybe the company wouldn't be in its current predicament of having to lay off employees.

"Here's the score, Tracy. Judy plays a submissive role when it comes to authority, leaders who have more power than she does. Judy is trying to become the chairman to free herself from the day-to-day running of the company. Judy isn't going to let anyone or anything stand in her way. Both Nora and Lauren are jockeying for the CEO position. The problem is that neither has established the level of credibility with the board to edge out the other. If Judy becomes the chairman, they know the board will elevate her choice to the CEO position. If you want my honest opinion, I think the company would be better served to go outside and recruit new blood," Leslie said, as she reached underneath her desk and pulled out two cold Diet Cokes from her mini refrigerator.

Tracy was mulling over what Leslie had shared. She hadn't been wrong. What Leslie said explained why Judy unquestioningly accepted everything Zahn had said and why Judy was reluctant to give her opinion during the meeting. Judy had played the role of Dr. Jekyll and Mr. Hyde. It was obvious that she played her cards close to the vest.

Judy was a different person one-on-one. She was more questioning and a little less direct. In her presence you knew what to expect. Judy came across as concerned about what you had to say.

In the group or with the team, Judy showed little support. She sought approval of Tracy's ideas and proposals from Sheila and the other executives before voicing her opinion. Judy didn't want to be the odd man out. It was obvious that Judy wanted the executives to weigh-in before she chose a position. The friendship between Judy, Sheila, and Nora was solid. Judy was protective of Sheila and, in a strange way, a mother figure for Nora.

"How does Gary Umar figure into the equation? I haven't spent any time with him. I sense that he's not well liked by the team," Tracy said, while taking a sip of her Coke.

"Gary joined the team about two years ago. I think Judy thought she was adding diversity to her team by hiring Gary. He is a smart man. Gary has both domestic and international experience. He was brought in to help get the company into international waters. I personally think Judy would love to step up to the chairmanship and let someone else worry about making Sunset an international company."

The phone rang, but Leslie silenced it with the press of a button. Her assistant stuck her head in the door and said good night, reminding Leslie of her doctor's appointment in the morning. Lynn handed Leslie a stack of messages and some letters that needed her signature.

She watched as Leslie told her assistant not to worry. Leslie was sure the building would survive until she returned. The chemistry was good between the two of them. They could read each other's mind, as each one would finish the sentence for the other. Leslie was lucky to have such an efficient individual covering her back. The skills and talents of the right administrative assistant were priceless.

"Look at all these messages I need to return," Leslie said, as she tossed the messages on her desk. "I think people just expect you to work day and night around here. Trust me, you can if you don't have the good sense to carve out some 'me' time."

Leslie was very frank when Tracy asked why there was no diversity with top management. She explained that Judy considered Gary, being of Middle Eastern background, a minority. It was a shock to Judy's system when Leslie explained that according to the census and federal government guidelines, Gary was classified and considered white.

"We must increase our diverse population. The board has added that as an objective for Judy. Going at the rate she's going, the company won't get there anytime soon. That's where you come in, Tracy. You need to make the necessary changes while your honeymoon is still going on."

They talked some more about the backstabbing tactics of Nora and Lauren. Leslie cautioned her to be careful sharing information with the two. Lauren was known for twisting information and taking it back to Judy. Leslie warned Tracy never to say anything she wouldn't want played back on the company's PA system.

"Before I go, did you get an email from Judy giving you the percentage by which you need to cut your team?" Tracy asked.

Leslie checked her emails, but there were no messages from Judy. At least she is true to form, she thought. Judy isn't going to stir up a hornet's nest.

It was after seven when she returned to her office. The place was deserted. Sharon had left her a stack of papers and messages. On the top, circled in red, was a note from Sharon asking her to please call Mr. Eric Sears. Sharon wrote in big bold letters that Eric had called twice, saying you know who he is. As Tracy picked up the phone to dial Eric, there was a knock on the door. She looked up into the eyes of Sam Mason from IT.

"I can come back in the morning if it's too late for us to meet," Sam said. Tracy had totally forgotten he was coming. She was so fully absorbed in her conversation with Leslie that she hadn't noticed the time.

"Come in, Sam. I'm so sorry to keep you waiting. I just left Leslie's office. We had a number of things to review. I'm OK meeting now if this time works with your schedule. My calendar is booked solid tomorrow."

They decided it would be best to get started and go as far as they could with her training. Tracy was a quick study. She was very familiar and used to working with computers. She knew computers were the world's work engines. There was no way to function in today's world void of technology. She remembered when having a cell phone was a luxury … a way to make a statement. Now you had to have a cell phone for security and safety, and to keep in touch with the world. She and Sam worked for half an hour. Sam felt comfortable that Tracy would have no difficulty whatsoever with their systems.

She really liked Sam. He had such warmth about him. They talked about where they went to school and how they spent their free time. Sam grew up on the East Coast and attended undergraduate school at Boston University, majoring in computer science. School was never his favorite, even though he went back to school to get a master's degree. He married his childhood sweetheart, who was a school teacher for a private preparatory school in Miami.

Sam and his wife had three boys with another child on the way. They were excited because the ultrasound revealed it was a girl. Sam kept his long hair neatly pulled back in a ponytail.

He wore one earring in his left ear, and just like the morning they met, he was wearing khaki pants and a polo shirt. He had a deep tan and slight wrinkles beneath his eyes. It was obvious he loved his job.

At about eight-fifteen, they heard a custodial staff member outside the office running the vacuum cleaner and talking on his cell. They called it a night as Sam asked if she felt comfortable walking to the parking garage by herself. Tracy thought she would be fine. He explained that if she called security fifteen minutes before she was ready to leave, a guard would walk her to her car. Sam left as she gathered up her things, making a note to call Eric from her car.

Her friend Don was en route, so she knew that tonight would be another long one. She had to prepare her speech for their meeting with the senior leaders. She didn't want to get caught off guard as she had earlier today when Judy decided to let her take the lead with the board chairman. There were also some changes she needed to make to the schedule of events.

Tomorrow afternoon she and Don would meet with her human resources team and the senior leaders who would have to lay off employees. Now that she was on the company's Intranet system, she could map out the things they needed on each employee who was scheduled to be let go, such as age, race, time with the company, and current performance rating. This would be needed to make sure there wasn't a disproportionate number of minorities and older workers leaving the company.

She was delighted that Don was coming. She would have someone in her corner who understood all that needed to be done. Additionally, once they got the approved budget, Don would be able to dispatch his people. She welcomed and needed his help. Next time, if there were a next time, there would be more people trained to assist with the layoff. Now the burden fell on her shoulders.

She took Sam's advice and called security fifteen minutes before leaving. The security guard was quite friendly. He told her that security was always there for the executives, 24/7, and that a guard would come immediately to escort her to her car.

What a day it had been. She had seen the other side of the rainbow and she definitely didn't like the landscape. Nothing had really changed. No matter where you went in life, somehow you always ran into the same type personalities. The personalities were just in different bodies. The game was always the same ... the winner took all.

Thinking about what Lauren, a perfect stranger, had said to her was mind-blowing—informalities so soon. She had to be careful of Lauren. She was sure Lauren took no prisoners. In her world Lauren probably valued conflict, chaos, and deception. Thank goodness Leslie was a friend with the inside scoop on all of them. For now, she would tread carefully, seeking Leslie's advice every step of the way.

She threw her things on the backseat of the car, unlocked the front door, and headed to the apartment, not stopping for anything. The traffic lights were all aligned tonight. She sailed through each and every one of them ... green all the way. She was glad she had chosen to lease a place with the option to buy. She still wasn't sure if her future was on the East Coast. There was something magical and surreal about the West Coast that she was missing terribly at that very moment.

Once inside the apartment, Tracy realized she hadn't stopped to pick up dinner. No way was she going back out. If she got started right away, she could probably finish up shortly after midnight. She opted for a grilled cheese sandwich instead of cereal.

Tomorrow she would check out the restaurants in the area that delivered. There had to be excellent restaurants with good food who would deliver. Since she wasn't a cook and hated the idea of preparing a meal, she had always allowed Rhonda or Stephen to do the cooking. She was responsible for cleaning up the kitchen and coordinating takeout and dine-in foods, which suited her just fine. She poured herself a glass of wine as the worries and stress of the day melted away.

Tracy spent the next hour revising the schedule as they headed toward "code red." She put the final touches on the diversity analysis profile, so all Sharon and the human resources team would have to do, would be to plug in the information on each affected employee. She was sure there would be a lot of healthy discussions around the employees who were targeted to go.

The team hadn't worked with her before, but would quickly learn that Tracy was definitely not a pushover and that each executive would have to justify his or her list of candidates. Often during the diversity analysis, certain employees would have to be traded for others if there was an imbalance. It was not legal to place all the older employees on the list, opting to keep younger ones who were less expensive due to their tenure with the company—just as you couldn't target all of the minorities in favor of non-minority employees. She was sure there would be a lot of ill feelings once she pushed back and asked that names be removed and lists be revised.

Next, she tentatively scripted out the messages that supervisors would deliver to outgoing employees. The key message to get across in the first minute was that the list had been reviewed at the highest level and the decision was final. Then the supervisor would leave, and it was up to the human resources manager and the outplacement representative to get the terminated employee focused on his or her future with another employer.

In so many cases, the outplacement representative could speak firsthand about the experience of being separated from a company, since many of them had been victims themselves. If an employee became emotional during the discussion with his manager, the outplacement representative would meet next with the individual, followed by human resources, explaining the benefits in the severance package.

These were always difficult discussions. It was never easy taking away someone's job. No matter how prepared the company was, there were always unexpected things that could happen. She remembered one downsizing effort when an employee started to shake and cry. The nurse was called in to make sure the employee's health wasn't at risk. It was always better having someplace the employee could go to the next day and every day after that during the job search campaign. It was difficult to wake up the morning following a layoff not knowing what to do next. The career outplacement center, which she would orchestrate with Brock, would make counselors and consultants available, people to help write resumes, workshops to get employees prepared for job interviews, and computers and phones for employees to make contact with the outside world.

She wrote guidelines for department heads when they met with the employees who were not affected. These meetings would take place after the last laid-off person had exited the company. This was necessary to reassure the survivors and to keep them from jumping ship. She crafted the messages for the media and for the meeting with all employees to explain any new organizational changes or procedures.

The final thing she did before calling it a night was to make sure that Don had checked into the hotel. She called Don's hotel and asked the operator not to disturb him. She needed reassurance that her friend would be there to help her navigate through the sea of details.

As she was about to turn off her computer, she remembered the orientation meeting format she needed to develop for the human resources staff. Instead of writing a new program, she quickly revised the last one she had used, changing the company's name and job title from human resources consultant to human resources manager.

Thank goodness for computers, she thought. What a time-saving invention. Tracy turned off the computer and the lights and laid down, hoping to get some shut-eye. Just then she remembered that she hadn't called Eric. She made a mental note to call him first thing in the morning during her drive to the office.

Tracy awoke alive and refreshed. It was almost scary, considering the lack of sleep she had been getting. She made her morning coffee and ate a bowl of cereal. She packed some snacks in her handbag, considering her hectic schedule for the day. She had to go grocery shopping soon. Snacking on nuts and crackers was beginning to get old.

On her drive to the office, she phoned Eric. He answered on the first ring.

"Hello, corporate executive. Do you make it a habit of not returning phone calls in a timely manner?" Eric asked.

She explained how busy her day had been and that she barely had time to go to the restroom.

"Please accept my apology. My company is in the middle of reorganizing some of the functions and redefining business goals and objectives," she relayed, as a call was beeping.

"Let me put you on hold, it's probably the office telling me I forgot about a 7:00 a.m. appointment." Tracy switched to the other line. It was Don, calling to let her know he was in the lobby of her office building, waiting for her arrival.

Don was like that. He was always prompt, organized, and direct. She hadn't met a person yet who didn't think the world of him. He had helped her employees out a number of times by continuing their outplacement service when company funds ran out. He never put anyone on the street. She had also called him when a number of her colleagues were let go with no severance and no outplacement service.

Don was one hell of a guy ... always there to support and make her look good. He rarely took credit for his efforts. When she'd had a limited company budget to work with, it was Don who convinced his superiors to readjust their payment scale. He was the shoulder she used to cry on when she had to deal with corporate demons. She told Don she would pick him up in the lobby in about ten minutes. She returned to her call with Eric.

"So sorry about that. That was the office calling to let me know my colleague has arrived and is waiting in the lobby for me. Now what were you saying?"

Eric could see that she was extremely busy. He had wanted to meet her at Starbucks. He thought that would be safe territory. However, he knew if he pushed too hard, she would probably run in the other direction.

She explained that a dear friend was in town who would be working on the reorganization plan with her. She realized that she probably had said too much, but it was too late to retract her words. Words were like arrows; once released there was no pulling them back.

As she talked about her friend, Eric wondered if it was a current or previous lover. What was he doing? He didn't even know Tracy. Why was he so spellbound by her? He had his share of women running after him. He wasn't short on dates, but somehow this one had gotten to him. There was no way he could tell her that. His infatuation with her was all consuming. He had thought about Tracy all night.

Tracy was self-assured, independent, and had a certain aura about her. When she looked at him, his heart melted. She was unaware of her true beauty. He could tell that her smile and laughter eased the stress of the day and surrounded people with positive energy. Tracy was high-spirited and the epitome of elegance, grace and charm. She was a great conversationalist. He wanted to know more about this fascinating woman.

CHAPTER 6

Tracy squeezed into the first available parking place, telling Eric that she was approximately three minutes from ending their call. He thought that was a peculiar way to say I'll have to hang up soon … but then again, she wasn't your typical woman.

"I'd like to take you to breakfast or brunch when your schedule permits," Eric said.

She explained that being new to the company she had little time to socialize. He was not about to give up.

"You have to eat like all the rest of us. Tell me what the window looks like for you."

She needed to go. She didn't have time for pleasantries. Her day would be long with endless meetings, while she navigated around all of the politics. She had to get going for last minute strategizing with Don.

She wasn't concentrating on what Eric was saying. She wanted nothing more than to end the call and get on with her day. She wasn't looking for a new affair or a new lover. She needed time and space to think about her long-term plans. Somehow she didn't see herself living on the East Coast indefinitely. There were distinct differences that separated the two oceans. It was like living on two different continents.

"I wish I had a little more time right now. My day starts at five in the morning and ends around midnight. I eat over mounds of paperwork, and I sleep whenever I can. I don't mean to sound evasive, but my life and job are unpredictable for the moment. I've got to get this train back on its tracks, and I don't have a lifetime to do it in," Tracy said, eager to hang up.

Eric knew he was losing ground. If he didn't think of something soon, this would be his last conversation with her.

"I have a brilliant idea. Join me on Friday and Saturday for Miami Events and Adventures. It's a great way to meet new people and learn about the various communities and cultures. It will be a lot of fun."

"What is Miami Events and Adventures?" Tracy asked.

"It's a group of people who come together to share two-way conversation and experience firsthand all the city has to offer. The group sponsors from forty to fifty events per month. Friday evening is wine tasting, and there's a moonlight cruise on Saturday. You should join us. We'd love to have you."

"I really have to hang up now. Tell you what, I'll come on two conditions: first, that this Miami Events and Adventures isn't a clever way to promote dating, and second, I can bring a friend."

Eric reassured her that the purpose of the group was to help single people get out and make new friends and enjoy all that Miami has to offer. He reluctantly agreed to her bringing a friend. Who would she bring to an event he invited her to? He was hoping it wouldn't be a date. Perhaps she would bring her friend who was in town. After all, since he was in town and would probably be there during the weekend, it would make perfect sense to have him tag along.

She and Eric agreed to talk on Wednesday or Thursday so she could get all of the details. She could stop working at the normal quitting time on Friday and get in the office early Saturday morning and work until noon. She would be able to accomplish a lot since most employees would be at home with family and friends.

Tracy turned off her cell so as not to be disturbed during her meetings. She and Don worked all morning, preparing last-minute details for the afternoon meeting with Judy and the team. Don had brought along some prototypes that would serve as the blueprint for their discussion. He was accustomed to working with human resources people, so she was quite comfortable having her staff join them at the appropriate time to finalize their key roles and responsibilities during the layoff. None of her direct reports were affected by the layoff, which made it easier to get things done.

First, she and Don met with Sharon so she could format the charts that would be used to collect the diversity information on each individual on the list. She reminded Sharon of the sensitive nature of the information and the confidentiality statement she'd signed. Sharon was like a sponge, soaking up and learning as much as she could. Sharon was inquisitive and delightful to work with.

Sharon was working on her B.A. at Florida International University. She had met with her professors to let them know that she might have to miss a class or two because of the demands of her job. Tracy assured Sharon that she would do everything in her power to get her to class on time. Tracy also told Sharon she would work around her schedule in getting things done. If she was scheduled to be in class, one of the other team members would take the lead.

Sharon was quite surprise by Tracy's honesty and concern for her well being. The department had gone through three human resources executives in the past five years, and there was a lot of dissension in the department. Discord ran rampant. It was every man for himself. The group was in for a challenge; Tracy didn't operate like that. Each person on her team had to pull his or her own weight. She used mistakes as teaching ground. She was forgiving of mistakes as long as people would own up to them and not repeat them. Life was too short to constantly be looking over your shoulder. She always wanted the heads-up so she could protect her guys from the political arena.

Sharon was going to be the point person for arranging and maintaining a calendar of all schedules and meetings. Tracy explained why the company had to take the layoff route and what Sharon could expect from the aftermath. She didn't pull any punches with Sharon. She told Sharon the separation of employees would be difficult, and some of her friends might be affected.

The next order of business was to reserve, for each executive and manager, two rooms that would be used for the event. The office of the executive or manager would be where the initial discussion would take place. The second office would house the outplacement consultant. The employee would remain in the executive's or manager's office for the initial discussion with his or her supervisor, followed by human resources explaining benefits. And finally, in the second office, the outplacement consultant would shift the discussion to life after Sunset Pub and Grill.

Sharon took detailed notes and promised to circle back if she had questions. She left Tracy's office with a better understanding of how the process would work and her role in keeping everyone on track. She knew that if she did this well, there could be some rewards for her efforts. Her personal objective was to become a human resources representative within the next year. This could be her ticket to make that happen.

Sharon's spirits had been lifted. She was glad she wouldn't lose her job. Deep within, she was praying that her friends wouldn't be affected. Sharon had to keep a stiff upper lip. It was just a matter of time before her friends and the other employees discovered that she had a pivotal role to play. This was a tremendous responsibility for someone so young.

Tracy saw potential in Sharon. Her previous supervisors never addressed her potential. Sharon was always relegated to menial tasks. She was never asked her opinion, and it was rare for them to seek her feedback. Tracy was exactly what the department and the company needed. Sharon wondered how Tracy would fare under the leadership of Judy and Sheila. It was apparent that Tracy would be both a challenge and a threat.

Once Sharon had received her instructions, she left Don and Tracy alone. After the door was shut, Tracy let out a sigh of relief.

"Hudson, I think you're well on your way. You should be happy that Sharon is a quick study. That hasn't always been the case when we worked on reengineering efforts in the past."

She had to agree with Don. There were a lot of balls to keep in the air when managing an assignment of this magnitude. One mistake could be costly. You would never want to announce to the organization that all employees had been spoken to if that weren't the case. The delicacy of the situation required precision and excellent craftsmanship. The plan had to be well executed. If anything went wrong, the command center had to be notified. Things that had derailed would be back on track within moments of the call. People would be standing by who could answer questions and make decisions. If a supervisor botched up the script, the human resources individual would always be in the room to get the conversation back on track. And Tracy would always be available by cell to step in for any executive who encountered an emergency.

The morning had sped by. Sharon knocked on the door around noon to bring in deli sandwiches, garden salads, tea, and chocolate chip cookies. Tracy and Don had met earlier with the human resources team to bring them up to speed and had held a conference call with Don's people to introduce Tracy to his team. Don had taken the liberty of sharing her biography with the outplacement consultants. He had explained that his team was just as seasoned and talented as the folks on the West Coast.

She shared with Don that they would only need to cover about ten states during the layoff. The bulk of the employees affected would be in Atlanta, New York, Chicago, and Texas. For those states he would have the separated employees work with one of Brock's regional offices. There each employee would receive top-notch outplacement service with the latest in technology. They would also meet individuals from other companies who had lost their jobs. As they were finishing lunch and finalizing the presentation, Sharon stuck her head in the door to let them know that Judy was running late due to a luncheon meeting at the Hilton Hotel in downtown Miami.

Tracy used the time to discuss the personalities of the executive team, knowing she and Don would share their notes after meeting with the team, over dinner and a glass of wine. The strategy was to let Don take the lead after she introduced everyone. He would show statistics and share with the team how providing outplacement services would help boost the image of the company. Outsiders looking in and valuable customers would see how humanely the company was treating its severed employees. A number of the severed employees would hopefully be future customers for the company.

At two-thirty she and Don moved to the conference room on the first floor. He led the conversation with the executive team. To her amazement, not only did Don get Judy to increase the weeks of severance according to industry standard and to set up the career outplacement center; he also got her to institute a severance policy for the company and to offer training to the survivors.

The meeting had been a huge success. They had gotten all they asked for and more. Don had carefully crafted his message as he shared with the executive team how market shares could be lost if employees who left were not treated fairly—not to mention the bad press. The team quickly got on board buying into the strategy. She shared with the group the announcements that would go out to the media, franchise community, internal employees, and board members.

Tracy reviewed the schedule of events with the executives, highlighting the changes. She encouraged all of the executives to attend the meeting with the senior leaders that would follow their meeting. At the meeting each senior leader would receive a copy of the script, which they didn't need to read, but needed to be familiar with the contents. There were also

Q&As to help explain the typical concerns, issues, and questions that employees needed answers to. The supervisors were what connected employees to the company.

She and Don suggested that Judy hold a town hall meeting with corporate employees to explain what the company had to do to remain profitable. The facts and the vision for the future needed to be shared with employees.

The executives asked a couple of questions followed by Tracy explaining when she would be meeting individually with each executive to determine which employees would be separated. Before adjourning the meeting, she cautioned the group about sharing any of the names on the list, since the list was subject to change after the diversity analysis.

It was clear that Judy and Sheila were uncomfortable with the diversity analysis. Tracy reiterated its purpose, which was to keep the company out of court and to make sure their decisions were legally defensible. She knew the executive team would push back and challenge the diversity report to the nth degree. Bring it on, she thought. She may have decided not to practice law, but that didn't mean she didn't understand its intent and purpose.

She ended the meeting as the executives got up and moved to the boardroom. Senior leaders had already started to gather around the table. Extra chairs had been brought in to handle the overflow. Judy's assistant, Elizabeth, had already set up the conference call with the field leaders.

Tracy opened up the meeting, had Judy to say a couple of words, and asked the group of senior leaders on the line to open the email she had confidentially sent to them. She encouraged each leader to change his or her computer password if any of their assistants had access to their email account.

The leaders appreciated the question-and-answer document she had attached to the email. One of the field leaders on the line, said the scuttlebutt was that the company was going to be sold. Judy spoke up and reassured the field and corporate leaders that the company was not on the auction block, that meetings with corporate and field employees were scheduled for tomorrow, and that each executive, along with the senior leaders, would hold face-to-face meetings with their teams.

The group was told to direct all questions and concerns to Tracy and that there were no "dumb" questions. Tracy gave the group her office and cell numbers and the name of her assistant, encouraging them to contact her at any time. She reinforced their need to get in front of employees and have a healthy dialogue with them concerning what was happening within the company.

She and Don returned to her office, created some additional forms and letters, and headed to Mark's Seafood Restaurant in South Miami. She wanted to meet in a place far away from the corporate office to avoid running into any familiar people.

They each ordered drinks before looking at the menu. She ordered red wine, and Don ordered vodka and orange juice with a twist of lime. As they cleared their heads, they each smiled at the successful day they'd had with both the executives and senior leaders. If only the momentum would continue.

"Don, it's like old times, working with you to make sure employees aren't screwed and the reputation of the company remains positive," Tracy said, sipping her wine.

She had made the right decision bringing Don in. He was charismatic, charming, and a true salesman. He was a smooth operator. He could sweep you off your feet, before you knew what had happened.

"How do you feel about the day's activities?" she asked, as the waiter appeared to take their orders.

Don suggested that the waiter return in about twenty minutes so they could look over the menu offerings. He ordered a bottle of chardonnay as they prepared to make their selections.

"I think your team is quite dysfunctional. I don't think it's even fair to call them a team. What you have are individual players fighting for their piece of the pie while the CEO sits back and watches the show."

She had to agree with Don. Judy had no backbone with the chairman of the board and wasn't going to do anything to mess up her relationship with Sheila. Judy was just buying time. She didn't want to rock the boat … she knew the chairmanship was within reach.

"I think I've made the wrong decision moving East. I'm not interested in another dysfunctional company or relationship."

She was sure Don had been astute enough to see how Sheila and Judy played off of each other. How sad to not trust your team, she thought. Why hire people you either don't like or can't trust?

"Hudson, you need to refocus. You knew this wouldn't be an easy move for you. They need you and your skill set here. Didn't you tell me that employees have to wait ninety days before they are eligible for health insurance benefits, and that most managers aren't on a bonus plan?"

"That's another mountain I have to climb. When you deal with finance people, everything is about the dollar and the bottom line. Judy and Sheila can't see the forest for the trees.

I'll have that discussion with Judy off-line. I'm sure Judy will run to her friend Sheila the moment I leave."

Before Tracy joined the company, she had gotten the verbal offer from Judy. Judy told the human resources director to let her make the call to Tracy. As Judy was discussing the benefits, Tracy was appalled that employees had to wait ninety days for health insurance. She placed that item on the agenda to discuss with Judy upon her arrival. She knew not to make it an issue or a condition of her employment so Judy and Sheila wouldn't think she was money hungry and wanted benefits to suit her personal needs.

She wondered why the previous human resources executives hadn't taken the initiative to get Judy and Sheila to rethink the waiting period for health care benefits. The industry standard was thirty days.

What Judy and Sheila hadn't analyzed, was the cost Sunset was paying when candidates negotiated for the company to pay the cost they were paying for an individual health plan or for COBRA; provisions in the law which provides employees the opportunity for temporary extension of health benefits due to a "qualifying event," such as a layoff. She had already calculated what the company had paid over the last three years. She couldn't wait to share those numbers with Judy.

There were so many things that didn't make sense to her. Why would a company not have a bonus plan for all its managers and supervisors? Candidates weren't comfortable shaking hands and hoping the discretionary bonus plan would address their needs. It was standard practice in the retail industry for managers and supervisors to be on an incentive plan.

By the time the waiter returned, they had decided to get the house special. It was a pound and a half of lobsters grilled to perfection with a buttery, lemon caper sauce. The lobsters were served with a house salad, with homemade dressing, roasted potatoes, and asparagus in a delightful dill sauce. The waiter placed a fresh basket of sourdough bread on their table. Their water glasses were refreshed, and a server brought a small plate of assorted olives.

The ambience of the restaurant was very relaxing. The lights were turned down low, candles graced each table, and soft music played in the background. In the center of the restaurant was a huge man-made waterfall that extended from the floor to the ceiling. It was done in an Italian rose marble. The granite bar curved around the waterfall like a snake waiting to take its victim prey. The waiters and waitresses wore black pants and white tuxedo shirts with red satin bow ties. The servers all stood at attention, waiting to make the customer's evening a wonderful dining experience. The servers were there to pick up the slack in case the waiters forgot anything.

As they waited, she asked Don about his love life. Don had been married only once. He and his wife had two boys. When their sons entered college and were out of the house, they decided to end their marriage. The flame had long since died, but they had stayed together for the kids. Being one of the regional officers for Brock, Don serviced the West Coast and the mid-Atlantic regions. Don had a home in North Carolina; a condo in Texas; and a townhouse in Pennsylvania. His dream was to return to North Carolina when he retired.

"Don, how is your friend in Boston?" Tracy asked, as he replenished their glasses of wine.

"She's fine, enjoying Boston and working independently. Life is good for her."

Don started his career in corporate America, working for an insurance company in Boston. He met Sheryl, a human resources executive, there. Sheryl fell deeply in love with him. She lived in the city in a spacious, four-thousand-square-foot home. Her house was incredible. Even though Tracy had never been there, from the details Don shared, it had to be an exquisite piece of real estate. He would faithfully visit Sheryl once a quarter. He and Sheryl had dated for some ten years, but Don wasn't the type to marry a second time.

Tracy wondered why women would latch onto men who just used them to fill the void. Sheryl would cater to Don's every need when he was in town. Sheryl was always too busy climbing the corporate ladder to make a personal life for herself. Don was her safe haven. Instead of having a man underfoot every night, Sheryl had decided to have a lover on the side whom she could love when the occasion and timing was right.

Why Sheryl would settle for seconds was puzzling to Tracy. It was like dating a married man, an area she knew a lot about. You wait and wait and hope one day it all works out. You make no commitments because they belong to or are committed to someone else.

Tracy had dated three married men while being married to Stephen. Stephen never found out about them. She was always careful never to keep any receipts. Paying for things in cash didn't leave a paper trail. She bought phone cards so numbers would not be traceable. She always kept extra underwear and blouses in her gym bag in case buttons were missing after she and her partner had enjoyed wild sex. She called all her partners "sweetheart or sweetie," as she did with Stephen, to not slip up and say the wrong name. She was clever and careful that way.

Tracy once saw pictures of Sheryl when Don's wallet flipped open. With Don's great looks, she couldn't imagine what he saw in Sheryl.

Don was six four with black hair and baby blue eyes. He ran five miles each day and had a physique that looked like one of those body builders on the cover of a sports magazine. Sheryl was five feet and about forty pounds overweight. She had an old-maidish look with long black hair that she kept pulled back in a ponytail. She wore no makeup and usually wore khaki pants with large pullover tops and sweaters. She often wore flats that were usually brown or black in color.

"I'm going to visit Sheryl next month. We're going to kick back, relax, and enjoy some crab cakes with wine."

Tracy commented that it sounded like lots of fun and quite relaxing. She admired Don for finding time to carve out a life for himself. Although he spent about 70 percent of his time on the road, he was never too busy to talk with a client, friend, or someone needing help. He had done an excellent job building up the eastern division for Brock. When everything was in place, they offered him more money to move west and straighten out both the west and mid-Atlantic regions.

Just as she loved the West Coast, he enjoyed the East Coast. When Tracy had requested Don to work with her during the layoff at Sunset, Brock's president suggested that she work with his replacement. When she refused, stating that she would only work with Don, the company's president agreed, for fear of losing the Sunset account.

Brock had made a lot of money working with Tracy on the West Coast. Not only did the company handle all of her outplacement work, but it had also created job success profiles, trained executives to be mentors, and implemented a training academy for executives and senior leaders. Refusing Tracy meant losing plenty of future business to their competitors. There was no way Brock would allow that to happen.

"Do you think you'll ever remarry?" she asked, as Don was looking around the restaurant, admiring how attentive the waiters were. The service was top-notch.

"I don't want to say never because you just don't know what life might throw your way, but if I were a betting man, I'd say it is highly unlikely. Marriage is hard. You have to work at it every day of your life. Humans are tough to live with. You think you know a person, and one day while sleeping in bed, you turn over and wonder who that is lying next to you."

She knew he spoke the truth. Look at her messed-up life with Stephen. She no longer knew him. Their love had ended years ago. She wasn't sure why she had hung on for so long. There were no kids … her parents were dead … why did she stay? She and Stephen would apologize to each other if they accidentally brushed up against one another. They hadn't made love in years, and she had no desire for him to touch her. They didn't even say the words, "I love you." Their marriage was a joke at best. She and Stephen were in a cold, dark, lonely place.

What happened to their dreams, all their dreams that would never be realized? She and Stephen were so cold to one another now. They didn't talk or have a life together. They moved in different circles. She was still bitter about losing her parents and Stephen not being there for her. Maybe when time permitted, she would seek professional counseling to get over her pain. It was just too much to think why her life had been spared.

Now having to face the realization they needed to dissolve their marriage was a strain on the relationship and a deterrent to moving forward. Gladys Knight had said it well in a song, "It's sad to think we're not going to make it. And it's gotten to the point where we just can't fake it. But someone's got to reach us ... because we just want say good-bye. I guess neither one of us wants to be the first to say good-bye."

Look at the chaos she created, sneaking away in the night like a thief on the run. She should have done the decent thing and told Stephen face-to-face about the job she had taken on the East Coast. She had been the biggest loser. She departed in a hurry, leaving Stephen to think she had simply moved across town. What in the world was she thinking? What a cruel thing to do to the man she had spent so many years with. No matter what Stephen had done to her and what had become of their relationship, he deserved better than that.

"Hudson, what are you thinking about? You appear to be thousands of miles away." Don always referred to her as Hudson. To Don, she wasn't Tracy or Ms. Hudson, but simply Hudson.

"I was thinking about Stephen and the nightmare I created, leaving with a note on the table by the door. As I think about it now, it seems like such a cruel and selfish thing to do. It makes me look like a sadistic person. It was never my intention to inflict that level of pain on another human being." She felt very bad, not for leaving Stephen but for the way she had left. She knew that her actions were uncalled for.

Don watched her closely as she shared her feelings. You never leave someone via a note. No matter how difficult life is or how unbearable the situation, the other person needs to hear the news directly from you. Don spoke up almost in a whisper. He didn't want to jeopardize their friendship, but Tracy had to face the music.

"Hudson, we've all made mistakes. Lord knows I've done some things that I'm not proud of. It's the lessons we learn in life that keep us grounded. It's OK to make mistakes as long as we learn from them. Maybe you need to make that call to Stephen and tell him that you chose the cowardly way out and for that you apologize. Let him know you have left and have no plans to continue with the marriage."

As much as she hated to hear the words, Don was absolutely right. You don't marry someone, share his bed, and then decide to run away with only a note left behind. It wasn't her style to run. She wasn't sure why she had chosen the coward's way out. Her actions had shown no courage. She had allowed her emotions to take over.

All the hurt she had built up inside over the loss of her parents and not being able to say good-bye to them had created an evil spirit within. Would it have hurt to tell Stephen in person and then have her attorney draw up the papers? There was nothing of his that she wanted. She had taken the family albums that held all the memories of her past and the time spent with her parents. She had to stop blaming herself for asking her parents to go shopping and Stephen for deserting her in her hour of need. She wanted to rid herself of all that negative energy and all those negative feelings. Life was too short to be mean to others.

"You're right, Don. Deep in my heart of hearts, I know you speak the truth. I just need to find the strength and motivation to say I'm sorry and good-bye. Stephen needs to find happiness and love in the arms of someone else. He's still young and quite attractive.

So much for my upside-down life. I think he'll be away for another two weeks. I got an email stating that the case was going a little longer than expected because of all of the witnesses who have to testify. Stephen loves that part of being a trial lawyer. I've seen him in court. He's actually good at what he does."

Don observed the sparkle in her eyes as she spoke about her soon-to-be ex. She was probably still in love with Stephen and didn't even realize her affection for him. All of the hurt feelings had suppressed her true feelings … feelings that she kept under control.

"Don," Tracy said, fighting back tears, "I've made a huge mistake coming here. I don't know what I was thinking taking this job. I was running away and trying to escape a life I knew I hated. I thought by moving to the East Coast all my problems would be solved. This company isn't one I plan to make my home. These people are so behind-the-times in their thinking and out-of-touch with how corporate engines run; and both Judy and Sheila are too close for comfort. I pity the day that Judy becomes chairman of the board. Between Judy and Sheila, they'll be able to treat people like they are insignificant and run the company with an iron hand."

She needed Don's guidance, for she had no plans to stay and play on a team and in an arena where the rules were made up and decided by queen Judy and princess Sheila.

"All mistakes can be corrected, Hudson. You were brought here for a reason. In time that reason will reveal itself."

Don was the only one she could talk with about her true feelings. He encouraged her to stay a little longer at the company. She knew he made a good point. It was atypical for an executive to take a new job and not be told during the interview process of an upcoming layoff. Most people had more scruples than that, especially given the fact that she was interviewing for the top human resources position. He was sure that even though the majority of the board members lacked corporate experience, they probably saw flaws in Judy, and perhaps that was the reason she wasn't running the board as chairman.

"Sometimes when we think people aren't aware of situations is when they surprise us and make the right decisions," Don said, watching her reaction.

Tracy knew he was dead-on, for she also believed in karma. Things had a way of coming full circle. The totality of a person's actions definitely decided their fate. You can do people wrong for just so long before the tables start to turn. She remembered what her mother always told her, don't dig a hole for someone else, you just might fall in it yourself. Fate has a way of rearranging things.

"My friend," Tracy said, as she finished the vegetables on her plate, "be honest with me. Would it look strange or perhaps weird if I left the company after three weeks of employment? I thought I would get Sunset through this layoff and then exit. I dread to think what will happen to the employees if I don't coordinate the layoff."

"You can always leave, but why would you want to do that? Sure we can craft a reason, such as having to return to the West Coast for personal reasons, taking another job with higher perks, or leaving to start your own company. I think you're needed here to steer this ship back on course. You may be the only one to help the board of directors see through the smoke and mirrors. Now the danger of that is Judy will probably be smart enough to see the motives behind your actions."

He was so right. Judy may have covered up some of her emotions, but she was one tough, insightful person. Beneath the exterior was a coldhearted, vindictive person. Judy had inhibited the company's progress. She had carved out a nice niche for herself and Sheila. The handpicked board saw Judy as a soft-spoken, caring person who was more concerned about the well being of her employees than herself.

That was so far from the truth. Judy knew exactly what she was doing. She knew her college roommate, Sheila, would never be in competition with her. It was Judy who convinced the board to elevate Sheila's position to second in command behind hers. It was Judy who convinced the board to compensate Sheila at the level of a president running a small to medium-size company, and it was Judy who convinced the board to enhance Sheila's executive perks. The board bought into every strategy Judy put forth. Judy's bottom line was to keep Sheila happy and satisfied.

Looking at Sheila, one would never know that she was a multi millionaire. She was married to a man from Chattanooga, Tennessee whom she met while on a business trip. They had been married twenty-two years and had two sons in college. Based on what Sheila said about her spouse during her interview, he didn't seem to be a mover and shaker. Tracy remembered Sheila saying her spouse worked for the county in the property tax department. Sheila was obviously the major breadwinner in the family. She brought home the bacon.

The waiter returned to their table with a tray of desserts. Tracy generally passed up desserts. She refused to work out for the length of time needed to burn up the five hundred calories that came with each morsel. Tonight she made an exception, which she seemed to be doing a lot of lately. Tomorrow wasn't promised. She had seen that firsthand with the early death of her parents. She chose the New York cheesecake with fresh strawberries, and Don couldn't resist the key lime pie with homemade whipped cream. She washed down the cake with a cup of cappuccino. Don decided on decaf coffee.

"Hudson, if you decide to leave this city, we should get together to strategize your exit. The last thing you need is for the industry to be afraid to hire you. CEOs and boards are reluctant to hire a problem or a person who ran away from a problem. We could always have a company come after you and explain that the offer was more appealing, and that you'd been in the early stages of negotiating with the company when Sunset Pub and Grill approached you."

That's what she loved about him. He would always share his feedback. He knew that the ultimate decision would be hers. Whether the decision was sound or not, Don was equipped with the tools and knowledge to make it work. She would need his counsel if she walked. She remembered when she started her career to always be careful to say and do the appropriate thing. She often took a backseat so her boss could shine. She definitely had the back of the company and truly thought the company had her back. It wasn't until she excelled in her career and made it to the executive suite when she realized it was every man for himself.

When you're an employee at a lower level, you don't see all of the infighting that goes on. You think that the executives care about you because of your contributions to the organization. Most executives don't know the names of the employees on their team beyond the senior leaders. Those frontline employees sweat it out each day, so the senior leaders can have those beautiful offices and make those high salaries. Most of the hourly employees at Sunset didn't have health care benefits. Not because they didn't want them; it was a matter of finances. They simply couldn't afford them. She had seen time and time again how hourly employees weren't only low on the totem pole but, were generally the aftermath of executive greed.

Tracy was now one of them. She wasn't a part of the employee group. What the employees didn't know was how hard she fought for their rights in every company that had employed her. She would do the same at Sunset. Judy and her sidekick, Sheila, hadn't seen anything yet. Getting the career outplacement center and severance packages for soon-to-be laid-off employees was the beginning of wonderful things to come. Being a part of the compensation committee of the board of directors would present an opportunity for her to enlighten them on the basics. In her estimation the basics included having succession plans in place, having salary ranges based on market analysis studies that showed what to pay people, and having benefits that people needed and wanted. Why make employees wait ninety days for their health insurance.

Now having full access to the human resources information system, she noticed that executive perks were all different for comparable levels. There would be no way to justify in a court of law why two executives at the same level, doing comparable jobs with similar experience, had such disparity in their pay.

Tracy surmised that if she dug deeper, there would be a host of problems in how managers were paid. She would have to open that can of worms soon. It was her personal objective to bring the company into the twenty-first century. She would work with the executive leadership to make the needed changes. She planned to keep Judy informed every step of the way to avoid any unnecessary outbursts, either publicly or privately.

Being the human resources head had many challenges. She had to be the master juggler balancing all the balls at the same time. She was paid by the company and had to protect the executives, the shareholders, the directors, the company and its employees. She was at the center of the action. Her law degree always served her well. Her goal was to uphold the name of the company, keep the company out of court, and keep employees engaged in the business.

She wanted employees to know they made a difference and that what they did added to the success of the business. Whether they worked on the front line or on the cook's line, each employee's job was significant. Over time she would encourage the executives to get out of the corporate office and travel the field. Traveling the field would give them an opportunity to see firsthand the sacrifices the employees made for the company. Even though it was unlikely that the company would ever have a total health care benefits plan for hourly employees, there were some things they could do like offering health and dental benefits at a reduced cost with affordable premiums and copays.

She planned to work with her team at Sunset to make sure the part-time employees understood the 401K retirement savings plan. Countless times she had worked in organizations where both part-time and salaried employees didn't enroll because of their lack of knowledge about the plan. She always made sure the human resources managers in the field and at the corporate office took the time to meet with employees to explain how having the company withhold a small percentage of their salary for retirement could start to build their nest egg in a relatively short period of time. Plus, the company offered a sizable match to the employees' contributions.

After they finished dessert, she drove Don back to the corporate parking lot to get his rental. The Miami air was pleasant. The ocean had cooled things down quite a bit. They talked briefly about the things they needed to work on the following day. He was flying to Texas on Friday evening on a six o'clock flight. With the Miami traffic, she felt Don should plan on leaving the corporate office around three-thirty. That would give him plenty of time to return the rental car and get a bite to eat prior to his flight. He would be on location for the next three weeks to set up the career outplacement center and to make sure he and his team were there to help her.

Her current staff, although very eager and supportive, hadn't pulled off a major layoff before. Even a seasoned veteran would be challenged because of the short amount of time to prepare.

After saying good-bye and giving Don directions for a shorter route to his hotel, she found herself sailing down Interstate 95. As she looked in her rearview mirror, she saw the flashing lights of a police car fast approaching. Not tonight of all nights, she said to herself. Can't you just past me by? To her amazement, the cop went around her car and continued on his way. The officer was after someone else and didn't have any time to waste. She considered herself lucky. All she needed was to get a ticket which would raise her insurance rate.

Her current record indicated that she was a safe driver—quite a different story from the maverick she was in college. Back then Tracy drove Corvettes. Her first Corvette was red; she was constantly being stopped and getting tickets. She always claimed that the cops discriminated against those who drove Corvettes. The reality of the situation was that she was a speedster with no time to waste. She was always running late to get to her next class or to some appointment.

She was counting her blessings when her cell phone started to ring. She couldn't imagine who would be calling her. Maybe Don forgot to tell her something.

"This is Tracy," she said, looking at the unrecognizable number on her cell. Clearly it wasn't Don's number.

"Hi, sweetheart," the person said on the other end. As she was about to ask who it was, he said, "this is Eric. Did I get you at a bad time? My day got away from me before I had an opportunity to phone you."

Tracy wasn't sure she was comfortable with the word "sweetheart." It seemed like an endearing gesture of affection and fondness. She felt the best thing to do was just ignore it and pretend she didn't hear the word. She hadn't given Eric any indication that she was his sweetheart. Maybe it was just his way of acknowledging people. He probably called all of his patients sweetheart for fear of not remembering their names. After all, she used that same strategy in her relationships so as not to slip up and say the wrong name.

"Eric, this is a perfect time. I'm in the car headed home. I just left a dinner meeting."

She felt saying "dinner meeting" sounded more appropriate and official. She didn't want to tell Eric, she had spent the last four hours spilling her guts about her unhappiness with Sunset. Eric probably would question her character and professionalism if he knew she was contemplating leaving the company she just started working for. She was sure he wouldn't understand why she would do such a thing. He had never worked in the corporate world. Politics and the workings of that world were all foreign to him, she was sure. Running his own practice had its headaches, but at least he didn't have to keep so many people happy. There were no shareholders breathing down his neck, no dysfunctional teams to deal with, no board of directors to contend with, or thousands of employees to look after and keep engaged in the business. Eric didn't understand her world, and she sure as hell didn't understand his.

"I want to confirm plans for this weekend. I thought I could pick you up or we could meet up somewhere."

She'd been so consumed with the upcoming layoff that it had slipped her mind to invite Leslie to attend the weekend functions with her. If Leslie had made any weekend plans, she would just have to cancel them. She wasn't going to show up by herself.

"That sounds good to me. I've a hectic day tomorrow and Friday will be totally crazy. I think I should meet you there. It would be easier for me and would allow me to wrap up some more loose ends,"Tracy said, hoping he wouldn't ask anything about the friend she was bringing.

Eric suggested she meet him at the entrance to the restaurant in Coconut Grove that was hosting the wine-tasting event. It was scheduled to start around six-thirty in the evening. She told Eric she would definitely be there by seven. Since she was on the phone, he finalized their plans for Saturday. She wanted to back out of the moonlight cruise; since it sounded too much like a lover's boat ride. He explained that over three hundred people were scheduled to cruise up and down the Atlantic Ocean. He told Tracy that she would have tons of fun and meet some great people. He had attended one last month and between the casino, dancing in the nightclub, singing karaoke style, and eating fabulous French desserts, there was never a dull moment. The ship left from Port Miami around seven-thirty in the evening and returned shortly after midnight.

If she found the conversation with Eric boring, Tracy thought she could lose herself in the crowd of three hundred people. Leslie had to come with her. The wine-tasting event and the cruise did sound like fun. She also needed an escape from work.

On Friday she could leave the office around six so as not to be too late. She knew how to take her business attire and transform it into the perfect after-five outfit. On Saturday she could get to the office early and leave by noon. That would give her time to get her hair done and get both a manicure and pedicure. She wanted to look fresh and alive for the affair. Miami was a lot like Los Angeles. Going out was a time to dress up and get it together. LA was known for wearing flip-flops during the day and mini dresses and stilettos at night.

Tracy loved clothes, and with her figure she wore them well. She was always tasteful and appropriate. She never let her guard down in a business setting. She only trusted her friends, and they were few and far between. The best way to remain private was to keep your personal life out of the limelight and to never make it the topic of conversation. She shared a little of herself so people would feel comfortable around her. Her motto was never share anything about your personal life that you wouldn't want to read on the front page of the newspaper.

After finalizing plans with Eric, she told him good-bye. Getting away early from the office on Friday would be good for her. She had things under control. It would have been great to take Don to the two events. They would have had a terrific time together. Don would also be able to size up Eric. She dialed Leslie at home. She didn't care that it was late. Leslie could catch up on her beauty sleep after their conversation. She was in luck; Leslie was free to attend both events. The only plans Leslie had were curling up in bed with a good book Friday evening and a hair appointment Saturday morning.

Leslie even thought she might be able to get Tracy an appointment early Saturday afternoon at her salon. Javier was open to taking walk-ins and new clients who had the money to afford the luxury of his services. Javier could make a plain Jane-looking person feel and look like a Hollywood star. Before setting up shop in Miami, Javier had styled hair and done makeup for some of Hollywood's greatest entertainers. Javier got fed up with all the bullshit he had to endure from divas. He was now doing what he loved and making more money. He always said that most of his clients, who weren't classified as rich and famous, tipped better than the major Hollywood stars. Go figure, he always said.

By the time Tracy got to the apartment, she was exhausted. She stepped out of her clothes and left them in a pile on the floor. She changed into a tee shirt, washed off her makeup, brushed her teeth, and jumped into bed. Since the corporate apartment provided housekeeping services, she planned to retrieve her clothes from the floor before leaving for work. For now all she wanted to do was sleep.

Tracy slept well that night, not even getting up to go to the bathroom. When the clock alarm sounded at 5 o'clock, she felt rested and ready to tackle the day. She hurriedly dressed, picked up the clothes off the floor, and threw them in the hamper as she grabbed a banana and bottled water on her way out of the door.

It looked to be a splendid day. Not a cloud in the sky. The temperature was in the low seventies with no rain in sight. Tracy loved this time of the year. The weather in Miami was similar to the climate in Los Angeles. When the North and

Midwest were struggling to stay warm amid snow and freezing temperatures, most of the people in the southern and western states were walking around in light clothing, clueless of those suffering during some of winter's coldest months.

She was meeting Don for breakfast, so they could pull together some additional plans before meeting with the employees at the corporate office. Field meetings would be coordinated simultaneously with the corporate one. Employees who weren't able to attend in person could "attend" by dialing into one of the meetings. It was critical for employees to understand that a reengineering effort would be taking place, why such drastic measures for the company were needed, and how decisions would be made regarding laying employees off. Following the employee meetings, the franchisees would be notified. Board members would receive copies of all correspondence before the company's announcement went public.

She and Don had warned the executives that the road ahead could become a little rocky. With the current national unemployment rate at 9 percent, the media might choose to have a field day. They both wanted the company to encourage employees to direct all media questions to the public relations department. That was the only way to have a single, one-voice, consistent message.

Don had taken the liberty of ordering breakfast for Tracy since their time would be short. As Tracy approached his table, she said, "Don't you ever sleep?"

"Only when it is necessary and my body starts to shut down. Then I know I've abused the privilege of playing with Mother Nature."

She admired him for his dedication to whatever job he was working on. He gave 200 plus percent of his time to the effort. He treated all assignments as if they were his first and only priority. She knew Don wasn't bringing in the dollars he should for this assignment. Sunset was getting a wonderful deal—getting the time of the top guy, a team of seasoned outplacement consultants, and a team of skilled writers to develop resumes for the laid-off employees.

Don pushed a piece of paper in front of Tracy as she was relieving herself of her purse and briefcase.

"What's this, my friend?" she asked.

The document was several pages with names of local companies in Miami and in other states. He explained that he had his staff compile a list of all companies in Miami and other cities in the state of Florida, as well as the other states in the country, who were currently hiring.

"This list, my dear, will help employees feel that the company is interested in their well-being and will assist them in obtaining other employment. The Brock database will also help to alleviate the fear that there are no jobs out there. For employees who can relocate, they will find the list invaluable. Employees who, because of commitments, can't leave the city will be able to contact local companies who are hiring."

Brilliant, she thought. The strategy at the meeting would be to talk about the number of companies that were currently hiring, and to let them know that each employee who would be affected would get a copy of the list.

"Hudson, today you need to call some of the local companies to apprise them of the upcoming layoff. I think if you speak directly with the executive vice presidents of human resources and some of the CEOs, you will score in two ways. First, your employees will be grateful that you made the call, and second, I'm sure these companies would love to get a hold of some of the talent at Sunset."

They agreed that the list of companies currently hiring would be discussed at the employee meetings, both in the field and at corporate. Field meetings would have a human resources representative present who would facilitate the discussion and answer questions. She would have loved to be at each and every meeting, but that was physically impossible.

After paying for breakfast, Don followed Tracy to the office. With a little over two hours before the employee meeting, she went to see Judy to make sure she was ready and prepared. Tracy explained that she would open the meeting, explaining why they were there today, and then turn it over to Judy who could deal with the specifics. She discussed the list of companies throughout the country who were currently hiring and how she would introduce the list. They then discussed the conference call with board members that would be held at noon before announcements went out to the franchisees and the media.

Judy seemed troubled about something. Tracy could see it in her eyes. "Is something wrong, Judy? You have a worried look on your face." The last thing she needed was to not have the endorsement of the CEO.

"Why is it necessary for us to notify the media, especially this soon and at this stage of the game? Won't that just cause confusion? The media will put a negative spin on the story. We've never had a layoff, and I think it would be best to first let the information sink in. Our employees need time to process the magnitude of this," Judy said, with anger in her voice.

"I understand your concerns, Judy. The strategy is for us to get ahead of this. Once we communicate the layoff to our employees, it's out of our hands. There is no way we can contain the information. By telling the media and crafting a positive message around the layoff, we stand a better chance of them printing a positive story. Otherwise, they might put a negative spin on it. By notifying the media of our plans, it gives us an opportunity to stay in control. The last thing we need is for one of our employees to jump-the-gun and notify the press."

After another twenty minutes, she had convinced Judy of the importance of notifying the press and inviting the franchisees to join the CEO on a conference call at 2:00 p.m. regarding the company's reorganization plan. She had to work hard at convincing Judy to do the right thing. Judy invited Sheila to join their meeting, which just complicated things. That was the problem when dealing with leaders who grew up in one company and didn't have the understanding of how corporate engines ran regarding a layoff.

If Tracy had followed Judy's initial directive and not told the media about the pending layoff, the media probably would have printed a very negative story. She could see the headlines now; Company caught off guard and in a last-ditch effort to save jobs of highly paid executives, the little people got the axe … board members force the company to lay off thousands of employees … employees are asked to walk with no severance.

To alleviate some of Judy's stress and tension, Tracy agreed to lead the meeting with the franchise community. Tracy surmised that most of the franchisees would ignore the email or continue with their plans for the day. Either way, the company would have made a concerted effort to notify the heart and soul of the company. With the company being 75 percent franchised, it was crucial to bring franchisees into the mix.

The conference call would only last half an hour and would be followed by all franchisees receiving a broadcast message and email labeled "time-sensitive" information.

The broadcast message to the franchise community was already scripted and would be recorded by Judy. Tracy left a copy of the script with Judy so she could make any minor changes that would personalize the message more. She was thankful for the time she'd spent earlier with Sam Mason, the IT guru, who would be critical in making sure the messages didn't meet with any problems.

When Tracy returned to her office, she had her administrative assistant send the schedule to the executives. She left a message on each of their phones, cell and office; explaining the schedule and when the franchisees and the media would be contacted. She asked that all questions be directed to her.

She then asked Sharon to have Sam meet her in her office as soon as he was available. Don watched Tracy's reaction and behavior once she had returned to the office. He was at her conference table, organizing meetings with his team and reading emails and correspondence scheduled to be released that afternoon. He knew her hands were tied on so many things and wanted to help wherever he could to reduce some of her stress and anxiety. Given what she had said last night during dinner about leaving the company, he wanted Tracy to experience some "wins." That was the quickest and easiest way to increase her loyalty to the company and to get her to rethink her plans.

Tracy closed her door and told Don about her meeting with Judy and Sheila. She was up for the task, but there was so much sacred ground, she felt like she had to tiptoe all the time. Don told her to keep things in perspective. Things would start to calm down after the event had taken place. The CEO and

CFO were not being difficult for the sake of being difficult, but because they were inexperienced in so many areas. This was their first time handling a layoff of this magnitude.

The task at hand seemed insurmountable in so many ways. Even a company with tons of experience in handling layoffs would be unnerved with the timing. She knew he was right. It was like working with young executives. Judy and Sheila were by no means young executives; they were in their prime.

The company was lucky to have Tracy orchestrating the series of events. She was experienced at taking jobs away from employees. Even though it turned her stomach and always caused her to throw up on the day of the event, she had to press on. She had to toughen up, keep her cool, and educate Judy and Sheila along the way. There was no sense in blaming them.

There was a soft tap on the door. Maybe one of the executives had decided to take her up on her offer to further explain things. The knob turned as Tracy said, "Come in."

Sam entered the room. She introduced Sam to Don before she explained her current needs. Tracy reinforced to Sam that what she was sharing with him was confidential, and she would need him when broadcast messages went out to the employees, board members, and franchisees. She didn't want to work with one of his direct reports; she wanted him. Sam told Tracy he would be at her beck and call. Whenever she needed him, just have him paged. He wasn't planning on leaving the building and would check in with her before leaving at the end of the day. She asked Sam to meet her in the office Saturday morning to work out some final details for the layoff. He agreed, took a copy of the schedule, and left.

Once out of earshot range of office employees, she asked Sharon to order file boxes. She explained that they needed to have them on hand for employees to pack up their things on the day they were notified.

The next half hour was spent with her direct reports and field human resources managers who had been conferenced in. She asked each to call up the email she had just sent with a schedule for today's activities. Tracy stressed once again that things were to remain confidential until she either gave the OK or the schedule signaled the approved timing. She answered questions from her team and told the group she sincerely appreciated their efforts. She apologized for not having an opportunity to meet the field human resources managers face-to-face. She promised to meet them within the next two months. If she couldn't get to the field, she would host a meeting at corporate.

"OK, Don, it's about time for us to head to the employee meeting. Are you ready to rock and roll?"

Realizing they had no other choice, they gathered up their things and headed out. Sharon joined them after she called Elizabeth, Judy's assistant, to tell her to let Judy know it was time. Sharon was instructed to take notes and follow up on any outstanding business that developed as a result of the meeting.

The employees started to slowly enter the room. Sam was up front testing all of the equipment. Sam didn't want any hiccups. The last thing they needed was to have a technical glitch. He checked the system to make sure the field leaders and employees were on the speaker system. He then put the system on mute as she and Don took their seats. Judy and Sheila entered the room a short time later. Tracy got up and met Judy at the podium.

"Are you comfortable with the script and the Q&A document?" Tracy asked.

Judy showed her the minor changes she had made. Tracy explained the order for the meeting and told Judy she should entertain questions from the employees. Judy was still comfortable with Tracy running the meeting. She surmised that Judy somehow wanted to separate herself from the layoff, giving the impression that human resources was responsible. She knew that approach would be disastrous for both her and the human resources department.

A look of shock was on the faces of many employees as the meeting got underway. It was difficult for employees to believe that the company was having financial problems and because of economic times the organization would have to downsize. Once Tracy turned the meeting over to Judy, she was holding her breath that Judy wouldn't say anything to further add stress to the employees.

Judy did a good job thanking Tracy and communicating to the employees that "we'll all get through this together." Judy shared the financial outlook for Sunset and stated that the survival of the company would be dependent on reducing headcount. She also talked about how the new organization would emerge and that employees would receive training in the new skills and direction of the reengineered company. She told everyone to continue to work hard and help the company move swiftly through the process.

Tracy was appreciative that Judy remembered to communicate when and how board members, franchisees, and the media would receive the news. Judy encouraged employees not to speak to the media but to refer them to Chutney Pepperberg, the vice president of communication and public relations.

There were only two questions during the Q&A period. Since Judy didn't spring to life, Tracy stepped up to the podium. The first question was whether or not employees would be receiving severance. Tracy responded that the company had developed a severance policy so affected employees would receive severance, had created a career outplacement center offsite, and that she was making personal phone calls to companies with job opportunities. The second question dealt with the timing of the event. She explained that the executives were working diligently to finalize plans, and that a specific date hadn't been established.

Next she introduced Don, who was fabulous with the employees. He started by saying that he understood their current level of fear and anxiety. He explained how he had lost his job twice and that each time he ended up with a better and a more demanding position. He got instant credibility when the employees realized he had gone through the experience twice. Don said it was somewhat ironic that he ended up managing the downsizing effort for so many companies. He told the employees that a positive mindset was invaluable when losing a job. He equated it to cancer patients whose positive attitude helped them defy all odds.

Once the meeting ended, Tracy let Judy know she'd done an excellent job. She sensed that Judy was pleased with the statement. Judy knew she had worked with major companies, so for Tracy to say a job well done carried a great deal of weight. After speaking with a number of the executives, Tracy went to Sam to thank him for managing all of the technical aspects. There had been no technical hiccups during the meeting.

She stayed in the room until all the employees left. She and Don went to Judy's office for the board of directors' conference call. After the conference call with the board and then with the franchise community, she pulled the trigger so all announcements could go out. Those targeted for board members were sent first, followed by the announcement to franchisees, and finally the press release to the media. She dropped off a copy of possible Q&As for the media to the public relations department.

Tracy was finally able to breathe after four exhausting days. She felt more in control as she ended the day. Don was having dinner with his team, so she decided to enjoy a relaxing evening in the apartment. She needed time to clear her head. She told Don goodnight as she headed for the parking lot. With any luck she wouldn't run into any of her colleagues. As she exited the building she saw Sam Mason.

"Hi Sam," Tracy said. "I see you're getting out of here at a decent hour."

Sam was as energetic and friendly as the day they met. "I'm leaving early to take the family to dinner. Thursday is our family night out, and Friday night is the time I spend along with my wife, Tonya. We're lucky that my mother-in-law is retired and is able to help us with the kids. I don't think Tonya trusts babysitters yet."

She and Sam spoke for another brief moment as she asked him to stop by her office on Friday for an update. Sam recommended a great take-out Chinese restaurant that was on her route to the apartment. She got directions and was glad to get the recommendation. She waved goodbye as Sam put his car in drive and headed out.

CHAPTER 7

Eric was finishing up with his last patient when the nurse stepped in to let him know he had a phone call on line 3. Eric left the patient with the nurse as he said good-bye and left the room. He was hoping it wasn't Tracy calling, canceling Friday night. He wanted to see her now more than ever.

As he connected to line 3, he heard the familiar voice. It wasn't Tracy, but his girlfriend Priscilla Braxton. Priscilla was confirming the time she would be at his place. Eric wasn't up to an evening on the town, so he asked her to meet him at his home. He told Priscilla he would have the Japanese Steak House prepare their dinner, which he would pick up on the way home.

As he hung up the phone, Eric wondered how he ever got deemed "Mr. Playboy". It wasn't something he planned. He never thought at age 42, he would still be playing the field. He never intended to be the "love them and leave them" type guy. He thought back on the many relationships he'd had while in college and after establishing his practice, and not one long-term relationship came to mind. For him, relationships were short-lived. While interning, he had slept with all the available pretty, young nurses. Each nurse was hoping to become Mrs. Sears. Even knowing his reputation, the nurses still gambled that the tables would turn.

Relationships and commitments were difficult for him. He enjoyed the chase, getting his adrenaline going. He knew how to romance the ladies. He took his time getting to know each lady as an individual. He never immediately hopped into bed with his dates. He was the perfect gentlemen, opening their car doors, lightly brushing against their lips, remembering and paraphrasing what they enjoyed doing, and not inviting himself into their homes. He understood the needs of women. He would listen intently to every word that was uttered. He was attracted to younger women half his age. In his field, women were everywhere he turned. He dated both his patients and office staff. The majority of his office staff were young, attractive and under the age of 30.

When the relationship went south, Eric would gradually disappear, blaming it on his practice and chosen profession with all of the demanding hours. Staff members who dated him would either leave his employment or hang on hoping he would change his ways, and return to their awaiting arms.

His life as a plastic surgeon, often lend credibility to the lies he told about late night and early morning visits to the hospital to see patients. He always had the perfect alibi to explain his absence. Many times he would receive calls from women that his answering service put through, while he was in the arms of one of his girlfriends. He was a master at creating fictitious emergencies and surgeries. He never had to justify his behavior, to let him tell it, it was all business. When Eric needed a break from a current relationship, he would create a scenario that sounded believable.

He loved the innocence and the simplicity of the younger woman. Life was so much easier and less complicated for them. They didn't have all the baggage of 40-year-old women, who had become wiser and more questioning in relationships. The younger women enjoyed life and looked forward to the next opportunity. For them, an older man, especially one who was rich, added stability and fun to the mix.

He wasn't sure dating younger women was always worth the perks. Many of his close friends were married. At first, he and his dates were invited to those small intimidate gatherings. After a while, it became awkward having to constantly introduce new girlfriends and new faces. The wives finally put their foot down, and over time the invitations were less and less. He was still close to his buddies, but their time together now was, just the guys. They usually met at the gym, on the golf course or for lunch.

He hadn't always scored well with younger women. About a year ago, he had dated a well-known singer, who lived on Star Island in Miami, a neighborhood of South Beach, on a man-made island in Biscayne Bay. The singer had an affinity for aggressive men. She and Eric had dated for about six months when he discovered her picture in the tabloids with her new billionaire French boyfriend. She dropped him like a hot potato. He quickly rebounded, mostly to save face, dating a very attractive actress who was on location in Miami filming a segment of her latest movie. The actress lost interest right away and started dating her co-star who was fifteen years younger than Eric. That was the first time he realized, that not all younger women preferred older men.

He was starting to find it difficult to have the stamina to keep up with women half his age. After a day of performing surgeries and seeing patients, many times he just wanted to enjoy the peace and serenity of his home. He would often walk up and down the beach in the evening to watch the sunset. Life was not just one big party full of fun and games, but an oasis to enjoy life's quiet moments.

Priscilla was talking with the security guard as he approached the gate. She followed him onto his property. She parked inside his four-car garage.

"Hi honey, how was your day?" Priscilla asked.

"It was quite hectic. I had three surgeries this morning and about twenty Botox injections this afternoon. In addition to that, one of my nurses had to leave early to pick up a sick child."

Priscilla kissed him hard on the mouth and cupped his face in her hands. "I'm sorry to hear that sweetie. Why don't you relax on the sofa while I fix you a glass of wine."

She turned down the lights, put on one of Lionel Richie's CDs and returned shortly with the wine. She removed his shoes and massaged his shoulders.

"Wow, that feels good. Just a little lower down on the middle part of my back," he said.

After dinner, Priscilla tidied-up the kitchen and eased into the shower with Eric. He felt alive after eating and taking a hot shower. He wasn't in the mood tonight for making love in the shower, and Priscilla could sense his distance. He seemed so distracted. What she didn't know was that his thoughts were on Tracy. He couldn't get Tracy out of his mind. He wondered what Tracy was doing and if her friend was more than a business acquaintance.

Priscilla was a gorgeous woman. At 25, her life had just begun. She was five feet ten with red hair and slight freckles on her nose. Her long eyelashes grew attention to her hazel eyes. Her skin was creamy white and her complexion was smooth and flawless. She had the perfect body with a bust measuring 34D, a gift from Eric.

Priscilla started her career as a model for Victoria's Secret. Now she modeled for some of the top clothing lines in Milan. She traveled quite extensively, and she and Eric saw each other when their schedules permitted. Unlike women who were trying to marry Eric, Priscilla was neither interested in marriage or kids. There was no way she was going to disfigure her body for nine months. However, she did want to cancel the lease on her apartment and move in full-time with Eric. She also wanted him to be monogamous. A trait Eric was sorely lacking.

At 2:00 a.m., Eric got up since sleep wouldn't come. He looked at the woman beside him. Priscilla looked so peaceful sleeping in his bed. Even though they had made love earlier, for him the passion had died. All he could think about was Tracy Hudson.

He and Priscilla didn't make love that morning. He wasn't in the mood and she had to rush off to her place to pack for a modeling assignment in New York. They kissed and said goodbye as he followed her out of the gated community, waving to the security guard as he left.

He was always smart to not give women a key to his place. Even though it would be difficult getting pass the guard without clearance from him, he didn't want to chance someone pretending to see real estate property, then secretly entering his home. Who knew what a scorned woman was capable of.

As he drove to his practice he was wondering what Tracy was doing at that very moment, and if she thought of him at all. He couldn't quite understand his feelings for this woman who was just slightly younger than he was. He estimated that her age was somewhere between thirty-five and forty. Although she didn't look her age; with her accomplishments she had to be at least in her mid-thirties. His greatest fear was that Tracy would show up at the affair on Friday with her business colleague, and have absolutely no time for him.

CHAPTER 8

Tracy felt like a new person when she woke up at four-thirty. She had time to shower and enjoy a cup of coffee in her bathrobe. She quickly went through her emails to make sure there were no emergencies. Once in the office she greeted all of her team as she walked around with her cup of coffee, listening to their concerns. She had no agenda, she wanted to see firsthand what was on their minds. She was amazed how well the team was accepting the pending layoff. Aside from her direct reports, the rest of her team had no idea of their fate, and if they were staying with the company or leaving.

She met Don in the first floor conference room at nine. She had mapped out the states and locations where the field layoffs would occur. She discussed with Don, the proximity of the field offices to the location of Brock's regional offices. In most cases, one of Brock's offices was in the locale. Where there weren't Brock offices, the consultants would either fly or drive to the location.

She phoned her assistant, Sharon, at ten-thirty, and asked that she join her and Don in the conference room. Sharon was standing in the door of the conference room within minutes. Sharon was able to decipher their notes, and suggested a format that would make it easier to understand where meetings would be held and which consultants and human resources managers would be teamed. After Sharon left, Don commented again on how professional and efficient she was.

"Hudson, she's a jewel," he said. "Did you notice how quickly Sharon was able to decipher the information and her excellent recommendation for formatting the data?"

"I agree 100 percent. As soon as I can get through this nightmare, I plan to create a career path for her."

Don corrected Tracy, telling her it wasn't a nightmare, but an opportunity. "I think you may be under estimating the board members. After being a part of the conference call the other day, some of the board members may not have corporate experience, but there's a reason why they are successful. The call was so short that I didn't have time to size any of them up. I'm sure reducing the headcount of the company by 8 to10 percent didn't sit well with them."

"I'm sure you are right Don. I can't wager an opinion, because other than Zahn Durk, I don't really know them or their pet projects and quirks."

"Hudson, in time you'll meet and work with all of them. Trust me on this one. Judy may be able to fool the board members some of the time, but it is nearly impossible to fool them all of the time."

She and Don worked through lunch. It was easier that way. In the afternoon, they met with Sam to let him know when additional broadcast messages would need to be sent.

Sam was always eager to help, and reassured Tracy that he was very confidential.

She and Don met with the additional consultants from Brock who had recently arrived. It was always in order, during a layoff of this size, to have as many eyes and ears focused on all aspects of the project. With so many tedious details, it was easy for something to slip through the cracks.

"Don, maybe we should run through our checklist of all of the activities that need to be done between now and the day of the layoff," Tracy said.

Don agreed that was an excellent idea. By going through the list as a group, they noticed that a couple of the human resources managers were slated to be in two places at the same time. He thought it would be a good idea for Tracy to debrief with Judy each day, highlighting the events of the day and next steps. Due to the sensitive nature of the information, he suggested that the sessions be in person.

Before she could say it, he took the words right out of her mouth, "Yes, Sheila should be present at the meetings to save time. Better yet Hudson, why don't you leave it up to Judy to make that call. If Judy wants Sheila there, it will be easier to explain her rationale to your colleagues. You shouldn't be the middle man."

For the next couple of hours, Tracy shared background information and current photographs of each executive with Brock's consultants. The profiles would help them get to know the executives' areas of expertise and to start to associate names with faces. She thought the consultants would relate well with the employees who would be leaving the company. Each consultant, at some point in his or her career, had either been laid-off or edged out by a company. They knew first-hand the inner trauma and inner struggle in finding a new job and accepting that your skills were no longer needed.

Don headed out at three-fifteen to Miami International Airport. He took along a stack of reports to review. All other information could be retrieve from his computer.

At four Tracy returned to the human resources department to briefly meet with Sharon. Tonight was a statistics class for her, and she wanted to make sure Sharon wasn't late. Even for a seasoned veteran, statistics wasn't a class you could miss and catch up on.

"Hi, Sharon. I want to get with you before your class this evening."

"I've already sent an email to my professor letting him know I might not be able to attend," Sharon said.

"You most definitely will be able to attend, and you'll be on time. I admire what you're doing, Sharon. I know it's not easy working and going to school with your family obligations, but believe me; you are doing the right thing. Your education will pay off."

Sharon was thankful her new boss was such a considerate person. Statistics wasn't one of her favorite courses. She was barely holding on to a B. Most of the students who were taking the class were struggling. The professor had a strong German accent, and at times it was difficult understanding what he was saying. Many of the students didn't drop the class because the professor was known to give extra credit and to work with students who didn't have the aptitude for statistics.

"Sharon, when the layoff is over, I'd like for us to meet to talk about your career goals. I see a bright future for you at Sunset."

The words brought tears to Sharon's eyes. She had never had a supervisor who cared about her career. When she broached the subject with previous supervisors, they acknowledged her comments, and that was as far as it went. She generally initiated the conversation, and felt that her supervisors weren't focused on the little people.

"Thank you so very much Tracy. I'll be looking forward to our discussion."

Tracy asked Sharon to put their meeting on the calendar and to schedule the discussion over lunch, away from the office. She wanted to make sure there were no interruptions. As long as Tracy was in her office, she had no control over her time and what fires she would have to put out. As a human resources executive, she was always on call. She shifted the conversation. She needed to know how the troops were really doing. With her short tenure with the company, she hadn't been able to develop trusting relationships.

"Sharon, how are employees doing in the company and in this department? I don't want you to break a friend's confidence. Just overall, how are employees fairing?"

Sharon wanted to be open and candid with her boss. She also needed to make sure that her supervisor didn't see her as someone who got confidential information and used it to her advantage or for personal gain. Sharon had many friends in the company who knew she was privileged to data regarding the layoff. She now walked a fine line, and as much as possible she stayed away from public areas, like the break room, copier room and the lunchroom. It was just easier not having to listen to the employees gripe about the layoff, knowing she couldn't comment.

Tracy noticed Sharon's hesitation. It was hard for Sharon to spill her guts, knowing that the employees perceived her boss, as the culprit. When she finally spoke, she chose her words carefully.

"Tracy, you're doing a great job. I admire you and I can't imagine how you're coordinating all of these moving parts so well. The employees, not all of them, but most, think you're responsible for causing this layoff. I know that might sound strange, but the company has never had to lay off any one before. The employees feel you're trying to make a name for yourself and somehow you encouraged and convinced Judy to do this. Human resources is being blamed."

Tracy respected Sharon's candor. She wasn't expecting to be perceived as the axeman, but she wasn't surprised. She hadn't had an opportunity to gain anyone's trust. She stepped into the company on Monday, and was immediately thrown to the wolves. There was no way she could defend herself. There was no use in holding up the flag and saying I'm not the guilty party, the condition of the company warrants this. She had to step up and take the blame until the tables turned. It was also a heads up that her colleagues hadn't stepped up and taken responsibility for the current state of the company. In time, the employees would understand that the financial state of the company led to such drastic measures.

"Sharon, thanks for your candor. I know this isn't easy for you. You have many friends in this company, who know you work for me. Layoffs are never easy. We'll weather this storm. Employees need to blame someone, and apparently I'm an easy target. What employees will see over time is that these are tough times not only for Sunset Pub and Grill, but also for America. The economy is bad and with high unemployment, emotions are running high. Employees are probably in a state of shock. It's hard for them to concentrate because they don't know if the job they are currently doing, will be relevant in the new organization."

"Tracy, I know you didn't cause the layoff. I think deep down inside employees know this too. They're hurt and frustrated, and having to wait for D-Day is killing them."

"How is the human resources team holding up?" Tracy asked.

"They're in a peculiar place. Human resources is probably the second most hated group, behind you, no offense, and they're scared. Not your senior leaders, but all the people below them. A couple of our team members have spouses who have been laid off."

Tracy told Sharon that she was doing all in her power to not prolong the agony. She could see the pain in the eyes of employees. The sadness and the high level of stress were ever so present, as she passed and spoke with them each day. She reassured Sharon that she would work with the company's leadership to help employees better understand how the company got into this financial crisis. With that, she said goodnight and told Sharon to do well in her statistics class.

She called Don on his cell. It was slightly after five and she knew he would be at the airport by now. Sharon had reinforced what she already believed. The company's leadership was trying to make her the scapegoat, and she wasn't going to stand by and let them get away with it. The company should have communicated the potential layoff before she arrived. Now she was left holding the bag; trying to explain how the company got into its current predicament. She was fuming when Don answered. She shared with Don, what Sharon had said.

He was by no means surprise. He had sized up the organization and the top leadership. There were no winners during a layoff. It was much easier to let Tracy be the fall guy and pretend human resources was responsible for life's ills. Employees were smart people; overtime they would realize that a new executive wouldn't be hired to start work on a Monday and 3 days later, be able to persuade the company's leadership and the board of directors to cut 10 percent of the organization.

"Hudson, take a deep breath and count to 10. You're over-reacting. Look at the big picture. If you hadn't accepted the job, employees would be on the street with no severance and no one to help them find another job. I'm afraid to think what legal action the company would be facing, if you weren't there. There definitely would have been a disparity between diverse and non-diverse employees, as well as with older workers."

Tracy spoke up in support of her friend Leslie. "One thing I know for sure, Leslie wouldn't have allowed the company to only cut diverse and older employees. Leslie is outspoken when decisions have legal ramifications. If Leslie had to, she'd go over the CEO's head and make the board aware. She's no softy when it comes to the law, and what's legally right."

Friday had been busy, stressful and crazy. Tracy was glad the day was finally coming to a close. She wished that she hadn't made a commitment to see Eric. What she needed most of all was time alone. It had been a grueling week. She was tired and exhausted. Somehow she found the strength to get herself out of her chair; with brief case in hand, and onto the escalator. When she got to Leslie's office, Leslie commended her for managing her demanding schedule and standing her ground in meetings with the executives.

"There she is, the hero and savior for Sunset," Leslie said. "If you weren't so damn good at what you do, this place would really be fucked up. I can't believe Judy didn't facilitate the Q&A session during the employee meeting. You and Don did a great job humanizing the meeting and answering employees' questions and concerns."

She was thankful for the positive comments. She knew Leslie called the shots as she saw them. Leslie didn't beat around the bush. She always spoke candidly and directly. She faced problems head on. Leslie went on to tell Tracy that she was doing an exceptional job managing all of the details. Tracy was good that way. Whatever she worked on was as close as you could get to perfection.

"So much for me. Are you ready to mingle with these great people?" Tracy asked.

Leslie said she was ready to mingle and to enjoy some fine wine. She tidied up her office and closed the door. She had a stack of papers in her hand that would serve as homework. She told Tracy that everything was set with her stylist. They would expect her tomorrow at one-thirty.

She handed Tracy a piece of paper with the address and directions to the salon. They proceeded to the parking garage. Tracy thought it would be best if they left her car in the garage and rode together, since she was still somewhat unfamiliar with the city.

Tracy removed her jacket revealing a tight-fitting Moschino dress. She slipped out of her pumps and put on D&G stilettos. She brushed her hair and put it up with soft ringlets cascading around her face. She clasped a gold necklace around her neck and put on gold hoop earrings. She looked stunning. She added a little more blush and a light coat of pink lipstick. Leslie couldn't help but wonder if there was more to Eric than what Tracy had shared.

"You look fabulous, darling, as they say in Hollywood. Are we going to sip wine or are you going on a personal date with Eric?"

"Just because we work in corporate America doesn't mean we can't glamorize. This will be a fun night out for us. It's been a long and difficult week. I'm ready for some wine," Tracy said, as she turned and looked at Leslie.

"I suggest you unfasten some of those buttons on your blouse, take you hair out of that school maid bun with its tight coil, and apply a little more makeup. After all, we're not going to a wake."

Leslie complied and was following orders as she picked up the expressway. She unfastened just enough buttons to show some cleavage. She released the bun and asked Tracy to get her makeup bag from the back.

"I will reapply my blush and lipstick at the next traffic light, I'm a pro at multitasking."

Forty minutes later they were pulling up in front of the restaurant. Leslie gave the car keys to the valet parking service. When the two of them stepped out of the car, all heads turned. A group of men standing in front of the door to the restaurant admired Tracy's exquisite beauty. It was amazing what stilettos did for the figure and to men's emotions.

She hadn't seen Eric approach the front entrance of the restaurant. He had watched the men admire her beauty. Tracy was totally unaware of how gorgeous she was. She looked more like a movie star than a corporate officer. The dress clearly showed her thirty-four bust, twenty-two-inch waist, and hips that measured thirty-five. She had that hourglass figure women spent hours in the gym trying to get. The dress she was wearing hugged all the right curves. The super high heels showed off her long, shapely legs. Eric wanted her but knew she was off limits. She waved Eric over once she recognized him as he stood in the doorway.

"Hi, Eric, I'd like for you to meet my colleague, Leslie Klein. Leslie is the general counsel for Sunset." She then turned to Leslie and made the necessary introduction.

"Eric Sears is a renowned plastic surgeon in Miami. He has his own practice."

Eric was so relieved that she had brought a girlfriend with her. He was afraid she would show up with the consultant who had flown in to work with Sunset. The very last thing he needed was to babysit a possible suitor. After the introductions were done, he escorted Tracy and Leslie inside, explaining that they always had a "meet and greet" first. Eric was a smooth operator. He got between the two of them, leading them by holding their hands. He introduced the two to some of the members as they entered the restaurant. As soon as introductory remarks were out of the way, he found a quiet spot in the corner of the restaurant away from the crowd.

"How on earth do you remember all of their names? I'm so bad with names and faces. There was a time when I could recall the names of everyone I ever met. Those days are over," Tracy said.

Eric explained that he was one of the board members and had been with the group for five years. "Tracy, I think you'll really like and fit in with this group. These people are professionals, and easy to get along with. No one is pretentious. They're just great people," Eric said, as he introduced Leslie to an equal, the general counsel for Burger King.

He was very pleased when Charles Steel, Burger King's general counsel, led Leslie away. Charles was in his late forties with gray hair. He had been the general counsel for Burger

King for the past ten years, which was a record for that company. The talk in the industry was that Burger King was a revolving door for executives. The company would spit them out as fast as they were hired. Most executives left or were fired after three to four years of employment with the company. Burger King was considered good training ground for up-and-coming executives, not for career focused leaders.

"You look stunning tonight, Tracy. It's incredible that you could look this way after a day at the office," Eric said, as he collected two glasses of wine from one of the waiters serving the crowd.

"Thanks Eric. It's been a long week, but it's over now. Maybe I should sip my wine slowly, so I can enjoy tasting the various brands at the wine-tasting event," Tracy said, taking another sip of wine.

He was still amazed and mesmerized by her beauty. There was an aura about Tracy, a quiet mystique that got his juices flowing. He had never had this reaction to anyone before. He was one of the most sought-after bachelors in Miami, not only for his money but his good looks as well. The women he dated dreamed of becoming his wife. He never let on that marriage wasn't in his current plans. He was having way too much fun in the company of the gorgeous creatures of Miami, although he often thought about the singer and actress who got away. That was water under the bridge now.

"Eric, I find it remarkable that you're not married. Have you ever been married?" she asked, pulling no punches. Tracy was direct, she didn't beat around the bush.

He knew he had to choose his words carefully. He didn't want to come across as a womanizer or a playboy. Younger women admired that quality in men, not older, more mature women. Professional and accomplished women would call the shots. They didn't waste time chasing the impossible dream. For them tomorrow offered no guarantees. One had to seize the moment.

"I know this sounds corny, but I always thought the right one would find me. I never actively went looking. I just thought it would happen," he said, hoping she would buy it.

"You've so much to offer to the right person. Take your time. Don't be in a rush. Marriage is a big commitment. As I think about all the married couples I know, I can't name one that is truly happy. My plastic surgeon that does my Botox and fillers was dead on the money. He said he couldn't understand why both married men and women took their looks for granted while they were married. He was always appalled by women and men flocking to his office after their divorce to get all pretty and dolled up. He made a valid point when he said, 'If only they'd worked that hard when they were married, they might still be married,'" she said, taking another sip of her wine.

Eric knew he had to tread lightly. Tracy knew more about relationships and marriage than he thought. Perhaps she had married young and caught her husband in bed with her best friend. Maybe she was a feminist and was waging a personal battle, although he hadn't seen any signs. He wouldn't dare ask her if she was once married after her brief speech. The best thing would be to change the subject and move on. Being too curious and prying into her business could potentially destroy a future relationship.

"You're so open about Botox and fillers. That's not always the case with my clients. They want to sneak in the back door and quietly leave by the side door. I'm sworn to secrecy, which is the oath I took going into the profession," Eric said, as he carefully watched to see if the statement would cause any veins in her neck to rise.

"I wasn't always like this. There was a time when I wouldn't dare let people know I colored my hair. I was a fanatic about my looks. I think back then to how excessive and irrational I was when it came to keeping up with the Joneses."

He found Tracy to be a fascinating woman. She was so sure of herself, unlike the twenty-year-olds he dated. She had rich conversation around almost any topic. She wasn't afraid to push the parameters and stretch into those "off" limit areas. There was still innocence, about her. Her smile radiated from within. There was also a sadness about her ... a loneliness ... a struggle with something bigger than herself. He knew in time she would open up. For now, he wanted to be her friend and later her lover.

"Eric, I'm told that plastic surgeons are always surveying the area and analyzing each woman they meet, offering their services, and explaining how they can make her more appealing."

"Tracy, I've a little of that in me. I think we do that to enhance beauty in the world. It's not because we're mean or think women need to have work done. I think it's partly because of our training and partly because we feel it's our duty to educate and share all we know about the human body."

She seemed satisfied with that. Her work, though completely different from his, constantly involved analyzing situations and people and trying to make them and the company better. She was always working with managers, trying to get more performance out of their people and trying to stretch them to the next level. They talked for another fifteen minutes before Leslie walked over and barged into the conversation.

"What are you two talking about over here all secluded and isolated from the group?" Leslie asked.

"Such an interesting choice of words. If I didn't know you better, Leslie, I'd say you're bored stiff with that group of attorneys you're with. I can spot a lawyer from a mile back. Conversations always become intense. From over here it looked like you guys were in court, trying to convince the jury that you're absolutely right without a shadow of a doubt. Am I right?" she asked.

"Close to the truth. Let's change the subject and talk about more pleasant things," Leslie said.

Leslie shared with Eric, that as quiet as it was kept, Tracy was also an attorney; the difference was, she was smart and got out of the game before it started. He wasn't totally surprised that Tracy was an attorney. That probably explained her directness and confidence. Attorneys were like that. So often it was difficult for them to see shades of gray. Their exactness often overshadowed options and other avenues that needed to be pursued. They continued to talk until they were ushered in for the wine-tasting event.

The conversation was lively among the three of them. Eric knew he had to move quickly if he wanted to get rid of Leslie and have more quiet time with Tracy. As he was contemplating who he could introduce Leslie to, Charles Steel reappeared. It seemed he had to make an important phone call to discuss the details of an acquisition he was working on.

"There's the most gorgeous woman in the room," Charles said, as he squeezed himself between Eric and Leslie. "What have I missed?"

"Some great wine, lively conversation, and relaxing music," Leslie chimed in and said.

"Why don't we go into the lounge and enjoy more of this relaxing music as we continue to taste some of the world's exceptional wines," Charles said, inviting Tracy and Eric to join them.

Eric told his good friend Charles to go and secure four seats. He wanted more time alone with Tracy. He wanted to crack the egg and get inside her head. He wanted her to let her guard down and trust him.

Tracy was having more fun than she thought she would. The stress and pressures of the day had long since gone. She was in a good mood, all relaxed and mellowed out. He led her to the balcony. The light breeze from the Atlantic Ocean and that delightful surge you get as the wine starts to take over made her feel even more relaxed. The wind was softly blowing her hair and there was a hint of men's cologne in the air as he got closer.

"I'm intrigued by you, Tracy. I don't think I've ever had these feelings for another woman. I realize how strange and foreign that sounds."

He'd put himself out there now. She'd either laugh in his face or encourage him to continue. She made light of his comments. She hadn't resolved her relationship with Stephen. How could she start another relationship when the ink wasn't even dry or better yet … before she had even made the call to her attorney to start the paperwork?

"Eric, that's the wine talking. We've probably overindulged. I think we need to flush down the wine with plenty of water. Let's get out of this night air, Charles and Leslie are expecting us."

Eric convinced her to stay on the balcony a while longer. As the waiter floated by with more drinks, he asked him to return with bottled water. The waiter returned within seconds with two bottles of Evian. She sipped the water like wine. It felt good oozing down her throat. It balanced all of those earlier glasses of wine she'd inhaled.

She was tipsy but not drunk. She had reached her limit. At cocktail parties and business affairs, she generally stopped at three glasses of wine or liquor. That way she got the scoop and dirt on those who became lushes. It was interesting the next day watching the reaction of those who had drunk too much the previous night. They were desperately trying to remember and recall what had transpired and if they had made a complete fool of themselves. It was also a way to get into and better understand the political arena as individuals opened up while under the influence of alcohol.

He wanted to get to know this beautiful goddess that stood before him. What made her tick? Who was she? Why was she so irresistible? And above all why wasn't she just as taken aback by him as he was with her?

Eric wondered if he'd perhaps spent too much time with teenyboppers and didn't quite know how to entertain a real woman. It was so much easier dating twenty-year-olds. All they wanted was to be able to charge clothes to your American Express card and party the night away. They usually slept late each day, got up in time to shop, and to get ready to dance till the break of dawn. Conversations were shallow, not rich and full of meaning. You often got the impression you were talking to an alien when speaking about worldly things.

Tracy was a real woman. Life had meaning for her. She cherished the moments with others and life itself. She was true to form, not fake. She felt telling the truth made more sense than lying or faking it. She understood people and appreciated life.

"I think we need to join Charles and Leslie. We don't want them to think we were captured by pirates," Tracy said, leading the way to the lounge.

When they got to the lounge, Charles and Leslie were in a lively conversation with a small group of attorneys. They didn't seem engrossed in nonsense but in topics that needed defending. Eric could see they hadn't been missed at all.

"Seems like your friend and the lawyers are hitting it off quite well. I don't think they've even noticed we are here."

She had to agree with him. "Eric, if you were my doctor, what would you recommend as the next steps in … let's say, beautifying my facial features? I'm not a fan of facelifts. I think they distort the face. It gives one a look of creepiness," Tracy said, and then wished she could take back the words. His profession was to alter the looks of women and men when necessary and to soften and enhance their features.

He was a real sport about it. He knew that plastic surgery was a mystery to so many women and men. So many surgeries had been botched up. The media was always showing and talking about entertainers who went under the knife and ended up looking scary, with disfigured faces.

Eric told Tracy that one of his primary goals as a surgeon was to educate his patients. He refused to perform surgeries on women who were addicted to going under the knife. For them it was a game of trying to relive an earlier part of their life while they remained stuck in the moment. He encouraged his patients to do the proper research and to take their time deciding. He had conversations with them about the pros and cons, and all possible side effects.

Eric was fortunate to have performed surgery on many of his staff. Although most of his assistants were very young, there were a couple of older women, who were the product of his skillful hands. He said the best way to increase your business was to have happy and satisfied patients, who were also a part of the office team. His staff would share with his patients the surgeries Eric had performed on them; patients who were somewhat reluctant or plain scared to have various procedures done. Tracy felt bad having phrased the statement as she had. She felt fortunate that he didn't seem to mind or hold it against her.

"Do you dance?" Eric asked, as he led Tracy away from Leslie and the attorneys.

She nodded, and a minute later found herself on the dance floor with him. He was a terrific dancer. He had all the right moves. He wasn't awkward or uncomfortable on the dance floor. The music was fast with a strong Latin beat. It didn't matter who your partner was on the dance floor; you could move about, choosing another willing person. She noticed that a live band was playing the music. The lights dimmed a little more, and a lady approached the mike. The female singer slowed the music down, singing Roberta Flack's number one hit, "The First Time Ever I Saw Your Face."

He wanted to whisper in Tracy's ear and tell her this would be their song, but he didn't dare for fear she would ask him to back off and leave the event. He pulled her close. Tracy was becoming uneasy with his firm grip. She could really smell his cologne now. She recognized the fragrance. It was D&G Light Blue cologne. She had purchased the fragrance for Stephen. She loved the scent the first time she sampled it in Neiman Marcus. Stephen never wore it. He claimed he was allergic to something in that particular cologne. He often asked her to not wear perfume.

To keep the peace, she would spray the perfume in the air and walk into its mist before it landed on the floor. This was an old trick she had learned. In the business world, no one wanted the heavy scent of cologne lingering in his or her office. By spraying the cologne in midair and walking into it, the scent became very faint.

Her body started to tingle when the singer song, "The first time ever I lay with you …" Maybe dancing slow to love songs wasn't the way to go. Before giving it another thought, Charles cut in and left Eric standing, looking for another willing partner.

"Your friend Leslie sent me over here to relieve you. She thought Eric was occupying too much of your time," Charles said.

"Truth is, I think Leslie is jealous that I'm on the dance floor having fun. Tell you what, on the next fast dance; we'll drag her butt out here on the floor. We won't give her a choice," Tracy said.

True to form, both Charles and Tracy got Leslie on the floor. The band played a salsa followed by a rumba. Leslie was better than Charles and Eric combined. She took the lead, showing hip and rhythm movement. She was quite the dancer. She moved around the floor, encouraging bystanders to join in the action. Her hair seemed to flow with her movements, and her feet seemed to lift off the floor.

Everyone was in awe of how good she was. Leslie left them dancing on the floor as she joined the band. Tracy had no idea that Leslie was a singer with a flawless voice. She had such sexy moves on stage. She flirted with the audience and all the members of the band, grabbing them in unusual places, all the time keeping it fun and clean. When the song ended, Leslie asked the band if they could play Michael Jackson's international hit, "Billie Jean."

The place went wild. People were on stage dancing as well as on the floor. Leslie took the microphone and joined the crowd on the floor. Everyone was on his or her feet. There were people trying to do the moonwalk, while others just stood and shook what they had. She was quite the entertainer. When the song was over, she thanked the crowd for indulging her.

Charles was grinning from ear to ear. He met Leslie as she was leaving the stage. He acted like a bodyguard protecting his star. The crowd asked for more, but Leslie yelled back saying, "You can't afford me." And with that she went back to her table.

"Wow, I didn't know you could sing like that or for that matter sing at all. I think you missed your calling in life. You were incredible," Charles said, as he softly kissed her hand.

Eric and Tracy were approaching the table. "Will wonders never cease. Here you think you know someone because you've worked with her for years. You've confided in her, and you've shared your deepest, darkest secrets … then you suddenly learn that she's been hiding a big secret. Where did you learn to sing like that and why didn't I know? Ms. Klein, do you want to explain yourself?" Tracy asked.

Leslie smiled and said it was the wine. No one bought it. They asked her to come clean. She admitted that she sang with a small band that played on campus while she was in college, and those gigs helped put her through law school. Leslie chose law, which her parents had instilled in her since the time she could walk. They didn't think singing for a living would pay the bills. If it hadn't been a dream of her parents for her to graduate from a prestigious law school, she probably would have moved to New York to pursue a singing career.

She was becoming uncomfortable with her friends going on and on about her magnificent voice. She tried several times to get them to change the subject but to no avail.

"It's never too late to pursue your dreams," Charles told her. "With a voice like that, you'd be competition for singers like Madonna, Streisand, and Celine."

Leslie knew deep in her soul that she'd like nothing more than to sing. The time had already passed for her to pursue a singing career. Today's entertainers were young, vibrant, and drop-dead gorgeous. Besides, her place was serving corporate America, where her skills and training could be utilized. She'd already accepted that part of life had since passed her by. Maybe if she had been stronger with more inner drive, her parents wouldn't have been so overpowering.

Eleven o'clock was fast approaching, and Tracy was thinking about all she had to do Saturday morning. She had to be done by noon in order to keep her afternoon appointment at the salon. After spending the evening with Eric, she was now looking forward to the moonlight cruise. For now she needed to bow out for the night. She looked around for Leslie, who had been standing by her side moments earlier.

"There you are Ms. Madonna. I think it's time for us to get out of here before we turn back into pumpkins," she said, pulling Leslie toward the door.

"Have we forgotten our manners? We were invited to this affair tonight, and the last time I checked we were having tons of fun," Leslie said, looking around for Charles.

The two ladies caught up with Eric and Charles, said their good-byes, and waited for the valet service to bring Leslie's car around front. Eric waited with Tracy while Charles and Leslie discussed the recent court decision in California regarding gay marriage. Before Eric opened the door for Tracy on the passenger side, he took her hand in his and thanked her for coming.

"You have a great friend, and I think you're pretty terrific yourself," Eric said, as he kissed Tracy on the cheek.

Leslie got behind the wheel and steered the car in the direction of the expressway. She barely stopped for flashing traffic lights. Leslie acknowledged the fun she'd had and couldn't understand why she'd never considered becoming a member of Miami Events and Adventures. Eric had been right. It was a great way to meet other single people and not feel like you had to go out on a date. You could spend time in a safe environment talking about yourself, your career, or whatever tickled your fancy.

"Wow, Leslie, I don't think I've had this much fun in ten years. I felt young and alive on the dance floor. Eric is such a great dancer."

Leslie agreed. She hadn't expected to have so much fun. Even the attorneys who initially came across as boring had a sense of humor. She now had a great group of attorney buddies she could call to discuss court cases, briefs, and corporate law. The attorneys were so open since they were not in competition with one another. They all had their area of expertise. No one was threatened by the other.

"Do I hear late-night walks on the beach and breakfast in bed for you and Charles?" she asked, looking a little concerned for her friend, who had broken out of her shell tonight and showed an entirely different personality.

"I think it's much too soon to know for sure. I'm glad to have colleagues I can call on to discuss legal matters. It's quite lonely in my area of specialization," Leslie said.

She was concerned about Tracy and her new found friend, Eric. She wasn't sure if Tracy's feelings were deeper than she let on. Her eyes gleamed when she mentioned Eric's name. She didn't think Tracy had shared with Eric the fact that she was married and had fled from California, not even discussing her departure with her spouse.

"Has Eric ever been married?" Leslie asked.

"No, he hasn't. We talked about that and his life in Miami. He seems like a super guy. He was so much fun, and he's a terrific dancer."

Leslie was worried about Tracy not telling Eric she was married. Men didn't like deceitful women. They wanted women who were upfront and honest. A man usually wanted to know where he stood. Leslie could see that glimmer of hope in his eyes. Eric was on the hunt.

She didn't want to burst her friend's bubble, but it was known in certain circles that Eric was a womanizer. He was good in a relationship for six months before he found fertile ground somewhere else. He would wine and dine a woman, being at her beck and call day and night. When the lust for his partner faded, the woman became a statistic. He didn't have a track record for sustaining a relationship and finding joy in that one person he wanted to be with. He dated for the sport of it. Eric never made a commitment. With the number of women he'd dated in such a short period of time running rampant, a rumor was circulating that maybe he was gay or bisexual.

She felt it was her obligation as a friend to tell Tracy about his background. She didn't quite know how to approach such a delicate subject. Maybe people were just jealous of all he'd accomplished. Maybe they were envious that he could get the beautiful women and never appeared to run out of possible dates. Even with the risk of losing the bond they shared, Leslie knew she had to tell Tracy what was being rumored.

"Tracy, does Eric know that you're married? I'm assuming since he invited you to this function for single people, he probably thinks you're single and unattached. Am I right?" Leslie asked, as she posed her question to her friend.

"It never came up. Eric had many opportunities to probe my background, but for whatever reason, he made the decision not too. I'm sure I was not the only one in there going through a divorce."

Leslie had to get her friend on solid ground and make her understand that she should have mentioned that important detail when Eric called to make plans. And now they found themselves invited to another singles' event tomorrow night.

"When do you plan on telling him you are technically still married and that you haven't filed divorce papers yet? Don't you think he has a right to know? You don't want to mislead him, or even worse, have him find out on his own."

Tracy had to admit her friend was right. She should have declined the invitation, saying she was not single. After all, one of the criteria for membership was being single and unattached. He hadn't played any games.

"I'll tell Eric during the cruise. I'd rather be face-to-face when I give him the news. I would want and expect the same from him. If he feels I've misled him, then I'll bow out, and he can go on with his fabulous life. How does that sound?"

As she turned to look at Leslie, Tracy could see that something was brewing beneath the surface. She had seen that look in the past just before a dark cloud fell.

"What's on your mind, Leslie? Your eyes tell me that you're not sharing everything with me. Spill your guts."

Leslie opened up and came clean. She shared the rumors that were circulating about Eric. None of it matched the person Tracy had met at Starbucks. Eric wasn't eyeing his prey. He'd been so devoted to her all evening. He had committed himself entirely to her. Maybe that was the hook that brought in his catch, she thought to herself.

A womanizer is clever. He makes you feel like you're the only one in the world who matters. What was she doing? She and Eric were friends. She wasn't his lover or his patient. She would let him know her situation on Saturday, and then she'd walk away and meet some of the other members. If he made a scene about her not telling him her relationship status, she would simply say she wasn't contemplating on becoming a member. If he became pissed off or upset, all the better. Life threw many curve balls, and even though life was sometimes unfair, it was still good.

Leslie was pulling into the corporate garage when Tracy turned and said, "I think you and Charles make a great couple. Even if you never pursue a long-term relationship, I think he's a good catch. Did you see how he admired you for stepping out of your comfort zone and singing for the crowd? And by the way, I haven't forgiven you for not sharing that feature about yourself with me," Tracy said, as she turned and waved good night.

Sleep didn't come easily for Tracy that night. She'd had too many cups of coffee at work and too many glasses of wine. Every time she looked at the clock, it had barely inched up a notch. She lay in bed for two hours before realizing that it just wasn't happening. She went to the kitchen and took a couple of all-natural melatonin tablets. The tablets were great at promoting sleep.

Saturday was going to be a very busy day, and she didn't want to take sleeping pills and not be able to function. As long as she couldn't sleep, she opened her computer and merged together some sample letters for public relations to send out on the day of the event. The letters would go to board members, franchisees, and the media. They wouldn't be sent out until all employees had been spoken to—those who were being separated and those who would still be employees of Sunset. She put in her zip drive and developed a scripted message that all managers would need to communicate to their remaining employees.

The message was simple: "We realize that this has been a most difficult time. Today we've lost a number of our colleagues and friends. Because of the reengineering effort that took place today, we'll emerge as a much stronger company with a clean balance sheet. We'll be reorganizing some of the functions, and all employees who will be going into new or different jobs will receive training. We also have counselors with us from Brock and our human resources managers who are available to meet one-on-one with employees. Brock's consultants will be here all week. If anyone would like to talk with them, feel free to let me know or call your human resources representative. Even though this has been a most trying day, I'd like to thank each and every employee for continuing to make Sunset a great company."

Her eyelids were becoming heavy as she started to write the Q&As for the session with employees. That would have to wait until tomorrow, she thought as she closed her computer and turned off the bedroom lamp. It wasn't a peaceful night for her. She had the strangest dream that Stephen and Eric were brawling to see who would win her heart. Then a dragon appeared and killed them both. She woke up in a panic before realizing it was all a bad dream. What a night she'd had. Too much wine and too many priorities wasn't a good combination. The clock was flashing five o'clock. She wanted to drag herself out of bed, but her body wouldn't give. She lay there staring at the ceiling until ten minutes to six.

"No coffee today," she said aloud, as if saying it would keep her from coffee. Her body craved coffee, but she poured orange juice instead. She also needed to eat something to balance all that unnecessary wine she consumed last night. She wasn't sure how many glasses of wine she had drunk; it was hard keeping count with so many wine samples being placed in front of her. She was sure she'd exceeded her limit. What in the world was she thinking? The wine felt smooth going down her throat, as it put her in a relaxing mood. The only problem was waking up with a hint of a headache. She took two extra-strength Tylenol tablets. That would ease some of her pain and help her get through the morning.

She would be able to work in peace. Leslie told her that few executives worked in the building during the weekend. Most executives stayed late during the week so they could enjoy a peaceful weekend with family members and friends. It was rare for Judy to come in on a Saturday. Judy would generally go to the office after church on Sunday for a couple of hours, unless she was traveling. If Nora or Lauren came in, it was all for show. They would do anything to keep the other one from getting ahead. They were cutthroat divas. Judy was aware of their self-centered, egocentric personalities, but chose to turn the other cheek. She was much too focused on protecting Sheila and jockeying for the chairmanship.

Nora didn't always use good judgement which was part of the problem. She'd accepted expensive gifts and many gift certificates from franchisees over the years. When the previous human resources executive brought it to Judy's attention that it was against company policy and could be considered a bribe or pay off—since Nora handled the marketing budgets for both the company and franchisees—that person mysteriously disappeared from the company. Apparently, the services of that human resources senior vice president were no longer needed.

Leslie documented the occurrence in the file and had an honest and frank conversation with Nora about the precarious position she'd placed the company in. Judy hadn't planned on talking to Nora. In her typical fashion, she ignored the problem and didn't address it because Nora was one of her favorites.

Nora and Sheila were the ones Judy confided in while she and her husband were in counseling. Supposedly, her son and daughter were away at summer camp when Judy walked in on her husband having sexual intercourse with another woman. Her out of town meeting had been cut short so she wasn't expected home until the following evening. What a rude awakening for her; so much for faithfulness and devotion in that marriage.

Another day, another dollar, Tracy said as she headed for the shower. Thirty minutes later she was in her car driving to the office. It was a very crisp morning. The temperature was seventy with a clear blue, almost transparent sky. The weather was perfect. This was the type of morning Tracy wished she could enjoy her Starbucks coffee outside and have lunch on the water. Traffic was very light. All the smart people had decided to sleep in.

She'd have that luxury on Sunday. She planned to vegetate. She was going to unplug the phone in the apartment, turn off her cell, and look at old black-and-white movies. She loved watching movies that were made before Technicolor. They had so much character. The movie studios had to turn out a movie each week. Now it was a major production to make a movie within six months. It took forever in comparison, and the cost was astronomical.

Once she parked her car, she got out to an empty garage. Leslie was right. The employees and executives may be working, but it was definitely not there in the corporate office. She said hello to the security guard and took the elevator to her floor. The office lights were off. Luckily, her office was not controlled by a master switch. Once inside her office, she closed the door—if someone decided to visit, perhaps they wouldn't stay long. There was a knock on the door. So much for wishful thinking, she thought.

"Come in, it's open," she said, as her assistant, Sharon, entered her office. "What may I ask are you doing here? It's Saturday; you should be having fun and enjoying your family."

Sharon explained that her daughter was with her mom and that she was available to spend the whole day if Tracy needed her. She told Sharon it was very considerate of her to give up her Saturday. She wanted to send Sharon home to be with her daughter, but knew she could use the extra help. With Sharon working with her, she was sure they would both be out of there by eleven. Although last night wasn't a good night for sleep, today was a different story. Getting a jump start on the PR letters and the scripted messages last night allowed her to doctor them up and make them all decipherable before she forwarded the documents to Sharon. In less than an hour, Sharon was done.

"How many words do you type per minute, Sharon? It must be at a phenomenal rate. I can't keep up," Tracy said, easing back in her chair and massaging her neck.

Sharon explained that she was once clocked at eighty-five words per minute. They talked about her eighteen-month-old daughter and her husband who was in the military. She was lucky to have her mom at home with her, who was a retired school teacher. Sharon explained how hard it was being married to a person in the military and the many hurdles they faced.

Tracy revised the schedule and had Sharon retype it and email it to all the executives. She asked Sharon if all the executives had dropped off their list of employees who were scheduled to be laid off. Sharon told her that all the executives had dropped them off except for Nora.

"Did Nora say when she would give you her list?" Tracy asked.

"Nora said she had to talk with Judy before she could finalize the list. Nora commented that she had to get Judy's approval on a couple of changes."

She could see that Nora was going to be a problem. She could only surmise what tricks Nora was up to now. She was thankful that Leslie had warned her about her antics.

"Well, that is Judy's problem," Tracy said aloud, for Sharon's ears only.

A short time later, Sam stuck his head in the door to talk with Tracy. She was thankful he'd come in. They talked for about thirty minutes as Tracy explained what she'd need from him on the day of the layoff. It was critical for him to cut off computer access for each employee who would be leaving Sunset after his or her discussion with the manager, human resources representative and Brock consultant.

To prevent any slip-ups, the command center would notify him when computer access would need to be denied. He'd also be notified if he needed to download any personal information that the employee had on the computer. It was against company policy for an employee to have access to company information once they were severed from the company. After Sam left, she went to Sharon's cubicle to see how she was coming.

"Sharon, I think we'll soon be home free. Maybe I should clarify that sentence ... we'll have things under control in about the next hour."

She had Sharon start the diversity analysis profile to make sure that the layoff wouldn't have an adverse impact on a protected group. Sharon knew the HRIS System they used in human resources and had access to all the data. Tracy made a couple of calls, leaving messages for Don, some of his staff, and a couple of the executives. She sent emails to the executives, bringing them up to speed on next week's plans and how important it was to adhere to the schedule and get their information to her in a timely fashion.

At five after eleven, she and Sharon were leaving the building. She thanked Sharon for coming in and once again apologized that she had to give up some of her Saturday. She told Sharon to put the overtime hours on her time card, and have her sign it on Monday.

To her amazement and sheer disbelief, Sharon told her that most of the administrative support staff didn't get paid for overtime hours. Sharon informed her that the company would allow the assistants to occasionally take extra time off or leave early to compensate them for the additional time.

Tracy was furious. Didn't the company know there were federal laws regarding overtime pay? She wrote a note in her Day-Timer to address the issue immediately with the executive team.

"Well, Sharon, that will change going forward. Overtime will need to be approved in advance by the manager, and all administrative assistants and full-time nonexempt employees will be paid time and a half weekly for hours they work over forty. That's the law, and this company will comply."

She wished Sharon a great weekend and said she'd see her on Monday. She thought about what Sharon had told her all the way to the salon. She was hoping that Leslie would still be there when she arrived. She wanted to know how the general counsel could turn a blind eye and not enforce federal laws. There was no telling what else she would uncover as she delved into the corporate workings of Sunset. The company needed to understand that the Department of Labor could shut them down and padlock the doors. They were treading on dangerous ground. It was the law, not a practice to be taken lightly.

Tracy stopped at a local deli for some lunch. She ordered a turkey sandwich on rye with a bottle of Voss water. She only ate half of the sandwich and ordered two chocolate chip cookies to go. She needed to talk with Leslie about how nonexempt employees were being compensated for overtime hours. As she pulled into the salon's parking lot, she looked around but didn't see Leslie's car. She took the first available parking space and grabbed her purse and the cookies.

She could see why Leslie loved the salon. The reception area was done in white with two huge white leather sofas with plush satin pillows. A waterfall fountain almost as tall as the ceiling stood in the corner. New Age music played softly in the background, which gave you the feeling of being near the ocean. Modern art adorned the walls. There was an area for coffee, tea, soda, water, and wine. The young lady who greeted Tracy told her the stylist was running on schedule. She offered Tracy, her choice of a soft drink or wine. Tracy decided on a diet Coke. With the evening she'd experienced last night, she knew she needed to refrain from drinking wine.

She asked the receptionist if Leslie Klein was still there. The receptionist checked the book and pointed to the room on the right. Unlike so many salons where stylists all worked in an open area, this salon had various rooms where clients could have as little or as much privacy as they wanted. Knowing Leslie, she probably opted for privacy and speed.

"Hi, Leslie," she said. Leslie looked at her watch. It was a little past twelve-thirty.

"Aren't you a tad bit early for your appointment, or did they have a cancellation?" Leslie asked, raising her head slightly to focus on Tracy.

She responded yes and no, explaining that she was early but the salon didn't have a cancellation. She offered Leslie and the stylist a cookie. Both of them declined, saying those would be useless calories.

"Suit yourself, ladies. I plan to eat up. I'll worry about the caloric intake tomorrow when I'm on the treadmill. For now it's all about the intake of calories and enjoying these fabulous cookies."

"I'm about done here," Leslie said, as the stylist sprayed her hair lightly with a mist of hair spray. "There is a coffee shop next door. I think we've time for a quick bite."

She wanted to decline the offer for lunch but decided it would be easier to talk at the coffee shop than at the salon. She agreed, and after Leslie paid, the two headed to the restaurant next door. She shared what Sharon had told her about nonexempt employees not being paid for their overtime hours. She wanted to give Leslie an opportunity to defend her position if she had any information on the subject. She'd worked with Leslie in the past and knew she had high standards, morals, and integrity.

"Tracy, there are a number of things that aren't working right at Sunset. I wish I could say that what Sharon shared with you isn't valid. I only found this out last week when an employee who'd left the company sent a letter demanding overtime pay and back wages. I was so sure that it wasn't true. I immediately met with Judy who claimed she had no knowledge of it."

"Do you believe Judy knew nonexempt employees were working off the clock? Did Sheila know?" Tracy asked, with an agitated and frustrated look on her face.

"I can't say for sure if Judy knew. Her assistant is an exempt employee, so Judy hasn't had to concern herself with overtime pay. My gut tells me that she had some knowledge of it. Whether it's ignorance or lack of information is anyone's guess. I'm sure the company has broken the law. Judy wants to address it with the leadership team first before we educate senior leaders and managers."

"Leslie, we don't have that kind of time to pussyfoot around. The penalty for a violation of this magnitude could cost Sunset thousands of dollars. Not to mention the damage to the company's reputation."

Leslie agreed with her. They spent the next ten minutes strategizing on how quickly they could bring all managers into the fold and give them the directive that nonexempt employees would be paid overtime pay if they worked more than forty hours in any given week. Tracy said she would meet with Judy first thing on Monday to let her know the implications for the company's actions given the pending letter.

Leslie reassured her that she felt the company could buy off the ex-nonexempt employee who was threatening a lawsuit. However, they had to carefully navigate through this one. If they announced to nonexempt employees that going forward they would be paid for overtime hours, it could send up some red flags.

"Leslie, maybe we could work with the managers and have them calculate how many overtime hours they think their support staff worked this past year and pay out that amount to the employees. This would demonstrate a good faith effort if someone leaks this to the press or the Department of Labor. I think the message and how we craft it will need to be well communicated."

"So that we've a consistent message, human resources should take the lead. I'm afraid to leave this in the hands of supervisors. There're too many opportunities for them to mess it up," Leslie said.

The time for her appointment was fast approaching. The salon was strict about clients being on time. After ten minutes your time was given to someone else. If it happened a second time, they would refuse service or charge you a fee to continue with the salon. After clients experienced rejection the first time, they usually got their act together. The salon was tolerable and more lenient when it came to situations beyond one's control.

"I guess I better get up and get myself to the salon. The last thing I'd want to happen is for them to give my time to someone else."

They briefly talked about the moonlight cruise and agreed to drive separate cars. It would be easier that way. When the ship returned to port, they could each get in their car and drive home. That would save time.

Leslie felt bad for Tracy. With everything that was on her plate, the last thing she needed was this. A problem surfaced with every rock she turned over. Leslie felt like she was betraying her friend. The job offer she had waited for arrived on Friday. Although she didn't relish moving to Minnesota, the offer was solid, giving her a chance to head up the legal department for one of the top ten retailers in the country. Unlike Walmart, Target was considered a premier retailer.

Customers loved Target. Their commercials were always great. The company wasn't in competition with the retail giant. Target's demographics were different. They went after a different type of customer. Their customers wanted more of a specialty feel with wide aisles, bright decor, and friendly sales people who knew the merchandise. Their customers didn't mind paying a little more for services and quality products.

The job offer would almost double Leslie's total compensation. She'd have access to the corporate jet, which was a luxury few had the opportunity to enjoy. Because the current general counsel was retiring, Leslie didn't have to start for two months. That would give Sunset a chance to find her replacement and her an opportunity to take some needed time off before starting her new job.

What Leslie hated most of all was not being able to tell her friend she was leaving the company. Somehow the time was never right. Since Tracy had arrived at Sunset, there had been one fire after another to put out. She was consumed with handling the pending layoff, a task that Judy should have mentioned to her during the interview process. In fairness to Judy, maybe because she was inexperienced in the area, she just didn't understand what was involved in a reengineering effort.

Judy hadn't quite grasped that the human resources senior vice president was her right-hand person. The head human resources leader helped to keep the company out of court and its employees engaged in order to satisfy shareholders, board members, and customers. Maybe she could tell Tracy that she was resigning her position on Sunday after the cruise and before her hectic week started.

Tracy looked fabulous when she left the salon. She had the stylist add highlights to her golden-brown hair. She went for a light pink nail polish and a strawberry margarita-pink polish on her toes, which was more Miami. She had planned on wearing a pantsuit on the cruise, but a boutique caught her eye as she was leaving the salon. She purchased a pale green sundress that was cut low in the front. She also bought a pair of Jimmy Choo sandals and a beige Gucci sweater in case the ocean breeze became cool. She threw her packages on the backseat of the car and drove to the apartment.

It had already been a busy morning, but she didn't feel as stressed out. Sharon had been a godsend, and the coming week was looking more manageable. She had a couple of hours to soak in the bathtub, finish the Danielle Steel novel she was reading, and unwind with a cup of hot tea. In looking through the desk drawer in the apartment, she came across a list of restaurants that would deliver. She felt she had died and gone to heaven. In California she lived on takeout food if Rhonda hadn't cooked a meal or Stephen hadn't prepared an enticing entree. Even when Rhonda was there, many times she told her not to cook since Stephen was either working late or out of town.

The list included restaurants specializing in ethnic foods, everything from Chinese and French to Indian and Italian. She loved Italian but thought it might be too heavy, given the spread of food on the cruise that Eric had talked about. She dialed the Chinese restaurant and ordered egg drop soup, orange ginger chicken with cashews, shrimp egg foo yung, and shrimp toast. It was definitely too much food for one person. The leftovers would serve as her dinner on Sunday.

She wasn't one to eat lunch at work. She carried healthy snacks with her and would eat small meals throughout the day. She loved cheese, peanut butter, yogurt, and all kinds of nuts. If she got hungry during the day, she always kept canned soup, popcorn, and canned tuna on hand. Her days were always full of pressing opportunities. Even when a layoff wasn't on the agenda, there were always supervisors and employees who needed some of her time.

All problems related to or stemmed back to people. If profits were low, it was because employees weren't performing up to job standards or hadn't been properly trained; if employees were disgruntled, it was because supervisors weren't managing them properly or engaging them in the business; if the shareholders had concerns, it was because the executives hadn't met their objectives, which generally tied to company revenue and profits; and the list went on and on. Employees and executives all wanted a piece of human resources. Sometimes she felt like a school teacher with demanding students. Employees would often follow her to the bathroom to discuss their problems.

Tracy never turned an employee or an executive away, no matter how pressed for time she was. She treated people with respect and dignity. If she was in the midst of a discussion with an employee and a manager, and the employee became emotional, she would stop the meeting and excuse the manager until the situation was under control. If the employee was too emotional to carry on, the meeting was rescheduled. Managers and employees had to work together and show respect for each other. She was fair and consistent. She would face the music and deal head-on with problems. Tracy didn't sugarcoat the message or coverup the truth. If the company was at fault, she said so. If the employee was not at fault or responsible, she spoke up and let it be known.

At the end of the day, she had to live with herself. She would rather leave a company than lie and not tell the truth. The truth was always easier to remember. She clearly understood that when you lied or fabricated the truth, your credibility was instantly destroyed. She knew that well. Over time board members, executives, CEOs, employees, and customers came to love her. The more they interacted with her, the deeper the relationship grew. Although they didn't always agree, each person respected Tracy for her honesty and for not having a hidden agenda.

She always followed through on her commitments and delivered results in a timely manner. Once given a project, she saw it through to completion. Even when she was a manager, her supervisors knew she would deliver an excellent product. She put in whatever hours were needed to get the job done.

The employees and senior leaders who had worked with Tracy at her previous companies all admired her. She never took credit for someone else's work. She learned early in life to give credit to those who deserved it. Publicly acknowledging others brought many loyal followers. She never understood why some executives didn't understand that they had already arrived and most employees understood that their jobs were more strategic, not doing the day-to-day tactical activities.

With some time to spare, she couldn't refrain from putting together a short PowerPoint presentation for Judy to review before she addressed the executives and senior leaders. For now, she would think of this huge mistake of not paying nonexempt employees overtime pay for hours worked past forty, as an oversight on Judy's part.

She called Leslie, who answered her phone on the first ring. "Are you sitting there waiting for your main squeeze to call?" Tracy asked.

"I could say the same about you. I seem to remember that Eric occupied all of your time last night. I don't remember you mingling with the other members," Leslie said, charging back, giving her a dose of her own medicine.

"Eric isn't a suitor for me. I've been thinking about what you said, and I'm going to tell him tonight that I'm a married woman who plans to file for divorce. I'll explain that it was not my intention to mislead him. Frankly, the topic of my marital status never came up."

Leslie coaxed her on not saying that last statement. She felt that any prudent person would have explained her status after Eric talked about himself and being single. They agreed that telling him tonight made sense before he developed feelings for her. Then if he wanted to hang on and linger that would be up to him.

After that motherly conversation was over, they talked about what they would wear. Since Tracy was wearing a sundress, Leslie decided to do the same. She opted for flats instead of sandals or heels. They synchronized their watches so they would arrive close to the same time.

"Hey, Leslie, before you hang up ... I've tentatively put together a PowerPoint presentation I plan to show Judy on Monday. I think we need to grab hold of this issue and manage the situation in order to stay out of the press. If the overtime issue hits the fan, I can see the executives pointing fingers and throwing blame."

Leslie agreed with her. One thing the team was good at was keeping their personal record clean. It wasn't a cohesive team with everyone pulling in the same direction; it was every woman for herself. Most of that had to do with the leadership at the top. Tracy surmised that the executives and managers probably resented the close relationship that Judy had with Sheila. When your best friend is the boss, there are perks that come with that, and they all understood that clearly. Preferential treatment was definitely given to Sheila and whatever crumbs were left went to Nora, then Lauren.

Leslie thought it was wise for Tracy to put her thoughts on paper. Tracy asked Leslie to gather the statistics around the cost that other companies had paid. Finance people clearly understood the numbers. She knew that the potential liability to the company would cause both Judy and Sheila to sit up straight in their seats. Leslie could easily get that information from her law journals. In the presentation she added how to respond to a variety of questions … Why now? Will I have to pay more taxes as a result of this change? Which employees are affected? Can I take time off instead of taking the overtime money? How is overtime pay calculated?

CHAPTER 9

On the drive to Port Miami, Tracy rolled down the windows and allowed her hair to blow free. She loved the cut and soft highlights. She looked gorgeous in her low-cut sundress. It showed cleavage but left something to the imagination. She would be celebrating her fortieth birthday soon. Turning twenty was wonderful. Turning thirty was devastating. She always thought that turning forty would be traumatic. Somehow she now respected the wisdom that came with age. She was at a very nice and comfortable place. She was sure of what she wanted from life, and she went after it with gusto. She didn't have to do the bar scene, and she was never one to go on those dating sites. Tracy always felt that she would end up with a mass murderer if she did.

Over the years she had worked with many employees who found happiness and love on dating sites. Some of them had even found spouses. She thought they were brave to take such chances. Thoughts of what Leslie had said were traveling through her mind. Leslie was right. She had to tell Eric that she was married and let the chips fall where they may. She hadn't led him on; they were two people trying to make some sense out of the universe. That sounded cliché, and whom was she fooling? A blind person could see his intentions. He didn't isolate her from the crowd for fear of her not fitting in. He had guarded and protected her for fear of someone else snatching her up.

It was probably best to end what might have been a swell relationship. She was married; there was no question about that. How she left in the night, like some criminal escaping from prison or her past, was questionable. No intelligent person would just pack up and go, not explaining themselves. Moving across town was one thing, but vacating a state was something entirely different. The rumors about Eric were troubling. What if he were gay or bisexual? She didn't think she could handle that.

She knew a great detective in California who could put his Miami office on the case. Maybe for the hell of it, she would call him on Sunday and leave a message for him to call her. She and Bruce Lamarr went way back.

When she suspected Stephen of cheating on her, she had Bruce put him under surveillance. The pictures told the whole story of his extramarital affair and weekend rendezvous. At first, she was very distraught and became quite hysterical when she broached the subject with Stephen. He denied everything and told her it was just her imagination. She still remembered how she had thrown the photos at him which Bruce had taken. The evidence spoke for itself. She became distressed and totally unglued. Counseling was out of the question for Stephen. He thought they could work through their problems, claiming the psychology classes he took in college would serve them well.

At first she blamed herself. Then her motives changed as she sought revenge. Her objective was to get even and hurt Stephen as he had hurt her. That was when she had her first affair with a married man. It was all so easy—a business trip with one too many drinks and too much time to spare.

Liquor has a way of easing the pain and clouding one's vision. Once you fall down, sometimes it's hard to get up and return to all you know to be true. Since that first affair, she had been involved with two other married men.

Married men were always a safe bet. Two people who were committed to someone else came together for moments of sheer ecstasy. When the excitement ceased, they said good-bye, going their separate ways. No one made a scene for fear of being discovered.

She had been careful to not be discovered by Stephen. Maybe he knew, but he never let on. Tracy always covered her tracks well, but she knew Eric would be a challenge. Deep within that inner voice said to tell him about her intentions. It was a double-edged sword. How do you say, "Oh, by the way, I'm married, have no intentions of us dating, but I'm going to have you investigated by a detective unless you come straight with me."

She was open-minded. Her parents had taught her to accept people as they are, not as you want them to be. She had many friends who were gay, but they weren't trying to sleep with her. Some covered up their sexual preference by dating heterosexuals. For them it was a safe bet, pretending and playing the game. People were relentless in their quest to get at the truth. Most people didn't understand their preference and were opinionated for no apparent reason.

She had fought for the rights of gay employees and their partners in every company she had worked for, encouraging the company to do the right thing, by offering benefits to their same-sex partners and job promotions when they were qualified. Some of the CEOs and executives had fought her bitterly. Tracy always won in the end, saying the fight for gay rights was just like the fight for individual freedom and who were they to play god.

In places such as California, Texas, Miami, and New York, individuals felt more comfortable displaying their sexual preference. So many came out of the closet, even though there were some who stayed in the closet for fear of retaliation. There were still many companies and businesses that discriminated even though it wasn't legal. Individuals usually didn't challenge those decisions for fear of becoming known or for lack of information. Those who took that leap of faith won big and put the bastards on display, for every citizen has the same constitutional rights and protection.

She put those thoughts aside as she approached the boat. It was more like a cruise ship that went on and on into infinity. The ship was decorated with lights that made it look like one of the ships in a holiday parade. The music was blasting, and everywhere she looked there were crowds of people talking, laughing, and just having fun. Tracy didn't feel out of place as she looked at the attire of the single women. Most wore skintight dresses or shorts that left little to the imagination. In comparison to them, she looked more like a school mom.

The moment of truth was fast approaching. She wanted to deliver the words to Eric, and then mingle with the other guests. She was there to have fun and enjoy the evening. She didn't want to be tied down to him all night. She was sure that once she told Eric she was married, he'd disappear, looking for new prey.

As she entered the ship, hostesses were giving out strings of gold, purple and green Mardi Gras metallic beads, and telling everyone to have a fun-filled evening. She slipped the beads around her neck as she looked for Eric and Leslie. Not spotting either one, she introduced herself to a group of men and women standing next to the stairs.

After enjoying their company, she moved to the upper deck. There was a nice breeze in the air, and people were dancing and swaying to the music. Waiters holding trays with a variety of hors d'oeuvres moved among the guests.

Food tables with feasts fit for a king were practically everywhere. She had never seen so much food. It reminded her of the cruise she and Stephen had taken on their honeymoon. She felt an arm pull her close. As she swung around, she saw it was Eric. He looked rich and powerful in his white pants, navy blazer, and an open-collar, light blue shirt. He looked very relaxed and comfortable in his black suede loafers.

"Hi, Tracy. I'm so glad you could make it. I got caught in that traffic jam on the turnpike. I barely made it. I called ahead and told them to hold the ship," Eric said, as he reached for two glasses of champagne from a waiter's tray.

What power, Tracy thought as she took the glass of champagne from his hand. She wasn't a fan of champagne; it tended to give her a headache if she drunk it too fast. Maybe she could keep sipping the champagne and stay away from wine and hard liquor. She was determined to eat more food and drink less tonight. She didn't want to spend her one free day nursing a headache.

"You look stunning. What a gorgeous dress," he said, reaching for her hand.

"This old thing," Tracy said, even though it was brand new.

She always had a problem accepting compliments. One of her therapists told her to acknowledge the compliment by saying thank you. Eric probably would have been pleased to know that she went that extra mile to dress up for the occasion. He loved her hair. He wasn't sure what she had done to it, but it looked magnificent. The lights from the ship seemed to bounce off the brilliant shades of gold and yellow. Her emerald green eyes matched the green in her dress. She looked casual and more lovable. He didn't want to share her with anyone.

She glanced up and saw Leslie and Charles waving their hands for her and Eric to join them. They moved swiftly through the crowd, reaching them seconds later.

"You look like the eligible bachelor. I bet all of these single women are dying to meet you ... you lucky fellow," Leslie said, as she asked Charles to get her a vodka and tonic.

Leslie thanked Eric for inviting them. Tracy was just staring at her. She had no clue why Leslie had called Eric the "eligible bachelor." Was she trying to send out a message?

She nudged Leslie away from Eric, as she asked, "Do you know where the restrooms are?" Eric pointed to the stairs, giving them directions. "Why don't you come with me, Leslie? That will save you some time later when the bathrooms get crowded with all the drinks that are being served," she said, grabbing Leslie's arm. Leslie knew Tracy probably had something she wanted to tell her, so she obliged.

"What are you, a matchmaker?" she asked, looking directly at Leslie. "I think Eric is aware of his attractiveness to women. I'm sure they gravitate toward him like bees to honey."

"Get a grip, my friend. I was merely making conversation. Besides, what do you care? Don't you plan to fess-up to the evils of deception? He's a good catch and we all know it. I don't think I have entered into uncharted waters," Leslie said, touching up her lipstick.

"If you want my advice, Tracy, I suggest you tell him the truth about you and Stephen, and let him draw his own conclusions. If you're smart, you'll forget him and mingle with the other singles."

She knew Leslie made a good point. The longer she delayed telling Eric about her situation, the more difficult it would become. Once back on the top deck with Charles and Eric, they talked about the makeup of the group. Supposedly, Miami was full of single people desperately looking for Ms. or Mr. Right.

The group had over four thousand members. Each month a calendar was sent out to all members who selected the events they were most interested in. There was a nominal membership fee, and members paid per event based on the cost of participation. The more members that participated in the events, the less the overall costs. For the past three years, the evening cruises, wine-tasting events, and overnight trips to the Bahamas had been a huge success.

Charles suggested they fly over to Nassau for an evening of dancing, eating, and of course, spending money in the casinos. He said the trips were fun. The flights left out of the Fort Lauderdale International Airport at six in the evening and returned the following morning at seven.

Leslie thought that sounded like fun. You didn't have to pack an overnight case ... it became one long night affair.

Charles told them that the next casino excursion was scheduled for mid-December prior to the holidays. Realizing that her time would be cut short with her soon-to-be new job in Minnesota, Leslie took a rain check. Tracy thought it would be fun, although she had no plans to attend.

"Let's dance the night away," Charles said, leading Leslie onto the dance floor.

Eric had other plans for Tracy. He wanted to learn more about this awesome woman who had landed in his lap. They moved to the railing as the sounds of the ocean echoed in their ears.

"What a perfect night," he said, taking her hand in his and kissing the inner palm.

She looked at Eric and saw love in his eyes. She wasn't ready to make a commitment even if he were single. She didn't want him to become the rebound guy. Falling out of love with one man and into the arms of another would be disastrous. Look at the mess she had made of her marriage. She should have left the first time she found out Stephen was a cheater.

"Eric, I don't want to mislead you. I'm not a free agent. I'm a married woman. I didn't have a chance to tell you this at the wine-tasting event last night," Tracy said, as she searched his face, seeing the disappointment in his eyes.

It was as if an explosion had gone through his body and he was experiencing the heat of the aftermath. That explained why she was hesitant to talk about herself or her childhood, Eric thought, as he was desperately trying to get his emotions under control. It also explained why there was a ring imprint on her ring finger even though there was no ring. He wanted to know more about Tracy Hudson. Where was her husband, and why did she accept a second invitation, knowing the event catered to singles?

"I knew I shouldn't have counted my lucky stars. A woman as gorgeous as you, had to be spoken for," he said, as he finished his drink in one swallow.

"To make a long story short, I left my husband and I'll be filing for a divorce. It's just a matter of time now. I should have left him a long time ago. When things aren't right, you just need to go," Tracy said, seeing the sadness in his eyes.

She told Eric about the car accident and losing both her parents two years ago … that her father was a lawyer and her mother a plastic surgeon. The memories of the accident still overshadowed her joy and happiness, especially during the holidays. She told him about being in a coma and missing her parents' funeral and the guilt she felt. He could see the pain in her eyes as she spoke.

"I've been given a second chance. The doctors had given up on me. I was supposed to be a statistic. I've so much to be thankful for, and I count my blessings each day. I do not take anything for granted. My husband, Stephen, is twenty years older than me. My mother tried to tell me that he was much too old, and over time he would be more of a father figure to me instead of a husband. My mother was right."

She explained to him that the timing was never right. "When I met you at Starbucks that evening, I thought we'd have a brief conversation and that would be the end. Now here we are, out for a second outing," Tracy said, choosing her words carefully.

She didn't want Eric to think she tried to use him. She was new in town, and he was quite aggressive in persuading her to attend Miami Events and Adventures. She was hoping beyond hope that he would accept what she said and move on.

Instead, he pulled her closer and put his arms around her waist. "I know what it's like to lose your parents. My father died in Vietnam when I was young, and my mother died of cancer five years ago. I lost my older brother to cancer last year. I've no other siblings. Sometimes I feel all alone in the world. I imagine there are times when you feel the same," he said, turning away so Tracy wouldn't see the tears in his eyes.

She realized they had a lot in common. She told Eric that her parents never had any other children. She had no brothers or sisters. Since she was spilling her guts, she told him about leaving the state with just a note left on a nearby table. She explained her legal training, which helped him understand why she was so direct and got to the heart of the matter instantly, not spending much time on the gray areas of life.

He was falling in love with her. He knew those words couldn't be shared. Eric only wished he could kiss away her pain. Here she was in a new city surrounded by people who had no idea of the burden she carried.

She told him about finding her husband in the arms of another woman, but she thought it would be too risky to give him the details of how she found out. Maybe in time she would mention her affairs with married men—a fact she was not proud of. In her quest for love, dating married men had been the safest route.

"Tracy, we've all fallen madly in love and had our hearts broken," he said. "For those who are lucky, they bounce right back and jump into the game again. I once heard that love is a gamble; you place your bet and hold on tight for the ride of your life."

"You're a wonderful person, Eric. There aren't too many men out here like you. I'm lucky to have this second chance in life. When you come close to death, you don't focus on the small stuff; you focus more on your objectives and what you want out of life."

"What do you want out of life, Tracy? By some standards you have it all; beauty, intelligence, a great career ..." he said, watching her body language.

She probably wouldn't make a good poker player. She wore her emotions outwardly.

"If you'd asked me that question five years ago, I probably would have said all of those things plus love." She turned and looked into his eyes. "But now I want good health, great friends, peace of mind, and happiness. I want to make a contribution to those who are less fortunate than me ... in some small way, I want my life to matter."

"What about love? Don't you want love, Tracy?" Eric asked, hoping her answer was yes.

"I think we're all hoping for love. Someone to cuddle up to at night, someone who will be there for us, someone to share our joys and sorrows with, someone who will accept us as we are."

He didn't want to push it. Her wounds were deep. After she was able to heal, he was sure the scars would be there indefinitely. She left a man who had turned his back on her in her hour of need. She had lost both parents in a senseless accident. He knew she was barely holding on and trying to make sense of it all.

"Hello, you two. Why aren't you mingling with the guests? Isn't that the whole idea of this get-together?" Leslie asked, as she put her arm around Charles.

She could see that they were becoming an item. The two looked good together. Tracy was so happy that Leslie had finally found someone who was just as smart and clever as she was—a man who would stand up to her, a man who wasn't a pushover.

She surmised that Leslie and Charles were about the same age. Charles was about three inches taller than Leslie. His deep blue eyes and golden-brown tan made him look both desirable and attractive. His gray hair didn't make him look old at all. She hated that about men. As they aged they became more distinguished looking, while when women aged with gray hair, they just looked out-of-vogue. The only people she felt aged well with gray hair were Nancy Wilson, the singer, and Emmylou Harris, the singer-songwriter and musician. All the other women who chose gray hair over hair color just looked dated.

As Charles and Eric went to get their dates drinks, she and Leslie seized the moment to get caught up. "Did you tell Eric you're still married?"

"I told him the short version of the story. You were right; I'd misled him last night. He thought I was available," Tracy said, feeling sorry for herself and her screwed-up life.

"You did the right thing, Tracy. The truth may hurt now, but it pays dividends later."

She wasn't so sure her friend was right. Her life was all up in the air. Technically, she was alone. Even if she decided to return to California, she and Stephen could never make a go of it. There were too many pieces of that puzzle that were missing. A broken heart is never whole again. All the marriage counseling in the world couldn't save their shell of a marriage. Thank goodness Stephen knew that by refusing to go to counseling. He must have thought she was a fool to let the Psychology 101 class he took eons ago offer advice and guidance in that area.

"Leslie," Tracy said, "I didn't tell Eric that I also cheated in the marriage. I couldn't bring myself to talk about the various married men I dated. I'm sure on some level that is being deceitful."

"Maybe it is and maybe it isn't, Tracy. Why do we women have to feel obligated to tell our mate or partner everything we did in the past? I personally think women share too much information."

"The problem develops out of fear that the other person will find out. Then it's too late, Leslie, to talk about honesty and to level with the person. Trust flies out the window and you spend countless hours thinking, if only I'd told the truth, would things be different? What if I hadn't had that extramarital affair? What if I'd come clean from the start?"

The two women knew firsthand the damage that being unfaithful in a relationship caused. Leslie's motto was never hump the help in the company that employs you. As the general counsel, she did the final sign-off on all those who were being dismissed for poor choices. If any of the employees challenged the action or decision of the company, she would be the one to defend the company in court or draw up the papers to settle out of court.

Even though Leslie never made it a practice to date married men, she too had slipped and entered into a relationship she regretted to this day. She was on a business trip with some of the executives from Sunset when she met Mr. Dreamy, an executive who had started his own multimedia company in Miami. The two sat next to each other in first class on a Delta flight from Miami to New York. She thought that would be the last she would see of him.

As fate would have it, the next week Mr. Dreamy was on the same flight bound for New York. She was working on a case for Sunset and had to meet with attorneys in New York, who were directly handling the case. Two employees had filed sexual harassment claims against one of the general managers in one of their New York restaurants. Another employee had come forward, claiming that she had worked off the clock and wasn't able to take her scheduled breaks. It appeared that the store manager was short staffed and had threatened to fire the employee if she didn't cut her breaks short.

The flight back to Miami had encountered some technical problems with the landing gear and had to be diverted to Atlanta. Atlanta was experiencing bad thunderstorms, so the flight didn't leave until the following morning.

Mr. Dreamy, whose real name was Craig Petty, found himself stranded in Atlanta with Leslie. Leslie never made it to her hotel room. Four drinks later she and Craig checked into a nearby hotel, spending the night together. She was so embarrassed by her actions that she woke up in the middle of the night, quietly dressed, and vacated the room. The next morning she opted to take a later flight to Miami. Till this day she refuses to take a direct Delta flight to New York. She also keeps a safe distance from Delta Airlines. Her administrative assistant knows not to book her on any Delta flights unless it is the very last resort.

The thing that bothered Leslie the most was the fact that Craig never called her after their one-night affair. She didn't know he was married until she looked him up on the Internet. She had never done that in her whole life. Since they hadn't used a condom, she had her gynecologist perform several tests to make sure she hadn't contacted AIDS or a venereal disease.

All tests were negative. She thanked her lucky stars. The very last thing she needed was to be infected with a sexually transmitted disease. That's what you get for having a one-night stand, she constantly reminds herself. That is exactly why they call it a one-night stand.

"Leslie, you seem a million miles away. What are you thinking about?" Tracy asked.

"We all have our secret doors that we lock and throw away the key. You're not the only one who has wasted precious time and years dating committed men," Leslie said.

She shared her story with Tracy, giving her all of the gory details. The two women laughed. Tracy thought it was wise and funny how Leslie ran to have herself tested. She thought about how much they had in common. When you make those horrible mistakes and end up in those awkward places, wisdom has a way of teaching you valuable lessons.

"You can do whatever you want, my friend. Have your 'come to Jesus' meeting with Eric and spill your guts; as for me, silence is golden. I plan to take my covert behavior of the 'heat of the moment' to my grave. What I did was the epitome of stupidity. As a grown woman, to this day I don't know what I was thinking. It must have been the wine that was talking and taking control." The two women laughed. "I think when the guys return, we should drink to wisdom and learning from life's lessons," Leslie said.

Eric and Charles returned with two glasses each of red wine. The wine felt good to Leslie as she tried to forget about Craig and the whirlwind one-night affair.

"I'd like to propose a toast," she said, to Charles, Eric, and Tracy. "Let's drink to good health, great friends, and wisdom. May life's wonderful lessons continue to nourish our minds."

"I will drink to that," Charles said, clicking his glass to Leslie's, Tracy's, and Eric's.

The night was alive with great music and a cool breeze from the ocean below. Everyone was having a great time. As the ship sailed from Miami to Fort Lauderdale and then to West Palm Beach, the party started to heat up. There were various groups of people huddled in corners, dancing on the top deck, and parading around in hopes of picking up a new catch.

This was the new and improved twenty-first century way of dating. You didn't feel like you had to stretch the truth on your profile or wonder if the person in the photo had the picture taken ten years earlier. Conversations were lively. When you got to the point where you were no longer interested in the person or the conversation, you moved on … no questions asked.

There were no calls to make to fabricate the truth. You didn't have to create a reason for not calling or an excuse to call. You could sample the goods, sometimes in groups of one hundred people or more. There were some unwritten rules that said respect the privacy of others and don't impose your sexual preference if there is no interest. Being a part of Miami Events and Adventures was a nice way to stay involved with the community and to have outings and events to attend.

Tracy found herself spinning around on the dance floor as Eric took the lead to the cha-cha followed by the samba. He was a superb dancer. He had removed his jacket revealing a muscular, toned body. She wondered how many hours he spent in the gym each week toning that body.

She was never one to visit the gym. She saved those extra minutes by installing exercise equipment in her home. She worked out at least six days a week in California. She preferred loose-fitting gym shorts and a huge pullover T-shirt to that skimpy stuff women wore in gyms. She always felt it was all a show, a type of parade to see who could out dress the other. To compete you had to have several outfits, rarely repeating them during the course of the week. The women were busy trying to get picked up by rich, influential men, while the men were trying to get an easy lay in most cases.

"Wow, you must have taken lessons," Tracy commented, as Eric led her away from the dance floor.

"This may sound weird, but when I was young, I took ballet and Irish step. I loved dancing and performing in front of groups. As I became older, my interests changed. I think some of that was because of me and mostly because of the teasing I encountered throughout elementary and junior high school."

"I hate that. Kids can be so cruel. I bet those same kids are high school dropouts," she said, empathizing with Eric.

"I think I did OK. I stepped away from dance and took on basketball and soccer. I was pretty good until my senior year."

"What happened during your final year of high school?"

"I injured my back. I didn't want to face a spinal injury and become paralyzed, so I decided to get out of the game and leave basketball and soccer."

"Are you sorry, Eric, that you didn't continue to pursue the sports?"

He told Tracy that he wasn't slated to compete nationally. He enjoyed competing when it was fun. Once it became a job and was no longer fun, it was time for him to quit. He explained that competing at that level helped him to develop lifelong skills. The time he'd dedicated to the sport allowed him to control a lot of his own destiny in life. He learned how to make sacrifices while keeping his eyes on the prize.

She and Eric took a walk around the upper deck. They had to squeeze between people who were dancing the night away. They noticed that Charles and Leslie were still on the dance floor. She was happy to see Leslie enjoying herself and having so much fun. She noticed Charles leaning in and planting a kiss on her neck. They seemed so happy together. She wished them well. If anyone deserved happiness, it was Leslie. All of the crap she had to put up with at Sunset was probably just the tip of the iceberg.

"Tracy, I never asked, but do you have any children?"

"No, I don't. I always wanted children, but the timing was never right. First, there was building the career, and then other things got in the way. One day you wake up and wonder where has the time gone."

He didn't want to press her to explain the "other things that got in the way." He was sure she was referring to Stephen's infidelity and losing her parents. He knew how devastating it was to grow up without a father and to lose the only family you've ever known. He would give anything to have a little more time with his mother and brother.

"Tracy," he said, "it's never too late to start a family. People have kids at all ages. There's always adoption as an option."

She was beyond entertaining the idea of having kids. Her lifestyle was all so different now. She wasn't afraid of being a single parent with a child, but it was scary thinking about how old she would be when the child graduated from high school. She was approaching forty, which meant she would be almost sixty. And the thought of having to determine who she'd want to take care of the child if something happened to her was very frightening. Maybe God knew best in her case.

"You're right, Eric, it's never too late to start a family. With all I have on my plate, I just can't think about that now," she said, hoping he would never find out that she had doubts about the long-term care of the child if she died. It was frightening enough having to think about who would be there for her in her hour of need.

They spent the next couple of hours chatting about life and things the country was facing. She shared with him how she loved old black-and-white movies and that her favorite actress was Bette Davis. She had seen *Whatever Happened To Baby Jane?* over fifty times. She also enjoyed playing the piano, which she seldom had time to do because of her job and the pressing priorities in her life.

He was a good listener, a skill he probably developed while in medical school. She could tell from his behavior that his patients probably adored him. He was handsome, not overbearing, and he listened intently to what she said. So many of her doctors didn't take the time to get to know her. Every non-necessary minute spent with a patient were dollars lost. It was sad how the system forced doctors to treat their bread and butter like a herd of cattle.

Before they knew it, the ship had returned to port. It had been a wonderful night. She still hadn't met many new people, even though this was her second outing with Miami Events and Adventures. There were so many people waiting for the captain to let them off the ship that it was hard for her to locate Leslie. She and Eric stood on the side of the ship until all the passengers had disembarked. There still was no sign of Leslie or Charles. Eric agreed to wait, but Tracy thought it would be best if she called Leslie on her cell while en route to the apartment.

Eric walked her to the car and kissed the inside of her right palm. He planted a wet kiss on her jaw.

"Thanks for a most intriguing evening. I feel so fortunate to have met you and to have enjoyed your company for two evenings. I don't want to push my luck, but maybe I'll see you tomorrow at Starbucks," Eric said, as he got Tracy into her car and on her way.

Tracy waved as she drove away. She felt she was the lucky one. Instead of spending two lonely nights stuck in the corporate apartment, she had been able to enjoy the time with her best friend and her two new friends. As she pulled out of the parking lot, she dialed Leslie's cell.

"Hello, Leslie, are you still on board the ship? There were so many people waiting to get off the ship that Eric and I couldn't find you.

"Are you still here? Leslie asked.

"No, I'm in my car. Eric and I looked for you and Charles, but the crowd was so large, we couldn't find you," Tracy repeated, practically yelling into the phone.

"Hey, Tracy, I'm almost at my car. I'll call you as soon as I can get away from this crowd." With that there was a click on the other end of the phone. Leslie was gone.

Tracy turned on the radio and decided to mellow out with jazz. After a night of loud music, she needed the smooth sound of jazz. She waited for about ten minutes and redialed Leslie's cell.

"This is much better," Leslie said, balancing the phone up to her right ear while trying to get chewing gum out of her purse.

"I was calling to make sure you got safely into your car. I wouldn't want anything to happen to you."

"Charles is coming over to my place for a nightcap. Do you and Eric want to join us?" Leslie asked, feeling like a schoolgirl waiting for the principal to say it was OK.

Tracy told Leslie to be careful. She hardly knew Charles. She reminded her of the one-night fling that never came back or had the decency to call. She thought Charles was a flamboyant guy, the kind that attracted women like flies.

"We aren't going to have sex, my dear. We just plan to continue our conversation," Leslie stated.

Once again she told her to be careful. Casual conversations at that hour, at her place, was treading on dangerous ground. Someone might get hurt. Before hanging up Leslie asked Tracy if she could come over to the apartment on Sunday after church. When Tracy asked what was so urgent, Leslie shouldn't have lied, but she said it was work-related for fear Tracy might continue to probe.

The apartment was dark and dreary looking when Tracy returned. She'd forgotten to leave a light on. She had to remember to go to the Home Depot soon to get automatic timers for the lamp in her bedroom and the two lamps in the living room. She always hated entering a dark place. She also needed to purchase some new pillows and throws to brighten up the sofa. Even though she would only be there a couple of months, she wanted to add some color to the decor. She could always take them to the condo when she moved.

She was too wired up to sleep. She got a bottle of Voss from the refrigerator and a piece of cheese. She flipped through the television channels, but nothing held her interest. She refused to do any office work. It had been a wonderful evening, and she had to admit to herself that she was growing fond of Eric. He was fun to be with and a perfect gentleman.

He didn't overpower the conversation and hadn't forced himself on her. He had a very calming way of making her feel special. He'd placed her on a pedestal. She knew he admired her and wanted more than she was capable of giving. In a peculiar way, he had gotten her to relax and not take life or herself too seriously, for she had a way of diving into situations with both feet whether at work or in her personal life. He didn't have her type "A" behavior with an assertive flair.

At around two in the morning, she drifted off to sleep. She slept until noon the next day. She was completely startled when she looked at the alarm clock on the nightstand. She hadn't slept that well since college. She felt good. She had been careful not to drink too much wine or champagne on the cruise. She had washed each glass she drank down with two glasses of water—a trick she learned in college when she had to stay up all night after partying to cram for an exam. She wasn't sure what time Leslie was coming over so she decided not to chance going to Starbucks.

She didn't want to admit it, but Eric was constantly on her mind. She was both excited and scared. What if he were gay or bisexual? If his preference were women, why would rumors be circulating about him? Did he enjoy both men and women, or did he have a preference? The more she thought about it, the more she wanted to know. She could call the detective she used to investigate Stephen and his mistress and put the issue to bed. It would be much better to know now while she could control her feelings and emotions for him. What if by some miracle it was just a vicious lie? Would she have to confess and let Eric know she doubted his masculinity? Would that act rob him of his manhood or faith in women?

She pondered the question, and then against her better judgment, she called Bruce Lamarr. He answered on the first ring.

"Hi, Bruce, this is Tracy Hudson from California. You did some work for me a while back," she said, hoping he would recall their meeting.

"Hi, Tracy. How are things with you?" Bruce asked.

"I'm fine. I'm working in Miami now. I left California about two weeks ago. I never thought I would move East, but it has been great; so far, so good," she said, talking a mile a minute and feeling like she needed to justify her existence.

"You sound great, Tracy. What can I do for you?"

She explained her current dilemma. She told Bruce that her marriage to Stephen had fallen apart and that she was filing for divorce, when the truth of the matter was she hadn't even told her husband.

He understood. He said in most cases where either one or both spouses had cheated, it was usually doomed from the time they learned of the affair. He said just in some rare and isolated cases the relationship survived … He estimated that approximately 80 percent of the investigations he conducted ended in divorce or separation. He knew why Tracy had called. Once she was confronted with Stephen and his mistress, she had lost faith and confidence in the institution of marriage. There was probably someone else now, and she didn't want to replay that same scenario.

Stepping into another relationship was tough. To be burned once was unfortunate; to be burned twice would be disastrous and traumatic. The crushing blow of her cheating spouse took a toll on her heart. In many respects she was just as low as Stephen, choosing to have three extramarital affairs herself. Maybe Stephen knew about them all and chose not to say a word. She would never know. Maybe he had pictures too and would pull them out for all to see when they met face-to-face with their attorneys present. Only time would tell.

Bruce took down all the information and her cell number and told her he would put his buddy, who worked out of his Fort Lauderdale office, on the case. Bruce said he would be working directly with his partner, which was exactly what she preferred. She didn't want to get to know another detective under these circumstances. She was comfortable with Bruce and felt they had a connection. If he couldn't come to her, then she would go back to California to meet with him. He didn't think that was necessary. They could talk over the phone if their schedules didn't permit them to meet up somewhere.

Tracy thought she would feel better after talking with Bruce, but she didn't. She felt like she was undermining her friendship with Eric. She didn't want to cripple their relationship. How could she ever convince Eric that she could trust another man if he found out. He probably would think she had commitment and trust issues. That would be a blow to his manhood and to the possibility of a successful long-term relationship.

She continued to hold the phone to her ear long after the call with Bruce had ended. She just stood and stared out the window of the apartment. It was a beautiful day outside. There were people in the complex coming and going. She saw tenants jogging, washing their cars, carrying groceries and other goodies, and babies being held by their parents. She finally placed the phone in it's cradle and turned on the shower. She felt a hot shower would put her in a better mood.

As she was about to step into the shower, her cell phone rang. Bruce must have forgotten to tell her something. She enthusiastically answered the phone.

"Hello," she said as she heard his voice, "Is this Trace?" She knew in an instant who it was. It was Stephen. Why was he calling her? What did he want? His timing was always off. He was so cold and formal.

"I sent you a couple of emails," Stephen said. "I thought I'd call since I didn't get a reply."

He hadn't changed at all. There were no more feelings of concern in his voice. He had become very formal and aloof now. She wondered how two people who were once in love now apologized for calling the other person when they had to talk or when they accidentally touched each other when in close proximity.

"Stephen, is that you? Is everything OK? You sound strange."

"I'm sorry, I must have been distracted. I have papers spread out everywhere in this hotel room. This trial is scheduled to go for another three weeks."

She wondered how Stephen could be so distracted since he called her. Surely, he could take five minutes out of his busy schedule to concentrate during the phone call.

"Stephen, we need to talk. Maybe in two weeks I could fly in for a weekend or a couple of days," she said, holding her breath, hoping he would agree. What she needed now most of all, was to bring closure to their marriage. She wished she'd gone to see Stephen before deserting him and their marriage.

"I told you I'm working both day and night. Whatever it is we need to discuss will have to wait until after the trial."

And with that he was gone. He didn't say good-bye … Can we synchronize our schedules? Can we discuss it over the phone? … nothing at all … just a click, and he was gone.

Stephen knew he had to keep Tracy in California. He also needed to check in periodically to make sure she didn't show up in New York unannounced. There was no way he was going to allow her to cheat him out of the few pleasures he enjoyed in life.

This time she threw the phone on the sofa and stepped into the shower as tears flooded her face. She had no idea why she was crying. She wanted out, and it appeared that Stephen did too. She felt like her father had just scolded her for getting into trouble. Here she was a grown woman allowing her husband to treat her so badly. She knew at that moment she'd made the right decision to exit the city and their marriage.

She stayed in the shower so long that her skin had started to shrivel. Her skin looked more like that of a newborn infant entering the world for the first time. She did her hair and put on a pair of jeans with a white shirt. She added a short Magaschoni jacket and alligator flats. She twisted her hair around a hair clip and added a pale shade of pink lipstick and large, gold hoop earrings. She looked gorgeous with just a hint of blush on her cheeks.

She was still fuming from her conversation with Stephen as she poured herself a cup of black coffee. She should have followed her mother's advice and married a younger man. Looking back on her life, she'd missed the best part. She didn't have an opportunity to enjoy the crazy thirties, doing all the stuff you regret later. Stephen was a homebody. He didn't particularly like going out or traveling for pleasure. He preferred staying home, cooking or bringing takeout food in. He spent his extra time reading law journals, watching documentaries, and playing golf. They had very little in common.

She enjoyed dancing, going to the theater, and visiting art museums. She also enjoyed international travel. The opportunity to see how people in other parts of the world lived intrigued her. So much for reminiscing about the past. She had to move on. She didn't want to be the fool who kept reaching back and living in the past. When you fall down in life, you have to dust yourself off and get back in the game. Tomorrow wasn't promised ... how true that statement was ... as she thought about her parents.

As she was about to pour herself a bowl of cereal, there was a knock on the door. "I'm coming," Tracy said, glancing around the apartment to make sure things weren't in disarray.

As she opened the door, in walked Leslie carrying a bag of bagels and muffins and two cups of Starbucks coffee.

"Thought you might want brunch. I hope you haven't eaten," Leslie said, moving past her going directly to the kitchen.

"I was about to eat cereal, but I'm sure what you have in that bag is more enticing."

She opted for a bagel as Leslie spread cream cheese on a chocolate muffin. "For a lady who spent the night in the arms of a man, you look great. You look well rested. I'm assuming you didn't get much sleep," Tracy said, as she watched her get up and go to her living room window.

"I felt like a teenager on a first date. Charles and I had a great time. He stayed until about three this morning. I don't know why I have so much energy. I should be exhausted," Leslie said, feeling overwhelmed with love in her heart.

"It's called being in love or infatuated with a person. When you find the person who makes your heart skip a beat, sleep deprivation is never an issue. It's that newfound energy that makes you come alive as you wait for his call, reliving all those special moments."

"Tracy, I haven't been this excited about someone since I was in college. Charles is a great person. He makes me laugh a lot. That is so good for the soul."

"The problem is that you're not in college now. Relationships can be tough. It's probably too soon to know, Leslie, if he's the one."

She wasn't convinced that Charles was the one for Leslie. She thought it might be the wine causing her to lose perspective. Things become cloudy after the second drink. She knew that well. She wanted to be happy for her friend but wanted her to be cautious.

"Can't you just be excited for me? Even if Charles isn't the one, I'll cherish our time together. We aren't getting any younger, my dear. When the moment comes, you have to be ready to dance."

"I'm happy for you, Leslie. It wasn't fair what I just said. I don't want my unhappiness with Stephen to spoil this moment for you and Charles."

"Charles and I are going for pizza and beer at three. We would love for you to join us?"

"I would just be in the way. Sounds like you two lovebirds have much to explore and be happy for."

One quality she admired in Leslie was her ability to take the leap of faith in relationships. Leslie was the direct opposite at work. She slowed things down a bit. She needed more than 99 percent of the information to make an intelligent decision. There were millions of dollars riding on those decisions. In her love life, Leslie was free as a bird and was more prone to take chances ... to make mistakes.

"Tracy, there is something I have to tell you. It's good news for me. I hope you'll be happy for me."

She couldn't imagine what Leslie had to tell her. Surely, she wasn't planning on eloping with Charles. She was crazy in her love life but not foolish. There was excitement in her eyes as Leslie intertwined her fingers.

"Don't keep me in suspense any longer," Tracy said. "What's this wonderful bit of news you want to share? Should I be sitting down for this?"

"I'm leaving the company," Leslie announced. "I received the job offer on Friday. It's a dream job and one I really want."

What Leslie said caused Tracy's heart to miss a beat. The last thing she expected was for her one and only friend at Sunset to be leaving the company. She wasn't prepared for the news. She couldn't be selfish and think of her own needs at a time like this. Leslie deserved the promotion. No telling how many times she was belittled by Judy or Sheila, not being able to perform the job to the best of her ability. Those two women were egotistical. It was clear that Leslie wasn't in the clique or sisterhood. That was one sorority she didn't want to be a part of.

The infighting between Nora and Lauren got to be old news fast. They made life at Sunset much harder than it had to be. If Judy ever left and one of them got the CEO position, fireworks would start. Over time she was sure they would bring about their own demise. How Leslie had lasted for seven years was anyone's guess. Seven years in corporate America was a lifetime. She was probably at the seven-year-itch point, like married couples experience on their way to a blissful ten. Working at Sunset was more like blissful ignorance.

"Leslie, I'm happy for you and sad for me. I wouldn't begrudge you the joy of leaving Sunset for greener pastures. Where are you going?" Tracy asked.

Leslie told her all about Target and the job opportunity. She didn't totally relish the idea of leaving Miami for eight months of winter in Minnesota, but felt a change would do wonders for her career. She had gotten herself in a rut of compromising some of her standards to appease Judy. She still had backbone, but the constant confusion and mixed signals had gotten to her. She wanted a company that the industry admired ... one that had a passion for its people, as well as for the business.

"Have you told Charles your exciting news?"

"I haven't shared my joy with anyone but you. I knew you'd be happy for me. I thought I would tell Judy on Tuesday."

"Why Tuesday? I'm sure she'll be saddened by your news."

"Don't be so sure. Knowing Judy, she will probably want a pushover the next time around. Someone she can mold, influence, and maneuver, a puppet. I'm still working through some of the perks with Target. We've agreed on what's most important; the base salary and long-term incentives."

"I think you're right. I've only been here for a short period of time, and I've observed how the in-crowd works; over time that has to be annoying and frustrating. I don't know how you stood it for seven years."

"I think I stayed to make sure the employees were taken care of. They have never really had a solid human resources leader, so as general counsel, I made sure the company followed state, local and federal laws. Judy knew how far she could push me and which buttons to press. I think deep down in her heart she knew my understanding of the law was far greater than hers, and she wanted to keep a lot of the inner workings of the company from our board of directors."

Tracy gave Leslie a big hug, telling her that she wished her only the best. They talked about her being with the organization for another two to four weeks before sailing off to her new life. She was thankful Leslie would be there to see her through the upcoming layoff.

"When do you plan to tell Charles about your new job?" Tracy asked.

"That's the sixty-four thousand dollar question. Because of loyalty and my allegiance to the company, I feel it's my duty to notify Judy first. She has to be the first to know. Although I trust Charles, this is still a small community. Everyone has a friend, and that person has a friend, if you know what I mean. Aside from that I always like to have the offer letter in hand with all the loose ends tied up."

Leslie was absolutely correct in her assessment. Something like this could blow up in her face. It would be unprofessional and embarrassing for Judy to approach Leslie about her new job with Target. Judy could mess up her reputation and ask her to leave the property immediately. Leslie had worked too hard building a name for herself to have it all destroyed in a matter of minutes.

"You're wise beyond your years, my friend," Tracy said. "Judy is the kind of person who would take you to the cleaners if she heard you were leaving before you told her. Plus, the last thing you'd want is for cutthroat Nora or Lauren to get hold of this information and charge up to Judy's office with ammunition in hand."

"We have to celebrate before you leave. This calls for a night out on the town. Just the two of us; like old times."

"That sounds wonderful to me. The guys can just suffer through one night without us."

She shared with Leslie her earlier call to private investigator, Bruce Lamarr. She was seeking advice more so than sharing information. She knew her secret was safe with Leslie. She wanted to hear what Leslie thought of the idea. If she thought it was a true invasion of Eric's privacy, she'd consider canceling the contract. She hadn't signed any papers, and at present it would be a nominal fee. She was still somewhat confused as to why she was investigating Eric, since she was still married to Stephen.

"You have my blessings, Tracy. I think it makes a hell of a lot of sense. The report will either dispel the rumors or show that Eric's sexual preference isn't just for women. You don't need the aggravation of dating an individual who likes both men and women. You've been a token wife for Stephen. You need a true relationship. You need to find someone who will be there for you."

She made a fresh pot of tea. She was so grateful that Leslie understood her pain. Marrying a man twenty years older had robbed her of much happiness and freedom. Stephen wasn't totally to blame. She had harbored so much hatred and suffered so much pain for his poor choices; which caused her to pull away from him and the marriage. Although her heart had been broken and her faith in the institution of marriage shattered, she still believed there was someone out there for her.

"Leslie, do you think I should let Eric know I'm having him investigated?"

"Now what purpose would that serve? I'm not like you, Tracy. I don't kiss and tell 'all' like those Hollywood books. I say let sleeping dogs lie. If you guys become an item, so be it. Telling Eric that you believed the rumors instead of having faith in him might be too much for his ego. I say start the story from Friday night. No one cares what he did in kindergarten."

"We're not in kindergarten, Leslie."

"You know what I mean. If you give guys too much information, they use it against you later when you're in the heat of the moment. Once you share that bit of information, I think you become susceptible to doubts, and soon confusion creeps into the relationship. After that it's all down hill."

Leslie was so different, in her opinion, concerning relationships. She didn't open Pandora's box. She dealt with current facts and information. She didn't labor over what one would think of her past. Unless her lovers did some investigating for themselves, they would never know all the secrets behind the doors she had closed so tightly. Maybe Leslie was right. What's the real purpose of sharing your past if what you divulge will only bite you in the ass later?

Looking at her watch, she knew it was time for Leslie to leave. "What are you doing this afternoon, Tracy? Tell me you're not going to sit here preparing documents for the lay-off."

"As a matter of fact I am. There is so much to do before week after next."

"Take my advice and get out of this apartment and enjoy this beautiful day. Trust me, Judy and Sheila aren't at home preparing documents. If Judy is at the office, she's probably catching up on company business and paying her personal bills."

She completely agreed with Leslie. What she had observed of Judy and Sheila didn't communicate individuals who were spending valuable personal time on company business. Sheila had a reputation of paying her people low salaries, working them like a dog, and keeping them on a short leash. Sheila saw no correlation between the millionaire lifestyle she lived and the penniless one most of them had.

Sheila wasn't from a wealthy family, but she had accumulated quite a nest egg. She and Judy weren't embarrassed about being listed annually as two of the highest-paid females in the state of Florida. Even though you would never be able to surmise their wealth from their attire; however, if you reviewed their bank accounts and income tax statements, you'd definitely see the disparity between their income and their appearance.

Tracy had noticed that Sheila played the game well. Sheila arrived at the office twenty minutes before Judy and always left after Judy. Judy was generally in the office by nine, unless an early meeting was scheduled, and out by six. This was always explained and justified because of Judy's hectic travel schedule, her speaking engagements, and all the committees and boards she served on. If the truth were told, when Judy was in town, she was at home with her family by six-thirty or seven in the evening.

The office building cleared out between five-thirty and six o'clock. Like boss, like employee. The company didn't have a grip on flextime and employees adhering to the eight-to-five workday. Tracy wasn't looking forward to tackling that one. She liked flextime options being made available to employees. What she didn't like was not having a written policy in place and holding supervisors and employees accountable. Flextime had to be fair, well communicated, and monitored. Where employees worked and when they worked was not the issue. Employees had to meet their objectives, work a full forty hours each week, and the company needed to monitor results in order to determine the true value of flextime.

"I'm leaving now," Leslie said, gathering her purse. "I'll call you later. Are you sure you don't want to have pizza with us?"

"I'm sure I don't want nor need those extra calories. My waistline is already expanding after Friday and Saturday night. Get out of here and have some fun."

Leslie went to the door and then turned around to look at her friend. "Tell you what … why don't you go to the Dadeland Shopping Mall or the Falls and spend some money. There are some great restaurants in those two malls. If you want cheesecake to die for, you have to go to the Cheesecake Factory at Dadeland Mall. The food is good, and the service is great." Leslie pulled out a sheet of paper from the living room desk drawer and gave her directions to both malls. As Leslie was leaving, she echoed the words again … "Get out of here and have some fun."

Tracy closed the door and sat down on the sofa. Watching a black-and-white movie suddenly didn't seem like a lot of fun. The day was young, and she didn't want to spend the afternoon vegetating. She was already dressed. She could eat at the Cheesecake Factory and worry about her caloric intake later. Monday would be here soon enough, she could gain points for not eating breakfast and lunch. She knew it wasn't wise to skip breakfast and then not eat lunch, but the race to the finish line was fast approaching.

Don would be in tonight with his total team, and she would have experienced people who knew what to do. They would relieve her of a lot of the grunt work. She could spend more time with the executive team, monitoring their words and actions to ensure things continued to run smoothly. She wasn't looking forward to seeing what Judy and Nora had agreed to. Leslie had filled her in on the closeness of that relationship and where not to step.

She got up from the sofa, went to the bathroom to freshen up her lipstick, and then headed out to the mall. Leslie was right. Why sit at the apartment planning for Monday? She'd have some time later in the evening to do that, if necessary.

On days like today, she wished she'd rented a convertible. The temperature was just right, not too hot and not too cool. Her cell rang as she was backing out of the complex.

"What did you forget to tell me?" she asked, assuming it was Leslie.

"I don't think I forgot to tell you something, unless … I miss you terribly would be inappropriate," Eric said, wondering whom she had spoken to before his call.

"I thought it was Leslie telling me other favorite shops to visit. She just left my place."

"Where are you headed?" he asked.

"I thought I'd go to the Falls Shopping Center, have a bite of lunch and shop for some handbags and casual clothes," Tracy said, hoping deep down, he'd want to meet her later. She knew that men generally didn't like shopping and waiting patiently on the sidelines as their spouse or partner found that perfect outfit.

"I need some things myself. A woman with your taste would enjoy the Shops at Bal Habour more. The shops are on the beach, and there's a small, quaint restaurant called Savarin where we could grab a bite of food; plus Bal Habour is much closer than the Falls, which is in South Miami."

She agreed to meet Eric at the Shops of Bal Habour. He gave her directions to take Interstate 195 East over to the beach, which he thought would be quicker.

Approaching the shops she could see why Eric had recommended them. The shops were exquisite. She could tell that you needed money and lots of it. If you were looking for bargains and sales, this definitely wasn't the place. She parked her car and entered the mall through Neiman Marcus.

While in Neiman Marcus, Tracy stopped at the cosmetic counter to purchase some Calvin Klein cologne. She had about ten minutes before she had to meet Eric, so she took the escalator to the second floor. She spotted a cashmere business suit in pink that she thought would be perfect for those cooler days in Miami. She made a mental note to go back and try it on. She wanted to see what other stores were there and to check out their merchandise prior to purchasing the suit.

As she was leaving Neiman Marcus, she saw Eric. He looked fabulous. He was wearing jeans with a pullover blue polo shirt and loafers with no socks. He wore a gold chain around his neck and an18k yellow gold Patek Phillippe wrist watch. As they approached each other, he gave her a kiss on the cheek.

"You look amazing. I bet you could wear a sheet and pull it off."

Everything in her wanted to say you must be kidding, but she was trying to follow the advice she'd received from friends and her therapist and just say thank you. She didn't want to discredit his comments.

"Have you been here long? I see you purchased something in Neiman Marcus."

"I arrived ten minutes early. There was very little traffic on the expressway, just as you said. I parked on the outside, in front of Neiman Marcus and couldn't resist buying some perfume."

She and Eric had a great lunch. She chose crab salad with a glass of raspberry iced tea. He had grilled salmon with a lemon caper sauce, red skin potatoes, and asparagus. For dessert they shared a piece of New York cheesecake. They sat and talked for a while before realizing that the shops would be closing around seven.

Eric paid the check, and they went to Roberto Cavalli where he purchased a pair of slacks and two light-blue business shirts. She bought a pair of stiletto heels with ankle straps that looked great on her legs. She had raised the legs of her jeans and paraded around the store before deciding on the shoes.

She loved being with Eric as they strolled hand in hand around the mall. He had so much patience, unlike Stephen who by now would be rushing her along. She tried on a suit in Chanel that didn't quite suit her needs and a sleeveless dress in Michael Kors that she thought would be great for work. Eric agreed. What he didn't tell her was that it accentuated her figure. He encouraged Tracy to take her time.

The last store was St. John. She loved their suits because they were easy to travel with. You could roll them in a plastic hanging bag, and they would be wrinkle free each and every time you got to your destination. She bought a mint-green dress with a matching jacket. She wasn't that fond of the blue trim on the jacket, but the dress went perfect with her eyes and figure. Eric loved it. He encouraged her to purchase one in candy apple red. She took his advice and went for it.

"Tracy, I've enjoyed being with you," Eric said. "You are so carefree and open. Thanks for shopping with me today. Lunch was great."

"The pleasure was all mine," she said, realizing he hadn't complained once or rushed her along. "Are you always this easy to shop with?"

"I think I owe that to my mother. She was a shopaholic. When I was young, my mother didn't like the idea of me staying with a sitter, so she took me and my brother everywhere with her. Her favorite pastime was shopping. Second to that were the arts. We constantly went to shows and art museums. Until this day, I enjoy both shopping for clothes and going to the theater."

A man after her own heart. Eric was so easy to please. He never questioned the amount of money she spent. Men she barely knew would complain about how much she spent on clothes. Eric enjoyed quality and was willing to spend money to get it. They sat inside the covered area of the mall and talked until the security guard politely told them that the mall would be closing in ten minutes.

She left in her car, following Eric to an ice cream shop two blocks over from the mall.

"If I continue to hang out with you, I'll be as big as a cow," she said, marveling over the wonderful and unusual flavors.

He ordered double chocolate supreme with almonds and cherries. She ordered a plain vanilla ice cream cone.

"I can't believe that with so many wonderful flavors to choose from you got vanilla. Where is your creativity? What happened to experimentation?" he asked.

Eric was right. Tracy wasn't the adventurous type when it came to her food. She only ate food that she recognized and was familiar with. She left the exploring to others. When it came to clothes, she would venture out with color and unusual styles and designs. Tracy hated traditional attire. She followed the stars and entertainers in Hollywood, not the ordinary people on the street.

"Call me plain Jane when it comes to ice cream. Next time I'm really going to step outside my comfort zone and order strawberry ice cream with a scoop of vanilla."

They both laughed as Eric asked her to taste his ice cream. She enjoyed the bite but confessed that she would never order it. When it came to ice cream she wanted simple. They talked for another hour until Tracy said she had to get some things done for Monday. He hated to see her go. He had never had such a fun-filled weekend. He felt as if he were floating on a cloud. She was not only charming and fun to be with, but a great listener as well.

He walked Tracy to her car and before closing the door, gave her a sweet, soft kiss on her lips. She was not expecting that. It took her by surprise. Somehow he had struck a chord and taken her to a place she thought no longer existed. She had long since locked that door. She had settled into a life of going through the motions in her personal life and trying to find enjoyment and fulfillment at work. When you're lonely at heart, somehow work never makes up for the loss.

She had to take it slow with him. She was still married. Maybe he also had a special person in his life. She didn't want him on the rebound. That wouldn't be fair to him or any future relationship they might have. The worst thing would be to leave Stephen and jump immediately into another relationship headed south.

As she drove home, she was thankful for Eric and her friend Leslie ... and perhaps Starbucks, which created the opportunity for her to meet him. Whoever was responsible, Tracy was just glad they had met.

She decided that tonight would be a free night for her. She had given all she planned to give to Sunset until tomorrow morning. She was grateful that Don and his team would be on site with her on Monday. She needed the expertise and skills of those who had already gone through a ton of reengineering efforts of this proportion. The enormity of the project, could only be appreciated by those who were on the frontline and had experienced it firsthand.

She slept well that night, never once waking up. When the alarm clock went off at five, she woke up ready to tackle her day. Don had left her a text message saying he and his team, were meeting for breakfast at a nearby Denny's restaurant. She texted Don back to let him know she would swing by at seven.

That would give them plenty of time to strategize on all that needed to be done. So as not to bring attention to the consultants, most of them were scheduled to work out of the career outplacement center, which was four blocks off-site in Brock's regional office. There was no need to cause any additional stress and anxiety to the employees.

CHAPTER 10

Tracy met Don and his team for breakfast at seven. She ordered dry toast and a glass of orange juice. She told him about the dilemma she had and that she wasn't looking forward to her conversation with Judy. He took the current list of employees who were slated to leave and told Tracy he would review the impact from a diversity standpoint. They agreed to meet in her office later that afternoon. That would give him an opportunity to organize things at the career outplacement center, so she could give her input and feedback.

Sharon was already busy at work when she got to the office. She asked Sharon about her weekend and reminded her to put the overtime hours on her time card. Employees were starting to fill up the building. There were several conversations about the weekend and the coming week. She moved around the department stopping at cubicles, speaking with her employees, as well as employees in other departments.

The company had moved the corporate office a year earlier to the top three floors of an expensive office complex on

Brickell Avenue with an excellent view of the Miami skyline. Sheila had negotiated the space with the option of expanding into two additional floors. The employees were excited to get to work in the new corporate facility. Judy had chosen the paint colors for the walls—various shades of green, brown and red, which she personally liked.

Only the executives and vice presidents were privileged to have offices. All other employees worked in cubicles equipped with a desk, file cabinets, phone, computer, and an overhead compartment for personal items. Tracy was surprised that the cubicles didn't have guest seating. The partitioned offices weren't inviting. They were cold, and the various shades of green, brown and red didn't make one feel welcome.

All the executive offices were relatively small for their level, with the exception of the CEO's and CFO's offices—a bone of contention with Nora and Lauren. Judy and Sheila had spared no expense. Their offices were decorated by some of Miami's top designers who shopped the world to find those rare pieces.

Tracy couldn't imagine what would ever possess them to be so elaborate and spend so much on their work space. Judy's office was so big that you could include two bowling lanes and still have room to house a desk, conference table, sofa, book case and chairs for guest seating. Tracy was sure the senior leaders saw the injustice in the arrangement. Tracy felt that all senior leaders should have their own office for privacy and to feel like they were sharing in the perks.

If the company ever relocated, she'd definitely give them her two cents provided she was still employed by Sunset. After she had greeted her team and listened to how they spent the weekend, she proceeded to Judy's office. She was thankful that no one asked any specific questions about her weekend. She killed those questions by explaining that she was in the office on Saturday with Sharon. Tracy didn't want employees to feel like they had to work on weekends, so she cleared the air by stating that she usually tried to get things done in the office before Friday rolled around.

Sheila and Judy were standing outside Judy's office as she approached. Judy invited her in, asking about her weekend and how she was adjusting to the area. Just as she did with the employees, she talked about spending part of the weekend getting things ready for the upcoming event. As Judy talked about her weekend, she mentioned that she was at the office Sunday afternoon clearing off her desk.

"Has Nora met with you regarding her cuts and the affected marketing employees? I need that information to complete the diversity profile on the company and to analyze the overall impact," Tracy said.

"I met with Nora late on Friday. Her argument is that since she's understaffed, she can't give up any employees at this time," Judy commented, as if that was acceptable.

"Judy, are you comfortable with that when each executive is making cuts with the exception of Sheila? Where will the remaining cuts come from?" Tracy asked, becoming very annoyed and irritated by the minute.

"I think Gary Umar can stand to make some additional cuts."

"I have reviewed the numbers, and that argument of being understaffed affects almost all the departments. I remember during my interview you commented that you kept the departments understaffed to meet budget constraints."

Tracy wanted to make sure she challenged Judy's thinking. A talented human resources executive would always push back in the privacy of the CEO's office and with the executive team when the situation warranted it. Judy was being unfair and unreasonable to Gary Umar. Gary was already down a number of field managers. She was determined not to leave Judy's office without a fair discussion. The executives were already buzzing about Sheila not having to cut her staff.

"Maybe we should look at the type of organization we're trying to create and the skills needed. That way we don't arbitrarily make cuts that might cause the company to lose the talent we need long-term."

Judy was pondering the question when in walked Sheila. Tracy invited Sheila to stay. It would be easier to kill two birds with one stone. Otherwise, Sheila would be summoned to Judy's office the moment she left. She knew that she'd need to handle the discussion with kid gloves. Sheila was a part of the group who didn't have to cut employees from her team. If she was too forceful with Sheila and Judy, they would alienate her from the team. It was too soon into the honeymoon for that. This was a situation that had to be handled delicately. She had to be tactful playing devil's advocate. It was unfair for Gary to carry the brunt of the cuts.

She saw how Judy allowed the team to run circles around him. She would change that over time. She was going to coach Gary and help him to be taken seriously by the team. Once she got through grooming and developing Gary, he'd be better able to speak up and defend his actions and position. He had to get a backbone to survive the corporate divas.

"Sheila," Tracy said, watching and analyzing her body language the entire time, "Judy and I have been speaking about the upcoming cuts. We find ourselves at a crossroads. I have reviewed the numbers for each department, and though it will be a hardship, I feel that if each executive carries some of the burden of reducing his or her team, then one discipline won't be weighed down unnecessarily. This will help us to minimize the loss of talent companywide."

She watched as Sheila mulled over her words. She was waiting for her reaction. Sheila would either join her camp or support Nora in an effort to go unscathed. Sheila knew Tracy understood human resources policies and the law. Sheila knew she was a fighter. Deep down Sheila didn't get all the laws surrounding human resources and its practices. Laying off employees was a big deal for Sunset. Never before in its history did the company have to resort to such extreme measures.

Sheila spoke up. "Maybe the thing to do is to have all of us share in this pain. I think Tracy makes a good point. We need the support of our employees. If they think the cuts are unfair, and we have favorites, I'm sure some may jump ship. Attrition never takes those employees who are underperforming. Generally, you lose your most talented employees. Those are the employees who are in demand. Other companies would love to have them on board."

She watched their eyes. Judy and Sheila had a special kind of language they spoke with their eyes. She had won this battle, but the worst was yet to come. She could see Sheila easing out of her chair in an attempt to exit Judy's office.

"Before you leave Sheila, there is one more item we need to discuss."

"I've a nine-thirty meeting I'm already late for," Sheila said.

"I can respect and appreciate that. Why don't you run along, and I'll try to swing by your office later this morning to bring you up to speed,"Tracy said, hoping Sheila would make herself available later.

Sheila turned and shared that she and Judy had a luncheon meeting in Coral Springs at noon and that Judy could fill her in during the drive over. How convenient Tracy thought. Sheila was sending a definite message that said we're still in control, we'll decide the best course of action for the company, and if we want your input, we'll call you.

Whatever, Tracy thought. She wasn't there to win immediate friends. She was there to help change the course of the company. The company had to get in compliance and follow the laws like every other company doing business in the U.S.

"Judy, are you aware that nonexempt employees aren't being paid overtime wages?"

"What specifically do you mean, not being paid overtime wages?" Judy carefully repeated, trying to buy some time.

"Most of our nonexempt employees are working off the clock. By that I mean once they exceed forty hours in a given week, they aren't being compensated, which is against the law. As leaders, managers and supervisors, we have to have measures and standards in place so nonexempt employees can get paid. Wage and hour laws have been established for that purpose. At present, we're not in compliance."

"How was this discovered?"

Judy was searching for the culprit who had brought this to Tracy's attention. She wasn't going to tell Judy that Sharon told her on Saturday. She was much too clever for that. "The issue isn't who told me or brought it to my attention; our concern should be coming into compliance with the law," she said, observing Judy's body language the entire time.

She had stepped into it now. Tracy had to take Judy out of the equation so she wouldn't feel compelled to go on the defensive. If Judy went on the defensive, the conversation would spiral downward fast. She needed Judy's support to manage through the legal nightmare.

"I realize, Judy, that you're probably unaware that this is going on within the company. Your assistant, Elizabeth, is an exempt employee, which means she's exempt from overtime pay, as are all other exempt employees. There are laws and rules that determine an employees' status."

Tracy went on to tell Judy that she had spoken to Leslie, who was managing a case in which an employee was suing the company for overtime wages.

"If we don't get in front of this issue immediately, we run the risk of other employees filing a law suit. With a pending layoff, it's highly probable that a disgruntled employee might take us to task."

After listening to Tracy, Judy agreed with everything she proposed. Tracy had educated Judy on the cost to the company if a lawsuit developed and how the company's image would be tarnished. With everything that was on her plate, the last thing Tracy needed was taking time to educate managers regarding employment law. Along with everything else, this too had to get top priority. A discontented employee, who lost his job, might want to see the company get hit with a lawsuit just for the hell of it.

Tracy assured Judy that she and Leslie would handle the meetings with the managers. First, they would meet with the executives and cascade the message to the vice presidents, followed by the directors and supervisors. So as not to blow this out of proportion, she thought it was best to train supervisors on how to have one-on-one discussions with their teams. She shared the Q&A document she had prepared.

Judy was impressed with how much Tracy was able to accomplish in such a short period of time. Judy thanked her again for joining the Sunset team, complimenting her on all the changes she was making. Tracy told Judy that one of her colleagues at another company said the organization was still feeling the pain from a layoff it did two years ago. Supposedly, it was botched up so badly that many talented managers and executives decided to exit, not to mention the bad press they received from the media.

"Tracy, before you go, I've made my decision. I'll email the executives and let them know that we'll make even cuts across the board," Judy said, completely taking Tracy by surprise.

Tracy spoke up. Since time was not on their side, having each executive feel the pain made sense. "I think a meeting or a personal phone call will humanize the discussion a bit more. Having that conversation in person will give you a chance to explain the rationale. I think the main reason, beyond fairness, would be not hitting one area so hard that we lose too many talented people. The employees who are left to continue building and growing this brand will be watching every step we take. We have to make sure everything is above the table and that cutting staff affects us all."

She left Judy's office with another pounding headache. The meeting was successful. Getting what was fair for the company came with a penalty. She was sure she'd pay dearly later. For now she was there to make sure employees didn't get screwed. She would love to be a fly on the wall when Judy shared their conversation with Sheila. Sheila was definitely going to be a challenge. The CEO and CFO were like two peas in a pod.

There were a million things to do when Tracy got back to her office. She had to run her department, while orchestrating the layoff. The pending layoff was consuming all of her time. She barely had time to meet with her team. She told Sharon to schedule a three o'clock meeting with her direct reports. She needed to keep all of those individuals motivated and supportive of the company's efforts. They each played a crucial role. Without them, employees wouldn't receive the direction and guidance they needed to be successful.

Sharon had placed Don and some of his team in a conference room on the first floor of the complex so as not to make their presence known to the employees.

Tracy didn't want employees speculating as to the day of the layoff. Employees needed to keep working and meeting their job objectives. She encouraged managers to be visible in their department. She wanted managers to be available for the employees. All too often when an employee's questions and concerns weren't addressed, rumors were created to fill the void and feed the grapevine.

By the time Tracy made it to the conference room, she thought her head would explode. Don suggested they leave and find a nearby Starbucks. Since he was driving, she didn't need her purse. Tracy called Sharon and told her if people needed her, have them call her cell.

Don packed up his documents, and they drove to a nearby Starbucks. She took two aspirins and downed them with a bottle of water. They got their coffee and took a short walk.

The fresh air felt good. She was thankful to have escaped her responsibilities for a moment. When they got back to the conference room, he reviewed the list of things that had to be done and relieved Tracy of about 70 percent of them.

"We're here to meet your needs and make you successful. You have a department to run. You have to mind the store, or the inmates will take over. With all you told me, you have to watch your back and carefully maneuver through this maze," Don said.

Don was dead on the money. Her victory today wouldn't pay off in future dividends. She was sure Sheila was planning revenge. Sheila was known to carry a grudge. She was clever not to wear her heart on her sleeve. Sheila knew how to keep a poker face and later go in for the kill. She was a master at deceit. Sheila only had one rule book, and it consisted of the rules she created. Once you got on her bad side, she wouldn't rest until she'd royally paid you back. The employees feared her. Sheila controlled the purse strings, and as far as she was concerned, no one was indispensable unless she said they were.

Sheila needed more time to figure Tracy out. Until then she would be partly agreeable. After that, she would set up traps for her to fail. With her friend Judy at the helm, payback would be swift and the timing totally unpredictable.

Both Judy and Sheila had learned firsthand that Tracy was definitely not a pushover. She held steadfast to her beliefs and what was right. For Judy and Sheila, the corporate rules didn't apply.

After she and Don talked, he encouraged her to go back to her office and run the human resources function. Being fairly new to Sunset, she had to watch her back and stay one step ahead of the executives. She went to Nora's office first. She thought Nora would blow a fuse with Judy's decision that they all cut their budgets by 10 percent.

"Tracy, what do you mean when you say I'll have to cut my staff? I've already had this conversation with both you and Judy. We agreed that since I'm understaffed, I won't need to cut any of my people," Nora said, fuming with anger.

"Things have changed, Nora. When I reviewed the numbers with Judy and Sheila, we had to make some additional changes. If each executive takes his or her percentage, then we'll refrain from laying off significant talent in one department."

"I respect what you're saying, Tracy, but you need to understand that the other departments aren't understaffed," Nora said, turning several shades of red.

"That isn't necessarily true."

She spoke up seeing how easily Nora twisted the truth. "If you review this year's corporate budgets, you'll see that Judy didn't approve increases in any of the departments with the exception of your department and Lauren's department. When I spoke with Judy, she said the agreement was to add staff after the fourth quarter if the company met its targeted goals. That hasn't happened."

"I'll need to talk with Judy. I'm not going to be able to cut any of my positions," Nora said, foaming at the mouth, venting her anger.

"Judy supposedly sent you and the other executives an email regarding this issue. Why don't you see if it has reached your email box, Nora?"

Nora was being unreasonable. Nora was still fuming as she went into her emails to retrieve one from Judy. Tracy waited so she wouldn't have to make a second trip and address the issue again. Nora had been caught off guard with the budget information. She'd been at the budget meetings and knew exactly what had been decided. What she didn't know and realize was Tracy's familiarity with the company budgets.

"I can't seem to find an email from Judy," Nora said, with a smirk on her face. "Do you want to check to see if you can find it?"

Tracy moved around to the corner of the desk. Sure enough, there wasn't an email from Judy. Hopefully, Judy delegated the responsibility to her executive assistant. She wanted to remain positive. Time was slipping away, and she needed to get on with the diversity analysis.

"Why don't we do this. Let's meet with Judy today and iron out this problem. The layoff will happen week after next. That gives us a very short window. I'm sure we can resolve this issue in a face-to-face meeting. I'll have my assistant schedule the meeting," Tracy said, wanting to end the conversation as soon as possible.

Tracy returned to her office giving Sharon instructions to call Elizabeth, Judy's assistant, to schedule an afternoon meeting with Judy, Nora and her. In the meantime she called and asked Lauren to join her in the boardroom. After explaining that each executive would need to share in the cuts, Lauren agreed. Lauren didn't think it was fair, but she wanted to be a team player. Tracy told her to be expecting an email from Judy explaining the rationale. She wasn't going to chance Lauren looking through her emails and not finding one from Judy.

She gave Lauren some pointers on determining which employees should be laid off. Lauren took copious notes. Lauren surprised her my criticizing Judy's management style. Tracy was careful to only listen and not make any comments.

"I would put some money on the table that Judy never sent that email. She's evasive when it comes to things like this. Judy doesn't want to step on anyone's toes. That's one of the deficiencies she needs to work on—that and vacillating on critical issues," Lauren said, venting her frustration.

"I'll keep that in mind as we move forward. I may be able to help her by providing feedback or matching her up with an outside mentor or coach."

"I'd love to be coached. Do you have a list of coaches I can call?" Lauren asked.

She could see that Lauren was aggressive when it came to things that promoted her interests. Lauren wanted everything she deserved and much more. Tracy explained how the process worked and told her that after they got through the layoff, she would train all executives and officers so they could coach senior leaders. She explained that coaches for the executives would be from outside the company.

Don would be great as an executive coach for the executive team. He had the style, experience, and training for the job. She could also work with Don to get a list of CEOs from larger companies who would be open to coaching Judy. Judy would have the option of working with an outside coach or a coach from Brock.

Before she and Lauren left the boardroom, they had agreed on a 10 percent cut in operations. The cuts would come from reduced services and headcount. She encouraged Lauren to consider reducing even more services whenever possible. Sometimes employees could do a little bit more by taking on new tasks, and sometimes services could be delayed by a quarter without any loss of income for the company.

The meeting with Lauren had been very productive. She had stepped up to the plate and was going to find the money somehow. Tracy thought that was amicable, given the fact that initially her department had been given a lower percentage. Lauren thought she would have a preliminary draft of the cuts in operations by either late afternoon or early tomorrow morning. She wanted to meet with her field directors and get their input, which Tracy thought was an excellent idea. The leaders and supervisors of those who would be affected needed to be a part of the process.

Tracy looked at her watch. It was only twelve twenty-five. It felt like she had already worked ten hours. She took the elevator to Leslie's office. Leslie was on a conference call with the chairman of the board. Her assistant offered Tracy coffee and told her, she would be happy to call her when Leslie got off the phone. Tracy opted to wait. Ten minutes later Leslie came out and invited her in, closing the door behind her.

"What on earth happened to you? You look like a train just ran over you," Leslie said, wondering what rock had toppled over.

"I think I survived my first run-in with Judy and Sheila. Those are two glued-at-the-hip women."

She told Leslie about her meeting with Judy and all the push back she had gotten. "I'm sure they're talking about me right now. They have a luncheon meeting, so Sheila decided to have Judy bring her up to speed during their drive to the meeting. Part of Sheila's strategy, I'm sure."

She shared with Leslie how Judy's email hadn't been sent to Nora and how that conversation went South. "Nora became irate when she learned that we all would have to trim our budgets by 10 percent. She was literally foaming at the mouth. It's obvious she wants special treatment," Tracy said, refusing to placate her conversation with Nora.

"Nora is always like that. Judy has given her preferential treatment since the day she arrived at Sunset. Nora thinks the rules don't apply to her. She's favored and privileged. Judy doesn't have the backbone to stand up to her. Sometimes Judy lets Sheila fight that battle for her. Once the tug of war starts with those two, watch out. In the end Sheila always emerges victorious."

"Thanks for the helpful advice. I don't plan to get in the middle between those two. That would be a no-win proposition."

"We need you here, Tracy. I'm so glad that you're providing the leadership and direction for the layoff. I shudder to think what would happen if you weren't here to intervene."

"Is that the royal 'we'? I seem to recall that a certain person has an offer she has accepted, which is not affiliated with Sunset."

They shared a laugh over that one. Leslie couldn't wait to tell Judy her good news on Tuesday. Sparks would fly, but she didn't care. This was one of those once-in-a-lifetime opportunities. She wanted to work for a more sophisticated company with seasoned executives. There was no such thing as utopia, but that didn't mean she had to settle for the war zone.

She was tired of fighting the battles. Older companies were beyond the pettiness and adhered to company policies. They knew firsthand how the company's public image could be damaged from a single lawsuit. Once the company was exposed, customers drew their own conclusions, generally opting to do business with brands that valued their people and were good corporate citizens.

Sunset had been fortunate. Whenever the company was in the news, the story was always positive. The organization had received a number of awards for its menu items and for expanding and growing the concept. Unfortunately, Sunset wasn't recognized as one of America's best places to work or as a great company for diversity and inclusion. Those prestigious awards had never been granted to Sunset. How Judy would love to be on the list of one of America's most admired companies.

"Have you received your offer letter?"Tracy asked, hoping all of the kinks had been worked out.

"I have. Let me show it to you," Leslie said, retrieving the letter from her briefcase.

Tracy read the terms of the offer letter. It was a sweet deal. Only a blind, stupid fool would walk away from it. If the company met its plan and continued to produce record sales, Leslie stood to earn millions long-term. That would give her a chance to retire early, if she chose, with a nice nest egg. The base salary of her new job would be 30 percent higher than her current salary at Sunset; and there was the corporate jet which would save an enormous amount of time as the team traveled throughout the country.

"This is your time. You have to take it and run with it. You can tell by the total compensation package that they definitely want you," she said, giving Leslie a hug. "If I weren't your friend, I'd be green with envy."

"So you think I should accept?" Leslie asked.

"Accept! You need to kiss the ground they walk on and laugh all the way to the bank. This is a hell of a sweet deal."

She asked Leslie to check her emails to see if Judy had sent her one.

"I was just on the system while speaking with the chairman of the board. He's a little long-winded. He tends to repeat himself quite often. So as he asks the same questions over and over, I paraphrase them while checking my messages. I don't recall an email from Judy, but let me check again," Leslie said, quickly going through her emails a second time.

"I spoke too soon. Here is one from Judy sent earlier this morning."

"What does it say?" Tracy asked, hoping that the email would clarify the decision she and Judy had reached and what each executive would need to contribute.

Leslie could tell by Tracy's expression that somehow she knew the email would be slightly different from her discussion with Judy.

"The good news is that it does ask all of the executives to find the 10 percent cut in their budgets. The bad news is the wording of the email. Let me read it to you … "Hello team, in a meeting with Tracy this morning, it was brought to my attention that we might be losing talented employees if the cuts aren't balanced across the entire organization. Sheila has taken the initiative to make the 10 percent cut in her department. I'll assume that each of you will do likewise. Direct your questions, should you have any, to Tracy. Signed Judy."

"At least she sent the email. I guess mentioning Sheila, as the leader of the pack, will motivate the others to jump on the bandwagon. I'm just glad she put it out there. I don't mind being the bad guy, encouraging the executives to do the sensible thing," Tracy said.

Tracy's cell phone rang, and as she answered, she heard Judy's voice with Nora's in the background.

"Hi, Tracy. I have Nora on the line. We've been discussing the cuts. Nora is having a hard time cutting her staff, being so understaffed at this point with our new marketing campaign about to roll out. What do you suggest?" Judy asked.

What a wimp, Tracy thought. She could tell that Judy was in her car as Sheila asked for the street number for the location of the luncheon. She surmised that Nora had connected the two of them by conferencing her in. Why Judy didn't wait until she returned to the office was anyone's guess. Tracy didn't want to have this conversation over the phone. Just for the hell of it, she decided to act as if Judy was calling from her office.

"Are you in your office, Judy? I could run up, and we probably can resolve our concerns in a short meeting. It shouldn't take long."

"No, I'm with Sheila", Judy said. "We're on our way to the luncheon meeting. Nora called me, so I thought we could discuss the issue over the phone to avoid holding up the process. Nora has been conferenced in."

She wasn't about to give Nora the benefit of winning the argument. "Nora, if you feel you can't cut your team by 10 percent, is there any way you could trim your budget by cutting back on services or delaying work with consultants by one quarter?" Tracy asked.

There was some hesitation as Nora thought about her offer. As long as the company got a 10 percent cut from each executive, it didn't matter where the dollars came from. She was sure Nora would opt for cutting marketing services. Nora reluctantly said she would find the dollars.

"Well, I'm glad, Nora, that you'll be able to pull your load. If you need my help deciding what to cut, you know where to find me," Tracy said, with disappointment in her voice.

"Seems like we're all good," Judy said. "See you guys when I get back." And with that there was a click on the phone line.

Tracy rubbed the temples of her forehead.

"Let me guess," Leslie said. "Little princess ran to mother to get out of cutting her team."

"You are absolutely right. I hope this isn't a sign of things to come,"Tracy said.

"I wish I could tell you with a straight face that this is a fluke, but I'd be lying. This is an everyday occurrence. Nora constantly runs to "mother" to get her way. I bet she's an only child. You know, the type of person who will collect her toys and leave the sandbox."

She wasn't up for the "mother may I" game. As an executive you had to be able to compromise. The game wasn't all about you. Since her day started, she'd had run-ins with almost everyone she spoke to, except Leslie. What was she going to do when her friend left for Eskimo country?

Lynn Davita, Leslie's administrative assistant, stuck her head in the door to tell her that Charles Steel was on line one. Tracy got up and motioned that she was leaving, but Leslie stretched out her arm gesturing for her to remain seated.

"Thanks, Lynn. I'll take it," Leslie said, with a big grin on her face. "Hi, Charles. What's up?"

"Eric and I would like to take you guys to dinner at Tango's, which is one of the newest restaurants on South Beach. I went there for the first time a couple of weeks ago. The place is a little noisy, but you can have decent conversation and hear what your partner is saying. The food is great, and the service is first-class. We could meet at seven-thirty and have you guys safely home and tucked in bed by ten. You will truly enjoy the ambience of the restaurant."

"Tracy is sitting here in my office with me. I'm not sure she's up for dinner tonight. She looks like she's been put through the wringer. Hold on, I'll ask her."

"I'm sure you got the gist of the conversation," Leslie said, covering the receiver with her hand. "The guys want to take us out. They promise to have us back home by ten. Are you in?"

"I have Don with me from Brock. Let me call and see if he can join us."

"Charles, I'm going to place you on hold. Tracy has a number of consultants here working tonight. The lead guy is Don Johnson. She's going to call him to see if he can join us. Otherwise, she'll not be joining us. Hold on."

Tracy called Sharon and asked that she dial Don who was working in the conference room on the first floor. His assistant told Sharon that he would have to take a rain check. He needed to fly to Atlanta tomorrow morning to meet with a client who was being difficult. He was planning on working late at the office tonight and returning to Miami on an eight o'clock flight tomorrow evening.

Sharon relayed the message to Tracy and told her that Don had stopped by twice to talk with her. He was en route to the career outplacement center and would be returning to the office later that evening. He had left specific instructions for Tracy to call him on his cell if she needed him.

She loved that about Don. He was working late into the evening with his staff in order to give her a much-needed break. He had worked in corporate America and knew how demanding and challenging it was. You didn't always know whom to trust. Many times enemies were disguised as friends.

She shared with Leslie what Sharon had said and told her she would be happy to join them for dinner. Leslie reconnected Charles and gave him specific instructions to order them chilled glasses of wine. Given the traffic, Leslie thought they would meet them at the restaurant by seven forty-five. Tracy continued her meetings with executives, answering their questions and preparing them for the layoff.

Sharon was still there when Tracy got back to her office. "Why are you still here? I'm sure your mother could use a break after spending the day with an energetic toddler. I bet she's standing by the door awaiting your arrival. Of course, I'm just kidding. Grandmothers get to spoil their grandkids and give them back."

Before leaving, Sharon brought her up to speed, reviewing the day's activities, scheduled meetings, phone calls, and invoices that required her signature. Tracy said good night to Sharon, reminding her to log in her overtime.

Tracy piled a handful of papers in her briefcase and locked her office. She called Leslie and told her to meet her in the lobby. Tracy followed Leslie to Tango's in her car and used valet parking once there. She wasn't going to try to look for her parked car when dinner was over. Almost on cue, she and Leslie entered the restaurant at a quarter to eight. The hostess led them to their table.

The first thing Eric did was look around the restaurant to see if Don Johnson was with Tracy. Charles hadn't shared his earlier conversation that Don wouldn't be joining them. Since Eric didn't see him, he thought Don might be parking the car.

"Hi, gorgeous," Eric said, as Tracy reached the table. "You don't look like you've had a difficult day. You look like the cover of Vogue."

"Thanks for the compliment, but if you had a day like the one I just had, you'd probably be on your second drink by now," Tracy said, eyeing the restaurant decor.

Eric was right. Not a strand of hair was out of place. Tracy wore a St. John knit suit that was impeccably tailored, accented with metal buttons with a tweed trim on the jacket. Her snake-skin, peep-toe, Christian Louboutin platform pumps added three inches to her height. She carried an envelope clutch bag. By any standard she was "dressed to the nines." She looked and acted like one at the "top of her game." Leslie was dressed in a navy-blue pantsuit with a baby-blue silk blouse. She wore pearls around her neck and navy pumps.

Eric reached out and kissed Leslie on the cheek as Charles said, "Watch out. Hands off."

"I love the ambiance of this place. It reminds me of one of those trendy upscale restaurants in California. By the way, I'm famished," Tracy said. "When do we eat?"

After the first drink, the stress of the day just seemed to melt away. Tracy was feeling very relaxed.

"Aren't you glad you decided to join us?" Charles asked.

"I am. Thanks for inviting us," Tracy said.

"Come to think of it, where is this consultant, Don, whom we've heard so much about? Will he be joining us?" Eric asked.

Tracy explained that Don was busy helping her keep the ship afloat and that his travel plans prevented him from joining them tonight.

Eric commented, "We need to make sure we meet Don before he completes all of your projects." He wanted to size up the competition. Eric felt she and Don were an item. His name had surfaced far too many times. Perhaps they were just colleagues and friends, but Eric had to make sure. With the pressure of her job and the pending divorce from her husband, she was vulnerable. It would be so easy for a man to take advantage of her situation, and before Tracy knew what had happened, she and Don might end up lovers.

Eric was going to make sure that didn't happen. If he could see the two of them interact with one another, he'd be able to tell if they were colleagues, friends, or something more. Men always knew when there was a deep attraction. If she did have feelings for Don, he'd have to work that much harder. At least Don didn't live in the city. Once the project at Sunset was over, maybe he would find another company to devote his time and attention to.

He'd waited too long for a woman like Tracy. He was becoming tired of dating the young chicks. He wanted a real woman. One who was very sure of herself and knew exactly what she wanted from life, a woman who had her own career and wasn't looking for her lover to carry the weight. Tracy was that woman. His fear was that she would return to California and continue the life she knew.

The waiter approached the table, rambling off all of the specials and the restaurant's favorites. Tracy told Eric to order for her. She craved seafood and would welcome anything fresh. She excused herself and went to the ladies room. She powdered her nose and reapplied her lipstick. She sprayed on a light mist of cologne and readjusted her suit. When she returned to the table, Leslie, Eric, and Charles were having a lively conversation and sampling a plate of appetizers.

"There you are. We missed you," Eric said, offering Tracy some of the appetizers.

"If I keep this up, wining and dining every night, I'll be twenty pounds heavier," Tracy said, helping herself to the appetizers.

"So that we'll be able to keep seeing you ladies, I personally spoke to the chef and asked that they get our orders out promptly," Charles said, serving each of them more wine.

And true to form, dinner was served within minutes. Leslie and Tracy had trout, Charles settled for a medium-rare steak, and Eric had lamb chops. They all feasted on the delicacies and traded stories about unusual things that happened during their travels to foreign countries.

The funniest story was the one Eric shared. It was the middle of September, and he had to go to Dubai on a business trip. Not thinking, and poor planning on his part, Eric had packed wool blended suits and long-sleeve shirts. He almost died in the heat while everyone else appeared comfortable at the meetings. He was drenched in sweat each day from head to toe.

"It's perfect we're talking about our international experiences," Charles said, "but I have to share a mishap I had in the states. It was in Minnesota about fifteen years ago. When I left Miami, the temperature in Minneapolis was in the low forties. Within an hour after my arrival, the city was hit with a snowstorm that turned into a blizzard. I didn't have an overcoat nor boots with me. All flights coming into and going out of the city were canceled for days. It took me five days to get out of there. I never understood why people choose to live there when there are so many great places with warm tropical weather and a decent climate year round. I guess they like brutal and harsh weather."

Tracy looked at Leslie. Charles had no way of knowing he was talking about Leslie who would soon become a Minnesotan. Leslie's life was about to change. Tomorrow she'd tell Judy it was farewell, and shortly thereafter Charles would be told. Tracy knew that would be a blow to his ego. In Miami there were so many takers, people who didn't want to work and were looking for a sugar daddy or a cougar. Charles had finally met a woman who was independent and carried her own weight.

"Well, I'm sure those people who choose the cold climate are happy to experience the four seasons, and they probably wonder how people in Miami and places like California tolerate the same type of weather year-round. They are probably aghast that some of us have never seen snow," Tracy said, hoping to change the subject.

Tracy glanced at her watch. It was twenty minutes to ten. Eric caught her eyeing her watch and knew they needed to bring closure to the evening.

"Charles," Eric said, "we need to get up, close out the check, and get these lovely ladies to their cars. If we don't, I'm afraid the slippers will turn to shoes and the coach will turn back into a mouse or something like that."

"I'll agree to that on one condition," Charles said.

"And what might that condition be?" Eric asked.

"We all agree to meet at the Hard Rock Hotel this Thursday evening for live entertainment with Diana Ross. I have four tickets in section 107, first row, middle seats."

She and Leslie watched as the guys bounced the discussion back and forth. Tracy hadn't seen a live show in so many years that she couldn't remember the last time she saw one. Leslie thought it would be fun. Diana Ross was beautiful and had so much magnetism on stage. The audience usually went wild when Diana entered the stage and sang "Reach Out and Touch (Somebody's Hand)." Not to mention her fabulous gowns and the number of times she changed during a performance. Diana gave you your money's worth.

"What time is the show?" Tracy asked.

Charles replied, "Most of the shows start at 8:00 p.m. and last for about ninety minutes."

Eric looked at the four tickets and said, "The show starts at eight."

Although she was having a wonderful time with Eric, Leslie, and Charles; Tracy didn't know if it was wise to be out so many nights during the week. She didn't fear not being prepared as much as not being able to navigate through the political maze at Sunset. Sometimes when you're lacking sleep, you miss the obvious.

Sunset and most of the executives were a challenge. She thought some of the challenges were due to lack of experience as opposed to meanness ... or at least she hoped that was the case.

Leslie's car arrived at the door first, followed by Charles' car. As Tracy stood with Eric waiting for the valet service to bring her car around, he put his arm around her neck and gave her a French kiss on the mouth. Her body and heart didn't resist, but her mind kept echoing, don't do it ... get in your car and go.

Eric tipped the driver who brought her car. He opened the door for her, and as she got in, he pulled her close for one more kiss. "I love and care for you, Tracy. I fell in love with you the moment you walked into Starbucks. Don't reply. Don't say I'm crazy. Take it for what it is. You have a guy who wants to be in your life. I know you don't love me, and that is OK. I think in time you will, and I'm willing to wait."

As she said his name, Eric placed his finger on her lips. "You don't need to respond. I just wanted you to know that you're loved. I'll never do anything to hurt or disappoint you. Sweet dreams, my love," Eric said, as he closed her door. He walked away and didn't look back as Tracy drove off.

CHAPTER 11

Leslie and Charles felt like two high school students. Leslie knew that her time was short. She felt guilty not being able to tell him about her plans. That would all change tomorrow when she delivered the words to Judy. She wasn't sure how Judy would react. She wasn't expecting a counteroffer. Many talented executives had left Sunset with little more than a good-bye. There were no send-off parties and no "thanks for a great job."

Judy was as cold as ice once you resigned. She saw it as betrayal. She felt you should stay with the company until she no longer had any use for you. She just didn't get it. Judy had led a charmed life, never having to do without and being handed everything on a silver platter. For now she had the board of directors tied around her finger. That could surely change in the future.

The board had recently appointed a new member who currently served on three boards of Fortune 500 companies. John Bailey was educating board members on their duties and responsibilities. John had over thirty years of corporate experience. He was currently the president and CEO of a multi-billion dollar consumer products company based in New York. Leslie had met with John several times regarding legal matters affecting the company. John was direct and always gave his input. He wasn't shy at board meetings. It had been rumored that he would be appointed the new board chairman at the May board meeting, which would be another blow for Judy.

Tonight Leslie would enjoy Charles completely. She'd accepted his offer to spend the night at his place. She planned to wake up at five, tiptoe out, and rush home to shower and dress. Then her hectic day would begin, starting with her nine o'clock meeting with Judy. She was surprised that Judy hadn't called her to see what the meeting was all about. That seemed so out of character and strange for Judy who didn't like surprises.

Charles had a magnificent two-story home on Miami Beach. He wasn't in a gated community, but there was a wall surrounding his property. In order to enter the property, a Venice electronic gate had to be opened. His gardens both outside and inside the property were well manicured. Everything was lush green with plenty of palm trees. His home was warm and inviting with light shades of blue, beige, and brown. He had a spectacular view of the Atlantic ocean.

She could tell that he'd spared no expense in having an interior decorator furnish the home with attention to detail. In the living room there was a black leather conversational sofa that seemed to go on and on. A bar area was situated to the left of the living room. Huge marble statues stood in the foyer, and the dining room had a massive marble table that easily seated twelve people. The artwork was unquestionably expensive in gold antique frames.

There were fresh flowers everywhere. She followed Charles to the kitchen, which was the size of her first floor. The kitchen floor was done in white marble that matched the white wooden cabinets and granite countertops. Hanging over the built-in circular kitchen island were copper pots of all sizes, which reflected against the glass cabinet doors like diamonds and newly polished silver.

Not a dish was out of place. Fresh fruit filled a basket on top of the counter, and a gorgeous flower arrangement sat on the desk in the kitchen nook area, which faced French doors leading to a sunroom. As Leslie walked into the pantry, she was amazed at how all the canned goods were arranged. They weren't just thrown in; they'd all been strategically placed.

"I have to tell you, Charles, that you're the first person I've ever met with a totally organized pantry. And by the way, this place is magnificent. I love the special touch of fresh flowers."

"I can't take too much credit for the flowers or the furniture choice. I had a decorator who pretty much decided on everything in this place. My housekeeper takes care of organizing the pantry and keeping the place stocked with fresh flowers."

"That must be some housekeeper to do that for you."

"We've been together for almost ten years. She's more of a friend than a housekeeper. She's like a mother. She's in her mid-sixties, a widowed mother with no family in this country. In her country she's considered wealthy for the wages she makes here."

"What country is she from?" Leslie asked, curious about Charles and his lifestyle.

"She's from Somalia. She sends money home to help her ailing mother and two siblings."

There was a short silence that filled the air. Leslie was taking in all that Charles had shared. She wondered how many other women had been in the exact spot where she was now standing. How many times had Charles played that same tape … over and over again?

"Honey, what would you like to drink?" he asked.

"What are my choices?"

"You can have whatever you want. I have wine, liquor, coffee, tea, and soda."

"I'll take some decaffeinated coffee if you have it."

"Two decaffeinated coffees coming up. How would you like it?"

"Black is fine with two packets of Splenda."

"Would Sweet'N Low do?" Charles asked, hoping it would since that was the only artificial sweetener he had.

"That's fine. I can take regular sugar if that's easier. After all the eating and drinking I've been doing for the past three days, I should be drinking water," Leslie commented, feeling guilty asking for a no calorie sweetener considering all the rich food she had inhaled in recent days.

After they finished their coffee, Charles led Leslie upstairs, using the excuse that he wanted to give her a personal tour of his home. She knew it was to mask the real reason for the tour, no doubt to end up in his bed where she wanted to be.

"You and your decorator have exquisite taste. I love what you've done with your office and the exercise room. You should have absolutely no excuse for not working out each day. All you have to do is walk up the steps."

He moved closer and kissed Leslie on the lips, placing his hands on her buttocks and gently squeezing. He was arousing her to levels she didn't even know existed.

"I suggest you watch yourself, Charles, or you might get more than you bargained for."

"I need you, Leslie. I desire you. Your body feels so good."

He slowly led her to his bedroom and laid her on the comforter. He took a step back and looked at her, eyeing and taking in her beauty.

"What on earth are you doing?" Leslie asked, wondering why he was looking at her strangely.

"You're a truly beautiful woman. Just look at you."

She sat up and pulled him down on top of her, and as they kissed, the fireworks exploded. She ran her hands up and down his spine, unbuttoning his shirt while fumbling to get the zipper of his pants undone. He was having too much fun to help her as he slid a hand inside her panties and felt the warmth of her secret garden. They made love and drifted off into a deep sleep.

When she awoke and looked at the clock, it was three-thirty in the morning. She made an attempt to get up, but he pulled her body close to his, kissing the nipples of her breasts. She smelled of their lovemaking. He desired and wanted all of her. There was no sacred ground. She totally gave herself as he entered her from behind. The soft groaning and moaning for more convinced him that he'd exceeded her expectations. They were both exhausted but still found the strength to reach new heights with a vaginal entrance.

She didn't wake up again until six-thirty. There was no way to make a quiet escape. He was standing over her with fresh juice and black coffee.

"I'll take the juice," she said, stepping into her clothes that were scattered everywhere from the night before. "It looks like a hurricane went through here," Leslie commented, as she picked up her things and placed his clothes on a nearby chair.

"You're right on that account, sweetheart. The weather report is smooth sailing for today."

She was afraid to stop rushing around for fear that Charles might lead her back to his bed, and she might not find the strength to leave. She had to get home to dress and get ready to face Judy. She would have to rush before the traffic picked up. She told him good-bye and headed for the door.

He spun her around. "Not so quick, my love. I need my morning kiss before you escape into the unknown. Those are house rules."

She gave him the French kiss of his life, gently massaging his genital organ. "Good-bye, and I'll see you later."

Within minutes she was in her car, backing out of his gate and heading for Interstate 195. She was feeling good. The night had been wonderful. She and Charles had connected on so many levels. She dreaded having to tell him about her decision to leave. Why hadn't she met him years ago? Why now when this wonderful job opportunity had surfaced?

As she entered her home, she put on a pot of coffee and went straight to the bathroom. She took a quick, hot shower. She wished she were still in Charles' arms. She felt so safe and secure there. His lovemaking made her feel alive. At forty-seven years of age, she felt like a kid again. She wanted more of Charles. Maybe they could have a long-distance relationship. Who was she kidding? Those relationships were costly and never lasted. In the end, either one or both parties drifted apart and found greener pastures.

It was a quarter to nine when Leslie pulled into Sunset's parking lot. Traffic had been slow due to an accident that had been pulled over to the side of the road. People in Miami always had to slow down or stop to see the victims of an accident. New Yorkers weren't like that. They kept moving regardless of the magnitude of the accident.

When she got to her office, there was a voice-mail message from Charles thanking her for the evening and a wonderful time. He told her he would call later that afternoon. As she was about to call and thank him for a great time, there was a knock on her door.

"Come in," Leslie said, placing the phone back in its cradle.

"Hi, Leslie. I didn't see you when you came in. Just want you to know that Judy is running a little late. She called from her car. Apparently, there's an accident on Interstate 95. Judy said she should be here around nine-fifteen or so," Lynn, her administrative assistant, said.

She dialed Charles, but he was unavailable. She phoned Tracy to let her know that this was the day. With any luck Judy would ask her to leave within the next two weeks, which would give her even more time to pack up and spend with Charles. She shared with Tracy how she was regretting having to tell Charles. Tracy assured her that he would understand. He was a professional in the legal field where confidentiality and integrity were mandatory.

They spent the next ten minutes discussing the overtime meetings and the upcoming analysis of the diversity impact. Leslie told Tracy she would be more than happy to help her with her rationale and justification for changes. Given the history of Sunset, she knew that some of her colleagues would attempt to lay off diverse employees before separating non-diverse employees. She ended the phone call and gathered her Day-Timer and headed to Judy's office.

Judy met her at the door, inviting her in as she placed her things on the desk. "I don't know why there are so many accidents on Interstate 95. You'd think people would pay attention to the road."

Judy asked Leslie if she needed anything as she told Elizabeth to get her a cup of coffee.

"Why don't we move to the conference table so we can be more comfortable," Judy said, as she closed her office door.

Without a knock Elizabeth entered, handing Judy the coffee and placing two bottles of water on the conference table. As Elizabeth left Judy asked, "What did Zahn Durk want when you guys spoke? I have to call him at two."

"He asked about our lawsuit in New York and where we currently stood. I also shared with him the overtime pay issue and our strategy. Zahn said you had briefly mentioned to him the other day that some of our nonexempt employees hadn't received compensation for hours worked over forty," Leslie said, noticing that the veins in Judy's neck had started to pop out.

"I did have a brief conversation with him, Leslie. I didn't make it out to be a major problem. I was just making conversation. I hope he got the message that we're on top of this one."

"Judy, he was very curious about this issue. He'd had a conversation with the new board member, John Bailey. John has tons of experience in this area. My guess is John said this was a serious matter that needed to be addressed immediately. I think Zahn was satisfied with our strategy of educating all of our managers regarding the overtime issue so they can have conversations with their teams."

"The timing of this issue isn't good. With the upcoming lay-off, some of the disgruntled employees might take revenge … I just don't know," Judy said, shaking her head.

"I think it's fortunate for us that Tracy is here. She has tons of experience dealing with employee relations issues. Just look at how she has orchestrated the reengineering effort. I think the career outplacement center is a brilliant idea. I personally feel your agreeing to severance packages will keep employees from suing the company. They will have to sign a separation agreement that will waive that right."

"They can still come after us for overtime pay, can't they?" Judy asked.

"The two are completely separate issues. Employees have the right to challenge our decision of not paying overtime in the past. What we have done is create a fair process for employees to be paid for wages earned last year and the past ten months of this year. We've no way of knowing the actual hours worked since we didn't keep any records. What the administrative assistants will do with their managers is to estimate what they should have been paid and, within reason, the company will pay it."

"What constitutes … within reason?" Judy asked.

"The estimation has to take into account the typical work day, the major projects that would have required overtime hours, and the reality of how many hours of overtime pay an administrative assistant could have earned in a given week. We have to show a good faith effort, so if we end up in court, that can be factored into the equation," Leslie said, hoping to end this part of the conversation, allowing her to officially resign.

"Do you think we'll have to face a court battle?"

"I can't say no with certainty, but if we do, I think we'll lessen the financial burden to the company by the action and steps we plan to take."

"I feel a little more at ease now, knowing that we're doing everything within our power to make things right for our employees," Judy said.

"Judy, I know you have a ten o'clock meeting with the finance team to discuss next year's budget, so I'll get right to the purpose of this meeting."

Leslie watched as Judy's body tensed up. She knew whatever Leslie had to say wouldn't be good news. She had seen that look on her face before. Leslie was all business. There was very little small talk. She hadn't even asked Judy about her evening the night before. Judy was bracing herself for the worst.

"I'll be tendering my resignation this morning. I've accepted a position with the Target leadership team in Minneapolis."

Judy's face turned pale. She stuttered as she asked Leslie what made her decide to leave. Leslie shared with her how the company had come after her. Target had been interested in her for the last two years. Leslie had initially said no to Target because she had so many things she wanted to accomplish at Sunset. She also didn't want to leave Judy and the management team in a lurch.

"I didn't want to abandon the ship, knowing you hadn't identified a human resources leader, and I hadn't fully developed the skills of my legal team. I'm confident now that things are moving in the right direction."

"I appreciate your modesty and self-effacement. You are a real trouper. I've enjoyed our friendship and your candor and honesty. Is there anything I can do to make you change your mind?" Judy asked, as color was slowly returning to her face.

"This isn't about anything you or the company have done to me. I've truly enjoyed my time here. You have a great team, and I'm happy to have been a part of it."

She was surprised that Judy was desperately trying to get her to stay. Protocol was to help the resigned executive vacate the premises as soon as possible. She had no idea that Judy would take it so personally. It was as if she felt a sense of failure. Leslie could see by her behavior that she'd been caught completely off guard. With the exception of the previous human resources leaders, she'd thought of her direct reports as solid. People didn't leave her until she decided their time was up.

The tables had turned. One of her top and most admired executives was leaving, and there was nothing Judy could do or say to keep her.

What would she tell the board chairman? The company was facing legal trouble in New York that could easily lead to a class action law suit, a huge layoff was about to happen, and now she had to navigate her way through the overtime issue. She needed Leslie's expertise now more than ever.

"Leslie, is it the compensation that's pulling you away from Sunset? I'm sure I could get the board to agree to elevate your position to executive vice president, which would increase your base by 10 percent and long-term incentives by 20 percent," Judy said, desperately grasping at straws to keep Leslie.

Judy was losing ground. Didn't she realize it was too late for all of that? Where was the sincerity? Leslie admired the fact that she'd go out of character and suggest a counteroffer, but Leslie had already been warned by the headhunter to not consider it. The executive hiring firm that had contacted Leslie on behalf of Target shared a recent Wall Street Journal article titled, "Counteroffers Seldom Work."

The article shared statistics on how companies made counteroffers to employees only to terminate their employment later. The counteroffer was like a death sentence; once the employee changed his or her mind and accepted the counteroffer, the company immediately started to look for his or her replacement. Most leaders were offended that an employee would choose another company to work for. They were often personally hurt by the gesture.

It was that very rare 5 percent of the time when the counteroffer was legitimate. In those rare cases, it was pretty much the skill set of the executive or the employee that was irreplaceable or the fact that it would cost the company more to hire a replacement in the open market. Companies were clever. There had to be something in it for them. Counteroffers were a way of putting managers on notice that something wasn't working as effectively as it could. Leslie wasn't willing to be a test case for Judy.

"Judy, I appreciate you trying to sweeten the pot to keep me. I know that it's usually not your style to make a counteroffer. I'm thankful that you think enough of my skills and abilities to go the extra mile. I've enjoyed my time with Sunset. We've become a family. We've grown together and made Sunset a great place to work. Like all families, there comes a time when you have to leave and spread your wings. That time is now for me."

Judy tried everything she knew to try and convince Leslie to stay. She felt that before Leslie departed the company she should talk with the board chairman. There were great things on the horizon for Sunset, and Judy wanted Leslie to continue to be a part of her team. She was also afraid that things could turn nasty quickly with a major void in the legal arena. There wasn't sufficient time to recruit someone and get that person on board to handle the major legal hurdles facing the company. She knew Tracy had a legal background but didn't have the legal license to practice in Florida. Tracy was also a maverick and an independent thinker who pushed the envelope to its limit. She was not a weakling or a pushover. Judy recognized that Tracy would definitely be her biggest challenge.

Judy wasn't about to give up when so much was riding on her own career. The last thing she needed was an inexperienced person making the wrong turn, causing the company to lose its competitive edge.

"If you don't think I'm being too personal, what was the offer from Target?"

"It equates to about a 30 percent increase in my base with significant long-term incentives if the company meets its objectives," Leslie said.

"Why don't you sleep on their offer while considering what I've proposed? You've done an outstanding job with the legal team and with managing our board members. I've always been impressed with how well you handle yourself."

The Wall Street Journal article, that she was given by the recruiting firm, pinpointed Judy's behavior perfectly. It talked about how the manager, in a last-ditch effort to keep the employee, would expound on how his or her skill set increased the overall performance of the company. The article said to be careful that you're not suckered into these superficial comments.

"Judy, I'll sleep on everything you've said. At this time I feel it's in my best interest to accept Target's offer. I know my decision to leave probably comes as a surprise, but I'm leaving you with a bunch of very talented attorneys whom I've personally nurtured and trained."

"You're right, Leslie, but they aren't ready to replace you."

"There's a person here who knows employment law and can help out in a crunch. Tracy isn't licensed in the state of Florida, but she knows the law. She has worked with many top companies that relied heavily on her skills and knowledge. She can't run the legal department, but she's one hell of a good attorney."

The two talked for another thirty minutes as Leslie tried to keep the conversation focused on company matters. She could see that Judy was becoming desperate. It wasn't about Leslie and what was best for her career; it was about Judy and the chairmanship.

She was relieved when Elizabeth knocked on the door and stuck her head in, urging Judy to move on to her next meeting. Judy reluctantly got up, encouraging Leslie to reconsider and stay with Sunset. Leslie nodded her head to pacify Judy as she left her office.

She called Lynn, her assistant, en route to Tracy's office, telling her she would return within the hour for the staff meeting. It had been a tiring meeting with Judy. She was exhausted. The last thing she expected was a counteroffer. She had no idea what brought that on. Judy wasn't known to do that. When people left they could hear her silently saying, "I'm glad to be rid of you."

Life had so many different twists and turns. Now Leslie had to craft her words carefully when she declined Judy's counteroffer tomorrow. Corporate America was nothing more than one big community. You never, ever wanted to burn bridges behind you. One thing she could do to ease some of the pain would be to extend her final departure date out four weeks, with an additional week being added if necessary.

She really didn't want to do that, however, for fear that Judy would turn on her once she felt comfortable with a replacement, Leslie was willing to make the sacrifice, for fear of being publicly slaughtered by Judy. She understood Judy's concerns. If that New York case went to a full-blown class action lawsuit, it would only be a matter of time before the board replaced her. With the employees not being paid overtime and that being a violation of the Fair Labor Standards Act, it could smear Judy's and the company's reputation.

Leslie also had to think about her reputation as chief general counsel. The last thing she needed was to be affiliated with a company facing a class action lawsuit. The media would have a field day as other secrets of Sunset became public information.

Tracy was on the phone when Leslie reached her office. It didn't appear that she was on a private call since her office door was open. Leslie entered her office and took a seat facing her desk. Tracy could see instantly that Leslie looked disturbed. She quickly brought closure to her phone call, telling the person on the other end she had to run to her next meeting.

"What happened to you? Was the news of your departure not taken well?" Tracy asked, as she pulled her door shut.

"I think I need a drink. I was taken aback by Judy's counteroffer."

"Counteroffer from Judy? I thought she hated those."

"I've never known Judy to make a counteroffer to any employee or executive. Her reasoning is that if they don't feel welcome here, then they need to go. I've tried through the years to convince her to reconsider but to no avail. Those conversations were always fruitless."

"What are you going to do now, Leslie? Surely, you aren't considering the counteroffer, knowing what you know about the dangers and how they can bite you in the ass."

"There's no way I'm staying. I need to carefully select my words so I don't insult Judy, causing her to become angry and make an attempt to ruin my reputation."

"Do you think Judy is capable of that? You don't think she would succumb to those nasty tactics."

"I would hope not, but the legal issues the company is facing could bring about her downfall. Judy would be devastated if she didn't get the chairmanship."

"I don't have a crystal ball to look in, but if I did I'd put my money on John Bailey. I think the board members are realizing more and more that they've just fumbled through the years. They need his leadership to help move the company forward. John brings tremendous experience. The members of the board are all millionaires. They probably took this gig to have something to do with their free time. Most of the members are retired. I don't think they want the headache of working through a class action lawsuit."

"Let's hope it doesn't get to that level and turn ugly," Leslie said, wondering how Judy would react when she announced she was definitely leaving.

"I'm with you, but let's look at the facts. We'll have from 8 to 10 percent of our employees on the street within about a week and a half. If any of these employees become irate, they may, just for the hell of it go to the media. I can see it now; large corporate giant steals money from the little guys."

"Tracy, don't you think that a lot of this can be circumvented with the career outplacement center? I mean it isn't like our employees are leaving with nothing. We are giving them severance packages and assistance getting their resumes together and finding jobs."

"Leslie, it's not about losing your job when you get notified. These are employees who put their heart and soul into making Sunset what it is today. They have given the 200 percent that we've asked of them. Most of these employees have only known Sunset from a career perspective. They left college and came here to work. Separating these employees will be one of the worst things they'll face in their lives. When they get up the day after their separation from the company, it will hit them hard that they'll probably never come back and work for Sunset. We won't have jobs to hand out. This is their life. It may sound strange, but many will go through the stages of death, asking questions like why me and what have I done? They'll also try to bargain with their maker. The only rainbow is that as these employees move to acceptance they will still be alive."

She got off her soapbox and focused on the immediate situation at hand. Judy had to be handled delicately. Leslie would need to shoot for a win-win resolution. There couldn't be a loser. She thought offering more time and being available by phone might soften the blow. Tracy was also willing to lend her expertise when necessary. To ease the pain of losing a talented executive, she planned to contact a number of executive headhunters to talk about how soon they could deliver a candidate if given the assignment. At that level the search would be put on retainer.

"Leslie, you need to look out for yourself and do what is best for you and your career. Judy had ample time in the past to praise you for your efforts. It's just a bit too late to charge into the cage as if she's going to save you from the lions. Sunset will continue with or without you, me, or Judy. Companies are thick skinned. You of all people should know that."

"You're absolutely right. I needed you as a my sounding board, so I don't trip over my own two feet."

Leslie left to go to her staff meeting. Tracy volunteered to join her with two of her directors to explain the overtime dilemma for the company. First, Tracy had to speak with the vice presidents of Human Resources at Ryder and Cigna about possible job openings. Don was going to have his consultants work with other local companies to add to the list that would be given to all separated employees working out of the career outplacement center and Brock's regional offices.

Tracy grabbed two of her directors and off they went to join the legal team. She wanted to role model how to explain the overtime issue, how the company would handle the issue, and how employees would be notified. Leslie's staff meeting was in session when they entered the conference room. Leslie acknowledged their presence and a short time later turned the meeting over to Tracy.

Tracy started by sharing a little of her background with the team. She knew that some of them hadn't had the pleasure of meeting her. She then introduced her human resources directors. The issue was a very sensitive one, and she wanted to make sure the attorneys and other senior leaders were all on the same page. Even though the attorneys were all experienced in their field, they asked a lot of very valid questions and felt it might help to have one of them present at each of the department meetings.

The legal repercussions from a misstep could be devastating to the organization. The company needed to minimize the risks associated with not paying overtime to nonexempt employees. She had already prepared Judy, Sheila, and Leslie for the challenge should an employee feel he or she deserved more than the 22 month grace period. It was best for the company to average overtime pay for a designated period of time, than to have the courts decide.

After the meeting Tracy checked in with Sharon for messages and asked that she schedule an attorney on the agenda of each of the department meetings. She instructed Sharon to contact the department executive in instances where meetings hadn't been scheduled. The drop-dead date to inform employees of the overtime issue was on or before the close of the business day on Friday. Sharon was asked to confirm all scheduled department meetings by the end of the day.

Sharon informed Tracy that her realtor, Linda Scott, had stopped by and left an envelope with papers for her to sign. Tracy asked her to put the envelope by her purse so she could review the information later that night.

Next, Tracy met with Don's team on the first floor in the conference room. They compared notes and hammered out the schedule for the day of the event. She would be teamed with him and would handle situations that were deemed slightly more difficult than others. Those would be situations in which employees' spouses may be facing a possible job loss, where the employee may have openly communicated major health issues, or where the supervisor may have observed signs of stress or high emotions in the past.

When it came to losing one's job, you could never be sure how the employee would react. Sometimes it wasn't the employee with constant emotional outbursts or stress issues. Often times, it was the employee who always appeared cool, calm, and in control. She covered all angles.

Whenever there was a scheduled layoff in one of her previous companies, there was always a certified nurse on the premises. The nurse stayed in the command center and dressed in casual clothes so as not to arouse attention. Tracy was thankful that they only had to use the services of the nurse once.

This situation might change all of that. The employees at Sunset weren't engaged in the business, and there seemed to be quite a divide between the senior leaders and the employees. Sunset had a very elitist mentality and culture.

She moved to the back of the conference room and dialed Don's cell, hoping she was not disturbing him with his Atlanta client. He answered as she was about to hang up.

"Don, how are you, my friend? I apologize for not being able to spend much time with you these past couple of days. Who would have ever thought I'd move East and during my honeymoon face a reengineering opportunity, which is more like a massive headache."

"I think if you stay on the East Coast a while you'll get to like it. You may not have the Pacific Ocean, but the Atlantic Ocean is at your back door. How are your meetings coming?" he asked.

"I just left the legal department where I discussed the company's position regarding overtime pay. The attorneys get it. They volunteered to shadow the human resources team and the senior leaders as they meet with their employees. I think that is a major breakthrough."

He agreed. In his short dealings and time with the executives, he'd noticed that the team didn't gel. It wasn't a collaborative team. There was a lot of backstabbing and infighting. Each woman was out for herself; while Gary Umar remained unmoved and untouched by their behavior. The close relationship of the chief executive officer and chief financial officer complicated things and constantly made people feel ill-at-ease. Both Judy and Sheila were joined at the hip like Siamese twins.

"Tracy, we did the first pass of the diversity impact, and it doesn't look good. The majority of the people who are leaving are diverse and older employees. This will never pass the test. You'll need to push back with the executive team."

"I figured as much. Quite frankly, I'm surprised they could find that many diverse employees to put on the list, given the fact that most of them occupy lower-level positions at less pay," Tracy said.

"The bulk of your work will be with operations and the finance department. I think the other departments will be OK with just some minor adjustments," Don said, hoping the executives would comply.

"I can just see Lauren and Nora now. The problem will be with Nora in marketing once she decides to place marketing employees on the list. Lauren will work with me. Lauren doesn't run and cry on Judy's shoulders like Nora does. I'm still trying to determine what Nora has on Judy."

"Over time that will surface. Remember that every dog has his day. Dirty laundry will surface at some point. Nora better just hope that Judy never leaves. I've sensed that Sheila is not as fond of her as Judy is."

"I have noticed that too. Seems to be some inside rivalry there. There's definitely friction between those two. I'm sure Judy has promised both of them her position when she gets promoted. I bet there are two succession charts, one that the board sees, which I think has Sheila's name listed as Judy's successor, and probably another chart that's kept in my department that lists both Sheila and Nora as possible successors."

"Boards are interesting. While the chief executive officer is in place, they tend to take his or her advice. If he or she vacates the position, then all bets are off. I've seen boards go outside and bring in someone new. You can just never tell," Don said.

"I'll circle back with you later, or tomorrow given your travel schedule. I'll start my rounds with our executives and see if I can convince them to adjust their lists so we don't end up in Judy's office."

Tracy tackled the easy ones first. She met with Gary in the real estate and franchising department. What a nice guy.

Gary was six feet two with black hair and light brown eyes. He was of dark complexion with slight wrinkles around his eyes. He was very accommodating. She asked Gary to make a minor change that wouldn't affect his percentage, and he made the change giving her no grief. She assured him that unless there was a major hiccup, his list should be final. Before leaving she promised to get with him for some one-on-one coaching for separating employees.

Gary wasn't that familiar with the process and didn't want to make any mistakes. She told him that he'd only have one employee to separate. His managers would be talking with their direct reports who would be leaving the company. Gary felt a little more comfortable once she told him that all messages would be scripted. He thanked Tracy for her time.

Her next challenge was Lauren, who by far had the largest group. Lauren gave the outward impression that she was a team player. She was like a snake in the grass just waiting for the right opportunity to strike. Tracy surmised that there were two sides to Lauren's personality; the somewhat agreeable one that smiled in your face and the snake that worked her devilish ways behind your back.

Lauren was outspoken with an autocratic style. She had high aggression with a dictatorial leadership style; always thinking little of the skills of others and feeling like she did all the work; a clear workaholic, with an unbalanced and unstable personal life.

Lauren was in the office of one of her managers when Tracy entered the department. She heard her voice and immediately came to greet Tracy. She told the manager she was meeting with to see her before leaving for the day.

"To what do I owe this pleasure?" Lauren said, as she led the way to her office.

"Do you have a minute? I'd like to discuss an issue with you," Tracy said, hoping not to alert those standing nearby that they were meeting regarding the layoff. Still, she felt that all eyes were on her and the other executives as the day was fast approaching.

Once the door was closed, Tracy explained that she was there to discuss the employees Lauren had placed on the list whose employment would be terminated. Lauren made small talk, sharing with her how Nora and the previous operations executive made her life a living hell. It was during the time she ran human resources. Tracy had heard the story before and wanted to get on with the diversity analysis.

"I'm so glad you're here, Tracy. I knew when we interviewed you for this job that you were the right person."

"Thanks, Lauren, that means a lot to me. I enjoy working with operations, and I like to have a solid relationship with all my peers."

"Good luck with that. When I had your job, Tracy, the guy who headed operations, Christopher Wood, along with Nora, were out to get me. I never understood why."

"Well, it looks like you've done all right, Lauren. You are responsible for operations and about 90 percent of our employees reside in your domain. In terms of importance from a job perspective, you rank up there with Sheila."

"I want to be paid as an executive vice president. I have the title and status, but if you check my compensation, I'm close to where Nora is. I want to be paid and compensated like Sheila. That's what you can do to help me, Tracy."

"Have you had this conversation with Judy?" Tracy asked, knowing that somehow the topic was never discussed.

"I have and Judy said that once we got the new human resources leader in place, she'd have the person look into it. Now that you're here, I thought I would discuss it with you. Has Judy mentioned this to you?" Lauren asked.

"To tell you the truth, Lauren, our meetings have been focused on the layoff and addressing the overtime pay issue. I can bring this point up at one of our next meetings."

"You may want to analyze executive compensation before your meeting. I personally think that Judy and Sheila have devised a separate plan for other executive vice presidents that's different from what Sheila is paid. Sheila is the only other executive vice president aside from me."

"What do you mean when you say they have devised another plan? Another pay grade … pay level?" she asked, realizing Lauren was aware of the injustice with executive compensation at Sunset.

"All I can tell you is that my perks are completely different from Sheila's. Sheila has a company car, while I've a measly car allowance that's the same as yours and the other senior vice presidents. My long-term incentives and annual bonus does not equate to that of an executive vice president. My bonus percentage is the same as yours, Leslie's, Gary's, and Nora's."

She'd gone to Lauren's office to discuss the diversity analysis list. The entire conversation had shifted to Lauren and her needs. If her compensation was such an issue, why hadn't Judy resolved it herself? Why wait for the human resources executive? Something told her there was more to the story than what Lauren was sharing.

"To be honest with you, Lauren, I haven't had an opportunity to review executive compensation yet and the policies surrounding pay. I'll have more time to review them within the next couple of weeks."

"I think what you'll find is that we're all compensated at the same level, if you exclude Sheila, even though some of us are operating at a higher level with significantly more responsibility. I think Judy kept all of us the same to keep Nora quiet. I don't think Judy wants to have to deal with Nora," Lauren remarked.

It was obvious that Lauren knew about the inconsistencies with how the executives at Sunset were compensated. She knew that her level was comparable to Sheila's and as such, her total compensation and perks should be richer. Tracy knew that for now she needed to refocus the meeting on the task at hand.

"Lauren, I've reviewed the list you submitted, and we seem to have an imbalance of diverse employees to non-diverse employees and a high number of employees over the age of forty on your list. What I'd like to do is work directly with you to correct this problem. Is that OK?" Tracy asked.

"Yes, I'd rather we work together and not have to involve Judy or the executive team."

One thing Tracy admired about Lauren was the fact that she always wanted to resolve her issues and keep them within her department. In front of Judy, she appeared to have a united front and to be a team player. Either Judy was blind to Lauren's tactics, or she enjoyed the level of infighting between Lauren and Nora. After trading and exchanging names for over two hours, they finally had a list that met the specs. Tracy was glad to not have to take the issue to Judy, and Lauren appeared satisfied with the changes.

Tracy told Lauren that she would confirm the list once she had an opportunity to roll it into the corporate analysis. They talked for a couple of minutes longer, then Tracy excused herself for her next meeting. She decided to tackle Nora last. Why not take on the challenge with Sheila? She was sure Sheila would be in step with her since she viewed employees like Nora, a necessary evil. It was so sad that Sheila didn't see the true value employees played in the success of Sunset.

Sheila was the least of her worries. Sheila pinpointed her superstars and those employees who were in jobs requiring special skills that would be too expensive for the company to replace. Her only stipulation was for those employees to remain in position; Sheila called them "untouchable." Tracy saw that as an interesting way to view employees.

Since Tracy didn't know the employees in the finance department, or for that matter most of the company, she suggested to Sheila that she work with her direct reports in order to create the list.

It was clear who the captain of the ship was. Sheila showed no respect for the schedules and priorities of her team. She told her administrative assistant to have all of her direct reports join her in the boardroom immediately.

"Tell them to cancel or stop whatever meetings they're in or whatever they're doing. Tell them they don't need to bring anything," Sheila instructed, gathering up her massive notebook that appeared to have company records and other confidential information.

Sheila probably would have made an excellent drill sergeant. She gave orders with precision and with focus on the immediate task at hand. You didn't have to second-guess what she wanted. She made it crystal clear.

Within minutes the boardroom started to fill up with Sheila's team. Some of the directors looked concerned, while others showed no emotion. Once they were all accounted for, Sheila told them the reason for the meeting. No one said a word or questioned her.

"Team, I know we're all aware that the company has some tough decisions to make regarding the upcoming layoff. In order to be fair and impartial, Tracy and her team will complete a diversity analysis on all employees who will be affected. This guarantees that we don't have a disproportionate number of people of color or older workers leaving."

Tracy decided to intervene so as not to confuse the group. "There are laws that we have to follow as we terminate the services of employees from the company. Some of these laws protect employees over forty and diverse employees. The purpose of our meeting is to make sure we're abiding by these laws and that as we select those employees who will be leaving, we're not crippling the business. By that I mean we'll have the right talent in place to meet our business goals and objectives going forward."

She was thankful that Sheila had turned the meeting over to her and didn't constantly chime in with her comments. It was best that she dealt with this group herself. As the meeting progressed, she challenged the names that were going on the list. With a list of all employees and their history with the company, Tracy could easily locate and access performance ratings, employment time with the company, specific training, education, and previous company experience.

She called Sharon on the conference phone at ten to five to ask her to have the restaurant next door prepare deli sandwiches and cookie trays. She instructed Sharon to leave after ordering the food since Tracy anticipated having to work late. She was surprised that Sheila hadn't even thought about feeding the group.

At five, Tracy asked the team if anyone had commitments that required them to leave early … and if that were the case, she'd work with them tomorrow morning to bring them up to speed and get their input, especially regarding employees they supervised.

The team was comfortable staying together to finish the task. One thing Tracy knew was that if the finance team was fed, their feedback would be more insightful, and the team would be more engaged. In the end the finance department was at approximately 8 percent cuts across the board, for both corporate and the field.

She thanked the group while explaining that if the remaining departments were under their 10 percent number, she might have to ask for two percent more. In the meantime she suggested that the finance team review the decisions they'd made, and consider if there were any services they could cut; that would definitely save employees' jobs.

It was almost seven when Tracy finished with the finance team. She went to central headquarters on the first floor and found Don's team working a way. Three of his consultants were preparing the details for the layoff. They had arranged for an on-site nurse, analyzed the diversity impact for three departments, reviewed the PR letters, and had compiled a list of all local companies that currently had job openings. There were over five hundred jobs listed. The lead consultant, Maggie Johnson, explained that there were still about nine other companies they had been in contact with who were getting their lists of open jobs to them.

Sharon had given the team the diversity analysis for Gary's, Leslie's, and Lauren's groups. Sharon was so efficient. She was like a sponge, sucking up information while constantly seeking and asking for more responsibility. Tracy was lucky to have her to keep things running in the office, given her hectic, demanding schedule.

She called Don from the first floor conference room, who was at the Atlanta airport waiting for his plane to arrive. The plane had been delayed due to a snow storm in Montana.

"Don, I don't know what I would have done if you and your very efficient and talented team weren't here to help me."

His team smiled and kept right on working. "That's what you pay us for Hudson. Don't think we're working for free."

He knew her day had probably been long and demanding. Knowing Tracy hadn't established herself with the executives presented concerns. She was the new executive on the team. The other players had been there for a while and knew how the games were played. They knew when to speak and when to coast. Don wasn't only her right-hand person, but a friend as well. Tracy had a lot on her plate. Decisions had to be made quickly, and everyone was looking to her for answers.

"How are you, Hudson?" Don asked.

"I'm fine. I had no idea what I was stepping into. This is a dysfunctional organization. It's every man for himself. I spent over two hours with Lauren who heads up operations. She spent half of the time telling me about the compensation she's due and what was promised by Judy."

"Be very careful and leery of her. It's not normal for someone this early in the game to trust you and to be so open. Her candor is scary."

"You're so right. Lauren has repeatedly talked about her true feelings toward Nora, who, by the way, she can't stand and how Judy has misled her. I haven't discovered what makes her tick."

"They should be glad that you decided to join them. If the company is hit with a class action lawsuit, the board will probably clean house, starting with Judy," Don said.

"You're so right. I don't think they see the writing on the wall. Leslie has resigned, and Judy is desperately trying to convince her to stay."

"It's certainly her decision, but that would be deadly and career suicide. If you want me to talk with her, I'd be glad to."

"I think hearing it from you, Don, would be better than me trying to convince her. I sound like a broken record. You have experience in that area. That's what you guys do for a living. The executive recruiter gave Leslie The Wall Street Journal article to read. I'm afraid with Judy's pushing and this new relationship she has with Charles, she just might make the wrong decision."

"Can you get her on my schedule for tomorrow?" Don asked.

"Consider it done. Can I take your team to dinner tonight?"

"You need to get out of there and relax. Sharon took care of the team. When Sharon went to order the deli trays, she called my assistant and asked if the consultants wanted sandwiches. I think their reaction to eating deli sandwiches for the last two days led Sharon to offer Chinese food. My assistant told her not to worry, but she said consider it done. She's a fabulous person and she is very pleasant to work with."

"I'm so lucky to have her. She keeps things running smoothly as I attempt to stay ahead of the fires. I'll have to thank her tomorrow and do something special when this is all over."

She and Don talked for another ten minutes before he brought her back down to earth regarding her own team.

"Hey, Hudson, before you go ... have you thought about your 10 percent cut in human resources? Just thought I would ask."

She'd been so busy attending to the needs of others that it had escaped her that she too would need to find the dollars for her contribution to the bottom line. She was at such a disadvantage. She didn't know the skills of her team or the folks in the field. Time wasn't on her side. She'd have to craft a creative strategy in order to be fair. She didn't want to arbitrarily make cuts to get to a number by playing dominoes with the lives of her people; like a game of chess.

"I have some thoughts, but I need your expertise. Let's grab some time in the morning, preferably before my meeting with Nora. That will turn into an all-day affair. She want be cooperative, so I'll have to involve Judy who will play gatekeeper and mother," Tracy said.

"Good night, Hudson. I'll see you in the morning. My flight should be leaving within the hour, at least that's what the monitor is saying."

"Good night," she said.

Tracy asked the consultants if they needed anything from her as she left the room. What a busy and hectic day it had been. She was glad it was over.

Back in her office, she checked her emails in a correspondence folder Sharon had left for her along with messages from callers. There were over thirty emails and twenty-two messages from people demanding to talk with her, all from internal people, except for three messages from Eric. He desperately wanted to see her. She didn't know if she had the strength or energy to talk to him, yet alone meet for drinks. She was physically exhausted.

There was a lot of unnecessary drama at Sunset. If Nora or Lauren could be removed from the equation, the company might have a little more cohesiveness. Why was she dreaming and who was she kidding? The solid relationship between the CEO and CFO clouded that sky.

She responded to all email messages and left about ten messages in response to callers who demanded to talk directly with her. She left instructions for Sharon to schedule a meeting at noon with her direct reports and stated that if they were traveling, it was fine for them to be conferenced in. She wrote two letters for Chutney Pepperberg in public relations to review, leaving specific instructions for Sharon to hand-deliver those. When she looked at her watch, it was a little past nine. She dialed Eric while packing up her desk.

"Hi, Tracy. I saw your name on my cell. How was your day?" he asked, sounding a little perturbed that she hadn't called him earlier.

"It was OK. I'm finishing up some emails and letters for my assistant to type in the morning. Give me another twenty minutes, and I should be on my way home."

"Don't tell me you're still at the office."

"OK, I won't tell you that. We'll just say that I'm trying to bring closure to my day."

"I hope they appreciate all you do for Sunset. You don't have a life. You're becoming a workaholic," Eric said.

"It will be fine. It's always this way when you start a new job. Typically, the position has been open for a while, and when they finally appoint someone, everyone lines up to tell you their problems. They have also paid dearly to get me, so they want immediate results."

"I'm glad I don't have to work in that mayhem. I just quietly exist in my world of plastic surgery."

"Consider yourself one of the lucky ones. Maybe I'll have that level of independence one day."

She didn't want to sound annoyed, but she was hoping he would end the conversation and say good night. She wanted some "me" time to kick back and do absolutely nothing. She loved his company and found him to be a fascinating person, but she just wanted to relax.

"Have you had dinner?" Eric asked, hoping beyond hope that the answer was no.

"I had to meet late with the finance group, so we ordered deli sandwiches. The good news is we were able to finalize one report. The team was cooperative and came through on short notice. So that's one down and many to go."

"I'd like to see you, sweetheart," Eric said.

As he spoke those words, she was becoming warm with desire. Her heart was in control, not her head. The day was over, and the night was young. She needed sleep and time to think. She also wanted to see him. Tracy didn't want to be too anxious. She still hadn't gotten the report from Bruce Lamarr.

Bruce worked fast and she knew he'd be calling her any day now. He had great connections. He also knew how to go underground and investigate the world of same-sex partners.

"Oh, Eric, that's very sweet. I'd love to see you, but look at the hour. It's almost ten, and I have to be back tomorrow morning for a seven o'clock meeting."

"Tell you what," he said, sounding as excited as a kid at Christmas. "Why don't you come to my place for wine and cheese? I promise I'll have you on your way within the hour. It's late, and if I were you, I wouldn't resume work until tomorrow."

Against her better judgment, she agreed to a nightcap. He gave her directions to his home on South Beach and told her to have the guard call him when she arrived at the gate. She hung up the phone and said good night to the security guard on her way out of the building.

The security guard offered to walk her to her car, but she declined. The guard watched her leave, standing in the doorway of the lobby. He warned her to be careful and to take the necessary precautions. Miami was a fun city, but it could also be a very dangerous one.

She arrived at his home thirty minutes later. The guard phoned Eric for clearance so she could enter. It was a short drive from the gate to his home, and what a magnificent home he had. She estimated it to be around nine to ten million dollars before entering the property. There were fountains in front with lights that reminded her of the Las Vegas hotels. He met her in the driveway with outstretched arms as he pulled her into his chest. He gently kissed her on the lips.

"Thanks for coming. I'll live up to my end of the bargain."

What a house it was. The floors were all done in a polished natural travertine stone. He gave her a tour of the place, which took about twenty minutes. All the bedrooms were suites. The master bedroom and bath were enormous. He had an indoor eight-person hot tub, an entertainment area with theater seating for fifteen, a music room with a grand piano, and an exercise room larger than most fitness centers.

The house looked like something in one of those exquisite magazines for bachelors. The colors were light, not dark, with far too many shades of brown and black. Glancing through his French living room doors, she saw a huge magnificent lighted pool with palm trees and tropical plants, and in the distance there was a lighted tennis court.

He led her to the game room where wine was chilling, next to a tray of cheese and crackers. Celine Dion was softly playing in the background. He challenged her to a game of pool. As tired as she was, when he said "game," her competitive juices started to flow.

"Let the games begin," she said, "and may the best man win."

She had a lot of fun even though she lost. She promised to do better next time. Eric offered private lessons, and she accepted with the stipulation that those lessons wouldn't start any time soon. He took her in his arms and held her there for what seemed like an eternity.

"Eric, you're such a great guy. I'm surprised that you haven't been swept off your feet. You've so much to offer. You're a doctor, well educated and have a warm inviting demeanor about you; you're rich and you're available. I bet the ladies are scratching and clawing to get next to you. Why haven't you found Ms. Perfect yet?"

"I'd never planned on being single this long. I was once engaged to what some would call a Brazilian beauty. She was the most beautiful creature God has ever placed on this earth, so I thought. The night before our wedding, I found out she'd been sleeping with one of my best friends and a couple of other guys."

"I'm so sorry. I know how painful that must have been for you. You did the best thing not going through with the marriage. Marriage is tough enough without adding to the confusion with drama. Starting out with a lie leads to more lies and more questions."

"What about you, Tracy? Do you think you will be able to follow through with the divorce? I think your spouse is going to want you back under any circumstance."

She already knew that he had fallen for her. He was now afraid that she would flee the state and go back to California. Stephen was a smart man. He had encouraged Tracy to marry him, and Eric knew he wouldn't give up without a fight. Women could forget and forgive much better than men. Women were willing to give men the benefit of the doubt. Men reacted differently than women. They would throw in the towel and keep stepping, looking for another love to serve as the replacement.

"It's too late for Stephen and me. There's no love there. When I needed him the most, he turned his back on me. I think I died in his heart when I went into the coma. We don't know each other any more. Our goals, wants, needs, and desires are so different."

Eric hoped she was right. He had no claims on her and couldn't force her to start the divorce proceedings. He was afraid that Stephen would have the upper hand. He wanted Tracy all to himself. He wanted to tell her. He feared that she'd give him the boot and confirm her suspicions that he must be a womanizer or a bachelor who loved playing the field. In reality he was a very lonely man.

There was no one to share his life with. There was Priscilla, but she was quickly becoming a relic of the past. On weekends he spent time with Miami Events and Adventures, on the beach and in restaurants.

He'd dated several women, but no one held his attention like Tracy. In the past he'd been afraid to date older, more mature women. What he found in Tracy was a sensible, giving, caring human being. A person who knew what she wanted and went after it. She wasn't a self-centered or egotistical person. She had her own life, a life she balanced well with work, friends, and fun. She was open to new adventures.

"A penny for your thoughts, princess. You seem miles and miles away," he said, as he gently stroked her face.

"I'm going to see Stephen in about a week or so. I have a major project that I need to complete first. I feel awful for the way I left. He deserves more than that. After ten years of marriage, I need to face the music. I don't know what drove me to flee in the middle of the night like some escapee."

"Do you think that's wise, Tracy? I'm sure Stephen will beg you to stay. It may be more than you wish to handle."

"It's not about Stephen and what he wants. It's about me and what I need. I'm not going there like a prize bull he gets to bargain for. I'm going there to say good-bye. I deserve someone who loves me for me. We don't have anything in common now. It's time for us to go our separate ways."

Eric did all he could to try and convince her to not return to Stephen. It was all in vain. He realized that given the circumstances and the way she left, she had to face Stephen and talk to him. If she didn't go back, she'd regret it later. Eric definitely didn't want to start their relationship on the wrong foot. They kissed and talked until the wee hours of the morning. She fell asleep in his arms.

He was very gentle as he lowered her head onto the sofa pillow and removed her shoes. He covered her with a blanket and planted a kiss on her forehead. He wanted to take Tracy to his bed but knew it was much too soon. He didn't want to frighten her. He set his alarm clock for five so she'd have ample time to go to the apartment and dress.

He wrote a short sweet note and slid it in her purse. He signed it with an "E." It simply said, "Thanks for a terrific evening … from a man who is truly fortunate to have so much sunshine in his life."

At five o'clock he went to wake her. Tracy was standing up, looking around for her shoes. "I see you're already up. I came to wake you so you would have time to go to the apartment to change in order to make your seven o'clock meeting."

"Thanks, Eric. I hadn't planned on sleeping over."

"You didn't. You work so hard with so many long hours. When you fell asleep in my arms, you looked so peaceful and beautiful that I didn't want to wake you. It was late and I didn't think it was wise for you to be on the road at that hour of the morning."

CHAPTER 12

Wednesday was quite a day for Tracy. She was approaching the halfway mark. She started her day with Don, looking at possible things that could either be cut or trimmed from the human resources budget. One thing that was working in her favor was the ratio of human resources managers to employees at the restaurant level. Sunset currently had twenty-five restaurants assigned to each field human resources manager. That was a luxury the company could no longer afford. The industry standard was seventy.

She decided to delay purchasing some of the off-the-shelf training programs. She also trimmed some of the features from the new human resources information system. The company just couldn't afford the BMW right now. She made a note to meet with Sam Mason. Sam was smart, quick, and customer-driven. She admired Sam and knew that the two of them could deliver a good product way under budget. She decided to delay the center of excellence, a training center for executives and senior leaders, by six months. During the interim she would train the executives to mentor senior leaders.

Her meeting with Nora and Judy was anything but professional. Whatever Nora had on Judy was causing her to make poor decisions, clearly affecting her judgment. Nora moaned and complained the entire time. There was just no way she could terminate any marketing employees. Unlike Lauren, Nora hadn't taken her up on her offer to help trim the marketing budget. The meeting was grueling, listening to a grown adult not play by the rules. She kept a poker face, not giving in to "little miss get everything you want."

The meeting lasted three hours. Finally, having exhausted all of her options, Judy agreed that Nora could delay marketing programs and trim the merchandise budget. Deep within, Tracy was fuming. With all she had to do, she didn't have time for crybabies. It seemed so unfair for Judy to not stand her ground. Even Sheila played by the rules regarding the layoff and separating employees. Tracy was sure that the executive team would think less of Nora knowing they had to cut people and she didn't.

That would also be a difficult message to deliver to the employees. It wouldn't take a genius to figure that one out. When all the departments started laying off people and there was no movement in marketing, employees would see the injustice. Tracy went back to her office after the meeting to calm down. After about an hour, she got on the elevator headed to Judy's office. Sheila was standing in Judy's doorway as she approached.

"Hi, Sheila, how are you?" Tracy asked.

"I'm great. I was just leaving, so Judy is all yours," Sheila said, closing the door behind her.

"Judy, I need to talk with you about what transpired with Nora. I know you agreed for her not to cut any employees, but I think that decision is going to come back and bite us."

"What do you mean?" Judy asked, sounding a little miffed.

"On the day of the layoff, it will be obvious to employees that marketing is the only department in the entire company that wasn't affected. I think employees will see that as unfair. Once that hits the fan, sparks will fly. Every department in this company is affected except marketing."

"Is there any way around the issue?" Judy asked.

"I think marketing needs to have some skin in the game. It will be almost impossible to explain that they found the dollars by only trimming programs and services. I suggest you sleep on your decision. I'll support the decision whatever the final outcome is. If you feel that Nora shouldn't lose people, then we need to get in front of this ASAP."

"How do we manage that?" Judy asked, as if she wasn't the one with the authority to change the landscape.

"At our next employee meeting, we'll tell the troops that marketing is currently severely understaffed and therefore, won't be eliminating positions. We'll need to build our case and have a united front. That means that all executives will need to support the decision. We can't have any executive or senior leader disagreeing in private."

Judy was beginning to see that excluding marketing from laying off employees would be a real issue. Tracy was determined to get Nora to contribute her share of employees losing their jobs.

"Judy, if you decide to have Nora reconsider her decision, you might want to have that conversation in private with just the two of you present. I can be there if you like, but it may be best if just the two of you spoke."

"Let me noodle on that overnight and I'll give you my decision on Thursday."

"Sounds fair. Talk with you then," Tracy said, as she got up and opened the door.

She knew it would be difficult for Judy to renege on her promise to Nora. She also knew there would be repercussions from the executive team if Nora didn't terminate the services of any of the marketing employees. Whatever Judy's decision was, they would have to get the executive team on board.

Tracy kept her scheduled meetings with all the executives and finalized with Don the list of companies that had job openings. Everything was on schedule for the event. Next week she would wrap up all the loose ends and train all the managers, senior leaders, and executives who would meet one-on-one with employees scheduled to be terminated.

She had to get to Leslie before the day ended. It had been a difficult time for Leslie regarding her decision to leave. In subsequent meetings with Judy, Leslie had stood her ground and refused to accept the counteroffer.

Things had become rocky with Judy as a result. She had lost the battle. Leslie had one foot out the door. Her commitment was to remain with Sunset for three weeks and to offer one additional week if both parties thought it was necessary. Judy was frantic, and it showed as she went about performing her duties. She knew how difficult it would be for a new general counsel to step in and handle the lawsuit facing Sunset.

Leslie was an experienced attorney and knew Sunset and its history well. She was a master at controlling the board and responding to their requests. She was always on point and well prepared for board meetings. Leslie knew the laws of Florida and various other states.

Up until the point John Bailey joined the board, Judy had the board members in the palm of her hand. The appointment of John Bailey changed the dynamics. John's experience and expertise was broader and more in-depth than any current board member. The board was now checking in with him before making any critical decisions. The landscape had changed, and it was obvious that the chairmanship was slipping fast through Judy's fingers.

Tracy found Leslie in her office chatting with an attorney. She motioned her in as the attorney communicated that outside counsel in New York had some new evidence regarding their case that he was emailing to them.

"Will wonders never cease, " Leslie said, instructing the attorney to see her as soon as he had the information in hand.

"Sounds like you're having a wonderful day," Tracy said, with a hint of sarcasm.

"Between our case in New York and the treatment by Judy, I feel like throwing in the towel."

"You're just a little stressed out. Remember you have the upper hand, and if Judy were smart, she would play by your rules. Judy and Sunset stand to lose, not you, Leslie."

"I know you're right, Tracy, but Judy's strong arm-twisting tactics are getting old."

"I think I may be able to help out. I was on the phone earlier talking with Korn Ferry International, an executive recruitment firm. They have identified four general counsels who are currently in the job market. All four have agreed to work internally with us until we can find your replacement. The good news is, you can leave in three to four weeks for your new job in Minnesota without feeling guilty that you've left Judy in the lurch. You'll not need to feel that you have abandoned the ship."

"How will that work?" Leslie asked, with a look of confusion. She could tell that Leslie wasn't familiar with the concept, "executives on loan."

"Executives on loan work with companies on a temporary basis to fill a void; generally a position that is open or one that will soon be vacant. Korn Ferry emailed to me earlier this morning, the resumes of four executives who expressed an interest in Sunset. I forwarded those resumes to Judy. Judy will conduct phone interviews with all four candidates and have her top two candidates meet with you and her in person. I have spoken to all four, and they are all highly qualified. Three of the four have been general counsels for multi-billion dollar corporations."

"That's an interesting concept. Would any of them be interested in joining Sunset full-time?" Leslie asked.

"All of them are currently seeking employment. It would depend on the chemistry between them and Judy, and their interest in the position. Let's face it; they're all overqualified for the position. By having them on loan, so to speak, you and Judy will be able to test their qualifications firsthand."

"If we decide that we're not interested, does that present any problems?" Leslie asked.

"Absolutely not. Korn Ferry will become their employer, not Sunset. Korn Ferry will farm them out to Sunset as consultants. We'll choose only one to work with us. However, if we see that the chemistry isn't good or they aren't the right fit, all I have to do is call Korn Ferry, and they'll send a replacement. But I will tell you that it's rare for these top-notch executives to not perform well."

Leslie seemed quite satisfied with Tracy's decision to get her some help so the transition wouldn't be difficult. She wanted a smooth transition for the company and her legal team. She was scheduled to tell her team on Thursday, which would be followed by an internal email to the employees. Judy had already communicated her decision to leave to the board, putting a positive spin on it, as if it were truly a once-in-a-lifetime opportunity for her, although, Judy was still hoping to persuade Leslie to change her mind.

"Have you told Charles about your decision to leave?" Tracy asked.

"Not yet."

"What are you waiting for?" Tracy asked, curious about her reason for not telling him.

"I want to make sure that Judy is comfortable with my decision first."

"You really don't think Judy will be comfortable with your decision to leave. Her first priority is Judy. She isn't thinking about your welfare; a blind person can see that. I've been here a short period of time, and I can read the writing on the wall. Let's face it, Judy is jockeying for that board spot, and nothing will keep her from attaining it. What she didn't count on was John Bailey."

"John called me this morning to discuss my decision."

"What did he say? John doesn't appear to be a person who would want you to rethink your decision."

"Tracy, John Bailey was wonderful. He was very understanding. He said there comes a time in all our lives when we have to make the decision that's best for us. He said once you make that decision, move forward and don't look back. I plan to do just that. I'll close this door so a new chapter can begin."

"That's the Leslie I know. Now back to Charles. When do you plan to tell him?"

She could tell that Leslie's loyalty was first to Judy and then to Sunset. She was made that way. She would never want to disappoint Judy in any way. Tracy wanted to relieve some of her anxiety by getting an "executive on loan" to temporarily join the team as soon as possible. She was grateful that Leslie hadn't fallen prey to Judy's ploy to keep her. If she had stayed, Tracy was sure her life would have become a living hell.

"I thought I'd meet him for drinks before the Diana Ross concert tomorrow evening. I didn't want to tell him until I'd finalized things with Judy. By the end of day on Thursday, everyone associated with Sunset will know. I felt that was the most appropriate thing to do."

"You're right. Once you tell Charles, then it's out of your control. How do you think he will take it?"

"I think it will hit him hard. My fear is that he won't understand why I didn't tell him right away. We've been intimate with each other. I think he'll construe that to mean a lack of honesty and trust between us."

"You may have misread him on that note. As an attorney, I think Charles will get it. After all, you guys have only known each other for a couple of weeks."

"Here I find a wonderful man, and I have to relocate to Minneapolis of all places. Where was Charles when I was sitting at home night after night watching television and reading legal briefs and journals?"

"It generally works out like that. You finally find the man of your dreams and a screw becomes undone. Maybe you guys can commute," Tracy said, trying to sound encouraging. She had done a couple of long-distance relationships early in her career; unless Charles decided to bite the bullet and move, the relationship would probably be doomed from the start.

"I would be open to that, but Charles doesn't seem like a person who'd go for it."

"What other options does he have if he wants to sustain the relationship? It's not like you went looking for this job. The job found you. The headhunter contacted you. There was no way for you to say no to Target. It's a great company to work for and they have won almost every industry award out there."

Tracy was feeling better when she left Sunset for the evening. For the first time in what seemed like an eternity, she was leaving early and feeling as if she was in control. Don and his team were just wonderful managing the various assignments. She had no idea how she would have survived without them. They were experienced and knew how to stay on top of things and get stuff done. Once they signed on with a company, they were committed and totally dedicated to the task at hand.

With the layoff now a week and four business days out, the real work would start. She was anxious to see what Judy's decision was regarding Nora. If the executives thought for one minute Nora was escaping the task at hand, all hell would break. She and Judy would be inundated with complaints and concerns. The credibility of the process would also be questioned. Not allowing Nora to have her way would be a big step for Judy. Whatever the outcome there would be someone who'd lose. The results probably wouldn't yield a win-win situation.

The drive home was relaxing. She stayed off the expressway as much as possible, opting for some of the back streets. She'd already spoken with Eric, and they agreed to take the night off. She felt she needed some time to herself.

Once inside the apartment, she ordered Chinese food, placed some clothes in the washer, and poured herself a glass of wine. When the Chinese food arrived, she devoured it, leaving only the fortune cookies untouched. She had gone the entire day on three cups of coffee and a carton of yogurt. Her eating habits were becoming seriously unhealthy.

She poured a second glass of wine and eased into a hot bathtub, where she was able to chill out for nearly an hour. She was drifting into a light sleep when her cell phone rang. She shivered hearing the sound. She wanted to ignore it, but what if Don or his team needed something. She got out of the tub, wrapping herself in a plush white robe. She thumped her toe on the end table trying to get to the phone as her breathing became irregular.

"Hello … this is Tracy."

"Hi, Tracy, it's Bruce Lamarr. You sound out of breath. Did I get you at a bad time?"

She thought her heart would stop. Now was the time to face the music. What had Bruce uncovered in Eric's background? She was afraid to ask. Her heart was beating at an unsteady pace. Her palms were sweaty, and she felt physically faint. She was speechless. The moment of truth had arrived.

"Tracy, are you there?" Bruce asked again.

"Yes, I am. I hit my toe on the table running to get to the phone. It's nice to hear from you. Have you finished the report?"

"My partner should be done by the end of next week. I could meet with you in Miami next Saturday. I've a meeting in Tampa early Saturday morning. I thought I'd get a rental car and drive over. Perhaps we can meet for dinner and discuss our findings."

"Next Saturday will be fine. Just let me know what time, and I'll make the arrangements."

"Why don't I call you next Wednesday or Thursday to finalize our plans. How does that sound?" Bruce asked.

"That's fine. If you don't reach me on my cell, call me at the office."

She gave Bruce her office number and the name of her assistant. She remained paralyzed in that one spot long after she hung up the phone. The day of reckoning was drawing near.

Why hadn't she asked for any details that he might already have? She was afraid to find out. Next Saturday seemed so far away. Her head was pounding, and she felt she was losing control. What if he'd already figured out that she cared for Eric and knew the news would shatter her world? She lay awake in bed all night. She read over the lease the realtor had left with Sharon, but couldn't focus on the words. When it was time to get up, she felt lousy. She needed coffee.

She entered the drive-through at Starbucks, relieved not to see Eric or his car. Her seven o'clock meeting had gone well with Don. They were way ahead of schedule. All signs were green. It was then that she made the decision to move the layoff date up to next Wednesday. Don was in total agreement. The employees were getting antsy. Everyone was anxious to get the event over with. So as not to alarm or arouse the employees too much, she thought it would be advantageous to have the human resources directors train the managers, who would deliver the message, in small groups. That endeavor could happen on Friday. The training session would only take about thirty to forty minutes. Since everything was scripted, the margin of error was greatly diminished.

Her only fear was that Judy wouldn't have made the decision to encourage Nora to add employees to the layoff list. Whatever the final results were, she was pressing on. She phoned Sharon to schedule a short meeting with Judy. She needed Judy's buy-in and blessings before proceeding. Don and his team had done an amazing job orchestrating all the tasks. They were the behind-the-scenes people who made it look effortless when, in reality, it had been a grueling and laborious task.

After meeting with her team to assure that each person understood the task at hand and his or her responsibility, she proceeded to Judy's office. Judy was on the phone as she signaled her to come in. Tracy had no idea what to expect. She was still holding out that Judy and Nora had reached an agreement to add marketing employees to the list.

Elizabeth entered Judy's office, bringing a pot of coffee, cups, and condiments. She also had a tray of fresh bagels and cream cheese. She was in need of coffee. She poured herself a cup as Judy brought her call to an end. After closing the door, Tracy moved to one of the chairs in front of her desk. She wasn't planning on being in Judy's office too long so going to the conference table seemed pointless.

"Hi, Judy. How is your morning going?" Tracy asked, hoping not to prolong the discussion with small talk.

"I was just on the phone with John Bailey. He's such a smart man. I think he's just what we need … a new set of fresh ideas. I think he is giving all of us a run for our money. John constantly questions the way we do things."

"Sometimes that's a good thing. I like having people look at processes and procedures through fresh eyes. That's how things become better," she said, agreeing with Judy's observations.

"I know you're right, Tracy, but with challenges come changes and time that we just don't have to spare. John is also quite loquacious. I think he must spend most of his day in conversation."

"I'm sure he's learning the ropes of how we operate. It might help to have John spend a day in the field with some of our senior leaders. I think the senior leaders would love it, and it would help John better understand our business."

Tracy could see she'd scored big with Judy. Getting John more acquainted with the business would be productive for him and the company. The senior leaders would also feel privileged to have an opportunity to work with one of the board members. At a later date, she would suggest that when the board was in town the senior leaders should attend some of the board lunches and dinners, and make presentations to the board regarding business developments. That would truly be a great way to boost their egos and increase the board's knowledge of the company.

"Judy, I've some great news. I've met with my team and with Don, and we're ahead of schedule. Given the tension and anxiety level of our employees, I think we need to move up the date of the layoff."

"What do you have in mind?" Judy asked, with an interesting look on her face.

"I suggest next Wednesday. This will give us two days after the layoff to meet with all of the employees who aren't affected; to refocus their efforts and get them on board with the new reengineered company, before they leave for the weekend. We'll need the two days to hold discussions and meetings so employees don't go home with too many unanswered questions."

"I think that's a wonderful idea and a great strategy. I can feel the tension as I walk throughout the building. This has really been hard on our employees, Tracy."

"I agree. Most have never gone through a layoff before. I surmise that only a small percentage of our employees were involved in layoffs at their previous companies."

She pulled out the diversity analysis and told Judy that even if Nora decided not to terminate any of her employees, the company would have met the criteria. They spoke for another ten minutes, before she excused herself. Judy said nothing regarding Nora and her change of heart. At this point Tracy decided not to rock the boat. If she didn't hear from Judy by the end of day, she would strategize with Don on the best way to get the message out to the executives and employees.

Leslie was waiting in Tracy's office when she returned. Something must have happened or gone wrong. There was a worried and depressed look on her face. Sharon had already gotten Leslie a diet Coke and a bottle of apple juice for Tracy.

"Leslie, are you all right? The color has completely drained from your face. What's going on?"

Leslie took a deep breath and told her how Judy had reacted when she confirmed that she was taking the job at Target. Leslie was appalled that Judy had behaved so poorly, telling her that if things didn't work out at Target, don't return to Sunset. She never thought Judy would be so brash and disrespectful.

"What have I ever done to deserve such treatment? She was so rude and her comments were insulting."

She had to calm Leslie down. That was the name of the game. When your time was up, the company generally had no use for you. Minor issues were blown out of proportion.

"Leslie, look on the bright side."

"And may I ask what side is that? I fail to see a rainbow in this scenario. What a nightmare." Leslie said, with a vengeance, as her color was slowly returning.

"The bright side is you didn't allow Judy to sucker you into staying. You didn't accept her counteroffer. Judy has broken one of the cardinal rules. She needs you. It's not the other way around. She's too blind to see that you're the one keeping this company out of court. Once she realizes that, you'll be long gone and enjoying life with a super company; Judy will have to eat those words. Just let that negative energy go," Tracy said, trying to calm her down.

"You're right, and so was the headhunter and Don. I took your advice and spoke with Don. Once you announce that you're leaving, you need to pack up your stuff and go. And that is exactly what I intend to do."

"This has been a learning experience for you, Leslie. In the future you'll be able to help others. That Wall Street Journal article is dead on the money. I always tell executives and employees to make the decision that's best for them ... the decision that's in their best interest, just like John Bailey told you."

Tracy felt bad that Leslie had to learn the hard way. Thank goodness Leslie was moving on. Staying with Sunset would have been a huge mistake. She regretted that Judy had been so egocentric. Judy was a self-absorbed narcissist. If only the tables were turned, Judy would get a dose of her own medicine.

"Just let it go, Leslie. Your time is short here. You can exit after three weeks and never look back. If I were Judy, I'd treat you like gold and try to pump as much information from you as possible. The company needs you. It's not the other way around."

She and Leslie talked about the evening concert and what they would be wearing. Leslie was scheduled to meet Charles at his home at six. She was leaving the office at four. Given the way things had gone thus far, Leslie was thinking about leaving the office at three. She would still give 200 percent to the job, but as far as her relationship with Judy, she was so over it.

Tracy met with Lauren and Gary to let them know that the date had been moved up. The two were quite pleased. Lauren commented that you could cut the atmosphere with a knife and that employees were spending most of their time talking about the layoff instead of performing their jobs. Gary was still a little apprehensive about delivering the message to one of his direct reports. Tracy tried to calm his nerves by going over the script with him. She finally asked Gary to get on her calendar so she could coach him one-on-one.

At around two, she and Don met over lunch to talk about the executives' reaction to changing the date of the layoff. She informed him that they all felt the decision was right. There were too many employees focused on the upcoming separation, and as a result, productivity was down.

"I still have to meet with Nora. Judy kept her poker face and didn't let on about the decision they had reached. When I leave here, I'm going to Nora's office. I'm tired of this drag-and-pull routine we're doing. Time is of the essence, and her time has run out. I'll give her my recommendation, and if she chooses not to play by the rules, then the aftermath will be hers to deal with."

Don jumped in and calmed her down. He knew her emotions were running high. He didn't want Tracy to forget her role or place. "Hudson, you still have to give it your best. Your role is to persuade and convince Nora to have some skin in the game."

"You're right, Don. I'm too emotionally tied to this. I need to step back and not take it so personally."

"It's up to you, Hudson, to play devil's advocate. You have to provoke that debate. Nora's peers will eat you and her alive if they think she's the favorite, and that you and Judy are showing favoritism."

"I hadn't thought about that," Tracy said, now realizing that her peers would think she and Judy were in cahoots.

"Well, my dear, you better think about it now. Nora, Judy, and you will be the black sheep of the family. You're a neophyte here. The team hasn't accepted you. If you can't persuade her to change, then I'm afraid your peers will think you're not driving the bus. You must win this challenge."

Every word of what Don said was true. She wasn't totally accepted by the team. If she wasn't able to get Nora on board, that would be a blemish on her record. The event was scheduled to move forward. All eyes would be on her and her effectiveness in handling the situation and keeping employees from suing the company.

With the overtime pay issue and the lawsuit brewing in New York, she didn't need any disgruntled employees. She would have to get Nora to change void of Judy. She knew Judy would go along with the program as long as her sidekick wasn't upset.

"Don, as usual you're right. I wasn't thinking about the perception that others would have of me. I completely made this Judy's and Nora's problem. The executives will be livid if they think Nora was able to escape by not placing any marketing employees on the list."

"Would you like for me to join you? I can bring an objective, unbiased perspective. Nora has to work with this team. I'm sure she doesn't want to be ostracized by the group," Don said.

"I think that's a great idea. Get your strategy together. We're on with her now. Shall we proceed?" Tracy asked, while collecting her things.

"Hudson, why don't you have her join us in this conference room. Let's get Nora away from her turf. We may be able to influence her more if she's not in familiar surroundings. Also, tell her that there has been a change in the date of the layoff and that you'll give her the specifics when you meet. Keep her guessing, and keep Judy out of this discussion. Can you do that?" he asked.

"I can. When I last spoke with Elizabeth, Judy was off-site at a board meeting with Spirit Airlines."

Tracy called Nora and asked that she join her in the conference room. After wetting her appetite with a change in the date, she seemed more eager to hear what Tracy had to say. Don's strategy worked like a charm. Within minutes Nora was standing in the doorway of the conference room. The plan was working. Now it was up to Don to convince Nora to add some marketing employees to the list.

"Nora, you remember meeting Don, who's spearheading the career outplacement center and working closely with me on the reengineering effort."

"I do. What's up?" Nora asked, totally in the dark that Don was there with the single purpose of persuading her to eliminate some positions in marketing.

"There has been tremendous progress in an effort to get things ready for the pending layoff. I owe credit to you and the executive team for diligently working with Don, the human resources team, and me to make it happen."

"I'm not sure what we would have done, Tracy, if you hadn't joined us when you did. This is new territory for us. We've never laid employees off at Sunset."

"Times have changed, and the economy hasn't helped matters. The reason I asked you to meet with me, is to let you know that we've stepped up the date of the layoff to next Wednesday."

"That soon," Nora said, with a hint of worry and concern on her face. She seemed to be searching for what to say next.

"I spoke with Judy this morning and most of the other executives about this change. They all feel it would ease some of the tension if we could bring closure earlier rather than later."

"I can understand that. As I walk the corridors, I hear employees talking about the event. Productivity has to be down."

"What I want to specifically speak to you about is the marketing organization and your decision to not lay off any employees. Don is here with me to help explain the effects of that decision," Tracy said, watching her reaction the entire time.

"Didn't Judy tell you? I've decided to add employees from my department to the list. I thought about what you said. I don't think we could come up with a justification as to why every department was affected except marketing. I'm not the most popular person with my peers. Something like this could alienate me even more from the group."

"Do you have the list with you?" Tracy asked, expecting her to pull another fast one.

"I dropped it off in your office in a confidential envelope. I left it with Sharon. I'm so sorry. I assumed that either Judy or Sharon would tell you."

"The important thing is that you've done the right thing. I'll get the list and roll up the numbers for the entire organization. I'll circle back with you and the executive team with the final analysis."

Once Nora was out of sight and out of hearing range, Don said he was pleased that Nora had done the right thing. "You never know people. As long as I've been in this business, I'm always amazed by human behavior. You brought that one home, Hudson. Congratulations for a job well done."

"I can't believe that Judy didn't mention it to me this morning when I met with her," Tracy commented, shaking her head.

"Don't try to psychoanalyze this situation, Hudson. Maybe Nora hadn't told Judy of her decision until after you left. Maybe Judy pushed the issue and decided for Nora. Maybe Judy wanted to give the impression that Nora is a team player. Who knows and who cares for that matter. The bottom line is a decision has been made, and it works perfectly well for us and the company."

"I stand corrected again. Let's move forward. Let's finalize the list, rerun our numbers, and prepare the packages. Let's get this show on the road."

She and Don worked through the numbers and reviewed all correspondence that would go out to the stakeholders regarding next Wednesday's event. Tracy circled back with all the executives, except for Leslie who had decided to leave early.

Judy was pleased that Nora had contributed her share. After speaking with Judy, Tracy wasn't sure who'd held back the information. As Don so eloquently said, forget the witch-hunt and press on.

CHAPTER 13

Leslie felt horrible knowing she would have to face Charles and tell him of her decision to leave Sunset. She had rehearsed her lines all day. Her stomach was starting to turn. She had found a wonderful man, and now she would have to end their relationship. There was no way she could turn back the clock now. Judy had shown her true colors. She thought how funny to practically live with a person and not know them. It would have been better if Judy had treated her like all the other lost souls who had departed Sunset.

The gate to Charles' property was open. The gardener was precisely manicuring the lawn and double-checking to make sure not a blade of grass was out of place. Leslie could smell the sweet scent of roses. As she stood outside his door, she was panic-stricken. She was sick with fear. She wanted to turn around and run and never stop. He spotted her through the sidelights of his mahogany door. Upon opening the door, he took her hand and led Leslie into the living room where wine was chilling on ice. He poured her a glass and softly kissed her on the neck.

"You look stunning," Charles said, wishing they'd enough time for a quickie. He could tell that something was wrong. Her eyes looked sad, and she seemed a little distracted. He chalked it up to a hectic day at Sunset.

"How was your day, honey?" she asked, hoping to prolong her unavoidable news.

"We got some good news on our case in California. The parties have agreed to settle. That was a very close call considering the laws of California."

Leslie took a deep breath and dived right in. "Charles, there's something I've got to tell you. I felt it would be best for me to tell you before the concert. I wish I could see my way clear to a solution, but at this point there isn't one."

He had no idea where she was taking the conversation. Maybe she had another lover she kept undercover, or even worse, maybe Leslie was married. He feared the worst.

"What is it, Leslie? I knew you weren't yourself when I opened the front door."

"I'm relocating to the Midwest. I have a terrific job offer that I just can't decline. I know you may think it's selfish of me, and I'll accept that. I'll be leaving in about five or so weeks. I plan to end my employment with Sunset in four weeks and just relax and coast for a couple of weeks," she said, without taking a breath.

"How long have you known? What company? Where in the Midwest? When did you decide to accept this offer?" Charles asked, rapidly firing questions at her.

"Target in Minneapolis approached me some time ago. The talks became serious a few weeks ago. The offer was extended on last Friday. I wasn't sure I could leave ... what I meant to say; I didn't want to leave you, Charles."

"Why didn't you tell me, Leslie, that you were considering relocating to Minneapolis and starting a new job?"

"Charles, I wasn't sure I wanted to go. I spoke with Tracy who convinced me that opportunities like this one only come along once-in-a lifetime. I also had to tell Judy first, and she's been a real bitch. I feel so bad. I've finally met a great guy, and now I have to relocate and end our relationship."

He took her into his arms, gently stroking her hair. "I'm not going anywhere. Haven't you heard of commuting? It's a well-known concept," Charles said.

"I have, but those relationships generally fizzle out within months. I've yet to meet a couple that made it work."

"That's because they're not us. These feelings I have for you won't go away simply because you are moving miles away. There has got to be a way to make this work," Charles said.

"Oh, honey, you're too much. I dreaded having this conversation with you. I didn't know if you would be happy for me or glad that I was leaving."

"How could you say such a thing?" he said, as he drew her close to his chest.

"I don't know. We aren't two teenagers who just met. We're two older, experienced people who have never really found true love. I guess I started second-guessing myself and the relationship; wondering if it were real."

"Let me reassure you that I'm not going anywhere, Leslie. We'll find a way to make this work."

She told Charles how cruel Judy had been towards her when she finally convinced her that she wasn't going to accept the counteroffer. He thought Judy acted very selfishly with her childish outburst. He was sure if the shoe were on the other foot, Judy would have done the same. As he gently massaged her shoulders, he planted a kiss on her neck, reassuring Leslie once again that they would find a way to make it work.

As she wiped her eyes and fought back tears, he made the ultimate gesture, getting down on one knee and asking her to marry him. Leslie didn't know what to say. How would a marriage work with two busy careers taking place thousands and thousands of miles apart?

"Charles, let's be serious. I'm moving to the Midwest. You're on the East Coast. When do we see each other … on weekends and holidays?"

Leslie truly loved Charles, but he was making entirely no sense.

"We can make this work. Others have done it."

"Name just one couple that made a long-distance arrangement work."

"Brad Pitt and Angelina Jolie. They have about a dozen kids, and each year they spend most of their time apart making movies."

"They're entertainers. They don't count. With all their nannies and jet planes, they're never apart for too long."

"Are you refusing my marriage proposal because you've another lover?" he asked, half joking. "Because if you do, I'll stalk you and your new lover. So are you accepting my proposal or not?"

"Counsel, it is my understanding that if you stealthily pursue someone or something, it is punishable by law."

"Come here. Just answer the question. Will you marry me?" Charles asked again.

She had no idea what she was getting herself into, but she desired him with every fiber of her being. She didn't want to let him go. After all these years and after giving up on love, love was knocking at her door.

"Yes, I will. But don't think you can lure me into staying here by asking me to marry you. My bags are already packed."

"Has anyone ever told you that you talk too much?" Charles asked, as he planted a wet kiss on Leslie's cheek.

"No, I don't think they have."

He released the buttons on her dress as he slid his hand underneath her bra and cupped her right breast.

"You should be glad we're meeting Tracy and Eric tonight. If we hadn't committed ourselves to this concert, I'd stay here and devour you."

"Lucky me," Leslie said, as she grabbed his butt and gently squeezed to arouse his inner passion. "I suggest we leave now."

"Good idea, my darling."

If they had remained in his home any longer, they would never have been able to leave. Leslie sat close to him during the drive to the concert. They French kissed at every traffic light like newlyweds. It was great having him so close. She had no idea how they would make the relationship work, but for now, she was game for anything as long as Charles was in the picture.

Tracy left the office early to go home and dress for the concert. She was meeting Eric at the Hard Rock Hotel in Hollywood at seven-thirty. As she reached into her purse, she pulled out his note. It had found its way to the bottom of her handbag under her wallet and makeup case. What's this, she thought. At the next traffic light, she read his note. How sweet and thoughtful of Eric. She knew he had to have slipped the note in her purse the night she fell asleep in his arms.

Tracy decided to wear a short, metallic, one-piece Gucci dress with a plunging back. She did her hair in a chic blown-out style, and to add a hint of drama, she wore shades of smoky-gray eye shadow. She wore a nude color lipstick and dangling turquoise and silver earrings. Stilettos in silver and black completed her outfit.

All heads turned as she stepped out of her car. She looked like a Hollywood movie star. She was fashionably and very stylishly dressed. After asking the valet service for directions to Hard Rock Live, Tracy headed in the direction of the theater to meet Eric. As she walked through the casino, she searched in her purse for coins to drop in the machines. Eric was waiting outside the theater looking gorgeous in a black Versace classic suit with a blue-cuffed shirt.

"Hi, Tracy," he said, as he embraced her in a tight hug. "How was your day?"

"Not bad at all. We made a lot of progress today. Things are starting to gel. Have you seen Charles or Leslie?"

"Not yet. We still have about twenty minutes before the performance. These shows generally start a little later than the advertised time. We should be OK. I have only attended one show that started on time, and I think it was when Kenny Rogers was here."

He was still counting his lucky stars that he'd met Tracy. He was still very concerned about Stephen and their relationship. What if Stephen refused to let her go? Maybe Stephen would convince her that he had changed and their marriage was worth saving. Maybe her feelings for Stephen were stronger than she thought.

"How are you adjusting to living here on the East Coast? I know it's not California," Eric asked.

"I've been pleasantly surprised. I didn't think I'd like it, but Miami is starting to grow on me."

"That is such a relief. I would hate for you to move and leave me here. I've grown so attached to you."

He regretted saying the words. Hearing those words out loud sounded like he was desperate. He didn't want to scare her away. He was hers, and soon she would be his. He needed more time to get her to see the light.

"Eric, I'm here. I'm not going anywhere. We've got to enjoy the moment."

"Tracy, I shouldn't have said what I did. I have no right to try and possess you. I'm just so taken with you."

"I feel the same about you. It's like a dream, and I'm afraid that if I wake up, the fairy prince will be gone."

Eric spotted Charles and Leslie standing beyond the steps and enjoying a performance by one of the outside bands. A small crowd had gathered, and they were definitely enjoying the live music. Hard Rock was alive and looked like a replica of the strip in Las Vegas.

"Hey, you two," Charles uttered, taking Tracy's hand and kissing her cheek. "You look divine, my dear. If I didn't know you, I'd think you were a hollywood diva on the red carpet."

"I have to agree with Charles. Tracy, you're stunning in … Don't tell me … Gucci," Leslie said, grinning from ear to ear.

"How did you ever guess?" Tracy asked.

"I tried that exact dress on in Saks, and it was definitely not a show stopper on me."

"I love what you are wearing, Leslie. We're obviously members of the mutual admiration society. So much for small talk. Lets go in," Tracy suggested.

They all went into the theater. Charles took their drink orders and asked if anyone wanted chips, popcorn, or pretzels. Leslie and Tracy decided to go to the ladies room since there was no intermission during the show. Once the concert started, there was no stopping Ms. Ross, and the best part of her show, was when she went out into the audience.

Tracy noticed that Leslie was acting like a giggling teen-ager. Leslie looked so satisfied and content with life. She hadn't had a chance to talk with Leslie before she left the office. It was obvious that something wonderful had happened in her life. Tracy couldn't imagine Judy apologizing or trying to make amends for the horrible way she'd treated her. She couldn't see Judy trying to compensate for what she'd done or trying to alter her behavior. Judy had wrongly inflicted so many people. At some point in life, she'd have to pay the piper.

In the restroom she turned to Leslie and asked her point blank, "What's going on with you? I've never seen you this happy."

"Are you ready for my news?" Leslie asked, overjoyed with excitement.

"I might as well be. Nothing will stop that train now."

"Charles asked me to marry him."

"Come again? Charles asked you what?" a shocked Tracy asked, assuming that Leslie may have had too much to drink before arriving.

"You heard me. Charles wants to marry me."

"What did you say to Charles when he proposed?"

"After some arm-twisting, I said yes."

"Leslie, you hardly know this man. Have you done a background check? And how will this marriage work with you in Minnesota and Charles in Miami?"

"I don't know. I'm taking this one step at a time. I'm on cloud nine. Maybe tomorrow I'll wake up and realize that this is all a horrible dream. But for now I'm celebrating."

Tracy felt bad about what she had said to Leslie. Who was she to pass judgment on her relationship with Charles? There were no guarantees in life. She had known people who dated and lived together for years before walking down the aisle. Then as soon as they said "I do," the whole marriage unraveled. Who was she to pass judgement.

Her life was a fiasco. She would soon have two failed marriages. Her first marriage had only lasted one year. Now faced with another divorce, she'd wasted another ten years of her life. She should have left Stephen after discovering his affairs. Who was it that said, "It's better to have loved and lost, than never to have loved at all."

"Leslie, I'm so sorry. Who am I to judge you and Charles? I'm not the poster child for successful marriages. You're right. Just go for it, and figure it out as you go along."

"Thanks, Tracy. I'm still relocating to Minneapolis. There's no way I'd reconsider Judy's proposal. I've seen her dark side. I was a loyal and faithful executive. I was always there for Judy. I never once disappointed her. Look at how she's treated me. She has practically thrown me out."

"Don't even give Judy a second thought. Target will make it all up to you. You're less than five weeks away from a blissful life. I'm happy for you. I'm so sorry I overreacted."

The two rejoined Charles and Eric as the usher got them to their seats. They had front row seats in the middle section. Diana Ross started the show at exactly eight. She walked on stage in a white fox coat over a gold sequined dress. Diana sparkled and glittered. The audience almost lost it when she left the stage and joined them, singing "Reach Out and Touch (Somebody's Hand)."

She was vivacious, and her bubbly personality showed through. Every fifteen minutes Diana changed outfits, each gown more elaborate than the previous one. The audience was on their feet when she entered the stage in a spectacular *Gone With the Wind*-type dress in a soft lilac color. Her diamonds sparkled, and her effervescent persona sent goose bumps up and down Leslie's arms when Diana ended the show with "Ain't No Mountain High Enough."

Diana returned twice for an encore performance. When she finally left the stage for good, the audience stood mesmerized, hoping the end hadn't come. As the band started to disassemble their instruments, the crowd slowly moved toward the exits, raving about the fabulous Ms. Ross. Even in her mid-sixties, Diana was still the reigning Lady of Song. Her beauty transcended time. It was hard to find any wrinkles on her face. She was still a size two, and her hair was styled as it had been during her youth. The only difference was the much shorter length.

Charles had his arm around Leslie's shoulders as she and Eric left the auditorium hand in hand.

"What an amazing show. Diana was unbelievable. I see why her shows sell out," Eric remarked, as they headed to Bluepoint Ocean Grill for dinner.

They got there in time to be seated before the onrush of concertgoers. Eric ordered a bottle of red wine and an appetizer platter of tuna, beef tenderloin sliders, calamari, and coastal oysters. When the waiter showed up to take their orders, Leslie decided on the Chicago-cut bone-in ribeye, Charles ordered the New York strip, and both Tracy and Eric ordered stone crabs. After-dinner drinks arrived at their table at eleven.

Checking her watch Tracy commented on the great evening and her desire to leave shortly.

"I hate to sound like Cinderella who has to leave the ball for fear of turning back into shabby threads, but I've some work I need to do tonight."

Eric was in agreement that it had been a wonderful evening, and it was probably time for them to end the night. He was in surgery the next morning at eight, and he always liked to review his patients' charts the night prior. Charles had an early morning breakfast meeting at the Intercontinental Hotel on Biscayne Boulevard. Leslie didn't have any early appointments and decided she could coast.

It was customary for the silent treatment to be applied once an executive announced his or her departure date. Most senior leaders didn't want to begin a project for fear of having to start anew when the new executive or senior leader arrived. Most would rather wait for the successor to be announced for fear of priorities being changed.

Eric walked Tracy to valet parking and gave the attendant her ticket first. It took about fifteen minutes for her car to arrive. Eric leaned in and kissed Tracy on the lips.

"Sweetheart, I'll be thinking only of you tonight," he said. "Get your work done and get some sleep. Doctor's orders."

Eric waved to Leslie and Charles as he got into his car. He watched the lovebirds as he put his car in gear and drove away. Maybe he should be more like Charles and Leslie and take chances. It was obvious that they'd fallen in love and enjoyed each other's company immensely. He had noticed that there was something different about them tonight. They gave the impression that the world was there only for them. Charles only saw and had eyes for Leslie. He watched them as they stole kisses throughout Diana's performance and during dinner. There was a type of halo surrounding them.

Their love appeared to be encased in a ring of light. They were so happy.

Mum was the word for Leslie and Charles' upcoming wedding. It wasn't Tracy's place to tell Eric or to congratulate Charles until they went on record and openly shared the news. After all these years, Leslie was getting married. There were now two noteworthy events she could look forward to. "I guess I should pat myself on the back," Tracy said, out loud in the privacy of her car. "If it hadn't been for me, those two would never have met. Count your lucky stars, Leslie, that you said yes when Eric invited us to Miami Events and Adventures wine tasting event."

Tracy started to undress the moment she unlocked the apartment door. Her shoes came off first, followed by her dress and jewelry. She grabbed her robe off the hook on the master bath door and draped it around her body. She stared at her briefcase on the table. She knew it needed her attention, but she couldn't muster up the energy. She found herself humming one of Diana's tunes. Over and over in her head the song replayed itself, " … Mama said, You can't hurry love … You just have to wait …"

She was in a deep trance when her cell phone rang.

"Hello, this is Tracy," she responded, in a half-conscious state. It took her a couple of seconds to gather her thoughts. She sounded disoriented and confused. She was struggling to get her words out.

"Hi, sweetheart. Is everything OK? You sound strange."

"Hi, sweetie. I must have dozed off. I'm trying to get my bearings."

"I just want to tell you good night and to be thinking about me in your dreams."

"I will. I'm just exhausted from all of the meetings. I hope you understand."

"I do understand, but that doesn't mean that I have to like it," Eric said, hoping she would invite him over. He needed to be with her tonight. He wanted to hold and caress her body. It had been years since he felt like this. The love bug had gotten a hold of him. He'd been bitten.

"I enjoyed the concert. You and Charles have been so gracious inviting Leslie and me to all of these affairs. If it hadn't been for the two of you, I'd probably be spending each evening in this apartment."

"I can't wait to see you. I miss you so much. You're so easy to be with. I only wish that … I'm sorry … I've no right to wish your divorce was final."

"Don't be sorry. You didn't break up the relationship. It ended a long time ago. I was too scared to take the first step. I've had two failed marriages. Maybe the institution of marriage isn't for people like me. I've made a mess of things, leaving the way I did. It's up to me to make things right," she said.

"You can't blame yourself, Tracy, because it hasn't worked out up until this point. You were too young when you first got married, and you married a guy old enough to be your father the second time. You know what "they" say."

"Who is "they" and what do "they" say?" she asked.

"The third time's the charm. Just give us a chance. No pressure whatsoever."

"I will, Eric. I've strong feelings and admiration for you. I just want to take it slow and be sure we're not rushing into things."

She'd already said and promised too much. She wasn't sure what the future held. She knew Sunset needed her, but she didn't necessarily need Sunset. It was too soon to tell if she'd stay on the East Coast. Leslie would be leaving the company soon, and she was losing her one and only supporter. At this stage in life, she didn't want to work for a dysfunctional organization.

"Can I hold you to that?" he asked.

He didn't want to pry into her life. Eric felt close to her, closer than he had ever felt to any other person he'd dated. She was now a part of his world. He felt as if they were on a merry-go-round traveling at an unimaginable speed. He was holding on for the ride and time of his life. He couldn't let go. He was afraid Stephen would win Tracy back, causing her to let go and give up on their possible future together.

"Good night, Eric. Think only pleasant thoughts. I'll see you real soon. Sleep well."

"Good night, my love. I'll call you at the office tomorrow."

She was on cloud nine when she hung up the phone. She admired Eric, but she didn't want to enter into a sexual relationship with him until she had released herself from her commitment to Stephen. Tracy knew she'd do things differently if only she could replay the series of events. Why she fled so swiftly would always remain the sixty-four thousand dollar unanswered question. Although she was tired and beaten down emotionally, that still didn't justify the route she'd taken.

Her life was confusing. Next time around she had to make sure things were better planned and that the love of her life wanted her with all her baggage.

As she turned off the lamp on the nightstand, her cell phone started ringing. She knew it had to be Eric whispering sweet nothings into her ear. It had been years since anyone paid this much attention to her. Even though it was scary, she loved it all. Her affection for him and his love for her, gave her the energy to endure the chaos at Sunset.

"Hey, sweetie, I'm here," Tracy said, in a rushed, hurried voice.

"Trace, is that you?" Stephen asked, almost knocking her off her feet.

Oh my god, she said to herself. It was Stephen. Why now when things were developing nicely? She was thankful she hadn't said Eric's name when she answered the phone. What did he want?

"Hi, darling. Is everything all right?" Tracy gasped, when she heard him. Stephen hadn't called her darling in years. Why was he calling? What did he want?

"Yes, Stephen, everything is fine. I wasn't expecting to hear from you so soon with the trial and all."

"I thought I'd call and let you know that closing arguments are coming up on Monday, and then the trial will be turned over to the jury. With any luck I should be home by next weekend. Given the nature of the case, I don't think the jury will deliberate too long."

It was time for Tracy to face the music. All bets were off. It was time to resolve their skeleton of a marriage. Life as they knew it was about to end. Things would get tricky going forward. If Stephen returned home next weekend and discovered she was gone, he could become irate and fly into a rage. She didn't need him showing up to an empty house. She had to think quickly.

"Stephen, why don't I come to New York next Friday. The case will be over, and we can have dinner in the city."

"That's not a wise idea. Trials like this can take a sudden turn for the worse."

"Stephen, I don't plan to take up too much of your time, but we have to talk."

"I'm sure whatever we have to talk about can wait until I'm back in California. It's not like we haven't been a part before for an extended amount of time. I'm working day and night here on this case."

"We need to talk. I'll not take up a lot of your time. I'll be in New York next Friday, and we can meet for dinner. If you don't have time for dinner, we can meet for coffee."

Stephen's double life was finally catching up with him. For the past two years he'd been dating Katherine Cochran, one of the newest and youngest attorneys in his office. Katherine was thirty-three, gorgeous and looked like she could be actress Julianne Hough's identical twin.

The two only got together during business trips; which was quite frequent. Katherine was committed to staying with her spouse, who had fallen from a ladder three years ago and injured his back while cleaning their outside windows. Her spouse was now in a wheelchair. There was no way she could ever leave him. Her family would disown her if she did; and Katherine knew she wouldn't be able to live with herself. She had accepted her fate. Stephen was her safe haven; she was married and so was he.

Katherine and Stephen had fallen deeply in love and knew that neither one would ever be free because of the chains that imprisoned them. Katherine made Stephen feel young and alive. Katherine had been in New York for the past few weeks working on the trial with Stephen. They spent their evenings having dinner together, enjoying the theater and experiencing all the city had to offer. Even though they each had a room at the hotel, they spent their nights together.

Stephen had to think fast; for Tracy to fly from California to New York to meet with him could only mean one thing. He had to devise a plan to win back Tracy's heart, even if it were only temporary.

He was beginning to realize that Tracy was slowly leaving his life and maybe this time she would follow through. It sounded like she was ready to call it quits. He feared that Tracy no longer wanted him or their marriage. He had neglected her for years, slowly pushing her away. They never spent any time together. When Tracy would try to prepare the dinner she had catered for him, he would claim he had dinner with one of his pressing clients. They never went anywhere together as a couple.

Plans she made for the weekend were always suddenly changed. When they occasionally went to the movies, he repeatedly complained about the film she'd chosen. He always picked up his cell phone, which kept him busy 24/7. What Tracy didn't know was that some of those conversations weren't business related. He used his cell as a crutch to fill the void, to fill the silence, and to talk with the women he dated. He had to get onboard or his wife would make the decision that divorce was the only option. He was finally able to discern that this was perhaps the last straw. To keep up appearances at the firm, it was just easier to stay married.

"Trace, I think you're right. Why don't you come to New York next Friday afternoon? I'll rearrange my calendar. Maybe we can see a play. I'm sure I can get some great seats. If I finish before Friday, maybe we could spend the weekend in New York."

"I'm not coming to New York to see a play. I'm coming so we can talk. I'll not take up too much of your time," she said, in a very direct and matter-of-fact voice.

"Why don't you come and at least spend Friday night here?"

He was becoming desperate. Her tone of voice was cold. His heart started racing. He was the one always in control; now Tracy had control of the situation. She was giving him one last opportunity to make things right.

"Bye, Stephen. We'll talk on next Friday."

Click and she was gone. He had to get clever now. He didn't want to lose Tracy. This time she sounded serious and if she wouldn't give him the benefit of the doubt. If only he could turn back the hands of time. How had he missed all of the signs?

His world was all about his work and the women he dated. His marriage never took center stage. They lived in two separate worlds. It had been more than two years since they made passionate love. During all this time, he never once thought about her needs. He was just never himself, after she slipped into the coma. He assumed that Tracy would become a vegetable, and the plug would be pulled. The day she came out of the coma was one of the worst days of his life. He still remembered receiving the call from the doctor at the hospital telling him to rush over. When he questioned the doctor, he refused to discuss anything over the phone.

He'd almost lost control of his Mercedes, driving at record speeds to get to the hospital. His heart was palpitating with terror and fear. He started to shake and tremble, totally out of control. He'd already said good-bye to Tracy and had buried her memories. He was content that now Tracy and her parents could be joined together in heaven. It was better that way. She was terribly close to her parents. They spoke on the phone each day. He knew she wouldn't be able to go on without them.

He could still recall when the doctors conveyed that a miracle had happened. Tracy had miraculously recovered without any scars. He started to cry—not for Tracy, but for himself. Why had her life been spared? It wasn't supposed to happen this way. The doctors thought he was crying tears of joy. He hated himself for wishing his wife dead. Since the day he brought her home from the hospital, he continued to blame her for not dying. Tracy had ruined what was left of his life. Her surviving that fatal car crash had messed up his plans to perhaps start a new life with someone else.

He hadn't come to grips with her overcoming that terrible accident. No one ever knew he'd wished his wife dead. He thought Tracy understood he needed time to adjust to her recovering from the coma. How do you say farewell to your wife and then have her return after you have made your peace and gone on with your life.

From her tone she wasn't coming to New York to convince him to make a go of it. Tracy had no more to give. Why had he been so selfish and so self-absorbed in his work and pleasing himself? Why hadn't he taken time to work on their marriage? Why was he desperately trying to hold on now?

Tracy tossed and turned for hours. Sleep just wouldn't come. Stephen had taken a perfectly normal evening and turned it upside down. Tracy wished that she hadn't answered the phone. It was just her luck that Stephen was on the other end at such an inopportune time. His calls were always poorly timed.

At three-thirty in the morning Tracy finally forgot about sleep. Why waste valuable time watching the clock? She wished Leslie was available to talk. She surmised that Leslie was probably in Charles' arms. If she hadn't moved up the date of the layoff, she could have approached Stephen this coming weekend. With all that was on her plate, she didn't need this. Don had been right. She should have faced him and asked for a divorce before taking the position at Sunset.

She was thankful that Stephen was on the East Coast. That would save her a great deal of time. She could work in the office until one on Friday and take the three-thirty flight to New York. That would give her plenty of time to meet Stephen for dinner or coffee … his choice. After they spoke, she could return that same evening on a ten-thirty flight. If things got hairy or awkward, she could leave early Saturday morning. She would take her weekender bag, which would hold all her necessities. Either way she planned to be back in Miami Saturday evening to meet with Bruce.

She tried to work, but her concentration was off. She kept reading the same paragraph over and over regarding a public relations correspondence she was attempting to write. As she checked her emails, there in bold print was one from Stephen. What now? Did he decide to cancel her out of meeting with him in New York, like a secretary canceling a meeting with a client? He didn't have many options. This was her last-ditch attempt to tell him the marriage was over. He could either let her tell him face-to-face or she would have the divorce papers served.

Why was he being so attentive now during the final hours? His email simply said, "Can't wait to spend some time with you. It's been too long, Trace, since we spent time together. Love, Stephen."

She quickly deleted the message. How dare Stephen think that mere words could make up for his treatment of her? Maybe she should have died after the accident, but she didn't. There were still things she needed to get done.

CHAPTER 14

Tracy knew that Friday was going to be a long day. Lacking sleep took her down a notch. She stopped by the drive-through window at Starbucks and ordered black coffee and the maple oatmeal with fruit and nuts. She ate the oatmeal while driving and finished her coffee just as she was pulling into the parking lot. She caught up with Don as he was walking towards the building.

"You look like death warmed over," Don said, wondering if she'd faced some turbulence with Judy or Nora.

"Thanks for the compliment. I trust you had a great evening," she responded, pushing her sunglasses up over her eyes to shield them from the sun.

"We'll talk inside," Don said. "Check in with your office, and I'll meet you in the conference room when you get a minute."

She did as she was told. She was pleased she'd gone by the office first. Sharon conveyed that Nora had stopped by in a panic over some information she'd left. It was still early, and

Tracy wasn't up for her foolishness. She dropped her things on her desk and marched herself directly up to Nora's office. She didn't want any time to elapse and have her complain about her not being reachable.

"Hi, Nora. Sharon said you wanted to see me," Tracy uttered, with a glued-on smile.

"I do. Come in. Can I get you some coffee?" Nora asked, as she motioned for her to sit.

"No, I'm good."

"Did you have a nice evening?" Nora asked, as Tracy was gently tapping her feet on the carpet. She was in no mood for games and unfocused conversation this morning.

"It was great. I went to Diana Ross' concert at the Hard Rock Hotel with some friends. Diana was great."

"I saw Diana about two years ago at the American Airlines Arena. She was amazing, and her clothes were fabulous. Diana packed the arena. What an entertainer."

She was losing her patience. She had to focus Nora's attention on the task at hand. Time was running out and she didn't have time to play the cat-and-mouse game any more. She was hoping beyond hope that Nora and Judy hadn't concocted another ridiculous plan.

"What did you need to see me about, Nora?" Tracy asked, knowing that whatever it was, it wouldn't be minor.

"I don't think this will present any problems, but I need to trade out my director for advertising with a senior manager for marketing. When I reassessed their performance, I think I may have inadvertently given you the wrong name. I hope that's not going to be a problem."

She could have kissed the ground that Nora walked on. Nothing at Sunset had been so easy to resolve than her request.

She was all set for a difficult session with Nora that she thought would have to involve Judy.

"That's fine. I'll change the master copy when I return to my office. The diversity numbers won't be affected since both employees are non-diverse individuals under the age of forty. There's also not a tremendous difference in their compensation. Once those revisions are made I'll get a revised copy to you," Tracy said, overjoyed that Nora hadn't created any more confusion.

She and Nora chatted a few minutes more before Nora was summoned to a meeting. Tracy swung by her office, gave Sharon some letters to prepare, and informed her that she and Don could be reached by dialing the first floor conference room. She asked Sharon to order lunch for Don and his team.

Before leaving her department, she spent a couple of minutes saying hello and entering into brief conversations with her team. The human resources leaders had done a phenomenal job in handling the details of the event. They were keeping a record of everything that was done for future reference. The director for organizational effectiveness had deemed herself the historian of records.

On her way to the conference room to meet Don, she was faced with the usual questions. She never got a break. Everyone wanted a piece of her. Employees and executives constantly commanded her time. They all had issues they either wanted resolved or that required her expertise.

When Tracy finally dragged herself to the conference room, even Don's staff knew something was wrong. She was always perky and cheerful. Today she didn't look "bright-eyed and bushy-tailed." She looked stressed out and troubled. To give her some privacy, the consultants excused themselves, pretending they had work to do at the career outplacement center. She could tell they knew she needed his guidance. Don had briefly shared with his team the challenges she faced day in and day out, working with an organization that had never experienced a full-scale layoff.

"Hey, Hudson, let's talk. You look miserable."

"I didn't get a wink of sleep last night. At around three-thirty or so I gave up. I just couldn't succumb to sleep."

"Did you stay out too late after the concert?" Don asked, hoping that would explain why she wasn't herself.

"No. In fact I was the one who brought the party to an end. I suggested to the group that we leave because of my early meeting with you."

"Hudson, what was the real reason you left? I didn't get off the boat this morning," Don commented, curious about what was really troubling his friend.

"It was a lovely night. Since I'm still legally married, I didn't want to encourage Eric, the plastic surgeon, by inviting him to my place. Plus, I'm just a bit confused. My emotions are running high. Everything is happening so fast. And before you say anything, I'll acknowledge that you were right. Nothing ever comes from running away from your troubles."

"Did Stephen call you, or did he show up at your door?" Don asked, wondering if her spouse was going to make life difficult for her.

"Stephen didn't show up. He called me acting like things were fine, and with the case in New York going to the jury next week, he wanted me to know he'll soon be returning to California. What an ass! Why did I ever marry him?"

"Keep things in perspective. It's not all that bad. The best thing to do is to face Stephen and tell him it's over. You owe him that much. I think you need some time between ending the relationship with Stephen and starting a new one with Eric. You don't want to enter into a relationship with Eric before you fully recover."

"I told Stephen I was coming to New York next Friday. He tried to talk me out of it, but I stood my ground. Then, as if we're great lovers, he suggested that we spend a couple of days in New York, just the two of us."

"How did you respond to his request for spending time together?" Don asked.

"I flat out said no. I wanted to tell him to take a hike, but I didn't want to upset him or mess things up for me," she said, as tears filled her eyes.

"You did the right thing. Calm down and take some deep breaths. I think Stephen knows why you are coming to New York. He realizes what he has … all too late. Stephen is trying to hold on and convince you to stay married to him. You need to be strong. This is your life he's messing with," Don said, as he watched her wipe a tear from the corner of her eye.

Don was right. It was her life. She deserved happiness at this stage in life. "Don, I'm so thankful that I'll be meeting with him in New York to discuss things. It would have been a horrible scene if he walked into our home and found the place deserted."

"Hudson, either way the discussion with Stephen won't be easy. Brace yourself for the worst, but keep hoping for the best."

"I now have two failed marriages under my belt. Should I even try for number three?"

"Life is too short to keep count. Look at Elizabeth Taylor. I think she gave up after eight spouses. Marriage isn't easy.

It takes lots and lots of work. Having to live with the same person day in and day out can be taxing, we both know that."

She and Don talked for the next hour while rerunning the diversity numbers. The corporation had met its goal. Next Wednesday would be a difficult day for all of them. In reality it was only two business days away. The event would start at 8:00 a.m. on Wednesday and conclude around two in the afternoon, Eastern Standard Time. They had to accommodate the employees working in the Midwest and on the West Coast. Tracy was thankful that hourly employees and managers at the restaurant level were not affected. Those were the real heroes. They kept the company moving.

She invited Don to dinner, but he had a seven o'clock flight to catch to Martha's Vineyard.

"You must be planning on seeing one of your special ladies," Tracy remarked, hoping to stir up some controversy.

"She's just a lady friend I see when I can," Don said.

"Does she know that? I bet she's written the script with a 'happy forever after' ending," Tracy said, knowing that he'd long past the stage of trying to tie the knot.

"We enjoy each other's company when I'm in town. I try to get up there at least twice a year. We like the crab cakes and fresh seafood. This isn't a serious relationship. I was married for twenty-two years. I'm done."

"When did you know your marriage had ended?" she asked, hoping for a little sympathy from her friend.

"After our second son was born things changed drastically. Kids are wonderful, but somehow they find a way to suck the life out of you. They zap all of your energy, making it difficult to find time to keep the romance alive. We stayed together because of our two boys."

"At least you guys stayed together because of the kids. I don't know why Stephen and I stayed together. I often wonder how I survived so long with no emotional attachment."

"The formula is different for today's couples. They flee when the relationship goes south. If talking and counseling doesn't work, they're on the next plane out of there. Frankly, I can't blame them," he said, realizing that it's tough trying to rekindle a burned out flame.

"Don that may not be all bad. Why spend those extra years together once you realize the relationship is doomed? Of course, I'm not one to talk. Can I at least offer to take your team to dinner?"

"I think they want an early start on the weekend. If you asked them, they would be courteous and accept, all the time wishing they hadn't. Three of them are flying home to be with their families. The others are hoping to sightsee on Saturday and do some more of the legwork on Sunday. We're meeting at 6:00 a.m. Monday at the Denny's restaurant off of Interstate 95 in Fort Lauderdale. Feel free to join us."

"I think not. I'll meet you here at eight."

"Suit yourself, my friend. Things look amazing during the early hours, just before dawn."

When she finished her conversation with Don, she collected a few of his things to keep in her office over the weekend. There was no need for him to travel with the reports, since most everything regarding the layoff was on his computer.

She followed Don in her car to the career outplacement center. She was quite impressed with the layout. There were small offices for the senior leaders to work in and cubicles for the other employees. Each cubicle was equipped with a PC and printer. There were four fax machines and three huge copy machines located in the center of the complex. There were three large and several small conference rooms, which the consultants would use to conduct meetings and training programs. The area was equipped with a small kitchen, and there were several restaurants within walking distance of the center.

Counselors shared offices that they used for meeting one-on-one with separated employees. Tracy was happy that the center was ready to go. On Wednesday after each employee was notified, he or she had the option of going to the center to talk with a consultant before going home. Next Thursday, when those separated employees woke up and realized that Sunset was no longer their employer, it would be comforting to know they had a place to go to. Counselors and consultants would be available to talk with the separated employees, as well as with their spouses and family members, if necessary.

Don's group would generate weekly reports on usage and those who had landed jobs. Separated employees would have access to Brock's database and the regional list of open positions. The consultants would help each person develop a resume and do some mock interviewing.

Tracy wished Don safe travels and watched him drive away. She went back to the office and met with senior leaders who were responsible for notifying employees. They each received a scripted message that they needed to be able to deliver next Wednesday. She asked each attendee not to read the message to the employee and not to memorize it word for word. There needed to be normal dialogue between the manager and the employee.

She confirmed with the group that each manager would have a human resources representative present at all times. The mechanics of the command center were also explained.

If anything derailed during the process, the manager or senior leader needed to call the command center. The center would be manned the entire day with experienced human resources leaders who could answer questions and get things back on track.

The senior leaders were told that a nurse would be on-site in the command center. The nurse was there to handle any health-related problems that might arise until medical help could be secured. The employees would never know that the nurse was on-site. The session ended after she told the group they needed to be in the boardroom by seven on Wednesday. The Q&A document she had prepared was handed out to the senior leaders as they left the room.

She called to see if Judy was available. She wanted to confirm where they stood as a company and invite her to dinner. Judy had already left for the day. She was expected in the office Sunday afternoon and she had cancelled her travel plans for next week. Tracy respected Judy for that. All executives needed to be visible during the process. The executives and senior leaders would need to meet with all of the employees who wouldn't be affected.

Tracy spent the remainder of the afternoon meeting with executives and coaching Gary so he would feel comfortable when terminating the services of one of his direct reports. Gary was starting to feel a little more at ease with the process. Tracy was pleased that things were all coming together nicely, with few problems.

She stopped by Leslie's office to check in. Leslie was standing outside her door talking with one of her attorneys. She asked Tracy to have a seat and told her that she would be with her momentarily. Tracy picked up Leslie's phone and dialed Sharon.

"Hi Sharon, you can leave at any time. We have things under control."

"Do you need me to come in this weekend? I have some time Saturday morning and Sunday afternoon. If those times aren't good, I can rearrange some things," Sharon said.

"I think we are in good shape," Tracy remarked, whispering into the phone. "I'm not planning on working in the office on Saturday. If I come in on Sunday, it will be for a short period of time. I want to bring Judy up to speed on the career outplacement center. It's a gorgeous facility and is well equipped with PCs, phone lines, printers, and fax machines." She and Sharon spoke a minute longer. A short time later, Leslie entered the office, asking who was on the phone.

"I'm talking to Sharon, whom I've instructed not to show up here this weekend," Tracy said, as she ended the call.

"Amen to that!" Leslie said, as she closed her door.

"How is our lucky, engaged lady doing today?" Tracy inquired, as Leslie beamed from ear to ear.

"I'm still on cloud nine. I haven't told a soul, not even my mother. It seems all so surreal. It's weird and bizarre. Don't you think?"

"No, I don't think it's weird. You've finally met a man who has caused you to feel something you haven't felt in years. It shouldn't matter if you've known each other for a lifetime or just a day. Only your heart can direct you now."

"What do I tell people? What do I say? The whole time I've been here, I've never really dated anyone. I've never spoken of love. Do I break out of my shell and say … oh, by the way … I'm getting married to my future spouse whom I've known all of two weeks?"

"I wouldn't tell them anything," Tracy said. "Why do you care what they think? You're leaving to start a new life in Minneapolis. I would exit and say nothing. Let them read about it in the newspaper or hear about it from a friend."

Leslie felt better after talking with her. Tracy was right. She didn't have to justify herself. Sunset was not a social club, and none of the executives, except Tracy, would be among the invited guests. She anticipated having a small wedding with only family members and a few close friends.

"Do you want to grab some dinner, or do you have plans to meet your future husband?" Tracy asked, already knowing the answer.

"We're going back to Tango's for drinks. Why don't you and Eric join us?"

"I think I'm going to call it an early night. I wasn't able to sleep last night. Stephen phoned late, sounding chipper and cheerful."

"What did he want?" Leslie asked, annoyed that Stephen had called and ruined a perfect evening.

"I think a second chance. His case will go to the jurors as early as Monday. Stephen feels the deliberations won't take that long. I told him we needed to meet to discuss things."

"That must have ruffled his feathers. That got his goose going, I'm sure."

"Leslie, I don't think Stephen has a clue. He assumes we'll just continue as man and wife."

"What are you planning on doing?"

"I'm going to New York next Friday to have dinner with him. He deserves that much. Besides, it will be easier to talk to Stephen in New York before he returns to that vacant house and goes berserk."

"You need to decompress my friend. I think you and Eric should join us at Tango's. It will be fun. Tell you what, call me on my cell if you change your mind," Leslie said, as she headed out of the office.

Tracy hadn't checked her emails or messages on her cell phone. She had been in a tailspin all day. She hadn't even had time to eat her snacks, which was definitely not good for her system. Eric had left several messages on her phone asking her to call.

She called his cell. He didn't answer. Maybe he was in surgery. It seemed odd to operate late on a Friday afternoon, but the world of medicine wasn't within her realm of understanding. She told the security guard to have a great weekend as she opened the door and felt a cool breeze on her face. Miami in November was wonderful. She had spent time in Miami as a student while on spring break when the temperatures were unbearable. She didn't know Miami could be so pleasant.

Her cell phone rang as she started the car. She was sure it was Eric inviting her to join him somewhere for dinner or drinks.

"This is Tracy," she said, expecting a warm, friendly greeting on the other end.

"Hi, Tracy, it's Leslie."

"Aren't you supposed to be on your way to Tango's to meet Charles?"

"I'm en route."

"So are you calling to see if Eric and I will be joining you?"

"No, I'm not, even though that would be wonderful."

"So what's up?" Tracy asked, completely in the dark as to why Leslie would be calling her. After all, they just saw each other about forty or so minutes ago.

"I just got the strangest message from Zahn Durk. He needs a copy of Judy's employment contract."

"What's so strange about that? With the calendar year coming to an end, the board probably needs to decide how much they want to increase her compensation by for next year and any additional perks they want to consider," Tracy said.

"Sunset's fiscal year ends in June," Leslie responded.

"Oh, that's right, the company's fiscal year isn't aligned with the calendar year. Yeah … then I agree … that's odd."

"Furthermore, Zahn would like to meet with me on Monday. I've already emailed Judy's contract to him."

"Do you think they are considering not renewing Judy's contract or forcing her to resign?" Tracy asked.

"I don't have any of the details. I'll know more on Monday. I do think that the board is questioning her leadership with the court filing in New York, the decrease in company sales, and not paying overtime to nonexempt employees."

"Do you think John Bailey is instrumental in causing the board to question her leadership? Is he leading the charge?"

"John has equal voting power right now. He doesn't hold a chairperson seat yet. I think John is challenging and pushing the board to step up and take on its fiduciary duty and responsibility to shareholders and stakeholders. With everything that has happened, the board might decide not to renew her contract."

"When does her contract expire?" Tracy asked, since she hadn't had time to review its contents.

"Her contract is up next May."

"I plan on being in the office on Sunday," Tracy said. "Hopefully, I'll run into Judy. I have to bring her up to speed on the upcoming separations and the progress we've made with the career outplacement center. I'll let you know if I find anything out."

"Tracy," Leslie said, in a high-pitched voice, "you should pull her executive file. You have it in your office file cabinet. Read it carefully in case you're asked any questions. Call me if you need any clarification or an explanation. You should also go into the human resources information system to get familiar with her compensation. If anything happens, you'll need to prepare most of the documents. I'll email a copy of her contract to you later this evening."

What a way to start the weekend. Tracy was thankful that the week had ended. All she wanted to do was go to the apartment, kick off her shoes, and chill out in a tub of warm water. She didn't need Judy to resign in the midst of the layoff.

Leslie had brought up a number of very valid points. It was the lag in sales that was causing the company to reduce its overhead. Additionally, the company was facing the possibility of a class action lawsuit which would definitely mean negative press.

With all that Judy had done to Leslie, it would be ironic if Leslie ended up preparing the legal documents for her departure. If Judy resigned, then karma would be in full force. What would Sheila do? She'd never worked for anyone but Judy. Get ready, Sheila … what goes around comes back at you.

This time when her cell beeped, it was Eric. She was glad to hear his voice. He had brought her so much joy and peace in such a short time. She knew he was worried about Stephen. She only wished she could find the words that would reassure him that her marriage was over.

"Hi, sweetie," Tracy said, searching for words to convey that she cared and wished she had more to give.

"How was your day?" Eric asked, hoping she would have time to see him later.

"Eric, my day was long, stressful, unbearable, and demanding. How about all of those descriptive words?"

"Tracy, I wish there was something I could do."

He felt bad knowing how awful it must be starting a new job and having to layoff employees. The local newspaper had done a damaging story about the greedy executives at Sunset who had taken their eyes off the ball, causing sales to plummet. A Wall Street Journal article had referenced the possible class action lawsuit in New York. Thank goodness the company had been able to keep the overtime issue from the press.

"Will I see you tonight, sweetheart? You know I can't stand to be away from you," Eric said.

He detected in her voice that something was wrong. She sounded vague and preoccupied. She wasn't focusing on the conversation. Her mind was a million miles away. It was obvious by her delayed response.

"Eric, I need to take a rain check. I didn't sleep a wink last night. I'm exhausted. Do you mind?" Tracy asked, hoping for some empathy from him.

Eric wanted to say yes he did mind. He wanted to go to her and kiss away all the pain. He didn't know how to comfort her since she still was legally married to Stephen. He wondered if Stephen had a mistress. Maybe Stephen wanted out too. He doubted that. Stephen had a good thing going, a younger wife who was both gorgeous and talented.

"Tracy, I hope we didn't keep you out too late after the concert and with dinner and all. I remember you commented that you couldn't stay out too late."

"Late last night I got a call from Stephen," she hesitantly said.

His heart skipped several beats. Stephen wanted to make amends. He wanted to atone for his mistakes. After all the pain he'd inflicted on his wife, he wanted a second chance. It was all a ploy to lure her back. It wouldn't last. It was nothing more than a cunning plan to entice Tracy, for eventually he'd leave her high and dry.

"What did Stephen say?"

"I told him I would meet him in New York next Friday for dinner." Tracy said, sorry she had ever mentioned her conversation with Stephen.

"Do you think that's wise?" Eric asked, sounding annoyed that she would even entertain the idea.

"Eric ... Stephen and I need to talk. It's best that we have that conversation now. It will be easier for me to fly to New York at the end of the week instead of flying back to California. Next week will be our busiest time, and I can't afford to be away. The following week I need to be here for the employees, our senior leaders and the executives."

"Will you be spending the night in New York?"

What he wanted to know was whether or not she would be sleeping in the same bed with Stephen. If that occurred, he might as well forget having a life with Tracy.

"That all depends on Stephen," Tracy said, realizing the moment she said it, Eric would assume she was hoping for a reunion.

"Should I be pissed, annoyed, or hurt by that statement? Do you want a reconciliation with Stephen?" he asked, now doubting himself. He was so unsure of himself or where he stood with her.

"Don't be so worried. If the shoe were on the other foot, wouldn't you want your spouse to tell you face-to-face and not send you an email?"

"What does that have to do with spending the night in New York?" Eric asked, quite annoyed with her unassuming response.

"If the conversation takes longer than I anticipate, I may not be able to get on Delta's last flight to Miami. I can't leave the office until early Friday afternoon. I won't be able to meet with Stephen until around seven on Friday evening."

She wished there was something she could do or say to alleviate his fears. She didn't want to hurt Eric or make him suffer. She wanted to be with him and not Stephen. The meeting would be a formality. She had to face Stephen and let him know that physically and emotionally she was already gone.

"Do you need me to come with you? I could rearrange some patients. I try not to do any surgeries after two on Fridays. I could be there for moral support."

"That's very nice and considerate of you. It's not fair to have you hanging in the wings. This is something I need to resolve."

"I don't want to lose you, Tracy, to Stephen's last-minute charms."

"You're not going to lose me, unless you tell me good-bye."

"Well, that's not going to happen."

"Trust me, Eric, you have nothing to be afraid of. After I see Stephen, my attorney can draw up the divorce papers."

He didn't have the same confidence level as Tracy. Men didn't like to lose. Stephen would take one look at her and know that she was in love or at least cared more for someone else. That's when he would turn up the heat and beg for forgiveness. Everything would be fair game. She might not be astute enough to see beyond the smoke screen.

"What if Stephen changes his mind after he sees you? What if he won't let you go?" Eric asked, in a panic.

"This isn't the dark ages, and we're talking about a divorce in California. That's one state that doesn't play when it comes to a legal decree to dissolve a marriage. It's not Stephen's choice. It's my decision. You don't think one dinner and a hour conversation will make me forget how I've been treated since the death of my parents? One hour can't make up for years of loneliness and isolation."

"I'm so sorry to be like this, Tracy. You have so much on your plate, and I know you're under tremendous pressure. I just want this to be over."

"We'll be able to put this behind us once I return from New York. I'm only going to be there a couple of hours, with any luck. How much damage do you think can happen in that short amount of time?"

He dropped the subject of Stephen. If he pushed any harder, Tracy might think he was obsessed. He didn't want to be preoccupied or consumed with Stephen and his reaction to their pending divorce. He had to trust Tracy to do what she thought was right. If only he could accompany her to New York. She'd have a shoulder to cry on … someone for moral support. Even if she got her way, there were still many dark days ahead of her.

He had to think quickly. He had to spend as much time as possible with Tracy before she sailed off to the Big Apple. He wanted to be the only pleasant thought on her mind when the plane landed in New York. He wanted to be the one she came running back to. Tonight was out of the question, but tomorrow held possibilities.

"Tracy, I want you to get your beauty sleep tonight. Would you like to go sailing tomorrow? I have a buddy with a boat, and he'd love to have us join him. We could sail over to the Bahamas for dinner."

"That sounds like fun but maybe another time. I'd like to spend a quiet, peaceful, weekend with you. Just the two of us."

"Sounds great to me. What time shall I pick you up?" Eric asked.

"Aren't you going to share your plans with me? Don't I have a say in what we do?"

"OK, I'll let you select what we eat. What time shall I call for you?" he asked again.

"How about noon? I have some errands to do in the morning. You know the typical stuff ... picking up laundry, dry cleaning, groceries ... all that fun stuff."

"Do you want some company? I'm great at grocery shopping," he said, hoping she'd take him up on his offer.

"You just be here at noon, and we'll take it from there."

Eric said good-bye as he blew her a kiss through the phone. He felt a little better after talking with Tracy. She was right to suggest that he not travel with her to New York. Her nerves would be on edge, and she needed her space to sort things out. He would only be in the way. The waiting game would start soon enough.

Chapter 15

Tracy got up early Saturday morning. After showering she had coffee, cereal, and toast. She then read Judy's contract. As Leslie had said, the contract would end in May of next year if not renewed by the board. It was a standard legal contract, and with her training and background, she understood it. There was no need for Leslie to interpret or explain any of the provisions. She also reviewed Judy's compensation and performance measures for the year.

At nine o'clock she left the apartment to pick up her dry cleaning and to get some groceries from the Whole Foods store. Since cooking wasn't her thing, she bought pre-packaged and semi-prepared food. The whole foods market was great for that as well as its array of fresh vegetables, fruits, and organic food items.

After leaving the market, she stopped at Target to pick up some needed household items. She also wanted to check-out the layout of the store and speak with some of the employees who were assigned to work. This would give her an opportunity to provide feedback to Leslie on her recommendations, if any, that might be helpful when she joined the Target team.

She was back at the apartment in plenty of time to get ready for Eric. She dressed in white jeans with an orange Valentino halter-top and matching orange sandals. She put on gold hoop earrings and a Pandora bracelet she had made for her in California. She had on very little makeup, which allowed her natural beauty to shine through. Even in casual attire, she was striking.

She called Leslie to let her know she had reviewed Judy's compensation and contract. Leslie answered the phone pronto, which was definitely an indication that she was waiting for Charles to call.

"Hi, Tracy, what are you up to today?" Leslie asked, knowing it was her by the number that flashed on her mobile.

"Eric and I thought we'd just chill today. He's picking me up at noon. I've no idea where he's taking me. How was Tango's last night?"

"It was great. The place was packed. It's a great hideout. We all have to go back there one Friday night. The atmosphere is totally different and the crowd is a bit younger."

"Well, I think you may want to make it soon before you start your new job in Minnesota."

"Remember I still have about five weeks here in the big city. Now that Judy doesn't relish the idea of my staying beyond three weeks, I'll have plenty of idle time to bum around. This will be the first time I'll have absolutely no responsibilities or commitments. The biggest decision I'll have to make each day is what shall I eat and what novel shall I read."

"Sounds like loads of fun," Tracy said, envying her friend for not only leaving the divas behind, but the fact that she had signed on to work for a terrific company.

"Leslie, I reviewed Judy's contract and compensation. It's rather straightforward and standard. I got the gist of her perks and performance objectives. Thanks for the advice to be prepared should I have to talk with the board or with Zahn."

"With your legal background, you don't need any coaching or an interpretation of the documents. I didn't want you to get caught off guard," Leslie said.

"I've been so busy putting out fires that I haven't had an opportunity to fully delve into her compensation or the compensation of the executives. Hopefully, I'll see her tomorrow afternoon."

She said good-bye to Leslie as her doorbell rang; realizing that Eric was slightly ahead of schedule, she glanced around the apartment making sure things were neat and not in disarray. She rushed to the door expecting to see him. Instead it was a delivery of yellow roses from him with a card that read, "You are the sunshine of my life, you're the gateway to my future, and you're the one for me." Tracy smiled as she took the roses and gave the guy who delivered them a generous tip. Eric was so thoughtful. He was both charming and a man with impeccable character and taste. He had shown her more love in a couple of weeks than Stephen had given her in the past two years.

The next time the doorbell rang Eric was standing in the archway. He looked relaxed and much younger than his forty-plus years, wearing blue jeans with a white blazer and polo shirt. He wore black suede loafers with the Gucci insignia. The moment he saw her, Eric threw his arms around her waist and pulled her close. He gave Tracy a kiss on her lips, taking her hand as she led him into the apartment.

"So this is where you spend your nights. Tucked away in this cozy spot," he said, glancing at her living quarters.

The place was nicely furnished, but he was sure it didn't meet her expectations. He was certain that her home in California was designed and furnished by some of the top designers in the area, if not the country.

Tracy offered him fresh juice from the Whole Foods store and a danish. He accepted the danish since he was famished. He hadn't eaten all morning. He was too busy making the arrangements for their afternoon excursion. He kept his fingers crossed that Tracy wouldn't be bored or preoccupied with next week's events. Even though he hadn't asked her directly, he could tell by her behavior that was the week Sunset would have one of its darkest moments.

He took her to Bayside Artists' Square where they walked and admired the work of local artists. They walked hand in hand as they talked and kissed periodically like two newlyweds. After purchasing some local artists' pieces, they walked around Bayside Marketplace where they browsed in stores, ending up at Waterfront Bar & Grill where they enjoyed tropical drinks.

Eric took the artwork to his car as Tracy made herself comfortable. While waiting for him to return, she ordered coconut shrimp, fried conch, which the waiter recommended, and oysters on the half shell. Tracy didn't think she would venture out and try the conch, but thought Eric might.

It was a perfect day. The temperature was in the low eighties with a perfectly clear blue sky. When Eric returned, he kissed her on her neck, sending fire below her waist. She wanted him as much as he needed her, but they didn't want to muddy the waters since she wasn't a free woman.

"There you are. I hope the art wasn't too heavy," Tracy said, not knowing what to say from the fire that burned within, so making friendly conversation instead was much easier.

"It wasn't bad at all. I think you got some great pieces. Better get them now before these artists become famous."

"Eric, I ordered some appetizers. I chose oysters, coconut shrimp, and conch. I'm not sure what conch is, but the waiter said it's a favorite here."

"Conch is one of the native dishes of the islanders. It's a tropical marine mollusk with a spiral hard shell. The shell is often blown like a trumpet to produce a native sound. Conch is served fried, baked, broiled, stewed, and I'm sure many other ways," Eric said, as he seated himself along side her.

"I ordered it fried," she said, now wondering if she'd made the best selection.

"Great choice, I personally think that fried conch is best served with limes and hot sauce."

The waiter returned shortly with the platter of goodies, along with fried sweet potatoes and fried onion rings. The waiter replenished their drinks. A band was assembling on stage after a short break. They played calypso music with a pleasant melodic sound. People were already on the dance floor moving and swaying to the beat.

"Shall we?" Eric asked, as he got up from his seat.

"I would love it," Tracy responded, thankful she'd worn her sandals and not her stilettos.

"You're definitely in step with the music. Where did you learn those moves?" Eric asked.

"Aside from taking various forms of dance while in school; I also took salsa, merengue, rumba and tango classes at By Your Side Dance Studio in California. There was a small group of us who met on Thursday evenings. It was tons of fun. We had a blast!"

"Did you have a favorite dance in school?"

"I loved classical ballet. It requires such concentration and focus. I learned self-control and balance. It's such a competitive dance. You should see the beauty queen moms trying to relive their lives through their kids. My mother wasn't like them. She always told me to dance as long as I loved it. She said when the fun dies, move on."

"Did the fun ever die?" he asked.

"No, it didn't. I just moved on to other forms of dance. I think the level of concentration and the mental effort that's required helped me get through law school."

He looked at his watch and realized that it was almost time for their sunset air tour. He was so excited about the tour, he could barely contain himself. He hoped that Tracy would love it as well.

Eric wanted to make the most of their weekend. He was still apprehensive about her meeting Stephen in New York. He had only today and tomorrow to show her that he was the man of her dreams, and that a life with him would always be amazing. Once the week started, he had no idea if he'd be able to see her before she left for New York.

"My darling it's time for our fun-filled, thrill-of-a-lifetime adventure," he whispered into her ear.

"I thought seeing the local artists and enjoying Bayside was the icing on the cake."

"Not quite. Shall we go?" Eric asked, as he led the way.

"By all means," she said, taking a final sip of her drink.

Eric drove a short distance before he stopped the car and took her hand. By then she had figured out that they were going up in the air. The excitement in her eyes told the whole story. She was falling in love with Miami and more in love with Eric each day. He had taken her by surprise with his kindness and charm.

"Let's do it," Eric said, as he led her to the launching pad. "Have you ever taken an air tour, Tracy?"

He hoped her answer was no. He wanted to make memories with her with some first-time activities.

"This will be my first sunset air tour," Tracy said, as she took a deep breath to take it all in.

The pilot welcomed them aboard, explaining that they would be joining another couple for a memorable sightseeing tour over the Everglades, Biscayne Bay, and Fort Lauderdale. The pilot explained that the tour would take one hour, and each couple would enjoy a complimentary bottle of champagne.

The pilot repeated the information as the second couple arrived. Tracy only wished she and Eric were sharing the plane with Leslie and Charles. The pilot explained the safety features of the helicopter and each person's responsibility in case of an emergency landing. The other couple asked if they ever had to do an emergency landing. The pilot shook his head and said no, explaining that the helicopter was only one year old and well maintained. After the couples were buckled in, the tour guide entered the helicopter.

"Hello, everyone, I'm Jessica. I'll be your tour guide for this flight. After we are airborne, I'll be serving chilled champagne. For now, sit back and enjoy the flight."

Tracy was spellbound. She knew the flight would be an amazing experience. This was going to be much better than skydiving. As they took off from Miami, the rich shades of amber, yellow, and red illuminated the sky. The view was breathtaking. She squeezed Eric's hand as she looked into his eyes.

"This is just what I needed after the horrible week I've had. Thanks so much for taking time to make it so unforgettable."

He had scored big. The hour seemed to fly by. Just looking at Tracy and the excitement in her eyes brought joy to his heart. The view was spectacular. It was a jaw-dropping experience. They enjoyed champagne over the Everglades as each couple made a toast. The first toast was general, drinking to good health and prosperity. Eric made the second toast as the other couple raised their glasses.

"May Tracy, my girlfriend, choose me for a life of blissfulness. May we find the rainbow to perfect happiness."

"I'll toast to that," said the wife of the second couple.

Tracy was a little embarrassed with his toast. Eric had never publicly shared his feelings. This was also the first time he referred to her as his girlfriend, and she loved it. She was thankful that the chopper had soft lights that shielded her blushing face. She was blown away with the entire tour. As the helicopter was turning around in Fort Lauderdale, heading back to Miami, she reached over and told Eric that no one had ever shown her so much affection or given her so much attention. He leaned in and kissed her.

As they exited the chopper, Eric tipped the tour guide and said good-bye to the other couple who were on vacation from Europe. Before the couple left, they asked Eric for recommendations for other tours in Miami and a wonderful place they could have dinner. He thought about asking the other couple to join him and Tracy for dinner, but quickly changed his mind for fear of having to share her.

"Sweetheart, we have one more stop, and that's for dinner."

"That sounds wonderful," Tracy said. "After that champagne I think I need to get food into my system."

He drove to the famous Mai-Kai Polynesian Restaurant in Fort Lauderdale for dinner and a show. They had reservations for eight-thirty. Tracy looked at the outside of the restaurant in awe. It was a tropical oasis with gigantic tiki sculptures, waterfalls, and lagoons.

"Eric, my love, you've outdone yourself. I'll need Sunday to recuperate. I've enjoyed every minute of this wonderful excursion. What an awesome day this has been."

"Shall we go inside?" he asked, giving his keys to the valet service.

They were seated at a table center front. The waiter arrived with tropical drinks and explained the entrees for the evening. Tracy ordered shrimp pad thai, and Eric ordered teriyaki chicken. For appetizers, the chef who went from table to table welcoming everyone, sent samples of crab rangoon, egg rolls, and Mai Kai house shrimp to their table.

"Are you enjoying yourself, sweetheart?"

She reached over and planted a French kiss when he was least expecting it. "I'll never forget today or this evening. You've been wonderful, and that breathtaking tour at the dawn of sunset was indescribable."

Just when she assumed that things couldn't get any better, the lights went down and the Polynesian dancers graced the stage in their native costumes. They performed the wedding dance, fire knife dance, and other native dances. The audience was invited on stage to participate. Eric tried to encourage Tracy to participate, but she declined.

"My brave one, why don't you try your hand?" Tracy said, in jest.

"Next time. I'm having too much fun watching you. The excitement in your eyes reminds me of a child in the candy store. I can't wait to spend the holidays with you," he said, hoping she would reassure him that was indeed a possibility.

"You may not want me by then. I may be too dull for you … I'm only kidding," she said, after seeing the hurt look on his face.

"When you come back to me from New York, I'll never let you go. I'm hoping for a miracle. Losing you now would shatter my world. I'd be traumatized. You're the best thing that has ever happened to me."

"Don't tell me … Gladys Knight and the Pips … 1965," she said, trying to make light of what he said.

"Go ahead and make fun of my words. You'll live to regret those words. You'll see, I'm not going anywhere."

"Eric, I'm scared just like you. I didn't expect this to happen. I'm totally surprise that you or anyone could love me. When I accepted this job, I planned on escaping love forever. Frankly, I'd had enough of false promises and shattered dreams."

He put his finger over her lips. "We both had given up. I assumed that I'd be a lifetime bachelor. I'd laugh inwardly at my friends when they talked about love at first sight and love ever after. I assumed they were either on drugs or under the spell. How could they know so soon?"

"It does seem like the impossible thing has happened to us. I know what you mean. I practically laughed in Leslie's face last week when she told me Charles had not only proposed to her but she had accepted. I thought how utterly foolish. I had to eat my words and apologize to her."

He was totally surprised to hear that Charles and Leslie had plans to wed. "Didn't Leslie accept a position out of state with Target?" Eric asked, wondering how their long distance relationship would survive.

"Yes, she did, and I don't have a clue how they plan to coordinate their living arrangement. All I know is Leslie is extremely happy, and I wish her and Charles the very best."

She and Eric held hands in the car on the drive back to her place. It was approaching midnight when they returned to her apartment complex. It had been a thrilling and exciting evening filled with fun, laughter, and excitement. She didn't want it to end.

It was awkward not inviting Eric in. She wanted to with all her heart. The passion inside her wanted to experience intimacy with him at the next level. If she started there was no stopping. Her moral ethics came into play. She didn't want Eric to think she would have sex with him while technically wearing another man's ring. If they continued the relationship, she feared he would always think she was promiscuous.

Leslie called Tracy early Sunday morning to invite her and Eric to an early dinner at Capital Grille on Brickell Avenue. She knew that Tracy had a busy week ahead and felt getting out of the apartment for a couple of hours would do her good.

"Hi, Tracy, did I get you at a bad time?" Leslie asked, desperately hoping her friend was up to it.

"Not at all. I just got back from Starbucks. What's up?"

"I want you and Eric to be my guest for an early dinner at Capital Grille. The restaurant is trendy and will satisfy any palate with its huge selection of steaks, which they're know for, as well as seafood, and lamb."

"I'm available. I'm not sure Eric is free. What time are you looking at?" Tracy asked, wanting to make sure she had time to stop by the office.

"I thought we could have dinner around six and a round of drinks, at say five-thirty. That would get us all back home by eight-thirty or nine."

"I'll call Eric and check in with him, and then we can plan on meeting you and Charles there at around five-thirty. Will the reservations be in your name?" she asked, dying to tell Leslie about her fascinating day with Eric.

Before they hung up the phone, Tracy told Leslie how Eric had surprised her by taking her on a sunset air tour and following that up with Polynesian dancers. Leslie asked about the investigation she was having done on Eric and if she planned to call it off. Leslie had concerns about Tracy not telling Eric he was being investigated, especially since she was planning on sharing the report with him.

"I respect what you're doing, Tracy. I think we should all conduct background checks and have each other investigated. I feel you should either tell Eric upfront that you're having him investigated or keep it to yourself. What happens if the results aren't what you want to hear? Then what?"

She felt in her heart of hearts, Leslie was right, but her mind said press on and get the results from Bruce. Tracy didn't know what had gotten into her, but she was making a mess of everything. First, she ended the relationship with her spouse via a note, not even acknowledging why she left and how he could reach her. It was bad enough to leave, but to relocate to an entirely new state was questionable. Then, she hired a private investigator to see if Eric was gay. She knew she could never do what Leslie suggested and not tell him. Eric deserved to know what her intentions were and the results of Bruce's findings.

She couldn't worry about all that now. There were bigger fish to fry. She had to get through next week. The layoff needed to happen without a hitch. If Judy was leaving, that might affect her plans to go to New York on Friday. And on Saturday she had to meet with Bruce Lamarr to get his investigative report. Yesterday with Eric had been wonderful. He was so attentive to her every need. She was falling for him, and the flame was growing stronger each day.

She called Eric to extend Leslie's invitation. They made plans for him to pick her up at five. That would give her time to send some emails and swing by the office to talk with Judy. She could also make sure that the notification letters were ready to go and that each person on the list was accounted for.

She arrived at the office at one. Judy usually stopped by the office after church and spent about three hours catching up on paperwork. Sheila seldom came in during the weekend. Sheila preferred to work at home or stay an additional hour on Friday. Sheila also had very talented people who did the heavy lifting and understood her power and influence, so they always got the job done. Miami wasn't like New York, Los Angeles and other major cities, which had an abundance of companies with corporate offices. Most companies that did business in Miami maintained a regional office. That translated into fewer jobs for corporate employees than most major cities.

Sharon had left a number of messages in her inbox. It was obvious that she'd worked either Saturday or early Sunday morning. She was so dedicated to the company and to Tracy.

Sharon always wanted to stay ahead of job demands and priorities. Tracy made a mental note to have her record her overtime hours and to make sure she was on the calendar to talk about her career at Sunset. Sharon was far too smart to spend her career as an executive assistant.

She took the escalator to Judy's office. Her door was open, but there was an eerie silence. She didn't hear any voices or any noise. As Tracy entered she noticed that Judy was signing a letter.

"Hi, Judy," she said, somewhat surprising her.

"Hello, Tracy. I didn't hear you come in. Have a seat. I'll be with you in one moment."

Tracy tried not to seem so obvious, but reading the letter upside down she thought she saw the word resignation. She couldn't be sure. There were files strewn on the conference table, credenza, and on the floor. It looked as if Judy had been specifically searching for something.

As Judy turned the letter over, she focused her attention on Tracy. "What brings you here on a lovely day like today?"

Tracy wondered why Judy had asked such a strange question. With the event happening within three days, why wouldn't she be there?

"Honestly, I was hoping to catch you. We have some new developments, all positive, that I want to share with you."

Judy seemed to be thousands of miles away as Tracy shared the layout of the career outplacement center and how the center would function. Judy listened intently off and on, never asking any follow-up questions. Something was either about to happen or had already happened. It wasn't like Judy to not give her opinion and thoughts, especially when money was involved.

"Have we had any fallout from the overtime issue?" Judy asked, while looking through her desk files.

"No, it's been pretty quiet. I think our senior leaders and managers did a phenomenal job explaining how we got here and the corrective measures we've put in place to address the issue. I think a number of the assistants think we were quite generous with paying back wages for overtime hours. I'd only say this to you; I think they saw it as a special kind of bonus," Tracy said.

"I hadn't thought about that, but with the holidays around the corner, I can see how the additional funds would be well received," Judy said, continuing to search through her drawer.

She and Judy spoke for another five minutes before her phone rang and Tracy excused herself. It was the oddest conversation she'd had with Judy since she arrived at Sunset. Judy had gone through the motions quite mechanically. She didn't seem to really care about any of the particulars. She wasn't excited or interested that the center was up and running, that Tracy had resolved the issues with Nora or that the diversity analysis document had met the requirements.

Maybe there was some validity to what Leslie had shared. Maybe the board of directors had become disillusioned with the company's performance, and stepped up to the plate, fulfilling their legal obligation. John Bailey had made them all aware of their fiduciary duty and had shared articles of executives who were facing serious legal problems for breaking the law. Being on a board these days was work. No longer could board members just coast. Just like the executives, boards were charged with overseeing the activities of the company and making sure it adhered to corporate bylaws, local laws, federal laws, and state laws.

John made it clear to all board members that they must act in good faith and on behalf of shareholders, make overall policy decisions and provide their oversight. She surmised that some of the board members were rethinking their decision to serve another year. The job of serving on a board had become complicated. It was no easy task, given the number of companies that had recently folded and those who had entered into bankruptcy due to boards being asleep at the wheel.

Before Tracy left the office, she called her realtor, Linda Scott, letting her know she had signed the lease and would leave it with her assistant. Linda agreed to stop by the office on Monday to pickup the contract. Before hanging up, they finalized plans for Tracy to move into the condo the week following Thanksgiving.

CHAPTER 16

Eric was returning home from Starbucks when gate security called and informed him that he had a young lady there to see him. Without asking who it was, he gave clearance for the guard to let her in. What an unexpected surprise he thought. Never in a million years did he think Tracy would come to him. Maybe the previous night had finally opened up her heart. Maybe he shouldn't have doubted himself.

He replayed the excitement in her eyes as the helicopter flew over Biscayne Bay and how good she felt in his arms when they embraced. His adrenaline was flowing as he recalled Tracy trying to convince herself that her marriage was over. He could only hope that maybe Stephen would call to end their marriage or she would decide not to fly to New York on Friday. Whatever her reason, he was elated that she took the initiative to come to him.

He was disheartened and shocked when he opened the door and saw Priscilla standing there with outstretched arms. She completely took him by surprise. The last person he expected to see was Priscilla. Wasn't she able to read the writing on the wall? Hadn't she noticed that he wasn't as affectionate when she was last there? Why had she returned from New York so soon?

"Hi, Eric. You look surprise to see me babe," Priscilla said, planting a kiss on his lips.

She brushed past him with bagels and coffee in hand. Priscilla was talking a mile a minute as Eric was desperately trying to maintain his composure. She looked fabulous in a leather mini skirt, black knee high boots, and a fiery red cashmere sweater. She hadn't paid much attention to the startled look on Eric's face.

"You won't believe that crazy flight from New York, I was on. The plane had taxied out on to the runway when it was called back to the terminal because the bathroom door in the first class cabin wouldn't close. Of all the idiotic things to go wrong, who'd think a bathroom door would delay a flight. Have you ever heard of anything so ridiculous?" Priscilla asked, as she started to peel off her clothes.

As she walked up the steps, in only her bra and panties, Priscilla asked Eric to be a dear and turn on the shower. She was in her own world, unaware that her boyfriend was paying absolutely no attention to her.

He didn't appreciate her undressing in the entrance hall, leaving a trail of clothes as she went up the stairs. Although he wasn't a neat freak or obsessive, he saw no need in tossing your clothes on the floor, only to retrieve them later and put them in their proper place. In a couple of hours, he would be with Tracy, Charles and Leslie. The last thing he needed was to have to explain to Tracy, why she couldn't come home with him tonight.

"Priscilla, what happened to your modeling assignment in New York? I hadn't planned on seeing you this soon," he said, hoping that her modeling engagement hadn't been cancelled.

"Neiman Marcus needs a model for their spring line, so I'm the chosen one. The model the agency had booked came down with the flu. I decided to fill in for her, since it's hard to get a top model on such short notice. A long story short, we delayed shooting in New York until early Tuesday morning. I'm scheduled to leave tomorrow night on a nine-thirty flight," Priscilla said, dropping her underwear as she reached for his bathrobe.

Before he could get a word in edgewise, Priscilla was in the shower relaxing her head against the marble wall and lathering her body as the bathroom filled up with steam. He closed the door, and neatly laid her clothes and underwear on his chaise lounge. The day wasn't turning out like he'd hoped. He was looking forward to a peaceful Sunday afternoon, followed by a relaxing evening with Tracy and their friends. His mind was traveling in all directions, thinking about what he'd tell Priscilla when he left at four-thirty.

With the water running in the shower, he called his answering service and instructed them to page him at four. Once the call came in, he'd take it from there. Priscilla was accustomed to him having to leave to see patients in the hospital. He decided this would be one of those times.

Priscilla stepped out of the shower with a towel draped around her head and another one around her body. Even with no makeup, she was a beautiful girl. She let both towels fall hoping to entice him to partake of her body. He was stalling for time as he stepped out of his pants and left her standing in the center of his master bedroom without a stitch of clothing on. There was a time, early in their relationship, when he would have been awestruck by her incredible body, totally unable to keep his hands off.

"Hey," Priscilla said, "Don't I get a kiss and a proper hello?"

She was becoming annoyed. With the cold shoulder she got from him on her last visit, and his avoidance of her now, she knew something was up.

"Did I do something wrong? You're avoiding me and giving me the cold shoulder," Priscilla said, moving into the bathroom to face him directly.

"You've done nothing wrong my love. With all the surgeries I'm doing and the opening of our new facility, I haven't had time to do anything else but work. I feel bad that we'll not be able to spend time together this evening. I'm meeting with the designers at four, followed by a round of visits to Mount Sinai Medical Center and Aventura Hospital. I probably want return until after ten," he explained, as he quickly jumped into the shower.

Priscilla said, "whatever." She was young, but not stupid. She knew when love had died on the vine. She was too exhausted to argue with him. She was tired and needed sleep. The modeling assignment in New York paid in the six figures, but working 12 to 16 hours a day, left little time for sleep and for a personal life.

She picked up Eric's iPhone, and readily noticed that a certain number had been called numerous times. She wondered if that was his afternoon appointment. She pressed the number into her phone for safekeeping as she returned his cell back to its original position on top of the chest of drawers. Maybe she'd dial the number later that evening to see if a female voice answered. She had no idea what she'd say since Eric was a free agent to date whomever he pleased, and so was she.

She hopped into his bed pretending to be asleep as she heard him turning off the shower. She could feel his presence as he swiftly moved around the bedroom, spraying cologne and taking extra time to select the right outfit. She almost couldn't contain herself as the fragrance of his cologne and the sweet smell of his shaving lotion aroused her inner emotions. She didn't believe for one minute that Eric was meeting with the decorators or that he'd be visiting patients.

Eric was relieved she was asleep when he finished dressing. He quietly closed the bedroom door and went to his entertainment room to catch the second half of the basketball game he'd been watching earlier. Tonight after dinner, he'd let Priscilla know that it wasn't working out between them. He'd blame his crazy work schedule and her demanding travel schedule. He wanted to end the relationship amicably. They were two consenting adults who had entered into the relationship knowing there would be no commitments or at least that was his understanding of the arrangement.

Tracy returned home from the office and took a hot bath before Eric arrived to pick her up. She dressed in a knee-length floral sundress and wore tan Gucci sandals. The dress had a short, pleated matching jacket that would be perfect if the restaurant became chilly. She pulled her hair back and up in a soft twist. She could hardly wait to tell Leslie about her weird conversation with Judy. She saw Eric pull up and practically knocked him over getting out of the apartment door, before he even had time to ring the doorbell.

"Were you watching for me out of the window? I don't think I've ever seen you move so fast," Eric said, squeezing her hand. "You look divine."

"Thank you, sir. If I may say so, you look like one of those entertainers on the cover of People magazine. Let's see ... George Clooney," she said, kissing him on the cheek.

They had a wonderful evening, just the four of them. Charles and Leslie were constantly making goo-goo eyes at one another. She was sure interesting things were happening under the table between them. The sparkle in Leslie's eyes clearly showed her love for Charles. Tracy was wishing that if Judy were forced to resign, her successor would keep Leslie. It would make life so much easier for her and Charles. Leslie would be able to stay in Miami, and Charles wouldn't have to commute between two cities. She knew long-distance relationships were generally doomed from the start.

As promised, she was back in the apartment by nine-thirty. She read some emails, drafted a few letters and decided to finish the Danielle Steel novel she had started on the plane ride to Miami. If she felt like it later, she would look at one of Bette Davis' old black and white movies. Realizing next week would be long and taxing, she needed to make the best use of her quiet time.

CHAPTER 17

On Monday morning, as Tracy was leaving the parking lot to enter the building, she had a weird feeling that something wasn't quite right. Her gut told her that things were different. The place looked the same, but she felt strange for some reason. Within minutes of entering her office, she received a call from Elizabeth Carmichael telling her that Judy needed to see her. She hadn't even had an opportunity to open her briefcase.

Leslie was already seated at the conference table when she arrived. Judy got up from behind her desk and motioned for her to join them at the conference table. There was no small talk about how each one had spent the weekend. Judy looked stressed, as if she hadn't slept in days. Elizabeth entered the room with coffee and water for everyone. Judging from Elizabeth's face, she already knew whatever it was her boss was going to discuss with them.

"I might as well get to my reason for asking the two of you here this morning. After careful thought and consideration,

I've resigned my position as CEO and President," Judy said, slightly choking on her words.

She quickly regained her composure and looking more in control as she went on; "I need this conversation to stay in this room until the details of my departure can be worked out."

Leslie had been correct all the time. She had called it right. The board of directors had become disenchanted with Judy's and the company's performance. That assessment must have taken her completely by surprise. Leslie was the first to speak. There was clearly no love lost between those two. The damage and hurt which Judy had caused was quite visible. The emotional scar would probably not heal anytime soon.

"Should I work with you or the chairman of the board regarding your contract and the announcement to the organization?" Leslie asked, hoping to have as little contact as possible with her.

"I think working directly with Zahn will be fine."

Tracy was more personable. After all, she didn't have an axe to grind with Judy. Her concern with Judy was the preferential treatment she showed to those who were in her privileged group. Most CEOs, like Judy, had their quirks … idiosyncrasies that were usually unorthodox behaviors that somehow, they hadn't eliminated.

"Judy, I'm so sorry to hear this. I just started here, and I was looking forward to working with you and the executive team to continue to grow Sunset. What are your future plans?" Tracy asked, wondering if she'd planned that far in advance.

"Tracy, I think I'll take a month or so off and travel and just enjoy life. I've been working since I was eighteen years old. I worked all the way through school to avoid those costly student loans."

"What will you do after your travels are over?" Tracy asked, watching her carefully to see if her plans were solid.

"I haven't sorted this all out. I've two job offers to join other retail companies. One is in manufacturing and the other one specializes in women's apparel."

"That sounds exciting, Judy. Do you think you'll be able to leave hospitality and casual dining?" Tracy asked.

"I plan to explore all my options. I may even start my own consulting company."

Tracy wasn't convinced that Judy had two offers on the table. Being asked to resign probably came as a complete shock to her. Why would she leave Sunset and her buddies behind? What would happen to Sheila?

"Judy, will anyone else be affected by your resignation?" Tracy asked, not wanting to name specific executives.

"For now, I'm the only executive who's leaving. I'm leaving all of you in good hands. You're a strong team with excellent skills."

Leslie, who had been quietly sitting listening to Judy and Tracy, chimed in. "Has the board hired an executive to replace you?" The moment the words were out Leslie could tell by Judy's reaction that she'd phrased the sentence all wrong. To save face, Tracy spoke up. The last thing Tracy needed was for the lines of communication to shut down.

"Judy, how will the board be handling getting your position filled? Will they look internally or externally?"

Tracy could see that the veins in Judy's neck were starting to relax. Her tone wasn't as loud, and her aggression was toned down. She wasn't as confrontational and as forceful as she'd been in the past. Whether Leslie realized it, they needed Judy's full cooperation for a smooth transition.

There was much at stake. They were two days away from the layoff.

The media and stakeholders had to be told the news of her departure in a timely fashion. Tracy had to make sure the employees and the public saw Judy's departure as her decision. There was absolutely nothing to gain by rubbing one's face in the mud.

"The board has asked Zahn, John Bailey and the chairman of the compensation committee to lead the search for my successor," Judy said.

"Who will be in charge of the day-to-day operation of the company?" Tracy asked, hoping that the board wouldn't be stupid enough to put Sheila or Nora in charge.

"Zahn is going to run the company until they identify a CEO to take charge. I recommended that the company be run by Sheila, Nora, and Lauren until they found someone, but the board wasn't too keen on that idea."

Tracy had to respect Judy's honesty. She was thankful that the board had rejected that idea. That would have been a disaster. With the friction between Nora and Lauren, who would be jockeying for the CEO position, the struggle would bring about the demise of the company she was sure.

What the organization needed was a turnaround executive who could get Sunset back on track. Hopefully, there would be no affiliation with any of the internal folks. A new face with fresh ideas would help move the company forward again and recharge the batteries of the employees.

"Judy, should Leslie and I work directly with Zahn on both the internal and external announcements, which I'm assuming will be made after the layoff?" Tracy asked. She didn't want people to think that the CEO's resignation was a part of the overall reengineering effort.

Judy agreed that was an excellent recommendation. They talked about the mechanics of her resignation so there would be no hiccups. By the end of their conversation, Judy was in good spirits. And why shouldn't she be, considering the millions and millions of dollars she'd be leaving with? If she chose to, Judy could retire and buy an island somewhere. Leslie and Tracy were sworn to secrecy. The executive team would be told on Wednesday about her departure. With so many loose lips, that was the only way they could keep her resignation quiet.

The morning seemed to fly by. Tracy and Leslie talked briefly after leaving Judy's office. They were scheduled to meet with Zahn at ten. All of the documents would need to be ready for him to review. She needed to draft internal and external announcements for Zahn's approval. They didn't want to bring in the company's public relations vice president, until after the executives were notified.

Leslie and Tracy met Zahn in one of the conference rooms at ten. Judy wasn't present. Zahn was always businesslike and very professional. He was talkative but focused. He wasted absolutely no time getting things organized. He was a quick study and could multitask extremely well.

"Judy told me that she met with the two of you earlier this morning regarding her resignation," Zahn said, while fumbling through some papers.

Tracy spoke first. She wanted to make sure that Judy's resignation was handled professionally and wouldn't be communicated internally or externally until after the layoff.

"Judy did meet with us. She communicated that the executives would be told first and that communication is scheduled to happen Wednesday morning."

"That is correct. It's my opinion that it will be best to separate her resignation from the layoff. However, I feel the media will link the two … cause and effect relationship; we'll never be able to control the press. It's critical that you and Leslie keep all of this under wraps."

Leslie spoke next, handing Zahn a copy of Judy's contract as she pointed out the specific areas he needed to pay close attention to.

"I've calculated all the numbers, and you have that worksheet at the back of her contract. All of her stock will vest immediately, including the equity piece. Her contract calls for three years of her base salary to be paid out in a lump sum amount. The company will pay her health benefits for a three-year period. She will have the option of purchasing her company car."

"Good work, Leslie, in such a short period of time. I'll review these documents and get back to you later this afternoon," Zahn said, placing the package in his briefcase.

"Tracy, I understand you have the internal and external communication letters for me to review."

"They're here. I've drafted letters to the media, franchisees, and employees. I have those for your review. I've also attached a timetable for each communication," Tracy said, as she slid closer to Zahn, explaining each document.

Zahn closed his briefcase after placing the letters and communication schedule inside.

"I want to thank you both for getting all of this information ready for me to review. I realize that your plates are full with the layoff that's scheduled for Wednesday morning. How is that coming? Are we ready?"

It was obvious that Judy hadn't kept Zahn in the loop. Tracy updated him on the reengineering process and invited him to drop by the career outplacement center later if his schedule permitted.

Before leaving, Zahn took a few minutes to let Tracy and Leslie know that he was looking forward to working with them. He shared that the board had three candidates they were talking to and would be making an offer to one of the candidates by the end of the week. Zahn communicated he would get their profiles to Tracy, who would be responsible for explaining executive compensation and perks to each candidate. If all went well, the individual would be on board within four to six weeks.

After Zahn left, Leslie and Tracy collected their things and left without saying a word. It was as if they felt the room was bugged. Outside the conference room, she asked Leslie to join her on the first floor. It was the quietest ride the two had ever taken together in the elevator. Neither one said a word. Once in the conference room, Leslie spoke first.

"Wow, I had no idea that this was in the works," realizing that Zahn had probably shared too much.

"Judy gave us the impression it was her decision, and that she'd just decided to leave. After meeting with Zahn, it's obvious she's being forced out," Tracy said, still in a state of shock and disbelief.

"These situations are always tricky. No matter how we alter the language, the press, our employees, and the franchisees will figure out that the decision wasn't hers when the new guy shows up," Leslie said.

"Leslie, there's a silver lining here. First, the job isn't going to an internal candidate, which means that Sheila will probably exit the organization soon. Second, the new guy will probably want you to rescind your resignation letter."

"I'm not sure I want to do that. I know I've Charles to consider, but I still remember the words of The Wall Street Journal article. That might get too complicated."

"That article refers to the current CEO remaining in place. The landscape changes when the old regime leaves. When the new executive takes the helm as CEO, one of two things will happen; One scenario is that the new CEO will ask all or some of the executives to resign in order to bring in new people or individuals he or she has previously worked with. The other scenario is that the new CEO will keep all the executives in position until he or she has time to assess their skills and personal chemistry."

It was never easy for a new guy to take the helm. There was always an adjustment period, just like there was in any type of union or relationship between two people. Not knowing the profiles and backgrounds of the three candidates, it was hard to say what his or her style might be. Tracy was hoping she wouldn't end up with a shit-head … a leader who saw little value in employees. Once she got her hands on those profiles, she could start snooping around to see what she could uncover.

Don would be of tremendous help to her in that regard. He knew the industry and players well. With all of his contacts, he could get the score on any executive or senior leader. Don entered the conference room just as Leslie was dashing out the door for a board meeting in Fort Lauderdale.

"Hello and good-bye," she said, all in the same breath.

Tracy told Don all that Zahn had shared. He wasn't a bit surprised by the news of the CEO's soon-to-be departure. Boards didn't like problems. With the possible class action lawsuit and Judy not meeting her performance objectives, they'd become disillusioned. John Bailey had enlightened them on their responsibility to both the shareholders and stakeholders. It was just a matter of time before turmoil set in.

Tracy shared the letters she had given to Zahn. Don suggested a couple of minor changes that would make them read and flow better. He advised her on how to address Nora and Lauren once the news broke of Judy's resignation.

"You don't need to worry about Sheila. She already knows Judy's fate. You can expect her to leave the organization soon. It seems like Zahn will be a good person to work with during the interim. When do you get the profiles?" Don asked, hoping to shed some light on the candidates' leadership styles.

"Zahn plans to share those with me this afternoon. Maybe I'll recognize one of the candidates," she said, anticipating the changes that would need to be made.

Don was always straightforward with her. He had a good business head on his shoulders and was quite insightful. He called the shots as he saw them. He didn't waste time fabricating the truth or dealing with hidden agendas.

"Tracy, if the board has three candidates in the hopper, you can be assured it's already out there in the industry that the CEO will be leaving the organization. It's just a matter of time before someone in this organization finds out. You probably have about a week or so to keep this news contained."

"I can't wait to see Nora's and Lauren's faces. They'll be pissed that they aren't on the short list for consideration for Judy's job."

Don told Tracy that she needed to give the board more credit. They were planning to replace Judy all the time. The best thing for Judy to do now was to leave on the day her staff was notified. After they were all told the news of her departure, she would merely be in the way.

As promised, Zahn dropped by the office a little after four. He dropped off Judy's contract to Leslie with some minor revisions and then went to Tracy's office with his changes to the letters, along with the three profiles. Having him in the building raised a few eyebrows. Most of the employees saw it as a sign that the layoff would be happening soon. Very few employees had been able to focus on their jobs. Everywhere you went there were small groups of employees huddled together talking about the upcoming event.

Tracy walked Zahn to the lobby and watched as he drove away. She immediately proceeded to the first floor conference room. As usual Don was in there working away. He had just finished talking with his team about the big day. With the upcoming news of Judy's departure, he was happy that the layoff had been moved up. Tracy couldn't wait to share the profiles with him.

All three of the executives were well known in the hospitality industry. The board had tapped the current executive vice president of marketing at Pizza Hut, the chief operating officer at McDonald's for its US operations, and the president and chief operating officer at IHOP. All three were well qualified, were from the restaurant/hospitality industry, and had excellent restaurant experience.

With all of Don's connections, he was able to get concrete feedback within the hour. Brock had offices in all fifty states and in over forty countries. With the wide span of offices, there were consultants who had worked on projects at some point with each of the candidates. In business it was understood that in order to get the real scoop on a candidate, you would confidentially call your contacts—not the references the candidate provided.

The prognosis was good on all three of the candidates. Based on what Don was able to gather from his colleagues, the marketing guru from Pizza Hut had a proven track record of placing people first. People enjoyed working with him, because he wasn't afraid to roll up his sleeves and get down in the trenches. The marketing executive had won numerous awards for the clever and creative marketing ads at Pizza Hut that had led to consumers returning to the chain time and time again, thus increasing same store sales.

On Tuesday Don and his team met with Tracy and her team for three hours, double-checking to make sure all employees were accounted for and that all the details had been addressed. Sharon personally delivered envelopes to the executives and senior leaders, asking the senior leaders to be in the boardroom at seven in the morning on Wednesday. The executives were to report to the boardroom at six-thirty. No one was suspicious that anything else was happening. Only Tracy, Leslie, and Sheila knew of the big announcement that Judy would make, followed by Zahn's remarks.

The command and career outplacement centers were ready to go. At seven that evening, "Do Not Disturb" signs were placed on all conference room doors and a supply of tissue and bottled water placed inside. Security had been notified earlier that afternoon that employees weren't to be treated like criminals. No one needed to be escorted out of the building. Tracy was surprised to find Judy still in her office at eight o'clock. She was quietly sitting, staring into space. She didn't hear her knock on the door.

"Hi, Judy. May I come in?" Tracy asked, half expecting her to be polite and informal.

"By all means. What's up?" Judy asked, as if it were just another business day which had come to an end.

"How are you feeling about telling your team of your decision to leave the company? You and Sheila have grown this concept to what it is today," Tracy said, knowing the decision to call it quits was not hers.

"In business, Tracy, you need to know when to leave. It's time for someone else to continue what we have started. I think you have a bright future here. You've a solid background in human resources and a thorough understanding of the law, and you don't back down from an opportunity. You're exactly what Sunset needs at this time."

She and Judy talked for a short time about the meeting with the executives in the morning, followed by the meeting with the senior leaders. She told Judy it was critical for her to lead those discussions and to present a united front when introducing Zahn and talking about his role during the interim. Tracy saw no point in talking about the layoff. She was sure that was the last thing on Judy's mind.

"Judy, I think it would make sense for us to throw you a farewell party. This keeps you in control, and it's an excellent way for the employees to say their good-byes. We don't have to do anything elaborate. We can have caterers pull something together for Thursday in the lobby of this building."

"I'm not sure that makes a whole lot of sense. What would I say? It seems awkward to me," Judy said, hoping that Tracy would drop the subject.

After about twenty minutes, she had Judy convinced that it made perfect sense to have a farewell party. Arrangements would be made for employees to drop in between three and five in the afternoon. There would be soft background music, lit candles, appetizers and cake for all. Because of the timing of the farewell event, Tracy thought she and and her staff could fill in and help the caterers in order to deliver a wonderful celebratory affair.

She knew Judy had agreed to the party after realizing the board would be announcing her replacement by the end of the week. Tracy told Judy that she planned to be in the building until nine in case she needed anything.

Before retiring for the evening, she called Leslie to get the name of a caterer. Leslie suggested Rubio's Restaurant, which was located two blocks over from the corporate office. Leslie offered to call the owner whom she personally knew.

"I'm so glad you called me. I think that's a super idea. We need to trade all those negative vibes for some positive ones. I agree, the employees need an opportunity to say good-bye to Judy. Mark, the owner of Rubio's, will take care of everything, including the cake," Leslie said, as she made some notes of what needed to be done.

Tracy told Leslie to order twenty stand-up bar tables so employees would have a place to put their drinks while they ate. Tracy wanted tablecloths on each table with a tall candle in the middle of a centerpiece of fresh flowers.

"Leslie, we need to present a gift to Judy. What do you recommend? I think it would be awkward not to have something from the company and its employees," Tracy said, hoping that Leslie would have some suggestions.

"That's a tough one … let's see … how about a crystal vase from Tiffany?"

"I think that is a fabulous idea. Do you have a contact there and do we have time to pull it off?"

"Tiffany does all of our employee service awards. I'll have our representative express the vase on Wednesday from their warehouse in California. In fact, I'll contact their office in California now. They are accustomed to working miracles."

Tracy couldn't believe her idea was so well received by Leslie and Judy after some coaxing. The bottom line was giving the CEO an opportunity to say good-bye. It would be terrible if Judy left the company without saying good-bye to the employees and senior leaders.

Early tomorrow morning, Tracy would coach Judy to say that she made the decision to leave Sunset some time ago, to pursue her dream of starting her own consulting company. That way, when the announcement was made at the end of the week regarding her successor, it would seem like Judy and the board worked hand-in-hand, more of a collaborative effort. Her departure would be more believable.

Tracy said good night to Don and his team communicating she'd be in the office tomorrow morning at 5 o'clock. On her way home, she phoned Eric to check in. He had ordered Chinese food and was waiting for it to be delivered. She wanted to see him but didn't have the energy. Her day had been most draining. Tomorrow would be even more hectic. With the layoff and the announcement concerning the CEO's resignation, employees wouldn't be able to concentrate. Productivity would be at its lowest.

"Hi, sweetie," Tracy said, as she pulled into the parking lot of the apartment complex. "How was your day?"

"Very lonesome since I haven't seen you in two days. The question is how are you surviving Tracy?" he asked, glad that Priscilla was back in New York on location.

"Barely," she said, hoping for a little sympathy.

"Any chance of me seeing you tonight?"

"Eric, I've got to be in the office tomorrow morning at five. It's going to be a short night. I'm afraid I wouldn't be much company tonight."

He didn't press Tracy. He knew without her saying a word that tomorrow was the day that some two thousand employees would lose their jobs. He felt bad for her. She had to deal with so much in her short time at Sunset. The company was in turmoil. What he didn't know was that it was about to get worse. Judy may not have been performing for the board, but in the eyes of most of the employees, she was their hero. She was the executive at the top looking out for them. Eric said good night and told Tracy to call him tomorrow.

Once inside the apartment, she ran the water for a long hot bath and poured herself a glass of red wine. She settled for a Weight Watcher's entree so as not to have to order dinner. The water felt good as she stepped into her bath. She just sat there for what seemed an eternity.

At eleven o'clock she turned off the lights as she thought about the day ahead. She didn't toss and turn. She slept soundly until two-thirty in the morning as her stomach started to turn. She got up, took some medicine, showered, and dressed for work. There was no use sitting home watching the clock or nursing her queasy stomach. Her nerves were definitely on edge.

Her cell phone rang at five while she was placing the packages in alphabetical order. All her field leaders and managers had synchronized their watches. At two in the afternoon all separated employees would have been spoken to. Corporate and the East Coast would be done by noon and the West Coast and Midwest by two. She assumed it was Don calling for information or regarding an issue that had recently developed. She was stunned. It wasn't Don, it was Zahn.

"Hi, Tracy. I didn't expect to get you this early. I was planning on leaving you a message. I'm in my car now. I didn't want to take a chance with the traffic from West Palm Beach to Miami. I should be there by six in plenty of time for the meeting with the executives."

"That sounds good, Zahn. I have everything ready to go. We'll meet with the senior leaders at seven, and the notification to employees is scheduled from eight to two."

"Is there anything that you need from me?" Zahn asked. "I emailed the additional corrections to you last night."

"I got your corrections, and they've already been incorporated. Zahn, we're having a farewell celebration for Judy tomorrow from three to five in the lobby," Tracy said, uncertain how he would feel about it.

"That's a great idea. I wish I'd thought of it. That will be a very nice and informal way for Judy to say good-bye. I'll invite all the other board members."

"Thanks, Zahn. I think it will be good if you made a short speech about all of the things Judy has been able to accomplish while at Sunset. That will be a great send-off and a perfect way to close. I'll try to get in touch with her spouse. Oh, Zahn, Tiffany is sending over a crystal vase as our farewell gift to Judy."

She was pleased that Zahn was in agreement that the celebration party was an excellent way to say thank you and best of luck from the Sunset team. It would be a defining moment for Judy, and with Zahn and all the other board members there, the employees will feel it was Judy's decision.

At six-thirty all the executives gathered in the boardroom. Many of the executives were shocked while others clearly read the writing on the wall. Judy delivered an eloquent speech. Zahn spoke next, reassuring everyone that Sunset would continue to prosper and grow.

The meeting with the senior leaders was a little more challenging. Most of them didn't have a clue. Zahn tried to reassure them that Sunset would continue to increase sales and grow. With their very limited contact with the board, you could see the fear in their eyes. Tracy stepped in to ease the stress of a difficult time by focusing on what Judy planned to do after leaving Sunset. Judy chimed in and told everyone that she still had stock in the company and was looking for them to do great things.

Tracy invited everyone to Judy's celebration on Thursday and asked that they not mention the party or Judy's resignation until after two o'clock when all of the discussions would have taken place. She was planning on sending the official announcement out shorty after two in the afternoon. With the executives and senior leaders in the room, she refocused them on the task at hand that would begin at eight.

There were no hiccups in the layoff process, although there were many teary-eyed employees. The consultants reassured the separated employees that they would be there to help them in their job search. Shortly after two o'clock each manager met with his or her team to answer questions and to let the employees know that Sunset would be stronger than ever.

The services of the nurse on call weren't needed, which was definitely a good sign. There were consultants stationed at the career outplacement center, but only ten of the separated employees decided to show up. It was understandable. There was a lot of information for them to digest and process. Tomorrow would be a better day.

At two-thirty, like clockwork, the announcements went out notifying employees, franchisees, shareholders, and the media that Judy had tendered her resignation. The press release talked about all of Judy's accomplishments and her desire to take some time off before starting her own consulting company. Because she was so well respected in the community, the press release invited friends and colleagues to her farewell celebration scheduled for Thursday afternoon. Leslie took the initiative and called the restaurant to order extra food and champagne. She felt a champagne toast to Judy's continued success was in order. Tracy couldn't agree with her more.

The company was buzzing with chitchat all afternoon. Judy chose to leave the office after speaking with the senior leaders. Her final appearance would be at the farewell celebration. What a day it had been. To say the employees were in shock with Judy's resignation would be an understatement. It was as if they were traumatized. Their faces were solemn. One would have thought someone had died. Tracy was so glad she had planned the farewell celebration. That would help employees accept the change and move on. Only time would tell the long-term effects of the CEO's departure.

Tracy was exhausted, tired to the core. She took two Tylenol tablets to ease a headache that was pounding at her temples. There were still many loose ends she had to tie up.

Eric heard the news about Sunset shortly after six. Now he clearly understood why Tracy had limited time to spend with him. She was coordinating a massive layoff and the resignation of the top executive. What an awful time it must be for her, he thought; to walk into a demanding job, having to do so much heavy lifting. He just couldn't imagine how Tracy was able to function so well given the level of stress and anxiety she had to endure.

She and Don met for drinks and dinner at Chocolates. She was physically exhausted. Between having to comfort the executives and employees, and meet the needs of the board, she was drained of all her energy. She wanted to talk to someone not affiliated with the company. Someone she could trust. Someone who didn't have an axe to grind, that person was Don.

"You did it, my friend. You and the company came out relatively untouched by the media. I know it's too soon in the process, but I think you guys will be OK. The board has the option of turning this situation around by bringing in a high-powered executive who can clean house, weeding out all the bad blood," Don said.

"My friend … we did it. Without you and your team, I would have faltered. This was a monumental task with an unrealistic timetable. This company was operating in the twilight zone. All I can say is thank you for all you have done for my career to make me successful through the years."

It was a lovely evening. She kicked back and enjoyed the moment. Don was always good for her. He was in control and handled stress extremely well. He wasn't judgmental and he shared the credit with others. What she needed was a couple of days off. With the state of things at Sunset, that probably wouldn't happen for some time. They departed the restaurant at about ten-thirty. She felt much better about the day's events. Tomorrow morning she would start her day at the career out-placement center. She wanted to be there to support Don and the employees whose careers had ended on Wednesday.

She knew all too well how the mind could play tricks on the body. If at any time the employees felt they had no way out, they might resort to some unorthodox behavior. She wanted to make sure they understood their severance package and had total support during their job search.

Don had promised the employees that the consultants would be there to help them develop their resumes, so they'd be able to start applying for jobs by the first of next week, as well as attending workshops to improve their interviewing skills.

At midnight Tracy found herself staring at the ceiling in her apartment. She couldn't sleep. She hadn't checked in with Eric but knew he understood. All the news channels had carried the story about Judy and the number of employees who had lost their jobs.

The media portrayed the story completely different. The headlines read, "CEO is forced out after major shakeup at Sun-set." In very small print at the end of an article by the local newspaper, there was a line that alluded to the farewell cel-ebration for Judy.

She phoned Eric at seven in the morning on Thursday as she was leaving the apartment. She was hoping to get his voice-mail. She was dead tired, drained, burned out, you name it, she felt it.

"Tracy, are you OK? I've been trying to get a hold of you. I had no idea that your CEO was going to resign," Eric said, wanting to know that she'd come through the storm with few bruises.

"Hi, Eric. I'm so sorry I didn't call you. After all of the events of the day, including the CEO's resignation, I was burned-out. Don and I went to dinner, and at about eleven we called it a night," she said, realizing that it may have sounded as if there was some attraction to her colleague.

Eric was still somewhat jealous of Don. He wanted to be the one to comfort her. He wanted to be there for her. He resented how Don consumed so much of her time. If only Don could disappear without a trace, he might have a chance to convince Tracy to walk away from all those things that reminded her of the past.

"Will I see you before your trip to New York?" Eric asked.

If he didn't have an opportunity to see her before she left Miami, he feared that Stephen would win and she would pack up and return to California. She now had the perfect out with the CEO's resignation and a new guy soon to be recruited to run the company. She could graciously step down, so the new CEO could bring a human resources executive on board he was comfortable with. Boards always gave the top executive the option of cleaning house.

"I'll try to manage that, sweetie. This afternoon I've the farewell celebration for Judy. This was planned at the last minute, so there are a number of details to attend to. I also have to be there for our internal employees and our senior leaders. Because we'll need to replace Judy fairly soon, I'm working closely with the board to make that happen. The chairman of the board will be stepping in until the executive is named."

Eric hung up the phone not feeling comfortable with their arrangement. He had to find a way to see her even if it meant camping out on her doorstep. He wasn't going to let Stephen win back her heart. He was running out of time and out of options. Tracy was leaving Friday afternoon. The only thing that would stop her was if a problem developed during the transition period at Sunset.

She drove directly to the career outplacement center. Only about half of the employees were there. It was still early. She spoke to all the employees who were present, reassuring them that everything would be okay. Tracy called the field leaders on the East Coast as she was driving to her office to check in and see how things were going in the field. All was quiet and calm. It was still very early on the West Coast and in the Midwest. If any of the terminated employees didn't reach out to a counselor or consultant within a day or two, one of the counselors would call and follow up with the individual.

Once in her office, she was putting out fires right and left. She had to coach the senior leaders since they were the faces of Sunset. Now wasn't the time for them to focus on selfish motives. Their primary job was to be there for the employees. She was thankful Lauren hadn't attempted to tie up all of her time. She was very cordial and professional with Lauren, letting her know that they'd talk when things calmed down.

She checked in with Leslie and Sharon to make sure everything was organized and on schedule for the celebration. The tables had been delivered, and there were fresh linen, candles, and pink roses on each table. In the center of the lobby was a mega, personalized photo cake of Judy imprinted with the message, "We Had the Ride of Our Lives." How thoughtful, she thought, wondering how Leslie ever pulled that off.

The caterers were using the large conference room on the first floor to house their equipment. She met Mark, the owner of Rubio's Restaurant, who was a fairly young man in his early thirties. Mark's youth didn't stop him from demanding and getting results. Mark was instructing the crew where to set up the tables and where to store the food. Portable refrigerators had been pushed up against the back wall.

There were many cases of wine and champagne with a flowing chocolate fountain. Seeing the setup, it looked like the party had been in the works for months. Tracy found Leslie out front telling the jazz ensemble where to set up. Leslie motioned her over, telling her that Tiffany had sent the crystal vase in their signature aqua blue box with the white ribbon. The printing company had printed a huge card that all the employees were signing for the three o'clock celebration.

She leaned over and told Leslie, "You are a genius. I can't imagine how you got a jazz ensemble on such short notice."

"This is all coming out of your budget my dear. I guess I failed to share that piece of information with you. Didn't anyone ever tell you that money talks? Before you leave Tracy, there's one thing you can do for me."

"Anything. You just name it," she said, looking around the lobby admiring the set-up.

"Call Sam Mason in IT and tell him to double-check that the mike is working. I'd hate to encounter technical problems in the middle of Judy's or Zahn's speech."

She agreed to call Sam who was there in a flash. As the employees came and went during lunch, they commented that the setup for the celebration was fit for a queen. That was exactly what she wanted to hear.

Tracy checked a final time at two in the afternoon to make sure everything was perfect. The lobby had been transformed into a magical wonderland. Waiters were dressed in black pants with white jackets. There was a huge ice sculpture on the end table, surrounded by a tropical flower arrangement. The jazz orchestra softly play contemporary music in the background; so conversations wouldn't be drowned out by the music.

At two forty-five Leslie took the board members and special guests to the lobby for the celebration. They needed to be in place before Judy arrived. Employees entered at three and at three-fifteen, Tracy escorted Judy and Zahn to the main lobby. The employees felt like royalty as the waiters walked around with appetizers and chilled wine. There was a steady stream of employees saying their good-byes to Judy and chatting among themselves. At four-thirty the formal presentation started. Tracy said the opening remarks and then turned it over to Judy. Judy was once again eloquent in her speech and with her farewell remarks.

When Zahn took the mike, there wasn't a dry eye in the place. He was a good sport acknowledging how difficult it was to say good-bye to part of the family. As champagne was delivered to each person, Zahn made the official toast to Judy, "a remarkable president and CEO."

After the toast, Zahn asked John Bailey to join him as the gift was presented to Judy, along with the gigantic card the employees had signed. Cake was then served to everyone. People lingered until about six o'clock. The caterers had done an outstanding job, continuing with appetizers until no one could eat another bite.

Tracy didn't leave until Judy and all the special guests had departed. Don was by her side, complimenting her on a well-orchestrated affair. She gave full credit to Leslie, who had remained in the background throughout the entire celebration.

"Hudson, if you ever get sick of your day job, you can always start a special corporate events service," Don said, while finishing his glass of wine.

"I don't think so. Besides, Leslie did all of this. She's so well connected. I think the employees believed that Judy's resignation was something she wanted."

"I think you're right. I was impressed with how well they accepted her resignation. The employees have been through a lot. This could have been the final nail in the coffin," Don said, looking around to see what else needed to be done.

Tracy said good-bye to Don who returned to the conference room to meet with one of his consultants. Tracy locked her office and headed for the parking lot at seven-fifteen. She knew there was still a lot of stuff to do. Tomorrow she would get an early start in order to make the afternoon flight to New York. She still needed to pack and tie up some loose ends in the office. Her cell started to ring as she unlocked the door of her car.

"Hello, this is Tracy," she said, hoping another crisis hadn't developed.

"Hi, Tracy. It's Bruce Lamarr. I want to confirm the time and place for our Saturday meeting. Are we still on to meet?" he asked.

She had completely blocked their meeting from her mind. She'd been so busy with Judy's resignation and the reengineering effort that she'd forgotten all about Bruce.

"Of course, Bruce. What time will you be arriving?" Tracy asked, realizing now she would really be pushing it if she stayed overnight in New York.

"I'll be driving over from Tampa. I should be in Miami around five or so," Bruce said, waiting to see if the time was convenient for her.

After Tracy said good-bye to Bruce, she just sat there in her car with the cell phone to her ear, looking out at the pavement. She was nervous to find out the truth. What if Eric dated both men and women? What if he were a womanizer? What if there was a dark secret in his past? She had to shake off these concerns. She and Eric weren't intimate lovers. She was not committed to him, at least not yet. Had she moved too fast with him? She hadn't filed for divorce yet. What if Stephen made her life hell? What if Stephen didn't want out? She didn't snap out of it until Don tapped the driver's window of her car.

"Are you OK, Hudson?" Don asked, watching her facial expression as she rolled down the window. "You look panic-stricken."

"Don, I'm OK. That was the detective. Bruce has the report on Eric. I'm not sure I want to hear it. What a week. I orchestrated, with your help, the layoff, worked with the board regarding the CEO's replacement, and within the next forty-eight hours; I'll ask Stephen for a divorce and find out the dirt on Eric. And may I add unbeknownst to him. What the hell am I doing?" she said, turning red in the face.

"Calm down and keep things in perspective. Don't get ahead of yourself. See what Stephen has to say before you read him the riot act. The same is true for the detective. You've had a rough week. You don't have to make any major decisions. There's nothing to resolve. Get the facts first and then decide your next course of action."

She wondered why she couldn't find someone like Don to love. He was kind, considerate, patient, and good-humored. He had wisdom beyond his years. He'd make an excellent companion. Don was leaving for Texas on Saturday to meet with some potential clients. Before their dialogue ended, he gave her the number to the hotel where he was staying. He knew she'd need a friend to talk with after her discussion with Stephen and consultation with the detective. He was certain that the facts wouldn't lead her to a conclusion.

She was in bed by ten. She was in desperate need of sleep. She took a melatonin tablet to help aid the sleeping process. She knew a sleeping pill would make her too groggy. She had to be alert and energized to get through the weekend.

She was tired when the alarm sounded at five. She forced herself out of bed and packed a small suitcase for an overnight stay should there be an unforeseen occurrence. Anything could happen flying to New York in November. After showering and dressing, she made herself a strong cup of coffee. She picked up her suitcase and purse and went to the hall closet to get her cashmere coat and gloves. She threw them on the backseat of the car and headed for the expressway. She was in the office by seven organizing her day.

Her calendar showed only two meetings, which were subject to change. When you worked in human resources, you were never in charge of your day. She was signing some letters that required her signature when the phone rang.

"Good morning, this is Tracy."

"Good morning, Tracy. This is Zahn. I wonder if you could meet me at the coffee shop next door at nine-thirty. I've a breakfast meeting at seven-thirty, which should be over by nine-fifteen or so. My meeting is only about five minutes from the coffee shop. Wait for me if I'm a few minutes late."

"Not a problem, Zahn. I'll be there."

When Zahn hung up, she immediately called Leslie who was in her car.

"Leslie Klein," she said, sipping on her morning coffee.

"Leslie, it's Tracy."

"Don't tell me you're already in the office," Leslie said sarcastically.

"OK, smart aleck. Remember it's the early bird that catches the worm."

"You can have it. What's up?" Leslie asked, hoping nothing unusual had developed since the farewell celebration.

"Zahn wants to meet me in about two hours at the coffee shop next door. What do you think he wants?" she asked, trying to probe her friend for answers.

"I haven't spoken to Zahn since the celebration last night, but if I were a betting person, I'd say the board is about to make an offer to one of the candidates. If that's the case, he'll need you to prepare the offer letter."

"I didn't think they were at that stage of the game. I thought we had a little more time," Tracy said, hoping beyond hope that she would still be able to make her flight to New York.

"Zahn isn't planning on taking his leisure time running this company. He's enjoying life too much to run operations for any company. I also think he doesn't want the responsibility that comes along with the title."

She walked next door to the coffee shop at nine-fifteen. She took a table in the back away from the crowd. Zahn walked in at exactly nine-thirty. She flagged him down, curious about what he had to say.

"Hi, Tracy. Thanks for coming. Can I get you something?" he asked, while fumbling in his briefcase for his notes.

"I ordered a cup of coffee. The waiter will be back in a minute," she said.

"We've made an offer to Gavin Reed. You may recall from the profiles that he's the marketing executive from Pizza Hut."

"That's wonderful. Gavin has a terrific background. I think he'll be great for Sunset. He was able to increase sales at Pizza Hut with those creative commercials and marketing ads. When will he start, Zahn?"

"Gavin hasn't accepted yet. He'd like to tour the area and spend some time with you regarding his compensation and perks," Zahn said, handing her the paper where he had scribbled his notes regarding the offer the board had made to Gavin.

"When will Gavin be in town?" she asked, praying that it wouldn't be during the upcoming weekend. She didn't need to add anything else to her schedule.

"He's going to fly in Saturday night and leave Monday morning. Gavin wants to do a quick tour of the area and talk with you about his compensation and the culture of the company. I thought he could meet with a realtor all day on Sunday and have dinner with you Sunday evening. He plans to return at the end of next week with his wife."

Tracy told Zahn she'd take care of all of the arrangements. Gavin could use the realtor she'd used, and they could have an early dinner or late dinner depending on his schedule. She told Zahn that she'd type the offer letter and send it over to him for review before she emailed it to Gavin. She was thankful she didn't have to meet with Gavin until Sunday evening. If he'd arrived a day earlier, he would have thrown off her plans. With her current plans, she could meet with Stephen tonight, Bruce on Saturday, and Gavin on Sunday.

To keep from encountering too many interruptions, she told Sharon to hold all her calls unless it was urgent or a board member trying to reach her, and to block her calendar in the system so no one could schedule a meeting.

At noon she emailed the offer letter to Zahn and left a message with his assistant to call or email her any changes. To be on the safe side, she mentioned to Zahn's assistant that she'd be leaving for New York after lunch, but would have her computer with her. If Zahn didn't have any revisions to the letter, she'd email it to Gavin before leaving for the airport.

She called Leslie after the letter was done, confirming that her analysis was right; the board had made an offer to Gavin Reed. She emailed Leslie a copy of the letter for her perusal and files. It was now just a matter of time before Sheila notified the board of her desire to leave. There was no way Sheila would allow her authority and power to be diminished.

The limousine service picked Tracy up in the lobby of Sunset shortly after lunch. She'd handled all of the emergencies and was taking in the scenery as the car drove her to the Miami International Airport. Traffic was cruising right along, so she was there in record time. After clearing security she purchased a sandwich and a cup of espresso from Starbucks. Upon arriving at her gate, she checked her emails to see if Zahn had sent her any messages. Zahn knew how to reach her or Leslie if he had any changes.

She phoned Sharon and asked her to change her reservation to a flight leaving LaGuardia Airport at seven in the morning on Saturday to be on the safe side. The change would give her ample time to relax before her meeting with Bruce. She could also swing by the office if Zahn needed to meet with her, since she had to pick up her car.

Sharon told her that she left for the airport at the perfect time. Almost all of the executives had stopped by her office to see her. Sharon supported them and answered their questions as best she could and insisted that they schedule some time on Tracy's calendar. She was grateful that Sharon had run interference.

The gate agent announced that the flight would be boarding within the next twenty minutes, and the flight was due to arrive in New York on time. Tracy thought she heard someone calling her name. The sound was faint and somewhat muffled. Perhaps she was hearing things. When she turned around in the direction of the sound, she saw Eric running to get to her with outstretched arms. He was totally out of breath.

"How did you find me?" Tracy asked, half believing he was there.

"I told Sharon who I was, even though she recognized my voice. She said I had just missed you, but if I called you on your cell, I might reach you before your Delta flight took off at three-thirty."

Thank you, Sharon, he quietly mumbled to himself. Eric gave Tracy a bunch of roses, which he knew she couldn't take on the plane. "These are for you my love. I'll keep them alive until you come back to me."

"Thank you, Eric. That's so very thoughtful of you. I'll only be gone overnight. I'll be in New York for less than twenty-four hours."

He and Tracy talked and held hands until the last passenger had boarded the plane. He gave her a kiss on the cheek and told her to return to him as soon as she could. The gate agent smiled at Tracy as she waved good-bye to Eric.

She slept the entire time on the plane. She didn't wake up until the plane had taxied into the New York terminal. She took a cab to the hotel where Stephen was staying and freshen up her makeup. She ordered tea to help settle her nerves. She wanted to be alert for their talk, which she wasn't looking forward to.

Stephen had called the front desk several times to see if she'd arrived. Each time he called, the response was the same; Ms. Hudson hasn't arrived.

Once she checked in, the front desk called to let Stephen know. With the jury trial taking weeks, he had become friends with the front desk and with the hotel concierge. They were on a first-name basis.

At seven-thirty in the evening, she called Stephen. She felt her heart was about to stop. Stephen answered the phone on the second ring. "Hi, Stephen, it's Trace," she said, feeling like she was talking to a total stranger. He was just as formal.

"Can we meet for dinner in the hotel restaurant? I made reservations for eight. They're expecting us," he said.

All she said was, "I'll see you at eight."

At five minutes to eight, she got her purse and closed the hotel door behind her, checking to make sure the room key was in her bag. Stephen was standing in the doorway of the restaurant waiting for her. He looked stunning in his navy Armani suit and leather loafers. He had grayed a little bit more; she was sure it was from the stress and strain of the trial.

"Hi, Trace. Did you have safe travels?" was all he could think to say. They had grown apart like two ships passing in the night.

The maitre'd' seated them next to the window in the far corner. He didn't hold back.

"Are you here to divorce me? Do you have the papers with you for me to sign? Is that your reason for flying here and not sleeping with me in my hotel room?" Stephen sounded off, not expecting any answers.

"Stephen, we need to talk. Since I came out of the coma after my parents' death, you haven't had two words to say to me. Do you blame me for living? I feel a part of us died the night of the accident," Tracy said, as tears started to fill her eyes.

"I'm so sorry, Trace. I was so wrong. When they told me you were in a coma and probably wouldn't survive, I felt sorry for myself and gave up."

"Did you still give up when I came out of the coma? I needed comfort when they told me my parents were dead. I couldn't grieve or say good-bye to them. They'd already been buried. After their death you were all I had Stephen, and you weren't there for me."

"Trace, don't blame me or throw us away. I know I don't deserve another chance, but we do. Our relationship should be able to weather this storm."

"It's not that easy, Stephen. I have gone on with my life. I live in a different world now."

She was shocked by what he said next. All this time she thought she had been so careful to not leave any traces of her whereabouts. He was the smart one. He'd tracked her down.

"Why would you leave town and not tell me?" Stephen asked. "I went home last weekend and saw the note. Some of the furniture was gone. When I called your office, I was told you no longer worked there. Your secretary told me all about your new life and job in Florida. How could you do that Trace? Didn't our marriage mean anything to you?" Stephen asked, as tears slowly fell onto the lapel of his suit jacket.

"I'm so very sorry that you had to find out like that. There is no excuse for my behavior. I wanted out, and when I was offered the job in Miami, I took it and ran."

"Give us a chance, Trace. I know I haven't been the best husband, the best companion, but I've learned from my mistakes. Please reconsider, darling."

"It's not that easy Stephen. I'm not the woman you married 10 years ago, and you're definitely not the person you were then. Time, distance, and silence drove a wedge between us; we don't even know each other now. We've nothing in common, the flame has burned out."

"Trace, don't do this. I love you. I want you. I desire you," was all he said.

At that moment he grabbed Tracy up from where she was sitting and held on tight. As she struggled to get free, he whispered in her ear that he was a changed man. She was his world, and he wanted her now more than ever.

When she was able to break free, there were tears in her eyes. If only time hadn't moved on. Tracy fought back tears as she relived all the pain and suffering he'd caused. She was young when they met, Stephen was the experienced one. The difference of twenty years was huge. Her mother had tried to warn her. He was a homebody. He was unadventurous. His idea of a good time was having dinner in a restaurant, reading a good book, reviewing cases, playing golf and occasionally cooking.

The last two weeks with Eric had given her hope for a better future. She'd had more fun with Eric than she had in ten years with Stephen. She felt sorry for him now. Why did he have renewed interest in their relationship? Why now? Too much time had passed. She wasn't the fool she once was. When Stephen broke her heart, the pieces no longer fit the puzzle. She knew her broken heart would never quite mend.

"Stephen, it's over. I'm so very sorry," Tracy said, walking swiftly away from his table.

She didn't stop, and she didn't look back. She returned to her room, got her overnight bag, called the front desk, and told them to email the bill to her office. She took the elevator to the lobby and walked out the front door of the hotel as the doorman hailed her a cab. She had no idea where she was going. Anywhere would be better than staying there with the possibility of running into Stephen again.

The fresh air felt good on her face as she cracked the window and told the taxi driver to take her to the airport hotel. If they didn't have any rooms, she would call around until she found one. If that didn't work, she was prepared to stay all night at the airport. She dialed information and asked for the number to the airport hotel. She was in luck; there were plenty of vacant rooms.

She didn't sleep well that night. She felt like a zombie when she got up to dress at five. She had no life in her and very little strength. When she got inside the airport terminal, she turned on her cell. There were several messages from Stephen asking her to reconsider and come back to him. After listening to half of the messages playing the same sad chorus over and over, she deleted the remaining ones. There were no messages from Zahn, which she was grateful for. That meant things were progressing nicely with Gavin.

When she checked her emails, there was one from Zahn. All was a go with the letter. He instructed her to email it to Gavin so he could review it before their dinner meeting on Sunday. She copied Leslie on the email from Zahn and attached a blind copy of the offer letter she'd emailed to Gavin.

She was back in her apartment by one on Saturday. What a night it had been. There was no way she would reconsider her marriage. She had given the best years of her life to Stephen.

He had discarded her and their love a long time ago. He'd rejected her, and now the scar would never fully heal.

Maybe marriage wasn't for her. Maybe she should give up on that institution. She stayed in the shower for over an hour just letting the water run down her body. She wasn't sure what she wanted. One thing she definitely didn't want was Stephen and his love.

She was no longer a caged bird. She would soon be free. She adored Eric, but maybe it was too soon to consummate a relationship with him. She didn't want to jump out of the frying pan into the fire. Maybe living by herself wouldn't be so bad. Sunset had grown on her. There was a lot to do with the new CEO probably starting by the end of the year. She wouldn't fight the new CEO if he wanted to bring in his own human resources executive.

Most CEOs had worked with people they trusted and would often take those executives with them once they accepted a new job. Tracy would often caution executives and senior leaders who followed their mentors to more than two companies. She felt at some point each leader needed to stand on his or her own two feet.

She ordered Chinese food at three. She wasn't meeting Bruce until after six. She was starving and knew she'd never survive the time on an empty stomach. She had no idea what Bruce had found out about Eric. Whatever the prognosis, she felt Eric needed to know she had him investigated. After all, what intelligent person would date today and not do a background check on the person?

Who was she fooling? Eric would either see it as an invasion of his privacy or be highly miffed that she hadn't mentioned it to him earlier. If he had nothing to hide, what difference would it make? … she thought, trying to reason and make a case for her actions. Maybe Leslie was right. Maybe she shouldn't tell Eric what she did if the report came back clean. What if he had two lives? How would she handle that? They hadn't had sexual intercourse, which meant she'd not cheated on Stephen with Eric.

What if Eric saw her as Ms. High and Mighty who used different standards in judging and evaluating people? Why was it OK for her, a soon-to-be divorced woman, to befriend and spend time with him, a single, unattached man? She had made a mess of things; fleeing from California to Florida, falling in love while married, and never telling Stephen that she had found comfort in the arms of married men. Whatever the prognosis of the investigation, she was determined to tell Eric the results.

CHAPTER 18

Bruce stood as Tracy approached the table. Even though she had others investigated, she never fully understood why anyone would want to pry into the lives of other people. It was tough enough just keeping up with one's own life. She recalled getting the report on Stephen. There were no bells and whistles. There was no one there to comfort her when she discovered a flaw in the character of the person she thought loved her. It was like waiting for the doctor to come out to the waiting room after a difficult surgery, and tell you everything would be OK. The fact of the matter was her life changed forever once she got the report on her spouse.

Bruce didn't have the image of a private investigator. He was six foot four with a slim build and hazel eyes. All of his suits and shirts were custom made. He had a very lucrative practice in California. He'd been hired by some of Hollywood's rich and famous people to get the exclusive story, to expose their intimate secrets, and to air their dirty laundry. The victims were usually clueless. How the information was used was out of Bruce's hands. He simply delivered the goods and closed the chapter.

"Hi, Tracy," Bruce said, indicating that she should sit.

He was seated at one of the back tables with his body facing the door. As an investigator you always kept your eyes on the entrance and the exit. Things could change at a minute's notice. Sometimes clients got careless and gave themselves away. When that happened disaster generally followed.

"Hello, Bruce. Thanks for coming. How was your meeting in Tampa?" she asked, making small talk as her heart pounded beneath her chest.

"It was very productive. I met with one of my clients and interviewed another potential investigator, a retired FBI agent who recently moved from Chicago. He seems perfect for the job."

The waitress came to the table and took their drink order. They each ordered wine and a tray of appetizers. While waiting Tracy talked about her new job and living on the East Coast. She was adjusting quite nicely under the circumstances. She told Bruce that Eric was a friend she met in Miami. Even though he didn't probe, he knew Eric was more than just a casual acquaintance. One didn't pay his expenses if they weren't somehow sexually, intimately or emotionally involved.

After getting liquor into her system, she became more talkative. It was easier to ask the questions, to expose and unmask the dirt. Bruce was the first to speak.

"Would you like to hear the report on Eric? Let me caution you that there can be an explanation for things we've uncovered. You need to balance this information with what you know or have learned about him," Bruce said, opening the door for his findings.

Tracy braced herself. She thought that was an interesting way to start the dialogue. "I'm ready. What did you find in your investigation?" she asked, holding her breath as if that would help her accept the information with ease.

"Eric made his millions as a plastic surgeon. He's never married, which has caused a bit of controversy in his professional and personal life."

"What do you mean … it's caused a bit of controversy?"

"Eric is forty-two years old. After you pass your thirties, if you are a man and still single, people have a tendency to speculate on your masculinity."

"Go on," she said with bated breath. The suspense was killing her. She was eager to get the facts.

"Not that it should matter, but Eric lives on South Beach and has a reputation for being a womanizer. He dates younger women and tends to end relationships fast and very abruptly. He doesn't appear to make commitments. Many of his patients are gay. Obviously, that doesn't make one gay, but for Eric it adds to the concerns about his sexual orientation."

"I see. So what does all that mean?" she asked, not quite sure of what Bruce was saying.

"That makes him a target for people to question his motives. Eric is a flirt, and he gets around. He's a board member of Miami Events and Adventures and that gives him a front row seat to young, single, beautiful women looking for Mr. Right."

"Does the data show that he's still dating several women?" Tracy asked, as she held her breath.

"Tracy, I think Eric has learned a lot. When some men are in their thirties, it's still a game, seeing how many women they can add to their little black book. In their forties, wisdom and experience generally makes them wiser. I think Eric may be reassessing that phase of his life."

"Wow!" was all she said.

"Eric lived with a gay roommate while he was doing his residency. There's no evidence that shows they were intimately involved. However, the stigma remains with him today. That has somewhat hurt his reputation. He was also once engaged to a model from Brazil. Eric was smitten with her. He was captivated by her beauty and charm. When he caught her cheating on him, he broke off their engagement. That sent her into a rage. His fiancee was obsessed and consumed with trying to damage Eric's reputation. I'd say she was pretty good at it. He's suffered to this day with that stigma."

Tracy was now totally confused. What was Bruce telling her about Eric? Was he gay or did he just run upon some bad luck? Was he still a womanizer? She couldn't think straight. She didn't even know what questions to ask Bruce. Maybe the best thing would be for her to end their relationship. Bruce could see she was struggling with the information.

"Bruce, what exactly are you saying? Is Eric gay?" Tracy asked, hoping she'd either misunderstood or misinterpreted what Bruce said.

"Before I continue, Tracy, you need to know that Eric is currently seeing a very young, attractive lady. The young lady appears to be in her early twenties. She's currently one of the top models in Milan. She has her own place, but she spends most of her time at Eric's home when she's not on location. My investigator took these pictures of them. Here you see the two of them kissing at the front door of his home. Here you see Eric and the young lady leaving his property in separate cars," Bruce said, as he handed the pictures to Tracy.

She couldn't believe her eyes. The man she thought she knew had a girlfriend on the side, or was she the side show. How dare Eric live a double life? Her mind was traveling in circles. How was he able to keep two women satisfied? How often did he see his girlfriend? She never heard voices in the background and his home definitely didn't look as if he had a live-in. The joke was on her. The womanizer had scored twice.

"Bruce, I'm the biggest fool here. Eric has outsmarted me. What else did you uncover?" she asked, feeling as if a dagger had been stabbed into her heart.

"Our findings are inconclusive," Bruce said, watching her reaction.

"What does that mean? Your findings are inconclusive."

"My partner, who has connections with the Miami and Fort Lauderdale communities, engaged in conversations with men who have seen Eric in a couple of bars with gay men. Eric and the men didn't arrive at the bar together, nor did they leave together. They think the men may have been some of his patients or perhaps friends."

She was on her feet. "I can't believe this. Don't you find that strange that a heterosexual man would be in a bar with gay men?"

"Tracy, maybe there's a logical explanation. Maybe Eric was invited there by some of his patients or friends. Maybe that's where they meet to discuss business or just to relax. Going inside a bar and having a drink with an individual with a different sexual preference doesn't make a person gay."

"Bruce, what other explanation is there?" Tracy asked, wondering now how she'd missed all the signs.

"Tracy, it means that there's some doubt about his sexual preference. Our report does not prove conclusively that his preference is for women … or that he prefers both men and women. I think his sexuality is still open to question," Bruce said, seeing the confusion in her eyes.

"Where do I go from here?" she asked. "Maybe I should just forget this. Maybe this is my cue to run."

"Tracy, if you run, you'll always wonder about Eric's sexuality. You have to confront him. There's nothing wrong with liking both men and women. Being bisexual is a preference. The question is … do you want to be in that triangle, if it's indeed a triangle. Eric is the only one who knows his sexual orientation and preference."

Bruce tried as best he could to calm her down. There was nothing more he could say or do. Eric was the one with all the answers. Tracy knew what she had to do. As much as she hated having the conversation, that was the only way to address the issue.

She felt like a fool knowing Eric had been unfaithful to her and his girlfriend. What she couldn't understand was his motivation. They finished their drinks as she thanked Bruce for delivering the report in person. Bruce had been able to address some of her fears and help her put things in perspective.

When she got back to the apartment, she sat in the dark staring at the wall. What an utter mess she had made of her life. She was still emotionally frustrated and distressed by what Bruce had said. Even though she wasn't thinking straight, she dialed Eric. She tried to sound upbeat and cheerful. He detected that something was wrong. It wasn't what she said but how she said it.

"Hello, Eric. I'm back from my trip. I thought I'd call and say hi."

"Sweetheart, when can I see you?" he asked, wishing she was in his arms.

"I'm really tired. I haven't been able to sleep."

Eric detected uneasiness about her. There was apprehension in her voice. She hadn't greeted him with any affectionate words. "Is anything wrong, Tracy? You don't sound like yourself."

Eric wanted to meet her for brunch on Sunday. He wanted to take her to the Biltmore Hotel in Coral Gables. The Palme D'Or was one of their signature restaurants. Since Tracy wasn't meeting him for food, she thought it would be best to talk sooner rather than later.

She needed to pose the question. She thought it would be best if they met at Starbucks and drove separate cars. If the discussion turned into a disaster, they could both walk away. She surmised that it wouldn't be as crowded at that hour and therefore, it would be easier to talk. Eric agreed to meet her at Starbucks at seven on Sunday morning.

He was in a state of panic all night. He knew he had lost her, and Stephen had won. She was too much of a lady to tell him over the phone. He didn't want to give up. How could she go back to Stephen after what he'd done to her? Maybe they were just too familiar with one another. He was sure it was all an act on Stephen's part. Stephen wanted Tracy back in California so he could manipulate and control her. Eric was determined not to let him win.

She was waiting for Eric at Starbucks on Sunday morning. She wore very little makeup. She had on Just Cavalli crop denims with a white shirt and Michael Kors wedge sandals. Without even trying she looked gorgeous. Eric had on denims and a polo top. He reached for her but received an icy greeting. He took the chair opposite hers.

"What's wrong, Tracy? I could tell last night in your voice that something was terribly wrong," Eric said, fearing she'd made her decision to stay with Stephen.

"I don't know where to start. Things have happened so fast," she said, breathing deeply to take in more oxygen.

"Take your time, love. Did you and Stephen reconcile?" Eric asked, bracing himself for the worst.

"Eric, there's something about me that you should know," Tracy said, as Eric took her hand. She took it back, placing both hands in her lap.

"What is it? Does it involve me? Does it involve us?"

"When I was married to Stephen, I had three extramarital affairs that he never knew about. I was able to keep them from him. Stephen never had me investigated so my secret remained safe."

Eric was relieved to know what was bothering Tracy. "Sweetheart, we all have things in our background that we're not proud of. Things we wish we'd done differently. That's not the end of the world. We can work through this."

She looked Eric in his eyes as she shared the report from Bruce.

"I had an investigator look into your background. At my age and with my history, I can't afford to be careless or irresponsible. There is feedback out there about your sexual orientation and the fact that you have a girlfriend," she stated. "Is it true Eric? Do you have a girlfriend? Are you gay?"

"Exactly, what are you asking me, Tracy," Eric asked, realizing she knew more about him than he thought.

"The report was inconclusive about your sexual orientation, but not the fact that your girlfriend lives with you when she's in town. A lot of the negativism in this report stems from your college roommate who was gay and the lady you were previously engaged to. Although nothing could be proven one way or the other, the report is quite alarming."

"Tracy, I wish you would have come to me first. I could have explained it all, if only you'd asked."

"I'm asking now Eric." She could see the hurt in his eyes. There was no way for her to comfort him. It was all out in the open. Her words couldn't be taken back. It was far too late to salvage the relationship.

"Tracy, I'm not gay. I never was. My roommate in graduate school was. I didn't hold that against him. This is America, people choose who and what they want to be. My fiancée never forgave me for breaking off our engagement. She made up a lot of nasty things about our relationship and me that has tainted my reputation. I'd give anything to change those things, but I can't. My old girlfriend, who's a model, doesn't live with me. Yes, my old girlfriend showed up two weeks ago and then last week at my home. We aren't lovers any more. I know on the surface it sounds suspicious, but she's no longer my girlfriend. I don't have feelings for her. I thought you and I could have a future together, I now see that's not possible. I'm sorry you didn't trust me, or our relationship enough to confront me in person before having me investigated. I'm not gay, just a guy who ran up on some bad luck. I need to go. I've got to clear my head. Being told by the woman I love that she believes I'm gay and having an affair with my ex-girlfriend is too much. You should have told me about the investigation … that was underhanded and dishonest of you to not tell me before you hired the detective."

With those parting words, Eric got up, took one final look at her and left without another word.

Tracy didn't know what to think of Eric's reaction. In less than forty-eight hours she'd managed to lose her husband and Eric. She was distraught. Her emotions were running high. She was becoming unglued. She left Starbucks, crying every step of the way. Her shirt was drenched with tears that cascaded down her face like a moving stream. When Tracy got in her car, she phoned Don for some advice.

"Hi, Don, are you busy? It's Tracy."

"Hold on, Hudson, I'm in the middle of a transaction." She held on, thankful that her friend was there for her.

"What's up? Sounds like you're stressed out."

She poured out her guts to Don. She told him about meeting Stephen in New York and the debacle with Eric. The whole relationship had collapsed right in front of her. She now found herself alone and miserable. She was questioning her motives and everyone else.

Maybe she should have put more time between getting the report from Bruce and confronting Eric. She was ready to flee Miami and return to California to start a new life without Stephen. She had the perfect out with the new CEO coming. She could simply say that Gavin Reed deserves to hire his own human resources executive.

"Hudson, I think Eric will come around. You hit the poor guy right in his balls. Excuse the expression. He was thinking you probably would stay with Stephen, and out of nowhere you tell him about your extramarital affairs and that you think he's gay and has a girlfriend on the side. That's a lot to digest."

"What should I do now?" she asked, looking for some advice and direction from her dear friend.

"All you can do is wait. If Eric's the man for you, he'll come around. It will take some time as he does some soul searching. He might be wondering if you can be faithful to anyone. Try to see it from his angle."

"What do you mean from his angle?" Tracy asked, totally not following what Don was saying.

"You are no longer pristine in his eyes. Your reputation is no longer spotless. There are blemishes and flaws. When you reconnect, you and Eric will have to learn to forgive and trust each other. You may always have doubts about his sexuality, and he may always feel that if the relationship goes south, you will have another extramarital affair. That's just life."

She didn't feel any better after ending her call with Don. However, she understood his assessment of the situation. If they reconnected, Eric would have a lot to overcome and accept, and so would she. If they couldn't forgive each other, at least a lifetime wouldn't have been wasted on a relationship doomed from the start.

CHAPTER 19

When Tracy left for dinner at six on Sunday evening, she noticed there were gray clouds in the sky. The meteorologist had predicted that a major thunderstorm was headed her way. She slipped an umbrella into her handbag and grabbed the folder with Gavin's offer letter, along with recent news articles on Sunset and a copy of the company newsletter. She was dressed in a black Gucci dress with a three-quarter-length sleeve jacket. She wore stylish tan pumps and diamond stud earrings.

Gavin was much shorter than she'd imagined. He looked to be about five feet six. He had brown hair, blue eyes and a mustache that was neatly trimmed. She liked him immediately. She knew he would be good for Sunset. He was full of humor and quite animated. He smiled and laughed a lot. The board had made an excellent choice. He wasn't stuffy and old-fashioned in his ideas. He enjoyed rolling up his sleeves and getting in the trenches. He had wonderful ideas and listened extremely well. Tracy was truly enjoying his company.

They talked about his contract and the culture at Sunset. Tracy was honest with Gavin, explaining that she'd only been there a couple of weeks and with all that had recently happened, they were all in survival mode. Gavin was impressed with her. He could see she was smart, witty, and knew her stuff. She didn't mince words. She spoke candidly. He shared with her that Sheila had already informed the board she'd be leaving the company by the end of the year. Tracy was neither alarmed nor surprised. She never felt Sheila would stay once her idol and confidant left.

With a new CEO in place, Sheila would lose a great deal of her power and influence. After working with Judy for so many years, it would probably be quite an adjustment for her to work with someone new. As Gavin probed Tracy for details about the organization, she was positive and careful about what she said and shared. She wanted to make sure he drew his own conclusions and did his own assessment of the executives and senior leaders at Sunset. She didn't want to influence his judgment.

"Tracy, I've heard great things about you. I want to make sure you remain a part of my team. Zahn has given you rave reviews. John Bailey continues to sing your praises. John was surprised that we were able to get you to come to Sunset. John has admired you and your work for years," Gavin said, hoping she wouldn't jump ship.

"That is quite flattering. I had no idea that John knew of my work and contributions. Thanks for sharing that. It means a lot to me."

"I want to run my plans by you for restructuring the organization," Gavin said. "I hope this won't be an imposition, but you have a good handle on the people. I'd like to make you chief people officer and have communication, public relations and diversity report directly to you. You have experience with both internal and external communication. You're a natural for diversity. Our diversity numbers are weak. You understand the business case for diversity. Zahn said you orchestrated all the announcements regarding the layoff as well as the diversity profile on Sunset. I could use your skills."

"Gavin, I wasn't expecting that, but I'm excited to be a member of your executive team."

"What are our chances of keeping Leslie? Zahn told me she's leaving in a couple of weeks. How can we keep her?"

She was impressed with how decisive Gavin was. It was great hearing a leader use the all-inclusive word "we."

"I'm not sure we can compete with the compensation Leslie will be receiving at Target. However, I don't think it's the money that's driving her to Target. I'd recommend two things: First, change her title to chief administrative officer and have real estate, franchising, and marketing report to her. With the title change, we'll come awfully close to the perks being offered by Target. Second, I think you should personally call Leslie tomorrow morning and let her know you want her on your team. She's generally in the office by eight."

"I can certainly do that, but it might be better if I did it in person. I'm back in town at the end of next week."

"Gavin, if I were you I wouldn't delay that discussion; the sooner the better. You don't want Leslie to mentally be in Minneapolis while you are trying to encourage her to stay at Sunset. My recommendation is for you to call her in the office tomorrow morning before your flight. Tell her it isn't your style to make such an important offer over the phone, but you didn't want any time to elapse. Take her out to dinner on your next visit."

Gavin admired Tracy's tenacity. She was persistent and determined. She gave good advice. He knew that time was of the essence and that he needed Leslie to stop her plans for moving to Minneapolis. Tracy made a mental note to call Leslie as soon as she got in her car to warn her that the new CEO would be calling to get her to rethink her resignation. Tracy needed to explain why Gavin's offer wouldn't be considered a counteroffer. The last thing she needed was for Leslie to make some flippant, impertinent remark.

The dinner meeting ended on a pleasant note. Tracy was excited that Gavin would be at the helm. She knew right away where she stood with him. She gave him some simple directions back to his hotel and Leslie's direct phone number. He promised to call her first thing on Monday morning. They shook hands and said good night. Tracy dialed Leslie as soon as she was in her car.

It had started to rain, and there were thunderstorms in the sky. She brought Leslie up to speed about asking Stephen for the divorce and the disappointing meeting with Eric.

Leslie said, "I don't want to say I told you so, but everything does not need to be shared or told, my friend."

"Leslie, you're probably right. At least my conscience is clear. I feel I did the right thing telling Eric. We'll just have to wait and see what happens. Changing the subject … I want you to know that I had a wonderful dinner with Gavin. You'll love him," Tracy said, not expecting Leslie's response.

"I'm happy for you and the company. I spoke with the chairman at Target today, and they're flying me up in their private jet next week to meet with the team. I'll be able to do some house hunting while I'm there. I'm getting the royal treatment."

"Leslie, Gavin is calling you in the morning to offer you a higher position with the company. Before you say anything, you need to hear him out. The position will elevate you to chief administrative officer with real estate, franchising, and marketing reporting in. Your compensation will increase significantly with this promotion. This will keep you and Charles from commuting back and forth across the country. It's a great offer, and you need to hear him out."

"I can't stay. I need to go. I'm getting excited about working in Minneapolis. I've been at Sunset for seven years. It's time for me to move on. As you said, the offer from Target is a once-in-a-lifetime opportunity. Don't you think that staying at Sunset will stall my career?" Leslie asked, wondering why Tracy would ask her to consider staying with the organization.

Tracy explained that the house of cards had all moved around and changed. Gavin's offer had nothing to do with Judy. The changing of the guard had taken place, and the slate had been wiped clean. After some coaxing, Leslie was starting to come around. Tracy told her to sleep on it and not to make a hasty or hurried decision. She was convinced that now, there would be a great future for Leslie since Judy was gone and Sheila had tendered her resignation. Tracy hung up feeling confident that Leslie would make the best decision for her and Charles' future.

As Tracy drove, she was becoming blinded by the storm. Her visibility was down to just a couple of feet in front of her. She could barely see the traffic lights as she drove to the complex. Once in the parking lot, she parked the car, opened up her umbrella and made a mad dash for her apartment, almost slipping on the wet walkway. That was when she thought she saw Eric ... standing in the distance waiting for her ... but it wasn't him. Unlike the movies, she wouldn't be swept off her feet by him as they kissed in the rain and expressed their undying love for each other. Their story wouldn't have a happy ending. This wasn't the big screen, this was real life. Eric was gone.

CHAPTER 20

The board made the right decision hiring Gavin Reed as the CEO. Gavin and his wife, Toni, along with their three children relocated to Miami the second week in January. Toni had found a lovely home in Boca Raton, Florida that she fell in love with the moment she saw it. To keep peace in the family, Gavin decided to commute. Their children, all under the age of twelve, were attending a private Catholic school. Tracy had taken both Gavin and his wife out to dinner during their second house-hunting trip. Toni was just as personable as Gavin. You could tell she loved her husband and would follow him to the end of the world.

Gavin met Toni when he was in graduate school and she was pursuing an undergraduate degree in elementary education. Before the kids, Toni taught first grade. After the kids, she volunteered her services weekly helping students improve their reading and math skills. She loved being a mom and hauling the kids to dance, soccer, football and gymnastics. She prepared dinner every night and refused to let the kids survive on junk food or fast food. Toni was five feet three inches with long, silky black hair and light brown eyes. Her complexion was olive and even after three kids, she easily fitted into a size six dress.

Tracy and Gavin spoke the same language. Gavin understood that employees were Sunset's bread and butter. He spent time both in the field and at corporate. Before officially starting the job as CEO, he trained for two weeks in the restaurant learning all the positions. He worked back of house as a cook, on the frontline as cashier and server, and as an assistant and restaurant manager. Each day after leaving the restaurant, he'd work for a couple of hours at the corporate office.

The employees greeted him with open arms. He was an effective communicator. He held quarterly town hall meetings and didn't shy away from employees' questions. He maintained an open door policy and didn't back down from issues that affected the business. He was a great sounding board and gave his executives equal say in solving problems and strategizing with him on Sunset's future.

Sheila left Sunset, the third week in December. She knew it would be much better for her to exit before the new CEO officially took over. After years of making decisions and deciding what was best for Sunset, she now took a back seat to Gavin. Prior to leaving, all her decisions were discussed with Gavin and Zahn before they were implemented. She was finding it harder and harder to get things done her way. True to form, her loyal servants hung in there meeting her requests until the day she left. Sheila and her husband moved to Nashville, Tennessee shortly after she left Sunset. No one was sure what she was doing now. She had simply faded away into a recluse existence.

Gavin had recruited the chief financial officer he had worked with at Pizza Hut, who was atypical of the finance profile. Zach Swift knew how to get the numbers and how to educate executives and senior leaders along the way. Zach wasn't about the bottom line at the expense of employees and customers. She and Zach worked hand-in-hand. All finance decisions had an impact on people, and between the two of them, they made sure executives knew what the implications were. When she and Zach disagreed, it didn't become a shouting match or a game of "let the boss" decide; they worked through the numbers and analyzed both the pros and cons, finally allowing the bottom line impact on company employees and customers to take priority.

Judy took a different route. She was doing speaking engagements around the country. Companies were eager to learn all they could about how she'd grown Sunset. They attributed the huge layoff to the depressed economy. No one questioned why Judy left or her reason for not accepting a CEO position to run another company. Her reputation hadn't been scarred. Although her marriage had continued to suffer as her husband played around, she became Teflon strong, ignoring the signs and refusing to get a divorce. Tracy suspected that Judy didn't want to split her millions with her husband and probably knew she would out live him.

At the end of February, Tracy and Gavin met with Lauren to let her know her services were no longer needed at Sunset. Lauren was in shock and gave the performance of her career accusing the CEO of favoring men over women. Tracy pulled her aside to inform her that the successor was a woman and that she had no basis for the allegation. Tracy suggested that Lauren put on a good face and tell the troops and her team that she had resigned her position and would be pursuing other opportunities. Tracy was always the considerate one, thinking of others first. She had convinced Gavin to allow Lauren to leave in mid March. Tracy told Lauren she should thank her lucky stars that the CEO had agreed to the additional time, and instead of bitching, use the opportunity to get out front of the problem and put a positive spin on why she was leaving.

Gavin saw though Lauren the moment he met her. She wasn't able to disguise how little she knew about operations. She'd been able to fool Judy, but her tactics didn't work well with him. He invited her direct reports to be a part of some of the executive meetings; asking them direct questions and for their feedback regarding issues affecting the field.

Gavin spent time in the field getting to know company operations and frontline employees who kept the business profitable. He was so different from Judy. When Judy would visit the field, Lauren was always by her side. Employees knew which stores they would visit and would often call ahead to notify the next store of their arrival time. When Lauren suggested to Gavin that they visit the restaurants together, he told her his style was to visit stores at random. He knew how the restaurant team would lose valuable work time preparing for the arrival of the CEO and COO, often distorting reality. Too much work time was often loss in preparing and making everything perfect.

Tracy had recruited the perfect replacement for the COO position. Olivia Sanchez was a native of Miami who for the past fifteen years had headed up operations for McDonald's, Ruth's Chris Steak House, and Blue Cross Blue Shield.

The board was already complimenting Gavin and Tracy for making diversity a business case. Gavin had given each executive, as one of his or her performance objectives, a diversity goal he wanted them to pay attention to. He was serious about diversity. He said that diversity was a priority for the organization, and as such Tracy would be hiring a Vice President with responsibility for improving diversity in the employee and senior leadership ranks, with franchise groups, with vendors, as well as with people Sunset did business with.

Tracy was charged with the responsibility of recruiting more qualified diverse candidates for both corporate and field openings. Gavin told executives that he didn't want to hear that diverse candidates were hard to find, they were less qualified or that they didn't want to relocate to Miami. He was doing and saying all of the right things for the organization. He was direct and decisive. When a problem had to be addressed, he brought the executives together to resolve the issue. He had no hidden agenda and didn't entertain executives complaining and talking about each other.

The word on the street was Nora was interviewing with companies in hopes of leaving Sunset. Nora was highly paid and companies in Miami were refusing to give her the dollars she was demanding. For an executive marketing guru with her years of experience, her skills weren't comparable to other executives who had worked for larger companies and had handled advertising and marketing budgets three times the size of Sunset's. She hadn't been able to win Leslie over as she had Judy. Leslie was fair and consistent. She had absolutely no time to listen to Nora whine and complain. Nora had to carry her own weight and be a team player.

Gary Umar, senior vice president, real estate and franchising was starting to come out of his shell. Don was his executive coach and had worked with him to speak up and voice his opinions during staff meetings. Gavin was great with Gary. At the executive meetings when Gary was quiet, Gavin would call on him for his thoughts. If he hesitated or was struggling to respond, Gavin would put ideas on the table and ask him for his opinion. Tracy would also reinforce what Gary said, by using his examples as she clarified and explained strategy.

The composition of the board had also changed. John Bailey was heading up the compensation and governance committees. It was rumored that John would be elected chairman at the May board meeting. He was great to work with. John had made several changes to the way the board conducted its meetings and had hired an outside consultant to work directly with the compensation committee. Gavin didn't feel the need to attend all compensation meetings as Judy and Sheila had. He trusted Tracy's judgment and knew she would let him know when his presence was needed.

Sharon was no longer Tracy's assistant. Sharon was working as a human resources representative with corporate employees. Sharon facilitated all of the employee orientation meetings at corporate and constantly received glowing reviews. Her energy level was high and she made sure it was a fun experience for new employees. Sharon was always offering suggestions to make human resources better.

Tracy saw loads of potential in her. Tracy instructed her director for organizational effectiveness to work on a development plan to get Sharon to the next level. She thought Sharon would be great in about a year as a field human resources manager.

It was now March and Tracy was looking forward to June when her divorce would be final. Stephen had reluctantly agreed to the divorce after realizing she'd gone on with her life. She moved into her condo on South Beach early in December. She loved the ocean view and the party playground life style of South Beach.

South Beach had everything she wanted; trendy cafes, art galleries, cool bars, famous restaurants and all the nightlife she needed.

Tracy was thankful she hadn't run directly into Eric. She saw him once while in the drive through at Starbuck's and in the shopping mall on ocean drive. She was thankful he hadn't seen her. She steered clear of Miami Events and Adventures. She had met some great people and she was starting to feel like Miami was her home. She was taking a French cooking class, yoga and had joined a book club. Tracy felt free as a bird. She didn't have to answer to anyone in her personal life.

She was enjoying working at Sunset. Although there were still office politics to deal with, she didn't have to constantly look over her shoulder. The executive team was a cohesive group. Gavin had no favorites, each executive had to carry his or her own weight.

The board took more of an active role in staying on top of what was happening in the company. Sales were increasing and the company was making money. As sales and profits increased, the company was able to rehire some of the employees who were let go during the layoff.

With Leslie at the helm of the legal department and approval from the board of directors, Sunset agreed to settle the New York case out-of-court. All managers and senior leaders were now required by the company to annually take an employment law class. Gavin understood and knew that negative publicity could quickly turn public opinion against the company.

Leslie and Charles were getting married at the end of April in a small ceremony with only family and friends in attendance. Leslie wanted to elope but Charles insisted that they marry in a small but elaborate ceremony. He wanted to see his bride walk down the aisle and give herself to him. Leslie was amazed everyday how the wedding had grown from 25 people to almost a hundred.

Tracy was truly happy for Charles and Leslie. The three still got together every other week at the movies, at some great club or restaurant, art show or for shopping. Charles was a lot like Eric when it came to shopping, he enjoyed watching Leslie try on clothes and parade in front of him.

With next month fast approaching, she didn't know how she would get through Leslie's wedding since she was the maid of honor and Eric was Charles' best man. She had begged Leslie to find another friend to be the maid of honor, but Leslie refused saying she thought it would be fun for the four of them to be together again.

Tracy wasn't so sure of that. At first, she thought about inviting Don, but what purpose would that serve. It was Leslie's day and her objective wasn't to make Eric jealous since frankly she didn't care if he brought a date or not. Maybe during the wedding rehearsal and dinner, she could claim she was sick and just show up for the main event, the wedding.

Tracy knew she couldn't do that to her best friend. She had to be there for Leslie just as she would want Leslie there for her. The past was over. What was done was done. It was quite obvious now that Eric's feelings for her weren't that deep. Her only regret was not telling him about the investigation upfront. What she couldn't forget or forgive Eric for was having a girlfriend while trying to entice her.

The pictures that Bruce had shared; clearly showed Eric in a compromising position with a much younger woman. Eric may not be gay, but the pictures clearly showed his affinity for younger women; and dating two women at the same time put him in the category of a Casanova. The question that would often trouble her mind was why did Eric go for her. She clearly didn't fit the description of the type of woman he was turned on by.

Leslie's wedding was now three days a way. All of the planning and preparation were coming to fruition. The weather in Miami was perfect, in the mid to upper 70s with an occasional cool breeze. The meteorologist had predicted that the temperature would be in the mid-seventies on Saturday. Tracy was meeting Leslie at noon for lunch to discuss last minute details and for her to try on her wedding gown one last time.

"Hey, Leslie," Tracy said. "How are you holding up?"

"I'm good … I can't wait to get this over with. Thank goodness the hotel took care of almost everything. All Charles and I had to do was hire the band, photographer and videographer."

"I'm so excited for the two of you. It seems like just yesterday when we were all together at Miami Events and Adventures wine tasting celebration," Tracy said, as she looked away.

Leslie could tell that her heart hadn't completely healed. It would take time for her to adjust to being single again and to accept Eric's lack of judgment.

"Tracy, are you going to be alright at the rehearsal dinner and wedding?" Leslie asked, wondering now why she hadn't listened to her friend when she wanted to opt out.

"Leslie, Saturday will be your day. I'll be in good spirits. I don't begrudge Eric. He did what he felt he needed to do.

Things happen in life for a reason and I can't continue to remi-nisce and ask why. He's moved on and so have I."

Leslie wasn't buying what Tracy said for a moment. She knew that Tracy's pain was great and seeing Eric again would conjure up those feelings.

When Tracy saw Leslie in her wedding gown it brought tears to her eyes. Leslie looked both sexy and elegant. She had decided on a Vera Wang gown that had intricately embroidered lace straps and a scalloped sweetheart-neckline bodice. The gown had a voluminous trumpet skirt with a floor-sweeping train for that fairytale finish.

"Oh, Leslie, you look like a fairy princess. Charles is one lucky man. Just think, you were about to leave him and go to cold country. Who knows what would have happened with that commuting arrangement the two of you talked about."

Leslie knew she owed so much to Tracy who had fought for her all the way. It was Tracy who convinced Gavin to keep her, and Tracy who encouraged her to stay. Never in a million years did Leslie expect to find love. She had taken a huge leap of faith and it had paid off.

Two days before the wedding, Tracy came down with some type of stomach virus. She'd spent the day in bed, too weak to go to the doctor. She was dehydrated and felt faint each time she got up to go to the bathroom, which was quite often. She wasn't able to keep any food down. What now she thought. Why had she ever said anything about being sick on the day of Leslie's wedding to avoid seeing Eric? She never meant it. It was said with tongue in cheek.

Leslie called her every hour, checking in to make sure she was okay. Tracy told Leslie, she'd be at the wedding rehears-al tomorrow evening, and the dinner that followed and that nothing would keep her away. Leslie was concerned for her friend and suggested that she not drive herself there on Friday. Leslie decided to send one of Charles' relatives to pick her up.

Tracy didn't start to feel like her old self until Friday afternoon. She made herself a cup of tea and heated up a bowl of chicken soup. These were the times she wished her mother was still alive. She desperately wanted to get her mother's opinion and advice.

Jennifer, Charles' sister, picked Tracy up at her condo at six on Friday evening and drove to the Biltmore Hotel in Coral Gables. The hotel looked impressive on the outside as they gave the car to the valet service. The Biltmore was one of Miami's most elegant, prestigious and historic hotels. The hotel staff understood that there was no such thing as one-size fits all when it came to that special day. For their six-figure wedding, Charles and Leslie had spared no expense. They wanted the very best, since the two had waited so long to find love. The wedding was going to be in the Danielson Gallery, a medieval-inspired ballroom with an open mezzanine. The rehearsal dinner was taking place in the Palm d'Or with after dinner drinks in the Tea Lounge.

There he was after all of this time, looking fabulous as ever. As their eyes met, Eric smiled and winked at Tracy. She wasn't expecting that. After five long trying months, she and Eric were now face-to-face. She didn't have a clue as to how she would manage the next twenty-four hours. She quickly moved into the Danielson Gallery hoping beyond hope she could escape the inevitable. There was nowhere for her to run and definitely no way to escape Eric. After all this time, she still had feelings for him. She was determined to never let him know.

The wedding planner, Marjorie Taylor, had everyone enter the gallery as she explained the order of events for the wedding ceremony. Marjorie placed everyone where they were supposed to be as they did a trial run. Marjorie was professional, organized and efficient. There was no messing with or second-guessing this lady; she knew her stuff. She had come highly recommended with impeccable credentials. She oversaw everything to the smallest detail. When Marjorie spoke, all eyes were focused on her. She commanded attention by the way she spoke and carried herself.

Within a little less than two hours, Marjorie had gone through the entire ceremony, telling everyone what time to be there and where they should go upon entering the Biltmore. Marjorie gave everyone her business card and suggested they keep it close for the next twenty-four hours. She instructed them to call her if anything went awry. It was Leslie's day and Marjorie wanted to make sure there were no missteps.

As family members and friends were moving towards the Palm d'Or, Tracy found Leslie and told her she was leaving to continue to nurse her virus, giving the excuse that she had to be in top shape on Leslie's wedding day. Leslie didn't buy it, for she had watched as Eric's eyes met Tracy's. Tracy had the hotel hail her a cab so Charles' sister could enjoy the rehearsal dinner.

On the day of the wedding, Tracy arrived at the church early so as not to run into Eric ahead of time. It was hectic in the dressing room. Clothes were everywhere as makeup was being applied and curling irons were being heated for last minute styles. The hour was fast approaching. She helped Leslie into her gown as tears fell from both their eyes.

"Leslie, you look gorgeous. Wait until Charles sees his future wife."

"I'm truly blessed to have found Charles," Leslie said as Marjorie, the wedding planner, entered the room, suggesting that each person use the bathroom to avoid any last minute emergencies.

The guests had all been seated when the minister, Charles and Eric entered the gallery. Five minutes later, the music started as the flower girl entered, followed by the ring bearer, bridesmaids and groomsmen. Charles and Eric moved to the center to face the bride as the traditional wedding song, Here Comes the Bride, was played.

The guests stood when Leslie entered the back of the room. Tracy was behind Leslie making sure the train on her wedding gown didn't bunch up.

Eric couldn't take his eyes off of Tracy. He watched her every step as she approached the platform behind Leslie.

The ceremony was beautiful beyond words. Charles and Leslie made a wonderful couple. As they said their vows, Eric wondered why things had unraveled so fast and completely out of control between him and Tracy.

At the reception, somehow Tracy was able to keep a smile on her face as Eric made a toast to Charles and his new bride. Now it was her time to toast the couple.

"Hello everyone. I'm Tracy. If you don't know the story, Charles and Leslie met each other one Friday evening at a wine tasting affair hosted by Miami Events and Adventures. I was new in town at that time, so I dragged my best friend along, so we could sample some of the world's finest wines and make new friends. Shortly thereafter, Charles' charm and sweet words won Leslie's heart, and she took the leap of faith and said I do. Please raise your glasses to Leslie and Charles. May the happiness you share tonight, be the start of a wonderful life together."

Charles and Leslie took to the floor to dance to their song, "Can't Help Falling In Love." They couldn't stop smiling and gazing into each other's eyes. Charles was whispering sweet nothings into her ear. He loved all of the attention, and most of all, he loved Leslie.

It was now time for Eric and Tracy to fulfill their customary role, and dance together as maid of honor and best man. Eric had already asked the band to play, "The First Time Ever I Saw Your Face". Tracy's heart skipped a beat when Eric took her hand and led her onto the dance floor.

"You look stunning tonight Tracy," was all Eric could think to say.

"The same to you," she said.

"Tracy, you never called me. I waited, but you never called. I don't want it to be like this between us."

Tracy didn't know what to say for fear of saying the wrong thing, so she said nothing.

With absolutely nothing to lose, he kissed Tracy on her lips, holding her in a tight embrace so she couldn't move.

"Don't say a word, sweetheart. We have a lifetime to figure this out. There's no need to rush into anything. I'm not going anywhere," Eric said, holding her close.

She knew at that moment that Eric had forgiven her and accepted those things that couldn't be changed. There were no grudges. The resentment and bitterness were slowly melting away. He had made some mistakes, and so had she. As they kissed, she was thankful that Eric had given their relationship a second chance. They'd weathered the storm.

There were no secrets between them now. As painful as it had been to tell the truth, Tracy was happy she had chosen that route. Whatever the future held, she knew Eric would be in her life.

ABOUT THE AUTHOR

L.G. Traylor is the CEO and President of L.G. Traylor & Associates, LLC, a premiere provider of senior-level services to promote the growth and success of client organizations. The author spent twenty years as Chief People Officer with some of America's most admired and recognized companies in the hospitality and restaurant industry. Traylor is a former administrator, teacher and college professor. She holds the B.S., M.S. and Ph.D. degrees from the University of Tennessee at Chattanooga, Florida International University and Union Institute and University.

Made in the USA
Charleston, SC
21 October 2013